CLASH OF KINGS

BOOK 3 THE BRUNANBURH SERIES

THE BRUNANBURH SERIES

MJ PORTER

First published in Great Britain in 2023 by Boldwood Books Ltd.

Cover Design by Head Design Ltd

Cover Photography: Shutterstock

A CIP catalogue record for this book is available from the British Library.

Paperback ISBN 978-1-83751-199-0

Large Print ISBN 978-1-83751-198-3

Hardback ISBN 978-1-83751-197-6

Ebook ISBN 978-1-83751-200-3

Kindle ISBN 978-1-83751-201-0

Audio CD ISBN 978-1-83751-192-1

MP3 CD ISBN 978-1-83751-193-8

Digital audio download ISBN 978-1-83751-195-2

Boldwood Books Ltd
23 Bowerdean Street
London SW6 3TN
www.boldwoodbooks.com

This book is respectfully dedicated to Athelstan, the first and only king of that name to rule England, in what is the 1100th anniversary of him being proclaimed king of Mercia and then Wessex, and then 'of the English'.

'The very mighty King Æthelstan enjoyed the crown of Empire.'

The Chronicon of Æthelweard

And the battle of Dùn Brude in his xxxiii year in which was slain the son of Constantin

— CHRONICLE OF THE KINGS OF ALBA

A great and lamentable battle fought between the Gaill and the Saxons

— THE ANNALS OF ULSTER

BRITAIN IN THE 10TH CENTURY

ORKNEYS
CAIT
SCOTTISH WESTERN ISLANDS
FORTRIU
Atlantic Ocean
DUNNOTTAR
KINGDOM OF THE SCOTS
DAL RIATA
SCONE
ST ANDREWS
ATHOLL
North Sea
KINGDOM OF STRATHCLYDE
BAMBURGH
Tyne
CHESTER LE STREET
EAMONT
KINGDOM OF YORK
YORK
Irish Sea
Humber
Ribble
KEXBOROUGH
Mersey
Don
MEXBOROUGH
CONINGSBROUGH
DUBLIN
CLONMACNOISE
BRUNANBURH
LINCOLN
CHESTER
NOTTINGHAM
GWYNEDD
IRELAND
Trent
DERBY
STAMFORD
POWYS
TAMWORTH
Welland
LIMERICK
EAST ANGLIA
OFFA'S DYKE
Severn
HEREFORD
NORTHAMPTON
DEHEUBARTH
MERCIA
Wye
GWENT
LONDON
WESSEX
Thames
KING'S WORTHY
KINGSTON UPON THAMES
WINCHESTER
KENT
EXETER
Tamar
English Channel

CAST OF CHARACTERS

(ALL HISTORICAL UNLESS UNDERLINED AND THEN FICTIONAL CHARACTERS)

The Family of Alfred the Great

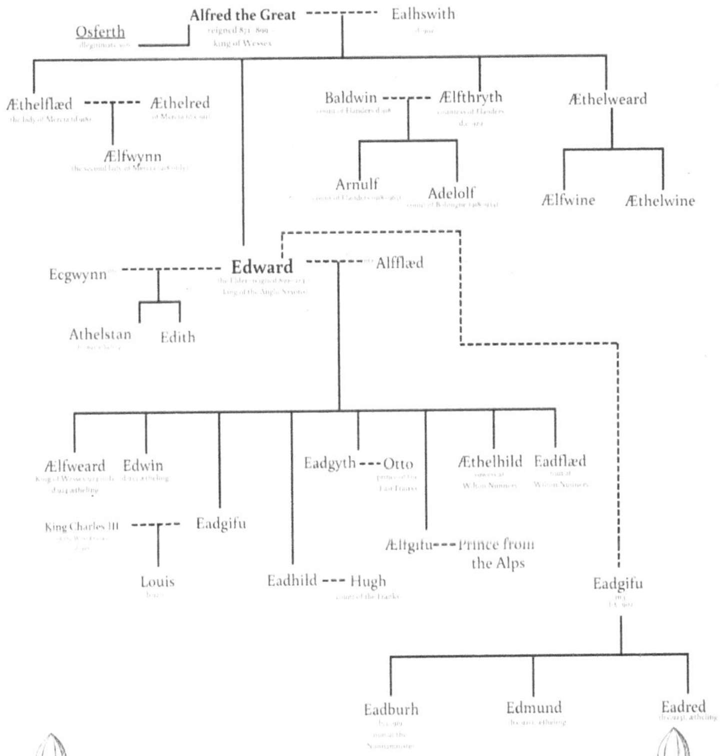

Alfred the Great --- Ealhswith
reigned 871–899 – king of Wessex

Osferth
illegitimate son

Æthelflæd --- Æthelred
the lady of Mercia — of Mercia

Ælfwynn
the second lady of Mercia

Baldwin --- Ælfthryth
count of Flanders — countess of Flanders

Arnulf
count of Flanders

Adelolf
count of Boulogne

Æthelweard

Ælfwine

Æthelwine

Ecgwynn --- Edward --- Alfflæd
the Elder — king of the Anglo-Saxons

Athelstan

Edith

Ælfweard
King of Wessex — ætheling

Edwin
ætheling

King Charles III --- Eadgifu

Louis

Eadhild --- Hugh
count of the Franks

Eadgyth --- Otto
prince of the East Franks

Ælfgifu --- Prince from the Alps

Æthelhild
Wilton Nunnery

Eadflæd
nun at Wilton Nunnery

Eadgifu

Eadburh
nun at the Nunnaminster

Edmund
ætheling

Eadred
ætheling

The English Ealdormen

Ealdorman Wulfgar

Ealdorman Athelstan of the East Angles (from 932), married to Ælfwynn, the lady of Mercia's daughter

Eadric, Ealdorman Athelstan's brother, ealdorman

Æthelwald, Ealdorman Athelstan's brother, ealdorman

Ealdorman Guthrum

Ealdorman Uhtred

Wulfheard, archbishop of Canterbury from 926

Wulfstan, archbishop of York from 931

Oda, bishop and archbishop of York after the death of Wulfheard

Elodwin, King Athelstan's warrior

Sigelac, King Athelstan's warrior

Wihtred, King Athelstan's messenger

Taliesen, scop

The Scots

The succession strictly alternated between two noble lines.

Constantin, son of Aed, king of the Scots (reigned 900 onwards)

Ildulb, son

Amlaib, grandson, son of Ildulb, died at Cait in 934

Cellach, illegitimate son, died at Brunanburh

Alpin, son, hostage at the English king's court

Mael Muire, daughter of Constantin (name is fictional, although we know she existed)

Mael Coluim, Constantin's designated successor, the son of his predecessor, Domnall

Strathclyde

Owain, king of Strathclyde, died at Brunanburh

Dyfnwal, Owain's son, now king of Strathclyde

The Welsh kings

Hywel, king of the South Welsh (Deheubarth), known as Hywel Dda

Owain ap Hywel, Rhodri ap Hywel and Edwin ap Hywel, Hywel's sons

Idwal, king of Gwynedd

Cadfan, his brother

Alun, Idwal's steward

Tewdwr ap Griffi ab Elise, king of Brycheiniog

Morgan ap Owain, king of Gwent

Gwriad, king of Glywysing

The independent kingdom of Bamburgh

Ealdred, king of Bamburgh (died 934)

Ealdwulf, his son, not ruler of Bamburgh at this time (might not be his son, but his brother)

The Dublin Norse and their allies

All claimed to be descended from Ivarr the Boneless, the Viking raider who led the Great Heathen Army of the 860s. Some would have been grandsons, others perhaps great-grandsons. The genealogy is particularly complicated.

Sihtric, king of York, died c.926, married Athelstan's only natural sister, Edith

Anlaf Sihtricson, his son, not the son of Edith

Rognavaldr Anlafson, Anlaf Sihtricson's son

Haraldr Sihtricson, Anlaf's brother

Gothfrith, king of Dublin, grandson of Ivarr, died in 934

Olaf Gothfrithson, son of Gothfrith, great-grandson of Ivarr

Camman, Olaf Gothfrithson's son

Rognavaldr, Olaf Gothfrithson's brother, died at Brunanburh

Blakari, Olaf Gothfrithson's brother

Gothfrith, Olaf Gothfrithson's brother

Olaf Cenncairech – Scabbyhead, king of Limerick – captured by Olaf Gothfrithson in 937, fought for him at Brunanburh, died
Ivarr, son of king of Denmark, Gorm, died at Brunanburh
Gebeachan, king of the Islands (as named in sources of the period), died at Brunanburh
Eric, one of Olaf Gothfrithson's warriors

The notable families of West Frankia
Charles III (died 929) m. Eadgifu, daughter of Edward and Æfflæd
Louis, their son, king of West Frankia from 936
Hugh the Great, married Eadhild (died 937), daughter of Edward and Ælfflæd

NOTE ON NAMES

The unwary traveller to this period will be faced with a profusion of names for the men and women in this story. Names may be given in Welsh, Gallic, Old Norse, Old English or with modern spellings. As such, you may find Olaf/Anlaf/Amlaib and be surprised to discover these are all the same person. You may find the name Eadward used, although the most common form is Edward. Equally, Æthelstan is the correct form of Athelstan. You will find names used interchangeably if you consult different sources, and secondary sources. The choice taken will depend, quite often, on the main sources the writer uses and on their own personal preference. I have attempted to use the names that are most recognisable for the individuals involved. Welsh and Norse convention usually names someone as the son of their father, e.g. Olaf Gothfrithson is Gothfrith's son; Owain ap Hywel is the son of Hywel. Names are often reused throughout the generations in all societies and, in England, families often name all of their children with names that begin with similar letters, e.g. Athelstan, Athelwald, etc.

All quotes from the Anglo-Saxon Chronicle are taken from *The Anglo-Saxon Chronicles*, M. Swanton ed. and trans.

PART I

AFTERMATH

1

SUMMER 937, WINCHESTER, THE KINGDOM OF THE ENGLISH

Eadgifu, the lady of Wessex

I eye the messenger before me. I wish I could tell who it is, but he's down on one knee, face pressed low to the ground, awaiting permission to speak.

I look to Eadred, my youngest son, and he shrugs his narrow shoulders. It seems he can't identify the man either. I huff softly with annoyance. I want to know that my king, and my son, are victorious on the battlefield against the might of the Norse and the king of the Scots.

Who then is it with knowledge of protocol and the respect due to me and to my son, as well as to Alpin, the son of the King of the Scots, who stands beside Eadred? He might be a prisoner, but Alpin is still esteemed according to his birthright.

'Rise,' I mutter quickly, deciding I've had enough of my fears and worries.

Vibrant eyes greet mine, even brighter cloth beneath the folds of the dull-coloured cloak, perfect for riding in, whether rain or shine.

'My lady, my lords.' The accent tells me straight away. This man is from West Frankia. Immediately my thoughts turn to King Louis. I can see Eadred opening his mouth to demand answers. The messenger beats him to it. 'I've been sent by King Louis, the fourth of his name, to inform my lord King Athelstan that Louis is now free from the fetters of his uncle by marriage. He rules in his name and with the support of his mother, Queen Dowager Eadgifu, and the archbishop of Rheims.' I feel a sour smile on my lips at the reminder of Eadgifu, my namesake and stepdaughter. It's been little more than a year since she left these shores, but I've forgotten her haunting presence quickly enough.

I lift my gaze to Eadred's and meet his fierce eyes. He and Louis were firm allies. This must please him to know that Louis is free from the louring presence of his uncle. We were all suspicious of the intentions of Count Hugh, and as it transpires, we were correct to be.

However, my deliberations run counter to this, and I notice the unwary expression on the messenger's face.

'Why now?' I almost whisper.

'Alas,' the man begins. 'Alas, Countess Eadhild met her death before the summer. She lies, now, entombed close to Paris.' I shudder at the thought. I consider if Athelstan will mourn his half-sister? I also realise that Eadhild's sisters must be told of this. I'll send to Wilton and ensure they know.

'And?' I realise there's more.

'King Louis has allied with Hugh the Black.' I wrinkle my nose at this. I don't know who he is. As England is served with too many Athelstans and Edwards, West Frankia has far too many Hughs.

The messenger must notice my confusion.

'He's the brother of the man who was king before Louis.'

Still, I'm perplexed, and I'd ask much more of the messenger, only now, from outside, we all hear the drum of fast-approaching hoofbeats, loud over the hard-packed road. My eyes swivel to the front of the hall, willing the messenger to hurry and enter. He's come from the north. I'm sure of it.

I notice that Scule and Osulf lumber to their feet now. The ealdormen, or rather jarls, were to stay here and protect Eadred and myself while Edmund and Athelstan rode to war. Osulf hastens outside. I wish he'd move faster.

A flurry of voices, the loud crash of someone dismounting in a hurry, and then a dust-stained man is before me. It's Wihtred, and I sigh with relief on seeing the victorious gleam in his eyes.

My gaze turns to Alpin, and I notice a haphazard smile on his lips at the sight of Wihtred. I consider who he wished to be triumphant, his father or the man who's kept him close all these years. Not that it matters any more.

'Victory, my lady, my lords,' he calls for all to hear, his eyes appraising as they sweep over Alpin with a knowing look. 'Victory at the battle of Brunanburh. Never yet,' he continues, as though he's a scop, and I smile at his exuberance, for it matches my joy, 'was there a greater slaughter of the bloody Norse.'

2

OCTOBER 937, DUBLIN, IRELAND

Olaf Gothfrithson, king of the Dublin Norse

I eye my brother with unease where he stands on the quayside of Dublin, festooned as though he's the king here and not me. Admittedly, I bid him rule here in my absence, but all the same, I didn't expect him to adopt the accoutrements of my kingship so easily. He returns my look without inhibition from beneath the thick wolf cloak he wears. He didn't agree with my decision to ally with Anlaf Sihtricson, giving him Dublin to rule when I was victorious and held Jorvik. No doubt, in the absence of both of us, Gothfrith has done much to win the support of the Dubliners. If Anlaf lives, I don't see he'll have an easy time of it now. I don't think that I will either.

'Brother,' he calls to me. No 'lord' or 'king', just 'brother'. Damn him.

'Brother,' I counter quickly. I hoped to come here in triumph but, instead, my ship has barely limped into Dublin's quayside. I'm defeated, but I'm not about to let on to that while Gothfrith watches me with his ambitious eyes.

The moans and wails of my shipmen sunder the tension between us.

'A triumph,' he offers sarcastically, coming forward, extending his arm towards me so that I stay upright after the days and days at sea as I place my feet on dry land – well, almost dry land. The planks beneath my feet extend over the reaches of the slurping water. It shouldn't have taken us as long to return to Dublin. The weather has been a bitch, the Goddess of the sea making her displeasure known only too well.

'Indeed,' I confirm, mirroring his tone, welcoming his support, although it shows me as weak, just like the wrecks of my ships. There are few of us. Two follow on close behind. We've not made this journey together. We came upon them only with the sunrise. Their wolf-headed sails proclaim them as my shipmen and warriors, but I've only seen a third of the number of men who should crew such a craft on board each one. How many, I consider, have been consigned to the depths during the perilous journey home? Too many. Too many.

'Where's your son? My brothers? Your wife?' The words are pointed. He knows that the battle wasn't a triumph. He knows I've lost. 'Tell me, at least, that Anlaf Sihtricson met his end?' His lips curl as he speaks. Gothfrith has no love for Anlaf, who thinks to rule Dublin in my name. Gothfrith would far sooner be ruling. But Anlaf is a great-grandson of Ivarr the Boneless as well. We're cousins, alas.

I can answer none of his questions. I'm defeated. I've lost all – well, apart from Dublin. I hope my son, Camman, lives. I know Rognavaldr, my brother, doesn't.

'Rognavaldr's dead,' I admit sullenly. 'He died fighting to save my life.'

'A worthless endeavour,' Gothfrith complains, his voice filled with sorrow all the same for our dead brother. There were once five of us, but now only three remain. His eyes are everywhere, watching the men limp ashore behind me. How has he heard tales of our failure? Have others made it home before me?

'Tell me what you know,' I demand.

'When we're inside, and these men have left their ships.' He surprises me with his concern for others, or perhaps it's merely a tactic to delay the inevitable of informing me of all he's heard of the battle.

I lean on his arm, all the same. I smell the too-familiar aroma of Dublin, and I could cry, I don't deny it. My dreams. My ambitions. My brother. They all lie dead on that battlefield, or rather, slaughter field, over the sea. That damn bastard, King Athelstan of the English, and his pestilent brother, Edmund. I must have my revenge against them both. I must. Although, right now, it all seems impossible.

I stink of battle, vomit, and the sea. I'm little more than a beggar I'd normally kick in the street to free my gutters from clogging with filth, the beggar included in that assessment.

Later, inside my hall, I meet the haunted eyes of the many women and boys who've come, seeking news of their men and fathers. I can scarcely hold their furious, blame-filled gazes. I promised much and have delivered bugger all. Worse. Men and boys are dead. In my name. I don't even have my new wife at my side.

Only now does Gothfrith speak.

'We've heard reports of the defeat. Two ships made it home before you did. The men were dead or dying, the storms finishing what the English scum began.' His words thrum with fury. He's said nothing other than that Rognavaldr's death in battle was a waste. He's cast no complaints my way. And then he does look at me, drawing my eyes to his with a hairy hand that I try to bat aside, but I'm too damn weak. I need to eat an ox or a boar, but right now, my belly still rolls with the swell of the ocean that's finally spat me out and allowed me home to Dublin. 'They blame the Scots' king, and your bitch of a new wife.' I wince at that. Gothfrith has always liked my first wife. He releases his hold on me, and now the very woman materialises before me. Her face isn't just streaked with tears but with claw marks where her nails have gouged her skin.

'Tell me,' she hisses, spitting into my face. 'Tell me that my son lives, my only son.'

I can't. I can't tell her anything. I don't know. He might yet live. He might even, and horror fills my gurgling stomach now, be a hostage of the English king, just as Alpin is, the son of King Constantin of the Scots.

'Tell me, you useless turd.' Her pinpoint nails snake down my face. I feel the burn of hot blood erupting from the strike, more wounds to add to those I've already gathered.

I'm too feeble to counter the unexpected attack. Now tears sting my eyes as well.

Camman. My son. Where is he? Isn't it enough to have lost my brother, to have lost my warrior reputation? I can't imagine, and haven't allowed myself to consider, what it will be like to know I've lost my son as well.

'Leave it, woman.' Gothfrith's words ring with conviction. I'm astounded when she backs away, still spitting and hissing as though a log in the fire or a snake under attack. I realise there's something else between the two of them, but I don't know what it is, and I don't care. I want sleep. I need to rest. I reach for a beaker of ale. The only way to sleep is to drown my sorrows and my fear, to curb my anger and resentment, to stop those blood-drenched visions of my failure from recurring time and time again.

But Gothfrith has my face once more in his hairy hand, eyes

blazing.

'You need to make this right, you damn fool. Make this right, or I'll take Dublin from you, and it'll be as though you never lived. Make this right, or so help me, Olaf, your wife won't be the only one prepared to rip your skin and shed your blood.'

I nod weakly, pull my head from his hands, and then startle at a sudden shriek.

I turn towards my first wife, her howling fury as she keens. But not for the dead, thank the Gods. No, my son yet lives, and his furious gaze meets mine across the room as his mother's arms clasp him tight while he shakes and shudders in his ripped, fouled clothes. Behind him, more broken men move into the room, bringing with them the smell of the ocean, and of failure. More women shriek and wail, some in delight, others in pain on seeing their husbands, sons and fathers.

All the time, Camman's eyes are on mine. His face is a grimace of unhappiness as his mother clings to him, her body shaking as violently as when she thought him dead.

His survival fills me with a resolve I thought lost. I know I must recover all that I've squandered if only to ensure my son receives his birthright. My father failed me. I'll not allow that deep wound to infect my son as well.

I will find my resolve.

And, God willing, my new wife as well, the daughter of King Constantin of the Scots. Mael Muire was only in my bed for one night. But she's still the bargain that binds us together. I can't see it was a good agreement, but she's mine, and I only hope she appears, as Camman has done, in one of the other ships limping back to Dublin. I won't lose her as well as everything else.

But first. I must drink until I sleep and then drink some more until I sleep yet again. I've wounds that need healing, and they're not just on my body.

3

OCTOBER 937, THE KINGDOM OF THE SCOTS

Constantin, king of the Scots

'My lord king?' The words are more query than greeting. I feel my lips curl. Bloody Mael Coluim. I shouldn't have left him to rule in my stead. It would have been better had he died on the slaughter field beside Owain of Strathclyde. Then, I'd face only the wrath of my sons that yet live and not my successor.

'Mael,' I murmur. I'm old, tired and broken. My body refuses to obey me, and I stagger, held up by my grandsons who've ensured I made it across the border and into my kingdom. We're all hollow eyes and filthy. Ildulb's not in much better condition. Mael's lips curl at the sight of me and, no doubt, at seeing that Ildulb lives.

'A great victory?' he questions, and if I could, I'd punch him. I wouldn't even care who witnessed the discord between the two of us. I'm amazed that Ildulb doesn't hit him on my behalf.

'No,' a too-bright voice answers, one of my grandsons.

'Indeed,' the odious man reiterates, his single word grating over my aching back and sodden clothes. In northern England, before and during the battle, the weather was bright sunshine. But since the sky darkened that night, covering the slaughter field, it's done nothing but bloody rain. 'Warm water, fresh clothes, hot food,' he orders my servants, as though he's the master here, and I'm not.

I'd kill him for that if my hand had the strength to lift a seax.

'Your daughter?' he questions, and I wince at the reminder that I don't know where she is. My grandsons and I fled north in a ship, over the Mersea river, to our encampment, but she was already gone. I don't know where, and I've hardly had an army of warriors to seek her out. 'Perhaps, my lord king, a marriage to me would have been more proper.' I brace, waiting for more invective, but he leaves my side. I'm rushed away by servants to the welcome heat and pleasure of being warm and clean and then into my luxurious fur bed. I sleep the sleep of the dead and curse on waking. How much easier would it have been to simply end it all here?

'Father.' I startle at Ildulb's tone.

My voice scratches in response. 'Enter, son, enter.'

Ildulb stands before me as a changed man. I can tell immediately. His eyes blaze with fury, and his stance is tight.

'Mael's a cock,' he exclaims and then settles beside me, unbidden. 'What will we do now?' His question is one I've been considering ever since I fled the battlefield.

'Keep out of trouble,' I caution. 'King Athelstan will send his demands for reparations, and they must be paid. The finest of our warriors are dead. It will be a surprise to find that Alpin yet lives.'

Ildulb absorbs this without surprise. He knows, after all. He saw it with his eyes.

'I thought I had him,' he growls. This has been an oft-repeated phrase since he found me fleeing the battle site whenever I mention King Athelstan. 'But it was his damn cousins. I killed them though, both of them. Bloody fools.'

'I know, son, I know,' I repeat. How much better would our current situation be if Ildulb had killed Athelstan of the English instead of his equally well-equipped cousins?

'We should retaliate now while they're not expecting it.'

'With what warriors?' I feel my temper begin to fray. Ildulb knows as well as I do that we left thousands of dead men of the Scots at that cursed place, close to the sea, hemmed in by the two rivers. We thought to be victorious, but we were very, very wrong.

'So what, father? You would have us lick our wounds and play the subservient? Allow Athelstan to claim dominion over our kingdom?'

'Yes.' My response is firm, for all Ildulb vaults to his feet and begins to pace.

'Mael has the support to replace you.'

'Mael thinks he has the support to replace me, but he doesn't. He has no warriors, just as I have no warriors. We've lost, Ildulb. We lost. You need to understand there's no immediate retribution. Not this time.'

'What of my sister?'

'What of her? We have no one to seek her out, not unless I send you or one of your brothers.'

Ildulb shakes his head at this, the snarl on his lips reminding me of a dog on the hunt. 'She's your only daughter.'

'And I want her returned to me, but she wasn't at the campsite. I don't know where she is.'

'But we'll find her?'

'We will, yes, hopefully.'

'What if the English have her?'

'They didn't cross the Mersea river,' I counter aggressively. I don't want to argue with Ildulb. I want us to be united in our approach to what's befallen us.

'Perhaps,' he admits, a shrug of his tight shoulders.

'For now, we listen, and we learn. We do what's expected of us. An apology to King Athelstan, reparations as demanded, and the hope that your brother Alpin yet lives, although if I were King Athelstan, he'd be long dead.'

'Forget about Alpin,' Ildulb dismisses. 'He's more English than Scots now. Whether he lives or dies is irrelevant. It would be better if he was dead, as harsh as that sounds. It's Mael Muire who concerns me. Her, and this union with Olaf Gothfrithson of the Dublin Norse.'

I startle at that.

'What of it? Olaf is just as ruined as we are if he yet lives.'

'Perhaps,' Ildulb muses.

He's misplaced if he thinks Olaf Gothfrithson will help us now. We enticed him to war with the promise of a bride and Jorvik. It seems he has none of those things. He might not even yet live. I didn't see him when I fled the battlefield. 'Rest,' my son orders me, as though I'm an invalid. 'Rest, my lord king. In time, we'll have our vengeance.' His words clang louder than the blacksmith's hammer. I feel no thrill in that. I don't believe we can ever have revenge for what's happened. But that doesn't mean that I wouldn't welcome King Athelstan's death. I would. Of that one fact I'm assured.

4

OCTOBER 937, MALMESBURY, THE KINGDOM OF THE ENGLISH

Athelstan, king of the English

Sorrow clouds my eyes. This should be my moment of triumph, and yet for all I know it is, I'm also wounded. My cousins, Ælfwine and Æthelwine, good men both of them, lost their lives fighting for me.

I know who killed them. I know only too well that it was Constantin's son, Ildulb, who stole their lives. I hope the bastard's dead but, somehow, I doubt it. Constantin and his ilk are lucky individuals – well, all apart from his grandson, Amlaib, dead on Edmund's blade at Cait. And another son, Cellach, dead as well at Brunanburh. And all the while Alpin remains as my hostage for his father's good behaviour. Constantin must care nothing for him. I pity Alpin.

I also know that others of Constantin's kin died on the slaughter field, but not Ildulb. And not Constantin. Even now, Edmund remains perplexed by the ease with which he killed

Owain of Strathclyde. I'm unsurprised. Owain was Constantin's creature, and yet he didn't wish to be. He didn't allow Constantin to kill him. Instead, he permitted my brother to end his life. I wish I'd known more of the rancour between the two of them. I could have done more to exploit it.

All the same, I believe the kingdom of Strathclyde will remain in the hands of Constantin, and one of Owain's sons. My triumph hasn't been complete enough to ensure Constantin, and Olaf Gothfrithson, no longer plague my borders. Yes, thanks to Hywel of the South Welsh the scop that Constantin employed to spread discord amongst the Welsh people is no longer able to disseminate his lies of a future when all rise up against the English. Yet, I can't help thinking much of the damage has already been done. My cousins are dead, and that's no one's fault but the coalition of the Scots and the Norse. I know my cousins died honourably. I know they died doing what they believed was correct for the future of my kingship, but it doesn't ease my grief at their loss. Or my fury at what Alpin's fate might now be.

'My lord king.' I turn and meet the gaze of Edmund. His eyes are haunted to be here, in the royal mausoleum I'm having constructed at the religious site of Malmesbury. No doubt, he doesn't wish to be reminded that one day my body will lie here, and in my place, he'll be king.

My thoughts tumble to my aunt, Lady Æthelflæd of the Mercians. Her body lies enclosed beneath the church in Gloucester. The monument to her life is impressive, and my own intentions are largely based on hers. All the same, I'd sooner she lived. Just as I'd rather my cousins did.

'What is it, Edmund?'

'A messenger from Winchester.' I feel my brow furrow at this as I stand from kneeling, my prayers forgotten about, although the priest's words continue to be heard in the background.

'What is it?'

His face clouds once more, but then he meets my gaze. 'Our sister, Countess Eadhild, is dead, and King Louis has cast aside the assistance of her husband in his kingship.' The words are bland, and yet I find a smile on my lips, even as I know a moment of sorrow for Eadhild. She had no children. Her husband will not take long to replace her, either. She'll be little mourned, perhaps, other than by her sisters living in the nunnery at Wilton. It's a poor assessment of her life. She deserves better. Once more, it's a sobering realisation that so many of my father's children are dead. Ælfweard, Edwin and now Eadhild. Not that my father didn't have an army of children. All the same, a flicker of unease trembles through my body. I want to know what killed her. Ælfweard died of contagion, Edwin on my orders, and Eadhild? I don't know. Perhaps it was in childbirth, although there's no mention of a child. Maybe it was some other cause. I shake aside the unsettling feelings that not knowing brings to my mind.

'Then we must have prayers said for more than just our cousins.' Quickly, I bend and return to my knees. This time Edmund joins me.

His words voice the familiar prayers, although, on occasion, he mutters only an 'Amen', the Latin too complex to fully understand, even with his schooling at Glastonbury.

My eyes stray from the wooden floor beneath my knees to the altar and the priceless relics ensconced beneath it, for all few know how to access them.

Our Lord God has ensured my success, but I can't deny the price has been heavy.

I should have my will rewritten. I must ensure funds are made available for the eternal praying necessary to escort my cousins and my half-sister as they make their way to Heaven. Only then my thoughts stray once more. It's imperative I reinforce the defences at

Chester in case Constantin thinks to make good on his failure. It's vital I ensure the contrary archbishop of York stays true to his oaths. Of necessity, I must consider the families of those men who died fighting for me. And, of course, I need to find out how affairs in Dublin and the kingdom of the Scots now stand. Does Olaf Gothfrithson still live? Does Anlaf Sihtricson? Do Constantin and Ildulb? I must have reparations for what they've cost England. I need to decide what to do about Alpin. Perhaps, I realise, I should have allowed him to fight against his father. Maybe, I should have allowed him to prove himself for who he is, and not his identity as his father's son.

Many will write of this battle. They'll write of the men who met their deaths there, but, I confess, I wish it had been some of the more important individuals rather than the son of the Danish king and Gebeachan of the Northern Isles. A pity it wasn't Olaf Gothfrithson who was struck down dead. A pity it wasn't Constantin of the Scots, but instead his son, Cellach.

The knowledge of what brought us to battle and what caused the resentment to form swirls in my thoughts. The scop that Constantin employed is a man of great skill. He still lives, transferred into my care by Hywel of the South Welsh on finding him. Perhaps I have a use for him that won't end in his death. Not yet, anyway.

5

NOVEMBER 937, HEREFORD, THE KINGDOM OF THE ENGLISH

Idwal, king of Gwynedd

Damn the bloody Norse. They're no good for anything. And damn Olaf Gothfrithson. If not for him and his failure to beat Athelstan of the English then I wouldn't be here now, in Hereford, once more forced to bend the knee to Athelstan in agreement to his onerous terms that assure the Welsh kingdoms of peace with the king of the English.

I eye him with unease. He's grown in stature since his success at Brunanburh. He was already an overbearing arse and now he's ten times as bad. And at his side his brother, Edmund, struts as well. The pair look like prize fools.

Hywel has also joined this little reunion of Athelstan and the Welsh kings. Once more, I growl low in my throat, he's come out of this looking better than I do. Damn him as well.

'My lord King Athelstan.' I bow low towards Athelstan but not respectfully. Rather, I wish to obscure my face until I can set it into one that's at least not contemptuous. I should have sought out Hywel first and called upon him as my cousin to ease relations with the English king, as he tried to do over a decade ago, when Athelstan forged two peace accords: one at Eamont with Constantin, Hywel, Owain of Strathclyde and Ealdred of Bamburgh; and one in Hereford, between Athelstan and the other Welsh kingdoms, my own included.

'My lord Idwal, you're welcome to Hereford.' Even Athelstan's voice is unctuous, setting my teeth on edge. I shouldn't have come here. Although, well, if I hadn't then Athelstan would likely have marched into my kingdom and demanded my submission, as he did to Constantin at Cait four summers ago. He's a man aware of his reach and power, his influence and the respect that his overwhelming victory against the combined force of the Scots and Norse gifts him. Rumours reach me of the retribution Athelstan means to take against Constantin, of the work being undertaken to reinforce Chester and York, of Athelstan's intentions towards Alpin, Constantin's son, who's a hostage at the English king's court. He won't be for much longer.

Damn Olaf. Damn Constantin.

'Please rise,' Athelstan continues, turning towards Edmund. 'You've met my brother before, I'm sure?' he asks.

I smile, but I deem it more of a grimace. Edmund is flush with his triumph and his youth. I don't think I was ever as young as him. Even his youthful countenance annoys me.

'And, of course, you know your cousin, Hywel, and the other kings of the Welsh people as well, Morgan ap Owain of Gwent, Tewdwr ap Griffi ab Elise of Brycheiniog and Gwriad of Glywysing.'

Damn him again. He even speaks our Welsh names well. Is there nothing that he can't do?

'Indeed, my lord king. Greetings to you all,' I call, trying to sound jaunty, although it sounds off, even to my ears. Searching eyes greet mine. I imagine Morgan, Tewdwr and Gwriad are as happy to be here as I am.

I'm the last to arrive at this meeting, by choice, not chance. Now I meet their interest. I respect none of them. There was a time I thought them worthy of my regard when they stood aside from King Athelstan and refused to attend upon him within England. But that time is long past. I imagine all of them pissed themselves with fright when Athelstan demanded their attendance upon him. Only the urging of my brother, Cadfan, has brought me here. He argued it was better to have peace than war. I'm still not sure I agree with him.

'Be seated.' King Athelstan is magnanimous as he speaks, his hand pointing to a seat that's been left free for me, next to my cousin, Hywel. Damn him all over again.

Ill-mannered, I sit roughly, the wooden legs scraping over the wooden floorboards. Hywel winces. I grin on meeting his gaze. He rolls his eyes at my antics. Good.

King Athelstan pauses for a moment while servants refill goblets of wine and place food before me. I missed this meal purposefully. I'd sooner not eat his food, and yet my belly growls angrily.

'Gentlemen,' Athelstan eventually speaks, his eyes everywhere.

I try not to meet his gaze, but it's bewitching, and I struggle to turn aside as his appraising eyes linger on me. I incline my head again, somehow compelled to be more respectful for all I don't intend to be.

'I've brought us together to reassert our alliances, variously agreed at Hereford, or since then, and to reveal to you the man who's caused us so many problems. King Hywel assisted me in tracking down Taliesen. I'm grateful for your help.' Again, Athelstan speaks respectfully, and I think Hywel preens like a bloody pheasant.

As he speaks, the scop I recognise only too well appears before us. I expect him to be bound, bloody and beaten, even now, months after the events of Brunanburh. But no, the man's dressed in court finery, and his boots gleam with fresh polish. His hair is cut into a pleasing shape, the nape of his neck shorn close, his fringe long and tied with trinkets that clatter together musically.

What is this? I was sure he'd be dead by now, or if not, have had his tongue severed from his mouth to prevent more tales being spread to sunder Athelstan's alliance forged at Hereford over a decade ago. Perhaps, I think, Athelstan might even have returned the man's remains to King Constantin. Maybe alongside those of his son's, Alpin. Everyone says that Athelstan will execute Alpin, if he hasn't already.

'Gentlemen.' I recognise the voice as the man bows low. It's melodic even now.

'This is Taliesen. I believe many of you will know him. I understand he's respected at every court upon this island, including mine.' The scop shows no fear in Athelstan's presence. Neither do any of Athelstan's attendant warriors look particularly on edge. I'm sure they are, but it's not for fear of what the scop will say or do. I look to one of the men and he grimaces, showing me his teeth in the process. Bloody marvellous.

'Good day to you all,' Taliesen continues. I nod towards him, determined not to allow Athelstan's warrior to fluster me, while Hywel smiles at the man. Why Hywel took it upon himself to apprehend Taliesen I don't know. Does he not dream of a time our kingdoms might be free from English interference? No, of course he doesn't. He thinks only of his precious laws, coins and justice. What's wrong with the edge of my blade to ensure men and women do as they should and obey my command?

'He is, of course, the man who constructed the scop song that all of your countrymen and women are humming and singing. I take it you don't need it repeated?'

All the same, Taliesen hums the familiar refrains. My foot taps along in time to the tuneful rendition.

'But, I've put him to greater purposes. When we've reaffirmed our alliance and reinstated the original terms of our peace accord, including making good on the missing years of reparations and tithes, I'll have him share his latest composition with us all.'

I startle at this. What has King Athelstan done? What has Taliesen done? And why must it be the original terms that are reinstated, and why must they be backdated?

'My lord king, I've had no opportunity to discuss this matter with you,' I rejoin too hastily, I realise, as Hywel smirks.

'It's of no consequence, my lord Idwal.' Athelstan's response is much slower. 'These fine gentlemen have agreed to the terms already, and so all you need to do is add your signature to the new agreement. Any time for negotiation has long since passed. All is decided. The terms are fair, are they not?' This Athelstan directs to Hywel, who nods, and also to Tewdwr, Morgan and Gwriad, who offer no complaints. Damn the fools.

My gaze flicks to Edmund, and also to the man sitting beside him. I squint, trying to place him. And then I remember. Of course, the English king has his prisoner at his side. Alpin, son of Constantin, as if I needed any more of a reminder of the might of the English kingship. I'm surprised his sisters aren't there as well – after all, Athelstan won York through marrying his sister to Sihtric who then had the misfortune to die. It's a fine warning, but a warning it is. I sign or lose a son or a brother. I'd rather lose my precious supplies than do that. King Constantin might be able to abandon his son, but I can't do that.

'Very well, my lord king.' I force the words through dry lips, not even the fine wine able to bring enough fluid to my tongue to make the words more than a harsh rasp.

'Bring the treaty,' King Athelstan speaks into the sudden silence. 'You'll be the last to add your signature. Alas, the roads must have delayed you.'

With quill to hand, I eye the scratches of my fellow Welsh kings, noting that Hywel's name is missing. No doubt his terms are more generous than mine. I pause, every bone in my body wanting to deny what needs to be done. The moment elongates, the words blurring before me, for all they've been penned in a handsome ink. They're easy enough to read. The terms not onerous, but unacceptable to me all the same.

'Come, cousin.' Hywel nudges me when I don't immediately sign. 'Don't keep your overlord waiting.' His words are whispered. I jolt at them. All too easily I understand that I've made a difficult situation even worse with my tardiness and refusal to engage in this new peace conference.

Growling while Hywel chuckles softly, I add my mark, careful to keep the ink away from my skin.

With that done, the cleric rushes to remove the manuscript, another taking the quill and the ink, and then I sit back, hands over my belly, legs stretched out before me. It's done. I'm once more subservient to Athelstan of the English.

'And of course,' Athelstan murmurs, as though he's about to say something inconsequential. 'Lord Alpin will be travelling to the kingdom of the Scots to enforce my dominion over them. Better to have a loyal man of the English than anyone else, keeping an eye on things.' The news displeases me, but I realise others already know it. Damn them all again. Not, I think that Constantin will approve of such an arrangement. Or his son. Or Mael Coluim.

And then Athelstan gestures expansively to Taliesen.

The man nods, plucking the strings on his lute, and then he

begins to speak. The words wash over me, and for every word spoken, my ire grows.

King Athelstan is victorious in name and deed, and no doubt, Taliesen and his scop song will ensure all in the Welsh kingdoms are only too aware of the monumental victory that Athelstan, and his brother, forged at Brunanburh.

I can hardly listen, and yet I do all the same.

Damn Olaf Gothfrithson. And damn Constantin of the Scots. And damn Athelstan, the bloody king of the English.

If he'd met his death at Brunanburh then the English kingdom would have crumbled, I'm sure of that. Young Edmund lacks his brother's reputation and military might.

Had Athelstan died at Brunanburh, but Edmund survived, then no matter the words of the scop, England would not have endured.

Not for the first time, I wish I'd allied with the Norse and Constantin of the Scots.

If I had my chance again, I would. I wouldn't even hesitate.

6

LATE 937, STRATHCLYDE

Ildulb, prince of the Scots

I eye Owain of Strathclyde's son with ill-concealed contempt. I know my father hated Owain, and for good reason. I hardly think his son is any better. The only thing Dyfnwal has that's an advantage is his grovelling welcome towards me. He's not Owain, to be haughty and difficult. No, Dyfnwal owes all he has to my father.

'My lord.' He bows low, as though he's my slave, not just my servant. I note it with a wry smile.

'Rise,' I order him, pleased to have some acknowledged authority here.

'Your father?'

'Is well,' I counter quickly. 'Hale and hearty.'

'That pleases me,' he simpers again. I note his thin body, his feeble arms, the tunic which seems to settle on him as though a dress. I'm unsure why my father chose him to rule after Owain.

'I've come to discuss the terms of the new peace accord with

King Athelstan,' I announce quickly, settling before the hearth fire, welcoming the warmth on this high peak. On any other day the views would be astounding, but with the cloud heavy and louring, it's a wonder I don't walk off the side of the hill.

'My lord?' Here Dyfnwal falters beside me, his goblet of wine hanging between his thin lips and his hand.

'The peace accord. With King Athelstan.'

'Is agreed, my lord. I have submitted to him, as King Constantin bid my father, all those years ago.'

'Without my father's agreement?' I feel my rage begin to build. The bloody fool. My brother, Alpin, more English than bloody Scots, has been sent to impose Athelstan's demands over our father. I'd spit in his face if I could. We must pay the wergild of the dead English men, we must make good on those tithes not sent to the English, we must sign a peace accord, promising to never again ally with the Norse. My father's relief that Alpin lives means he's all too happy to oblige. But with Strathclyde, he means to be more obdurate. Or he did. It appears he's too damn late.

'My lord, your father bid me reach an accord with the English messenger. I've done as he said.'

Dyfnwal's correct, my father did bid him that. But not so bloody quickly.

'And what were the terms?' I exhale. I should have come sooner, but I didn't wish to leave my father with Alpin. I don't trust him despite my father's pleasure at seeing his son once more.

'As to be expected. An alliance against the Norse. A promise never to break the peace.'

'And the reparations?'

'A resumption of the tithe.'

'What of the wergild?'

'No, my lord, your kingdom is to pay the wergild. The English king was adamant about that.'

I feel a growl on my lips, and stand abruptly.

'Then you'll pay half of the amount levied on my father,' I announce angrily. 'You're his to command, and he'll agree with me.'

I notice the dismay on Dyfnwal's face, the way his hand shakes as he holds his goblet.

'And never again make an agreement with the English king without my father's permission.'

Furious, I stride from the hall, the grey clouds cloaking me, but I know my way back to Scone, to where my brother sits at my father's side, as though he's the prodigal son returned and not the viper in the nest.

I've a mind to send him back to King Athelstan cold and marbled in death. He's not my brother. Not any more. He's not even a man of the kingdom of the Scots.

7

CHRIST'S MASS 937, EXETER, THE KINGDOM OF THE ENGLISH

Eadgifu, the lady of Wessex

I eye the scop. So much trouble can be laid at his feet, and yet King Athelstan has determined to reprieve him. And not only forgive him but allow him to compose a scop song in praise of the battle of Brunanburh.

The man is tall and wiry, well-clothed at the king's expense, trinkets clattering together in his long hair. He looks very good for a man who should have been executed as a traitor.

I think it's too much. After all, men died because of the words this man disseminated. I've tried to make him welcome within Athelstan's household, but I mistrust him still, no matter Edmund's instruction that I shouldn't. The scop was once in the pay of King Constantin of the Scots, and now he does King Athelstan's bidding. I wish the king could see that men who allow their skills to be paid for by the highest bidder can't be counted upon.

And yet. Well, it'll be good to have King Athelstan's virtues extolled before the court. His reputation grows daily, even without the aid of the scop. Athelstan has accomplished much. The kingdom of the English is united against the Norse and the Scots. Even the kingdom of Bamburgh looks to Athelstan for leadership, although Ealdwulf, Lord Ealdred's adult son and heir, is rumoured to still live. A pity he didn't meet his end on the slaughter field at Brunanburh. Ealdorman Guthrum holds Bamburgh for the time being.

'My lady.' I turn and meet King Athelstan's shining eyes. He's excited for all to hear the words the scop has composed.

'My lord king,' I reply, noting his finely stitched tunic, bedecked with the wyvern of Wessex and the eagle of Mercia. I notice too the head of Kent's horse and the snake of the East Anglians. Athelstan claims all and displays it in the embroidery and imagery that adorns him, his warriors, servants, slaves and even his horses. He's truly a magnificent king. Not that the inclusion of Kent doesn't rankle. I confess, it does. Kent was my gift to Athelstan's father alongside my body in marriage. Athelstan has done nothing to earn it, other than respect me and my sons.

'How's Eadred?' Athelstan sits beside me. Eadred's not long returned from the school at Glastonbury. He thinks himself too old to learn more, but boys who might one day be king should always be learning. King Edward had five sons between three wives. Two of those sons are dead. Life is precarious. Not that a boy of his age will understand that.

'He's grown,' I laugh. 'Taller than me now by at least the width of my hand.'

Athelstan nods as though it's to be expected. And it probably is. Edmund is taller than Athelstan. I think Eadred will be taller yet.

'And his affliction?'

'It's passed, or so I'm told. A problem with his belly. The monks have told him what foods to eat. It'll be a tedious diet, but better than the pain he's experienced.'

Again, the king nods, as though pleased to hear this. Only then he leans closer. 'They say my grandfather was affected by the same affliction. It's a shame for Eadred. It's to be hoped he finds a better way of contending with it than spending all his time praying.' The words are followed by a soft chuckle. Athelstan is perhaps more spiritual than his grandfather, but his faith is a light cloak, not something to quench all fire from his soul. 'And what of the news from Louis in West Frankia? And my half-sisters and their husbands?'

I know a moment of sorrow to be reminded of Eadhild, dead for half a year. Her husband replaced her immediately. I think little of him, and not just because of the problems he causes Louis, king of West Frankia.

'Eadgyth sent word from Aachen and wished us well. I've not heard from Ælfgifu for some time. Eadgifu also sent greetings for Christ's Mass, but reading between the lines a little, I fear there's unease between your half-sisters, or rather, between their husbands and sons.'

Athelstan nods. I know he's pleased not to contend with all of his sisters. I don't blame him. However, Edmund is concerned for Louis, and I share those worries. Athelstan's cousins in Flanders are not the most loyal, but I keep this to myself. For now.

'The others are safely about their prayers at Wilton. Eadburh is extolled for her virtue.' I'm proud of my daughter, even if a life of quiet prayer doesn't appeal to me.

'Then we can relax and enjoy the words of the scop,' Athelstan announces. A sharp glance at his pensive face, and I realise he's doing the very opposite.

Athelstan understands the twisted and tangled threads his sisters' husbands and sons weave. He would, I think, do well not to become involved. But I know he will. He would think it unkingly to abandon them to the machinations of East and West Frankish politics.

Edmund hastens to my side then, a swift bow towards the king, his brother, and Edmund pants softly beside me. I don't wish to know what he's been doing. He's dishevelled but I don't detect the smell of horses on him. No doubt he's been amusing himself with women or ale elsewhere. I forgive him this once. After all, it is a time for celebration.

With a sharp clap of his hands, the scop draws the eye of all.

He bows towards King Athelstan, so low his nose almost touches the ground. And then, in a rich voice used to such displays, he begins his tale of the events at Brunanburh.

'Here King Athelstan, leader of warriors,
Ring-giver of men, and also his brother,
The ætheling Edmund, struck life-long glory
In strife around Brunanburh, clove the shield-wall
Hacked the war-time, with hammers' leavings,
Edward's offspring, as was natural to them
By ancestry, that in frequent conflict
They defend land, treasures and homes
Against every foe. The antagonists succumbed,
The nation of Scots and sea-men
Fell doomed. The field darkened
With soldiers' blood, after in the morning-time
The sun, that glorious star,
Bright candle of God, the Lord Eternal,
Glided over the depths, until the noble creature
Sank to rest. There lay many a soldier
Of the men of the North, shot over shield,
Taken by spears; likewise Scottish also

Sated, weary of war. All day long
The West Saxons with elite cavalry
Pressed in the tracks of the hateful nation,
With mill-sharp blades severely hacked from behind
Those who fled battle. The Mercians refused
Hard hand-play to none of the heroes
Who with Olaf, over the mingling of waves,
Doomed in flight, sought out land
In the bosom of a ship. Five young
Kings lay on the battle-field,
Put to sleep by swords; likewise also seven
Of Olaf's jarls, countless of the raiding-army
Of seamen and Scots. There the ruler of
Northmen, compelled by necessity,
Was put to flight, to ship's prow,
With a small troop. The boat withdrew,
Saved life, over the fallow flood.
There also likewise, the aged Constantine
Came north to his kith by flight.
The hoary man of war had no cause to exult
In the clash of blades; he was shorn of his kinsmen,
Deprived of friends, on the meeting-place of peoples,
Cut off in strife, and left his son
On the place of slaughter, mangled by wounds,
Young in battle. The grey-haired warrior,
Old crafty one, had no cause to boast
In that clash of blades – no more had Olaf –
Cause to laugh, with the remnants of their raiding-army,
That they were better in works of war
On the battle-field, in the conflict of standards,
The meeting of spears, the mixing of weapons

The encounter of men, when they played
Against Edward's sons on the field of slaughter.
Never yet in this island
Was there a greater slaughter
Of people felled by the sword's edges,
Before this, as books tell us,
Old authorities, since Angles and Saxons
Came here from the east,
Sought out Britain over the broad ocean,
Warriors eager for fame, proud war-smiths,
Overcame the Welsh, seized the country.'

The hall is silent, all listening to this tale, and I confess, the inclusion of Edmund beside Athelstan fills me with pride. My son risked his life for Athelstan. I'm pleased that the king's prepared to acknowledge this. Perhaps I forgive him for showing Kent's emblem on his tunic after all.

While Athelstan's reputation has grown so vast in a relatively short space of time, he's determined not to take all the acclaim for himself.

I allow a smile to play on my lips. This accounting might not be quite as Edmund told it to me, but it is a truly magnificent rendition.

I hope King Athelstan lives for many years to enjoy his triumph, and certainly so that he can counter the threat from the Norse and the Scots, when they regroup and recover themselves, for, just as when King Constantin bent the knee after his failure at Cait only to rise against Athelstan once more, I know that this present calmness over Britain will not last forever.

8

938, DUBLIN

Olaf Gothfrithson, king of the Dublin Norse

'Brother.'

'What?' I drawl, from where my head rests level with the table before me. My ale jug is empty. I'd ask for another, but instead I've welcomed the sleep that's claimed me.

'Get up, your worthless shit,' my brother glowers at me.

'Why? What is there for me to do today?' I demand, wishing Gothfrith would leave me alone. Since my defeat at Brunanburh, my life has been the same, one of endless drinking. I lost many of my warriors in the battle, and have nothing of value with which to tempt new men to serve me, not even my battle prowess. I rewarded my warriors with little more than death and failure. I don't even have my wife, lost to me since the battle.

'Your wife?'

'What of her?'

'There's someone here who says they have Mael Muire and will return her to you.'

Now I force myself upright, wincing at the bright light spilling through the open doorway. She's been missing for many months now. I've spent the winter without her, my bed filled by any willing to take my drunken advances.

'Who is it?'

'Haraldr.'

'Haraldr who?' I feel my temper fray at his obtuseness.

'Haraldr Sihtricson.'

'Brother of Anlaf?'

'Yes, brother of Anlaf.'

I allow a small smile to play on my face at that news. Anlaf is my ally still. He too survived the slaughter field of Brunanburh. If his brother has my wife, then it should be nothing more than a matter of him handing her over to me. My lips curl and I pause, my ale-addled mind slowly working its way through the words and the intent behind them. 'Why is she not here?' I question, reaching for a jug of water and swigging from it, only to gag at the sour taste. Once more I wish there was more ale.

'I believe, brother dearest, that there's something needed in exchange for your wife.'

I stand abruptly at that. 'But his brother is my ally.'

'Anlaf is your ally, yes. But Haraldr isn't allied with Anlaf.'

My head swirls at this, not that warring brothers should surprise me, and I stagger towards him. 'Have them brought before me.'

'You're to meet him on the quayside, when you've cleaned yourself up a bit.' Only then do I realise that my hand rests on the head of a hound who licks away the spillages of my excesses which mar my stained beard and tunic.

'Get away with you,' I growl at the animal, offering it a swift kick to go with the words, greeted by a whine of pain. I glower at the dog, and it slinks away. Damn thing is always stealing my ale.

I call for a clean tunic and dunk my head in the water barrel, wincing at the bite of the cold water, before pulling the tunic over my head with a sniff for my armpits. Gods, I stink. All the while, Gothfrith watches me, his expression unreadable. If not for him, I'd have lost the rule of Dublin after Brunanburh, but I'm not about to tell him that. If I let him know I'm grateful for his steadying hand while I console myself in ale and women, he'd do more than just govern in my stead.

With a grunt of unhappy acceptance, Gothfrith leads me to the quayside. I growl at that. It's depressing to see so few ships moored along its edges. Even more sobering is the realisation that many of them aren't seaworthy. Not even the taverns ring with the cries of men too deep in their cups. No, Dublin is not what it used to be before the slaughter of Brunanburh, and I've only myself to blame for that.

'At last,' a stout man calls from where he's sitting beside a ship, perched on a barrel and gnawing the meat from a chicken leg. Beside him, I startle to see my wife. She's bound and a gag is around her mouth, her eyes furious, as she twists on seeing me.

'Remove the gag,' I demand, moving towards her to do just that. I've not seen her for over half a year. I note her belly isn't filled with another man's child. That pleases me. I confess, I feared whoever had her would use her poorly. I mean, that's what I'd have done if the situation had been reversed. She rears back from me, and I'm tempted to kick her, as I did the bloody dog.

'Now, now, my lord king.' Haraldr's voice is gravelly, but his grip on my arm is fierce. He looks like his brother. Perhaps older. Or maybe not. A scar mars his right cheek, pulled tight, forcing his eye half-closed. I step backwards, although I don't take my eyes off Mael Muire's furious face. I try and calm her with that look, but she's having none of it. If she's not careful, she'll tip herself into the watery depths. 'We need to barter first, and then you can have the lady returned to you.'

'Where did you find her?' I ask before I can stop myself. Really, I should have been outraged at the thought of bartering for my damn wife.

'It little matters. She's mine now, and she can be yours, when you give me Limerick to rule.'

'What?' It's my brother who splutters at those words, not me. Anlaf Sihtricson, Haraldr's brother, holds Limerick in my name, for the time being. Anything to get the annoying fool away from me ever since his return from Brunanburh. I promised him Dublin, but he can't have it. I need it. For now.

'I would rule Limerick, and you can have your wife.' Haraldr's eyes gleam with triumph at his ploy, as his words slow with the pleasure of saying them. I close my eyes, considering how this might aid me. I mean, I want my wife back, but if it also brings Anlaf back to Dublin, I'm not sure it's a good bargain. That said, Constantin of the Scots has sent me messengers demanding to know the whereabouts of his daughter. It would at least solve that problem for me, and might repair our fractured alliance.

'Fine, you have Limerick, and I'll have my wife.' I wince to hear Gothfrith's outraged shriek at my hastily made decision. But I'm king here, not him, no matter what he thinks. Yes, Gothfrith aided me in sending Anlaf to Limerick. He won't be pleased to have Anlaf returned to Dublin, and that's sure to be where he'll come, furious and outraged, demanding that which I've refused to give him. But, I want Mael Muire restored to me. Then, perhaps, I can amuse myself with begetting more children, rather than drinking myself insensible every day. And of course, I can have her working for our future as well. I was promised much in exchange for her in my marriage bed. With her here, I can begin to make more demands of my own on Constantin.

With a mocking bow, Haraldr stands, and unties my wife, removing the gag last of all and pushing her towards me so that she stumbles and I flounder to catch her. She lands in my arms, and we meet one another's eyes, hers blazing into mine even as running steps come to an abrupt stop close by. She stinks worse than I do.

'Father.' Camman's words ring loudly, and I wince, the pounding of my head finally making itself known. I need ale to quell the bitterness of last night's drink. 'We're under attack. The Northern and Southern Ui Neill have allied against you.'

I close my eyes, even as I try not to smell the foulness of my wife's dress and hair. Wherever she's been, I don't think she's washed since Brunanburh. She bucks in my arms, her hands pounding on my chest, tears slipping down her face to force the muck aside. I almost gag, but swallow heavily instead, and grip her hair tightly, so that she's forced to peace or risk losing her hair.

'Wonderful,' I announce, looking at Haraldr, imagining I can scent the smoke from buildings burning on the extremities of my landholdings where they abut the Southern Ui Neill. 'Now, my good man, you can prove your loyalty to your lord king by joining the coming battle. After all, you're my man now.' I allow a slow smile to spread on my lips. 'If you want to hold Limerick, you'll have to fight for it.' Haraldr's grin of triumph turns into a grimace of displeasure. I note how many ships he has, and how many shipmen – more than me, which depresses me further. So few ships to call mine in the quayside. But, a fight with the Southern and Northern Ui Neill will prune that to a more acceptable amount.

I need to shave, and stop drinking, after I've banished my aching head, that is.

I must consider the future. I have my wife, and she needs cleaning up. I'm also to go to war with Haraldr's men, and then it's to be hoped, when we triumph, that other warriors will once more flock to my side.

I eye my brother and my son. Both grunt an acknowledgement of the fight to come. I nod. I might have been forced to hand over Limerick to Haraldr, but it's filled with the dead Olaf Scabbyhead's remaining allies, and they're all pestilent boils. I'll be glad when Haraldr's won them over or killed them. I don't mind, as long as Limerick becomes easier to rule.

9

939, WINCHESTER, THE KINGDOM OF THE ENGLISH

Edmund, prince of the English

I eye the woman before me and her small children. They look terrified, although she holds herself haughtily. I'd ask my half-brother for more details but now isn't the time. His triumph at Brunanburh means he's lauded by all, and the island of Britain is quiet. Constantin has been forced to bend the knee, with his son, Alpin, watching all he does, as have the Welsh kings, all apart from Hywel, who's still Athelstan's subservient, but allowed more freedom of action than the others.

The same can't be said for affairs in East and West Frankia, where my half-sisters and cousin are involved in continual war, or so it seems. This woman is the wife of Herluin, count of Ponthieu, and I should call her countess, or so I've been informed.

'My lady, countess.' I incline my head, determined to offer her respect, even if she is a hostage at the English court. I didn't believe Athelstan would involve himself in such discord, but I think he's been left with little choice. Affairs in East and West Frankia are fraught with family strife. Not for the first time, I'm grateful that our half-sisters are married into families far from England, for if not, I think there'd be constant war.

'My lord.' Her words are sharp and edged with flint. I wish my mother were here to meet her, but she's visiting my sister, Eadburh, in her nunnery at Wilton.

'I would welcome you to England. A pity it's not under happier circumstances.'

'I'm a prisoner, my lord.' When she offers nothing further, I falter.

I wish Athelstan were here, but he's embroiled in conversation with the messengers and warriors who brought this woman and her children to Winchester. It's my cousin's fault. Arnulf of Flanders has attacked her husband's holdings in Montreuil and needs to keep her somewhere safe until peace can be negotiated with her husband. Why Cousin Arnulf would think Winchester the place to do that, I'm unsure, although I suspect he means to embroil England in the war between East and West Frankia. This is his way of doing so because Athelstan has so far managed to keep his distance.

'You look like your cousin,' she announces, words filled with spite.

'Count Arnulf?' I query, just to be sure.

'Yes, and King Louis, the fourth of his name, I think. They'll tear themselves apart, Arnulf, Louis and Otto, who's the husband of your half-sister, Eadgyth,' she murmurs. 'Your king won a great victory against his enemies in Britain, but there are no better enemies than family.'

I encourage her to sit, the children gripping her skirts tightly so that the movement is awkward.

'Perhaps,' she continues, 'it'll be safer here, after all. Your king is a magnificent warrior. None will dare to attack England while he lives. Not again. And I doubt that the fleets of your cousin, my husband, or Otto of East Frankia would be a match for Athelstan's.'

I don't miss that there's some respect in those words. And also some ambition, which is solidified with her next words.

'He has no wife?' She arches an eyebrow suggestively at me, and I swallow heavily, feeling a sheen of sweat on my forehead. I should have allowed Ealdorman Athelstan to keep her company while the king was absent. Or my younger brother, who is too young to appreciate a beautiful woman. I fear she's ambitious.

'No, the king will not wed. I'm his heir,' I reply, only to wish I hadn't as her gaze appraises me. She's gone from being angry at her capture to plotting her future. She's as quick to think as any of the king's most able politicians. As quick as my mother as well.

She licks her lower lip, and I find myself unable to draw my gaze away from such a wanton action. Only then the door opens, and in strides King Athelstan, followed by a host of messengers, as well as his ealdormen and the archbishop of Canterbury.

'Ah, I see you've met Lady Beatrice,' the king begins.

I manage to tear my eyes from her and notice the knowing look in my brother's eye. He might have no wife, but he's not immune to the charms of women.

'You're my guest, more than my prisoner, I assure you.' Athelstan speaks with confidence. 'I'll do all I can to bring the problems between East and West Frankia to an end and see you returned home,' he confirms. 'Count Arnulf means you no harm, and neither do I.'

The haughty expression has returned to her face, and I'm grateful that Athelstan arrived when he did.

'Now, Edmund, I would have you join us. We must discuss what will happen next. Lady Eadgifu's servants will see you and your children settled,' he confirms to Lady Beatrice, and I bob my head towards her and hasten to catch the end of the line of ealdormen as they follow the king to a small room to continue talking.

I'm hardly in the door when Athelstan begins to speak. His face has lost its placid acceptance of the position Count Arnulf, our cousin, has placed him in.

'They say that West and East Frankia are at each other's throats. My foster son Louis is antagonistic, as is my brother by marriage, Otto of East Frankia. And in the middle of it all is Count Hugh, my former brother by marriage, and Count Arnulf, my cousin. Tell me, what should be done?' His exasperation is impossible to miss. Here, far from West and East Frankia, it's difficult to see any means of bringing the warring family members to heel.

Silence fills the room as I try and make sense of all the family relationships at play. Our half-sisters are at war against one another. No, that's not right. My half-sister's husband is at war against my oldest half-sister's son, and in the middle my other half-sister's widowed husband is playing the two against each other, and my cousin is there to pick over what he can. I think. I feel a pulsing in my head at such a tangled mess.

'Count Arnulf places you in a difficult position,' the archbishop speaks consideringly when no one else does.

'Yes, he means to drag me into all this, no matter what.'

'And Louis of West Frankia?'

'I received a messenger from him only yesterday, requesting I send my fleet to aid him against Count Arnulf and King Otto of East Frankia, his uncle by marriage?'

'Then Count Arnulf knows Louis was likely to ask for your support. He's sent this woman here to make that impossible.'

I watch Athelstan carefully. I've never known him to be someone who took kindly to being told what to do. He certainly doesn't appreciate being forced to take a stance.

'If I could, I'd bring this to a peaceful end, but it seems impossible. I'll send the fleet to aid Louis. He's my foster son, and I promised to support him, no matter what happened. And the seas around our island are quiet.' Resolved, Athelstan's face lightens a little, especially when no one complains at sending the fleet so far from England. The shipmen played their part in the aftermath of Brunanburh. They hunted down the Norse who thought to flee over the sea. Since then, they've been restless. Not even affairs in the kingdom of the Scots demand their attention. 'I pray to God every day that my half-sisters are either holy women or far from my shores.' His grin widens. 'Can you imagine the problems if they remained at Winchester?'

I laugh along with him, as do the others he's sought opinions from.

'Indeed, my lord king,' Ealdorman Athelstan offers. 'There'd be no peace in England. None at all.'

10

27 OCTOBER 939, GLOUCESTER

Athelstan, king of the English

The words of my priests blur around me. I feel my time growing short and curse the frailty of my body. There's so much more that I can accomplish, but I'm not to be given that time.

My eyes blink open at the scene before me. A week ago I was hale and hearty, and now I can feel death calling to me. I know some will think this a just punishment for all those killed at the battle of Brunanburh, but I know better. This isn't punishment for that. The contagion which has stolen my strength and my breath has affected many others as well. I didn't think I would avoid it, as the king, but I did hope I'd somehow escape its ravages. But it seems not.

I've bid everyone leave my side. I don't wish others to sicken as I have, but my priests remain with me, as do my most loyal servants. My half-brothers have been banished from my side. The House of

Wessex must continue to thrive, even if I'm no longer here to direct the governing of England, and her involvement in East and West Frankia. My actions in supporting Louis have driven a wedge between my Flanders cousin and me. But I have no remorse. Louis is my foster son. My cousin is merely that. And he's a brutal bastard as well. Lady Beatrice has been returned to her husband, against Count Arnulf's wishes, but that doesn't concern me, and no longer will, anyway. I didn't enjoy being forced to take a standpoint, and now, it's Edmund who'll have to contend with affairs in East and West Frankia.

I spare a thought for my dreams of a united England. I hope it will prevail without me, but I know some will sense England's weakness. I consider Edmund. Many would still think him a child, but he's not. In the coming days and months, he'll need to prove that.

'My lord king.' The voice of one of my scribes reaches me, recalling me to the here and now. I've not allowed him inside my room, but he shouts to me from behind the closed doorway where he lists my dying wishes when I can remember what they are. I meant to fulfil this task after Brunanburh. I erred when I delayed the task.

My body has been hot and cold. I've been wracked with fevers, shivering until I had to clasp my teeth together, only to throw clear all my furs a moment later. I crave sleep, but every time my eyes close, a cough erupts from my mouth, and it's all I can do to breathe.

'My lord king.' The voice again.

'Where was I?' I demand, my voice thin and reedy, whistling through my tight lips.

'Your books, my lord king,' he offers. I know we've been working on my will for some time now. But I have many priceless books. 'The Gospels,' he prompts, clearly not for the first time. I hear his huff of frustration that he must tell me again. But this time I have an answer for him.

'To the archbishop of Canterbury,' I manage to whisper.

'And the smaller Gospel book?'

I wish I didn't own so many books. I'd sooner lie in peace. But no, this must be done.

'To the monks at St Augustine's, Canterbury,' I decide, although my voice grows weaker and weaker. 'And the relics.' I speak urgently, my breathing is becoming more and more laboured. I fear I won't get through all my books and there are other things to consider. 'The relics should be distributed amongst my holy establishments,' I whisper, only my scribe is talking.

'The letters of Alcuin,' he demands. A smile touches my lips at the memories of the wisdom found in those letters between the scholar and his friend, Charlemagne, a king that many have said I resemble. I've done what I could. Alcuin's demands that Charlemagne be staunch in his faith have been something I've striven to accomplish; his words, that the blessing of the heavenly king may strengthen me against the pagans, have guided my actions in contending against the Norse.

'Edmund. Edmund,' I murmur. 'Edmund must have the book,' I say louder, but I don't think my attendant priest hears me, for he leans over, his ear close enough that I can see where he's been cut with the shaving knife. He's a brave man to remain at my side. He's also a disobedient one. Even Flodwin and Sigelac have heeded my instructions.

'Edmund,' he repeats, and I try to nod but find I can do nothing but blink. Only then my eyes don't open again. My last breath rasps through my chest, and I hear nothing else.

PART II

THE DEATH OF KINGS

'Here King Athelstan passed away on 27 October, 40 years all but a day after King Alfred passed away. And the ætheling Edmund succeeded to the kingdom; and he was then 18 years old. King Athelstan ruled 14 years and 10 weeks.'

— ANGLO-SAXON CHRONICLE, A TEXT (THE D VERSION ADDS THAT ATHELSTAN DIED AT GLOUCESTER)

11

27 OCTOBER 939, GLOUCESTER, THE KINGDOM OF THE ENGLISH

Athelstan the ealdorman

It's a dark day for this fledgling kingdom of the English, and I'm not the only one to feel it. Young Edmund is haunted, his face shut down. For all that he's now king, he'd not have wanted it to come so soon or at the expense of his half-brother's life.

A hush has fallen over the entire court at the news that Edmund has shared from his place beside the royal chair Athelstan always sat within, and which travelled with him on his many journeys throughout his kingdom. Athelstan, so well only a week ago, is now growing colder in his bed next door. I know he'd rather have died in battle than go quietly in his bed, and his death is not as he expected. Not as any of us anticipated.

To wither and die from illness is a terrible way for a warrior king to lose his hold on life. And with such haste as well. He inspired me to be a better man, to look closer for my God and to defend my people and my lands. I'll miss him, not just because he was my cousin by marriage, but because of who he was.

I know I have a part to play here, but the suddenness of it all makes me slow to react until I feel a nudge in my ribs and a press on my foot from my brother, and suddenly I remember.

Hastily, I drop to my knee; my two brothers, Eadric and Æthelwald, the one huge and hunkering, the other not much smaller, both of them warriors, beside me doing the same. We incline our heads towards our new king. A wave of scraping feet and creaking knees signals that everyone within the room is now on their knee, even the new king's mother, Lady Eadgifu. She's not as old as some might believe she should be. She was young when wed to the old king, and young when her husband died. And now she's young to be the mother of the king, but that's what she surely is. Once, I thought she had some warm feelings towards Athelstan, but whether she did or not will never be known.

A touch on the back of my head, and I look searchingly into the new king's red-rimmed eyes. I hold Edmund's gaze, trying to convey my sorrow, even as I hold my shock in place. I've known him since he was no taller than my knee, and now he's my king.

We must mourn his brother. He was, after all, a great and mighty king. But we must also ensure that Edmund is as potent as his half-brother, like his father, Edward the Elder, and like his grandfather, Alfred, who some say saved England from the Viking raiders, although I know many who'd argue with that in Mercia. All the same, there's a great deal for Edmund to emulate.

The new king clears his throat, the sound grating above the stunned silence.

'Please all stand. A witan must be convened with urgency at Winchester, and until then, I'll act as the king, but I'll need to be voted into my position and confirmed as your king.' His voice breaks as he speaks; his traitorous eyes straying back to the door behind which his oldest half-brother's body lies, growing chill, his priest still in attendance.

More priests will come soon. Now that the healing work is done, the praying must begin. I wonder what Edmund thinks. Does he thrill to know he's the king of the English, or does he quiver at the responsibility that's been thrust upon him so unexpectedly?

His brother was only just into his forties and in excellent health, training every day with his shield and axe. None would have thought that he'd die so suddenly. None, and certainly not his younger half-brother, who adored him and looked up to him and hoped one day to be like him.

One day.

Not this day.

And I shared the thrill of his older half-brother and strove to be as great as I could in my capacity as an ealdorman. Now I, too, feel unsteady. The hand that guided the English through the unifying of the Mercian and the Wessex lands, the regaining of York from the grasp of the Viking raiders, who united the peoples of Britain at Eamont and fought for that peace in Cait against the king of the Scots. And then once more, against the might of all at the battle of Brunanburh, is no longer here to guide us. None of us is wise enough to act without Athelstan. None of us.

And yet, Edmund will have to be. And we'll have to aid him. My brothers and I. My wife as well, cousin to Athelstan, and also cousin to Edmund, and his brother, Eadred.

I can almost hear the cries of joy from Constantin of the Scots, and Olaf Gothfrithson. Both men, so soundly beaten only two summers ago at the mighty battle of Brunanburh, will crow with delight to hear that their most dangerous enemy, the man who dared make them his subjects, has breathed his last. I can see them forming their war bands, calling their best warriors to arms, and my future suddenly looks bleak too.

Those two men will do all they can to undermine Edmund, forgetting in their delight and haste that while Edmund might be young he fought at Cait and Brunanburh. He tasted those triumphs and much of it was his, as well as his half-brother's.

The pair will launch attacks on England, and send people to whisper of Edmund's unworthiness to all who'll listen, especially amongst the Northern Welsh under Idwal, who all know is as unhappy and disgruntled as the Norse and the Scots. Together, they'll make a push for York. The prized York, or Jorvik as some of them will name it. It's the land that Olaf Gothfrithson wants as his own, the kingdom that King Constantin may help him claim if only to keep the English from his borders.

I'm not the only one to be thinking as such. I can see the same fears and worries running through Edmund's eyes. He knows there's much to prove in the coming months and years.

There's also the matter of his half-sisters, and the family arguments that create such discord in East and West Frankia. Edmund's cousin, Count Arnulf, has refuted any alliance between his holdings and that of England. Athelstan's ship army made a mistake, ravaging his lands instead of those of King Otto's last year. It's caused much unease, not that Athelstan seemed unduly concerned. He paid reparations and renewed his support of King Louis of West Frankia. I don't believe Count Arnulf has the resources to do more about it. Flanders isn't as rich as England. Count Arnulf doesn't have Athelstan's reputation. Ah, but of course, neither does Edmund. The realisation is unwelcome.

Slowly, the hall returns to some normality, the men of the witan in attendance huddling to discuss this dire news and the women returning to their crafts, spindle in hands as well as the nursing of the small children present.

Not all of the ealdormen are here in Gloucester. Some of us were close enough to be summoned and to share a few final words with Athelstan, shouted through the doorway when the finality of his illness was known. But others were far distant. They'll hear this news in the coming days and weeks. They'll mourn and hasten to attend the king's witan in Winchester.

Some, I'm sure, will also anticipate some gain to be made here. Olaf Gothfrithson and King Constantin of the Scots aren't the only two who'll underestimate Edmund. Idwal of Gwynedd will do the same.

I walk towards Edmund, each step heavy with pain and grief. He still stands beside Athelstan's chair, eyeing it warily as if it might somehow bite him. I know he fears to sit there and take the reins of his people and kingdom. I don't share his fears of being inadequate, but I understand them.

'My sympathies,' I whisper, my voice breaking. None have yet dared to speak to the new king since he made his announcement.

His eyes are tear-shrouded and yet clear at the same time. The murmur of the summoned priests' prayers reaches our ears for they're not allowed to enter Athelstan's bedchamber for fear the contagion will spread.

'He told me he didn't fear death, not that Athelstan welcomed it, not yet, but that he'd go to his God with a glad heart knowing that I'd rule in his stead.' Edmund's voice breaks as he speaks, and I pity him again. The words between the half-brothers were hardly private, shared through the barred door so all could hear in the hall.

'And you'll be a powerful king,' I state simply.

He quirks a sad smile my way, tears leaking down his cheeks to pool into his thin beard as he absorbs my reassurance.

'I have the potential.' He grins wryly. Like me, he must be thinking of his grandfather, his father and his half-brother, who've all ruled before him, and not of his other two half-brothers who died before they could do much of anything.

'Yes, you certainly do, and I know you'll fulfil it.'

'My thanks, Athelstan,' he says, his voice breaking a little over the name I share with his dead half-brother and predecessor as king.

'At least no one will confuse us any more,' I offer with a shrug. He laughs then, a slow noise, almost a sob, but his mouth is turned upwards even as his shoulders shake. We embrace in grief and joy and the possibility of the future.

Both our bodies tremble, and we don't care what other people say, do or think. Around us, I feel movement, and then the arms of my two brothers wrap themselves around us, and we're all laughing, crying and embracing. This is a good day for Edmund and a good day for my brothers and me. We'll govern with our king. We'll support him in any way we can and will be remembered for our deeds. My king is dead, but my new king is just as much my ally and my friend.

All the same, I fear for the future.

We must keep England secure and united. And with Athelstan's enemies still unhappy after the events of Brunanburh two summers ago, and with the onerous reparations demanded, and with the time to rebuild their support with warriors who'll fight on their behalf, it'll not be an easy task. Alpin's last report from the kingdom of the Scots didn't make for pleasant reading. Sent there to keep his father under the yoke of the English king, he warned of his brother Ildulb's ambitions. I fear for him now, as I never did before.

12

LATE 939, THE ROYAL PALACE, THE KINGDOM OF DEHEUBARTH

Hywel, king of the South Welsh

The messenger comes into my presence slowly and despondently. Instantly, my heart sinks. Wihtred is one of the English king's regular men; his unhappiness means that something is seriously amiss. I wonder what's happened now? It's only been a few days since my last messenger visited me, and then everything was well. Yet, I've held a sense of foreboding for some time.

There's been nothing further to report about Olaf Gothfrithson and affairs in Dublin, although I fear that he might be about to do something unexpected and catastrophic. The near-constant stream of Dublin 'traders' and 'men of God' making their way to my shores in the last year hasn't gone unnoticed. Nor their interest in King Athelstan's actions. But recently, that's faded away to nothing. If I know these Viking raider bastards at all – the Norse, as I'll term them – having them jumping up and down is better than them laying low and causing my kingdom no problems.

There's nothing to report from my cousin Idwal, either. In his kingdom to the north of mine, he has as much open coastline as I do and the land is fertile as well. I'd like to add it to my domain. Idwal's been distant of late, his fury concerning Athelstan's reasserted control over his kingdom making him lose his usual 'good cheer'. But, the Norse and my cousin, behaving themselves? It makes my skin crawl with unease.

I gesture for food and mead for the English messenger and wait to see what he'll do next. He's ridden hard. He's drawn and tired.

'My lord king, Hywel of the South Welsh,' he intones from his kneeling position on the floor. I arrest my interest in the legal documents arranged before me to truly look at him and listen to what he has to say.

'Yes, rise. Tell me what ails you, for something surely does.'

'It's with deep regret that I must inform you of the sudden and unexpected death of Athelstan, glorious king of the English, emperor and overlord over the island of Britain.'

My eyes widen in shock at his words. Of all the things I was expecting to hear, this wasn't one of them. Athelstan? Dead? How can it be? He's younger than me, and as I say, only a week ago he was hale and hearty, according to the previous messenger.

'Quickly, tell me everything. Is Edmund king?' A sense of urgency guides my questions, despite my sudden grief for the man who's dead.

Wihtred swallows hard over his sorrow. He was a huge favourite of Athelstan's. They'd often joke about his role as our go-between. It was a position of great trust, albeit a covert one. Few knew of the matters we discussed. Many thought him just a messenger boy, and not the mouthpiece of two kings trying to rule well, and in accord.

'It was a sudden contagion. He went from life to death in a

matter of days. And yes, Edmund has been declared king by the witan in his place.' Even those words are edged with regret. I'm unsurprised. Edmund is a boy. In my eyes, he'll always be a boy, somewhere in age between my sons and grandsons. I pity him for his advancement to the kingship.

This changes everything. I nod to catch the eye of my oldest son, Owain. He knows what I need him to do: ride with all haste to the coast for news about Olaf Gothfrithson. Does Olaf know of Athelstan's death already? Did he even arrange it? Is that why his agents have been so quiet in the last few months?

I signal for Wihtred to sit beside me. He must have quiet words to share besides the official pronouncement. A hush of silence greeted his initial words, but the general flood of conversation has restarted. I keenly note those who sneak from my presence nonchalantly as though their sudden departure isn't untoward.

There, the man I know spies for my cousin, Idwal, ever resentful of Athelstan and his claim to power over him. By nightfall, Idwal will be aware that Athelstan's dead. By daybreak, his thoughts will have turned to revenge against Athelstan's far younger replacement. Idwal will seek to gain from Athelstan's death.

A woman also stands and slides out of view. She's one of my youngest son's bedfellows. He's not here but hunting in the nearby woodlands. She'll ride and inform him of this new development. Not that it will unduly concern him. Not until we know what Olaf Gothfrithson of Dublin has planned. And Constantin of the Scots? What will he do now? His alliance with Olaf, cemented through a tie of marriage, means he must be watched. That wily old bastard has outlived yet another of the kings from the House of Wessex. Some think he'll never die, but all men are mortal. Some are merely longer-lived than others. Regrettably. Mael Coluim, his acknowledged successor but not his son, must pray for his long-overdue death.

Others hoist themselves upright and also leave the hall. I narrow my eyes, trying to place them and mark them for future reference at the same time.

'The men of your witan have formally chosen Edmund?' I ask, just to confirm the news in my mind.

'Yes, and he'll have an official coronation at Kingston upon Thames in as short a space of time as possible.'

'He has a younger brother?' I inquire. I can't always remember the facts of the old King Edward's horde of children. Many are dead.

'Yes, he does. Eadred.'

'He's a good prince?' I ask. I mean no harm by my questions but my political arena has changed with a spoken word. I must decipher where I stand. Does England remain the power she was or is she now weak?

'Eadred's young, my lord king. The last of old Edward's children.'

So much has happened since Edward's death that I forget his children might still not be men. This is one of those occasions. My children are men grown, with their children to bedevil them and ask for treats and toys. Edward's youngest son, Eadred, must have transitioned to manhood barely knowing more than his father's name. I've not given that much thought before.

Wihtred watches me closely. He comprehends that I'll have questions. He's been sent to give me the answer to anything he can if it's politic to do so. I imagine he has questions to ask of me as well.

'King Hywel.' His tone's formal. He's more likely to call me Hywel, especially when pressed so close together as we now are, where none can hear us. 'Will you support the new king?' He voices the question in barely a whisper. I feel a flicker of a smile turn my saddened lips upwards to hear the concern.

King Athelstan won my support with his view of a united England and a concerted approach to the menace of the Norse, and with his love of good law, which I emulate. Edmund has played a part in the negotiations and in the ensuing battles. I know he'll be a good king, imitating Athelstan, but there's obviously a concern within the witan.

'I stand with England, as I always have,' I reply quickly. It's the truth. I have my eyes on others much closer to home. I need England and her king to be as supportive of me as I am of them. Now's the perfect opportunity to show my loyalty and backing. I didn't fight at Brunanburh. I confess I feared that Athelstan would lose the battle. That he didn't and welcomed me back to our alliance was a testament to the man he was. And also because I made myself useful in hunting down the troublesome scop, Taliesen, who spread such discord within the Welsh kingdoms with his incendiary words and call to arms.

'King Edmund will be pleased,' Wihtred responds, the worry lifting from his shoulders, allowing him to sit taller beside me. I consider whether such concern was for his king or if it was fear he might run messages between two kings who were no longer as comfortable with each other. It would make his life far more difficult if he didn't have my permission to race through these lands and if he didn't carry my token to show any who might seek to question him. My writ makes his position much more tenable. 'And Olaf Gothfrithson?' Wihtred continues.

I sigh. I've kept a careful watch on Olaf. Or as much as a man can when a large, great, heavy swell of the sea, an unruly one at that, divides our lands. The sea between me and the misty ancestral homeland of my people has never played fair with us. It claims the lives of heroes and spits out bloodthirsty warriors with no thought for the people of my kingdom or of England. I sometimes hate it more than I do the bloody Norse.

'I hear things, as you know. But there's been silence for some time, which concerns me more than Olaf's constant interference. He's up to something, but what that something is, I don't know. Neither, I think, does Constantin of the Scots. Olaf's held himself apart from his father by marriage. I believe they have an uneasy alliance now, although I hear, as you know, that Olaf's wife, Constantin's daughter, works hard to bring allies to Olaf's side since she was reunited with her husband. She uses her influence on anyone and everyone she can, reminding them of her father's exile in their lands, for all he was a babe at the time.'

Wihtred nods with understanding. In the two summers since Brunanburh, we've both grown a little paranoid about Olaf's next moves. King Athelstan shared my concern. Brunanburh was a great victory, a huge blow for both Olaf Gothfrithson and Constantin, and yet they weren't utterly destroyed. They live and breathe, and while they can do that, Olaf foments trouble whenever he can, now that he's put his failure behind him. Men died fighting for him, many of them, but he's busy ensuring the Norse know the true fault lies with King Athelstan and never with him.

'Owain has gone to seek news. If there's none, I imagine he'll attempt a sea voyage to the islands of the Manx to see if they know Olaf's intentions. If I hear anything, I'll send word.'

This is the way Athelstan and I have conducted our affairs. We respect each other, or we did, and we allowed each to rule as we saw fit. But we watched each other's backs, ready to intervene and send word of any coming attacks. It's been quiet since Brunanburh, but Athelstan's death is all Olaf needs to prepare himself for war once more.

Wihtred stands and bows formally.

'I must return with all haste. My thanks for your support of King Edmund of the English. I'll revisit as soon as I know more.'

I'm nodding without really listening as he walks from my presence. My thoughts are twisted and tangled. Athelstan is dead. England is in danger now until Edmund can prove himself as king. I can almost hear the delighted laughter of Constantin and Olaf Gothfrithson, and just faintly, I hear my cousin Idwal as well. He had no love for Athelstan.

My peace is shattered by the news, but it's also opened new possibilities for me. I'll support Edmund, I didn't lie about that, but there might be more for me to gain here.

13

939, ST ANDREWS, THE KINGDOM OF THE SCOTS

Constantin, king of the Scots

I'm on my knees praying to God for the souls of my sons and grandsons and all the other men I lost on the slaughter field that should have been my triumph. The battle of Brunanburh, as I know the English name it, although in my tongue it's called Dùn Brunde, is too vivid a scar on my memory not to rise every day and immediately turn my thoughts to what I could have done better. What I should have done better.

Athelstan was the nobler man, the better warrior, the more Christian king, and I must live with that for the rest of my life. I hope I don't have a score of years before me to continue waking with the weight of failure and grief laid upon me, but I don't know. My God has kept me hale and hearty for this long. I don't believe he plans on me joining him anytime soon. I wonder if this is his punishment for my aggression.

So many times before I made and broke pacts with Edward,

king of Wessex. Never, ever, did I think the son would punish me so magnificently. If I'd known, If I'd realised, I'd have kept my word on this occasion. I gained nothing and lost far too much.

The church is a magnificent monument to my kingship. I enjoy its calming nature and the monks' soft, shuffling feet over the wooden floorboards. Still, I must seek the resolution to continue every morning. If I didn't visit every day or seek advice from my God, I'd not manage to pull myself from bed each sunrise. Grief would take me, and I'd die a sad and lonely man.

Every night, I lie awake and replay the battle in my mind. Sleep is elusive and hard to find. Each day, I wake up more and more tired and increasingly convinced that I'm unworthy and always will be. I strive to do more in the name of my God, in the name of my dead children and grandchildren, but I fall far short of His expectations of me.

Grief pinches my tired and lined face. I no longer seek the comfort of a warm woman in my bed each night. There's little point. That moment of pure joy and exhilaration is followed by a crushing return to the reality of what I set in motion to cause the battle. The assaults on my thoughts and senses are too much. The smell of sweat on my skin reminds me of my frantic retreat to safety after the battle. The smell of candles reminds me of the days I spent after the battle praying for forgiveness and for the souls of my son, Cellach, and my grandson whom I left to rot on the field of death.

I'm alone in my grief, Ildulb somehow finding in the aftermath of Brunanburh the strength to overcome the death of his own son, Amlaib, at the hands of Edmund of England five summers ago. I admire his resolve and wish I had the same vigour. I doubt that in five summers' time I'll have rediscovered my determination to live as well as he does. But then, I'm an old man. He's younger, more buoyant and far happier to make the best of his life now that he appreciates the threat that Athelstan is. He's uneasy around Alpin, sent home to ensure my loyalty. Alpin has English warriors to protect him, here, in his homeland. I don't welcome them, and yet Athelstan was right to safeguard my son in his homeland. I fear for him even while he lives.

I sigh deeply, opening my eyes and taking in the surroundings of my church with the richness of the altar cloths and the shimmering candlesticks of gold and silver. Only then do I note the respectful stance of Ildulb. He's alert and keen to tell me something, a smirk of joy playing at the corners of his mouth. I wonder what has him so excited, and something springs afresh inside me, a feeling that perhaps this might be excellent news to hear. Why else would he have come here to disturb my daily vigil? All know to stay away from me until this part of my routine is complete.

Thanks to my old and creaking knees, two men assist me to my feet. I don't allow the comfort of a cushion beneath them when I pray. One day, I think I'll pray for so long that my body will stick and remain in this position. Then I'll have to be escorted everywhere I go crouched. Age is a terrible judgement on a man, especially in the depths of an ice-cold winter. I long for some summer sun and warmth on my cold face.

As soon as I'm upright and able to stand without assistance, Ildulb walks towards me, his smirk growing with each step. I'm suddenly desperate to know what information he brings me, but I know a moment of obstructiveness. Before his mouth can form even one word, I point to the front of the church. Abruptly, he stops walking, a momentary flash of annoyance on his familiar face that brings an unbidden smile to my lips.

He bobs his head respectfully, a perfunctory motion, but I let it go. He doesn't share my love of the Lord God. He doesn't believe a God such as mine would take children from their fathers.

'Father, I've great news for you.' His tone is firm, his exhilaration compressed, as Alpin rushes to join Ildulb, his face shadowed in grief.

'And what is it, Ildulb?' I ask slowly, letting the moment drag between us, not meeting Alpin's eyes, for fear he'll see my joy at what I hope Ildulb will tell me. Ildulb grins widely, not caring that he stands within the hallowed ground of the church and should be respectful.

'King Athelstan of the bloody English is dead,' he crows with delight, and my feeling of righteousness swells and bubbles within me, even as Alpin buckles at the knees, sobs ripping from his mouth. Dead. How can it be? Athelstan's only a young man, almost half my age. But I'm as delighted as Ildulb and allow his foul-mouthed word without remonstration, although I hear the sharp intake of breath from my priest. He's a prude but a good man all the same.

I slap Ildulb on the back in delight, aware of my weak arm and soft motion, but doing so before I can stop myself. Before I consider Alpin's sorrow.

Ildulb grins and grins. I think his face might split.

'And that means that sodding Edmund is now king. I hunger to kill him even more than Athelstan.' Ildulb's eyes darken as he speaks, thinking of the future that's suddenly opened up before him, and not just for him, but for the kingdom of the Scots as well. Alpin gasps at Ildulb's words. I wish he wasn't here to witness mine and Ildulb's delight.

'Send word to Olaf Gothfrithson immediately. Let him know what's happened and ask him what he wants to do now. I think… I hope that we'll have a war to fight soon.'

'And I too, father, and in that war, I'll ensure that Edmund dies, his guts spilling from his torn and shredded chest, with the sure knowledge that I'm the one to end his life.'

My son's bloodlust should sicken me, but for the first time in two summers, I share it, and the thud of my heart warms my face as it hasn't since that day on the slaughter field at Brunanburh.

'And you.' Ildulb looks at Alpin. 'Stay silent or die on my blade,' he menaces, already calling his own guards to ensure Alpin can't escape, and neither can his English guards.

I'm an old, old man. Older even than the wise men of my religion, but the prospect of war thrills me, if not the idea of my son murdering his brother. But I'll hold a sword and shield this time. I'll stand side by side with Olaf Gothfrithson and my son. Vengeance will come. Athelstan, and his self-righteous ways, will not override my beliefs, my work, and my long life. I allow a smile to play on my lips. Athelstan's God has struck him down, and that, in the words of any of my priests, can mean only one thing. He wasn't righteous. He didn't have God's support for his actions.

I'll vanquish all that has gone before. I'll overawe the English, even if I die in the attempt.

14

939, THE ROYAL PALACE, THE KINGDOM OF GWYNEDD

Idwal, king of Gwynedd

The messenger finds me in the practice yard, teaching my sons how best to hold a sword and a shield. They're good boys. Sturdy and well made, for which I thank their mother, but they need to learn some guile. Every move they take, I know they're going to make at least five steps before they do. Their bodies, faces, hands, and their posture, everything about them gives them away.

There's no point in being able to hack the head from a man when he knows what's going to be attempted. It's too easy to counter that intent by raising a shield in an almost leisurely way while my sons would expend all their energy and leave themselves wide open to attack.

The boys listen intently to my instructions but then do as they want anyway. It'll be their deaths one day, not mine. I labour not to show my frustration. I'm not very successful at it, but my rants are so renowned that they have no impact on them any more.

The messenger's sweaty and hot for all that it's chill today, almost at the darkest time of the year. I do know him, although I struggle to remember his name, but he has a grin on his face. I believe I'll enjoy what he has to say as my brother, Cadfan, steps closer to hear as well.

I'd like nothing more than to return to my warm hall and sit before my smoking fire and warm through from the chill of watching my sons spar. But I don't think I want to be in an enclosed space with the man. He smells, even in the crisp air. I won't endure that after such a trying morning.

My steward, Alun, also wears a grin. No doubt, he's already grilled the man as to what he wants and why he thinks I'll want to hear it from him.

'King Idwal,' the man lisps, his voice overloud even outside. Does he struggle to hear or is it just the thrill of whatever news he carries? 'King Athelstan of the English is dead,' he announces without asking for coin or being remotely coy with the information he carries.

And that's it. My day has suddenly improved beyond imagination. I didn't even know Athelstan was ill. Beside me, my brother startles at the news, even as the shriek of one of my sons, frustrated with the brother he fights, flings himself against the wooden shield, knocking it to the ground. I know he'll be watching me to ensure I've seen, but I don't turn away from my messenger.

'In battle?' I seek to establish. Is there a war in the lands beyond my borders?

'No, an illness. I heard it from a messenger at King Hywel's court who came directly from the new king, Edmund.'

My sudden elation deflates. I'd have loved to be the one to inform my bloody cousin, Hywel, about his good friend Athelstan's death. I've been wary of their friendship for a long time. I hope the younger brother will be less of a threat to me and my kingdom.

Especially as, with the death of Athelstan, my kingdom is no longer subject to his, no matter what his brother might think.

'My thanks for bringing such welcome news to me,' I offer, trying to hold my joy in check. Eagerly, I signal to Alun that the messenger is to be rewarded.

The man smirks with pleasure.

Turning to Alun, I indicate he should take the man away. 'And see he bathes before leaving here,' I add in an undertone. Alun smirks at my fastidiousness.

'I'll see to it at once, my lord king.'

'And call together the highest men of the land. I must inform them of this.' Cadfan nods along with me.

Alun simpers at my obvious pleasure and hastens to be on his way. He's a man who thinks as I do. He knows my dreams of the future.

My son looks at me expectantly, the one snivelling, the other triumphant. I send them away with a wave of my hand and no words of censure or praise.

Along the way, I discard my equipment into the waiting hands and arms of whichever servant currently follows me, while Cadfan hurries to keep pace with me. Sometimes I find the press of people irritating and annoying, but today I have other things to occupy my mind. I'm pleased when I feel hands around my neck, and my mailed coat is lifted from my shoulders. Somehow, despite its weight, I'd almost forgotten it was there.

My hall's merry with laughter, and those inside don't yet know the news. It's warm and bright, filled with pleasant smells and my observant warriors. They know what the little bounce in my step portends. Already, busy whispers fill the space, even though I should have been the first to know. No doubt Alun has spilt the news. His mouth runs away with him.

I haven't yet decided on my future plans, but there are suddenly possibilities where moments ago there were none.

I bent my knee to Athelstan, king of the English, and for my obedience, I was rewarded with a massive tithe to burden my people. His success at Brunanburh was most unwelcome, preventing my attempts to distance myself from him. After our meeting at Hereford last year, his bloody scop, Taliesen, has been doing his best to poison the minds of my people against my kingship, pointing them towards the men of the English who'll fight the Norse for them. The scop's words, so successful at turning the Welsh against the English, have now done exactly the opposite. How I hate the man. It would be better if he sat at Athelstan's knee and merely repeated his lies about him rather than traipsing through the Welsh kingdoms.

People speak of Athelstan's holiness, but as far as I'm concerned, he was a grasping bastard, with eyes bigger than his belly.

A new king signifies that my kingdom is no longer bound by the terms agreed at Hereford. I have nothing more to fear from England, and neither do my people. With a new king, England is vulnerable once more. Whole for barely fifteen summers, England might not remain England for much longer.

'What will you do?' Cadfan questions me.

I think of the golden wheat fields I've seen growing on the island of Mon to the west, part of my kingdom, and how they're mirrored on the sheltered plains of the English lands that border my own. If they were mine, my warriors would be more amply provided for. If that were to happen, my kingdom and possessions would have much more stringent guards to watch for our enemies. I could even assign my brother lord over the stolen lands of the English. I'd trust Cadfan to keep true to me. Perhaps he senses that.

'I'll think about it,' I deflect. I don't know my plans. Until a few heartbeats ago, I thought I was stuck in this alliance with the English, but suddenly that's no longer the case. And, if I'm no longer tied to an alliance with the English, then I could find new allies. Olaf Gothfrithson would, no doubt, welcome allying with me. Perhaps I could even unite the Welsh kings against the English, and against Hywel. Maybe even King Constantin of the Scots would welcome overtures of friendship. My mind thrums with the possibility, and Cadfan adds to that fire of hope.

'War would be good for your warriors,' Cadfan suggests.

'War could be very good,' I confirm, nodding as I speak, thinking of claiming Hywel's kingdom, of taking part of the English kingdom as mine, and of uniting with the Norse and the Scots. Why not, I reason, take inspiration from all Athelstan accomplished, and turn it on its head? 'England could crumble under the hands of its young king if we go to war. I could take my share. Too long the English, and before them, the Mercians, have hounded my borders. Perhaps today is the beginning of the end of that,' I announce, and a smile spreads across Cadfan's lined face. I smile, and his lips broaden in return.

After all, today has brought me some pleasure.

I wonder what tomorrow might bring.

15

1 DECEMBER 939, KINGSTON UPON THAMES, THE KINGDOM OF THE ENGLISH

Edmund, king of the English

If I close my eyes, I could think myself a child once more at my half-brother's coronation fourteen years ago, but it would be wishful thinking. I know that this is my coronation, and while I should be enjoying it and absorbing the acclaim of my people, I feel none of those things. Even now, a month after Athelstan's death, I feel hollow and overwhelmed by it all. My brother. I somehow thought he'd live forever, not die abruptly at barely over forty winters old.

My mother has been coaching me through my grief. She liked Athelstan, admired him even, and basked in the reflected glow of his success, but she doesn't grieve as I do. Instead, she's a woman with intent, and that purpose is to make me a better king than my brother. More just. Wiser. More militarily dominant. But I know she labours under a false illusion. Athelstan was a great king. I'll be a pale shadow in comparison.

Worried messengers have already ridden to my witan to inform me that Constantin of the Scots has greeted the news of Athelstan's death with delight. I thought the tough old goat must be dead, but no. I fear that his bitterness at losing the battle of Brunanburh and his son will make him desperate to exploit my new kingship. That, and the knowledge I killed his grandson five summers ago in Cait. I imagine Ildulb greeted the news triumphantly. Ildulb didn't manage to kill me or Athelstan at Brunanburh. But I know he lives. He must be desperate for another chance to face me on the battlefield. While Athelstan lived, that wasn't going to happen. But now? Now everything Athelstan laboured to accomplish is threatened. And I fear for Alpin as well, in the kingdom of the Scots, without Athelstan's backing. I worry for the English guards who accompanied him too.

I know Olaf Gothfrithson of Dublin will hold the same hopes when he hears of my brother's death. While York remains part of the English empire and Olaf continues to breathe, he'll yearn to reclaim what he considers his birthright.

Only Hywel of the South Welsh has sent words of condolence and congratulations. Although he's not attending my coronation, despite the invitation. But he, too, becomes ever stronger on my borders with Athelstan's death. He was my brother's ally. I can't be assured he'll remain mine, no matter his reassurances. My brother proved himself a strong warrior king before seeking the allegiance of others. That loyalty won't simply be inherited, unlike the golden crown that will soon grace my head.

I fear the united kingdom of England, made strong by my brother, will crumble without him. How am I to see things before they happen as he used to? How am I to play the role of a mighty warrior, a devout man of God, father, husband and king, all at the same time? How am I to be Athelstan?

England's neighbours squeeze her. War will come, and no doubt before I discover the means to a successful kingship.

The words of Archbishop Wulfheard drag me back to the here and now. I focus on my surroundings and not my worries and fears.

The church is the same one within which my brother held his coronation. Nothing has changed in the few short winters that have passed, only the man who sits on the royal throne and who'll have England's crown placed upon his head. When Athelstan was consecrated, I was a small child, bored with the length of the service and unsure why my father was no longer proclaimed as Wessex's king. I didn't know Athelstan as more than the distant half-brother that few mentioned in the presence of my father or mother.

I hope I sit dispassionately looking on while the holy men do their work around me, aware that all who attend my coronation must be thinking as I am. They watch me, waiting to see how I compose myself.

I've spent time practising my kingly face for this unexpected service, conducted so soon after my brother's death that, despite invitations sent to Hywel, Idwal, Constantin and the Welsh kings, none have had the time to make the journey, or so I reassure myself. Hywel, I thought, might attend, but he hasn't. I pray that doesn't speak of his intentions towards England. Wihtred has assured me of Hywel's loyalty. Word was also sent to East and West Frankia, but if men couldn't travel from South Wales in time, they certainly couldn't come from Laon, Aachen or Flanders, and not at this time of the year when storms ravage the coastlines.

For those in attendance, my bishops and archbishop, the ealdormen and their families, the nobility, my mother and my brother, I hope not to reveal my dismay and pride. For I can't deny that I'm proud to be king, I merely wish that it hadn't come at my half-brother's loss.

I'm from a kingly line; my ancestry can be traced back through the ancient kingdom of Wessex, through the ravages of the Viking attacks and my grandfather Alfred's accord with them. I never knew my grandfather, being born many years after his death, but he looms large in my life, as does my father and my half-brother. All three men were magnificent kings, ruling with equal parts force, benevolence and religious might.

I quake to know that I must follow in their footsteps while thrilling at the challenge being presented to me.

I'll not fail.

I'll not fail, I think, a little more quietly. My resolve still falters at the most inappropriate of times.

As with my brother before me, the coronation service gifts me with symbols of my new position. I'm anointed with holy oil and given a thick gold ring with a flashing ruby to prove that I accept my role as protector of the one true faith. It's not my brother's ring. That will remain with him in death as it did in life, and not just because of the contagion that killed him. A finely wrought sword is placed in my hands, with which I'm to defend widows and orphans and with which I can restore things left desolated by my foes. This is mine as well, a new sword for a new king, not an old one already put to good use.

Further, I'm given a golden sceptre with which to defend the Holy Church and a silver rod to help me understand how to soothe the righteous and terrify the reprobate, assist any who stray from the Church's teachings and welcome back any who have fallen outside the laws of the Church.

I wonder how my brother coped with the heavy responsibility; whether he embraced it immediately or whether he too fought against it? I imagine not. He was keen to be king after our father's death, eager to be given the opportunity to prove himself, the chance he felt our father never allowed him. The hastily flung words of another of my half-brothers, Edwin, before his execution made Athelstan reassess the relationship he'd had with our father, but even then, there'd been too much hurt to fully heal. Athelstan respected our father. I don't know if he ever loved him.

My mother, for all that she's been the king's de facto mother throughout Athelstan's reign, is now actually the king's mother. I don't think she'll be shy about it. She sits before me, dressed in beautiful clothes so stiff with golden embroidery I fear they'll creak when she moves, smiling gently at all the magnificence and formality that surrounds me. She's younger than Athelstan was. I pray she lives for many long years to come. If I should lose her too, I don't believe I'd have the strength to undergo this transformation to become England's king.

I eye my brother as well, Eadred. Of all the many sons born to my father's three wives, there remain only me and him. Should I die, he'll be king in my place.

Eadred's a few winters younger than me. His face is still boyish, the first fuzz of beard and moustache just starting to show. I try and catch his eye, but his gaze is elsewhere. Perhaps, I think, he considers the future when he's here in my place. Or perhaps he mourns Athelstan. Eadred looked to Athelstan as a father, having no memory of our own.

The prayers of the archbishop finally cease, and I look in confusion as the rousing cheers of the congregation proclaim me as their king, and eventually, I remember to smile, while remaining regal. I meet the gaze of Ealdorman Athelstan, of his wife, Lady Ælfwynn, and notice how my mother beams with pride, a tear shimmering its way down her cheek. I hope I live up to their expectations.

Inside I'm quaking. I'm now officially king of England, in more than just name.

I hope I'll make my brother and my father proud of me.

And my grandfather, King Alfred.

And to do that, I'll have to fight England's enemies. It's just a matter of time until one of them rears their heads. I consider who will be the first to strike out of Olaf and Constantin. Perhaps, it will be both of them.

16

DECEMBER 939, THE NORTH SEA

Olaf Gothfrithson, king of the Dublin Norse

Following the frantic retreat after the ignominious defeat at Brunanburh, I've licked my wounds and made my plans. I vowed revenge, and for the last two summers, that's exactly what I've been working towards. I defeated an alliance of the Northern and Southern Ui Neill to retain my control over Dublin, and allowed Haraldr Sihtricson to take Limerick in exchange for having Mael Muire, my wife, returned to my bed.

I heard the cries of my wounded men and watched my allies cut down before me. Still, I escaped and returned to my land and kingship, no matter the complaints of Anlaf Sihtricson, and his petulance that Dublin would be his. It only increased when his brother was given the prize of Limerick, which Anlaf had thought to hold when I refused him Dublin. Once more my constant companion in Dublin, Anlaf Sihtricson has been a constant thorn in my side, as I feared he would be.

But I vowed I'd not be made a laughing stock. I'll not forever be remembered as the man who gained nothing but a wife from his alliance with the king of the Scots and lost many men in battle against the English king.

Messengers and spies have made their way to Jorvik in the last two summers, as well as to the Welsh kingdoms. The things I've learnt have committed me to regaining what I've lost. My people are there, the Norse, ruled by Athelstan of the English. I'm convinced they'll turn their back on the English king and once more look to me and my successors as their rightful rulers. All I need do is make my way to Jorvik and overwhelm the ancient walls that provide a half-hearted defence from all who might think to attack.

The news from the king of the Scots, my father by marriage, is perhaps less retaliatory towards the English than I might like. But the old bastard will support me, and willingly as well, or so his daughter, my wife, assures me. While I left her in England after the battle of Brunanburh, we've since been reunited thanks to Haraldr Sihtricson, and all it cost me was Limerick and a blazing row with Anlaf. I wouldn't think the two of them were brothers.

Still, it was worth it. She's done much for me with my dismayed allies within Dublin. She's called on all her father's one-time allies, men who knew him as a child, or rather the sons and grandsons of men who knew him. There are few alive to remember Constantin in the flesh, but the words of the scops and the presence of his daughter have refreshed many half-remembered memories of Constantine's childhood exile in the lands of the Irish.

I'm pleased with my wife. She's not the most exciting in bed but does her duty, and I enjoy that more than I thought possible. I hope to be a father again soon. Until then, my oldest son's smouldering resentment at my remarriage can be contained. The same can't be said for his mother and her relationship with my brother,

Gothfrith. Still, I've left them in control of Dublin. That will make them happy for the foreseeable future.

Now, I prepare my new warriors to return to the land of the English king and reclaim that which I failed to win two summers ago. I'll attack in the winter months when few should be waging war. When the English will be warm in their beds. When the Norse will think nothing of facing the raging seas and the torrents of foul, cold weather. After all, it's what we'd expect in our homelands.

Athelstan.

The name fills me with revulsion and some grudging respect. He was the more able warrior; he controlled his men better during the battle at Brunanburh and accomplished what needed to be done.

He arranged his men, considered how to counter the attack and then read the ebb and flow of the fighting while mounted on his horse. He made changes as and when needed. Athelstan of the English knew how to work the battlefield and did it so well that an entire generation of men were killed there and then. So many, and yet I don't grieve for them. No, I'm furious with them for failing to support me as they should have done. For refusing to heed my words and follow my orders. For allowing themselves to be overwhelmed by little more than a crevice in the ground. I'm incensed at the son of the king of the Danes, Ivarr, at Olaf Scabbyhead and at Gebeachan of the Outer Isles, and at everyone else who arrived with their eye only on the treasure and not on what needed to be accomplished first.

And I'm angry with myself as well.

I shouldn't have gone to war with my allies as equals but instead as my subordinates. Olaf Scabbyhead of Limerick wasn't the brave warrior he pretended to be. His men didn't fight on my behalf to ensure his life, as they were oathsworn to do, and that fool, Ivarr, was precisely that. He didn't know his arse from his seax.

If they'd been true to their words, I'd have had the power I needed to win. I ought to have humiliated every man who pledged their support to me in battle and blood and who disappointed me in breaking their promises. It's a pity so many of them are dead that I can never take vengeance against them.

But Athelstan of the English won't defeat me again. No. I'll fight him. I'll win back Jorvik. It'll be returned to the Norse who won it from the bastard Saxons so many decades ago.

This time, my allies are fewer in number. I've made the conscious decision to involve less men. I won't deplete Dublin of her finest warriors, not when they've been so hard to win over. The reports I've received suggest that the people of Jorvik will rise and fight for me anyway. I don't need the vast numbers I took to Brunanburh.

There are fewer to gossip and spread rumours and a smaller number who could alert Athelstan of the coming invasion. Anlaf supports me. Better to have him where I can see him, anyway. Not that my brother Gothfrith wouldn't be able to overwhelm him if he did try to take Dublin from his control, but I prefer it this way. I can rely on Gothfrith to return Dublin to me. He's done it before, even if it was unwillingly.

I have thirty ships filled with men under my command. Not as many as I took to Brunanburh. Unlike two summers ago, our journey will round the coast of Constantin's kingdom. We'll journey north to come south. We won't risk alerting the English to our presence by landing close to Brunanburh. We won't involve the Welsh kingdoms, for with the intelligence I've gathered about them, I doubt every single one of their kings, even Idwal of

Gwynedd – though I know he wishes to be free from the overlordship of King Athelstan.

No, I'll happen upon Jorvik from the sea, visiting the kingdom of the Scots to inform Constantin of what's going to happen rather than asking his permission. His daughter will smooth my unexpected arrival. We might even venture to visit the holy island of Lindisfarne, where my forebears first defeated the weak Saxons over a hundred and fifty summers ago before passing the stronghold of Bamburgh. I might find allies there as well. I don't know where Ealdwulf, the heir of Bamburgh is. Perhaps I'll find him at Bamburgh. Or maybe not. He's so far been unsuccessful in claiming his inheritance.

King Athelstan of the English will have no time to raise his force to counter the attack. Not during the winter. Winter isn't a time for war. I plan on taking advantage of that.

I've spent days and days considering how best to take back my kingdom and reunite Jorvik with Dublin. I've sought advice from everyone, even from the lowliest boy in the stables. From them all, I've picked little snippets, and now I have my plan. I've ignored much that Anlaf Sihtricson demanded I do. He's not the warrior I thought him to be.

It's a good omen that the wind whips the wolf-headed sails on the ships. It'll speed my ships on their way. It'll get us to Jorvik sooner, and perhaps it might ensure we arrive before the true advent of winter snows, while there's still a watery paleness to the nights to make the attack possible.

I smile. I love the feel of the biting wind on my cheeks and the dancing of the ship beneath my feet. Others might heave their guts over the side, cursing my ambitions to attack while the sea threatens to turn into a howling torrent. But I feel as though I control the sea, I've made my peace with the Goddess of the sea, and soon I'll count Jorvik amongst the dominions under my control as well.

And with it, I hope, to add the death of King Athelstan of the English.

17

DECEMBER 939, WINCHESTER, THE KINGDOM OF THE ENGLISH

Eadgifu, the lady of Wessex

The volume is weighty in my hands, and yet I won't allow another to hold it on my behalf. I seek out my son, the new king, frustrated by his ability to hide from me, his mother.

I know my son is scared. I confess, I am as well. Athelstan is dead, and England mourns, but that doesn't help my son who must now rule in place of his half-brother, my dead stepson. I can only hope the gift I carry will aid him, for something must bring him the resolve that's needed to rule England as Athelstan did before him. I'm not immune to the whispers of the nobility. I hear what they say about my son, Edmund, and how he is too young to rule, too immature. How he needs others to rule on his behalf until he grows into his kingship.

'At last,' I announce, sighting my son before me. I've been here before, I'm sure of it. Perhaps, I consider, my son is trying to evade me. The smell of hay is redolent in the air. I should have realised he'd seek comfort in the stables.

'My lady mother.' He inclines his head, but I detect the unease in his voice all the same, and his bowed head means he doesn't meet my eyes.

'Are you avoiding me?' I query, determined to resolve this.

'Perhaps,' he murmurs. 'Or mayhap shunning my responsibilities.' He offers a sad smile. I know pity for his plight. He's young. He should be ploughing women and drinking himself insensible, not that I approve of either, but instead he must rule a kingdom swathed in grief. That said, when I was his age, I was wed to his father, and had adopted the responsibilities of being the wife of a king. I understand the weight of expectation.

'Then I've brought this for you.' I hold the heavy book out to him. Edmund knows the value of books, and not only for preventing an assassin's knife from ending a life, as Athelstan once used the life of St Cuthbert to defend himself from Edwin's fury. But Edmund doesn't take it, instead gazing at it with unease. 'Take it. It's heavy,' I urge him, wishing my arms didn't tremble with the burden of the words etched on to the vellum contained between the leather covers.

'I don't want it.' Edmund shakes his head, eyes downcast.

'It was a gift from your brother. It will bring you solace.'

'I don't want solace. I want Athelstan.' The words are sharp and edged in pain. I hear the scrabble of others fleeing the stables, not wishing to hear this argument between the king and the king's mother. I hold myself firm, clasping the book tightly once more to my thick fur cloak which shields me from the cold weather outside. Athelstan has been dead since 27 October. That's less than six weeks ago. But, in political terms, six weeks is an eternity.

'I know, son, I know,' I offer softly. I grieve for Athelstan as well.

I miss his confidence and conversation. He was a fine man. His death was too sudden and too soon. But I harden my resolve against feeling compassion for my son. There is no choice in what he must do. 'You may offer your prayers for his soul, but you must not abandon his legacy. He kept you close. He taught you all he knew. Don't waste his legacy.'

'I do no such thing,' Edmund counters angrily.

'And hiding in the stables is ruling England, is it?' I know my words are sharp. They're meant to wound.

'The ealdormen and archbishop know what they're doing.'

'The ealdormen and archbishop gave you their support. Relying on them indefinitely will not make you a wise king.'

'I have no wisdom, Mother,' he murmurs. 'What do I know of ruling and kingship? Athelstan was the king. He should still be the king.'

I snap back my immediate reply. 'Athelstan wasn't born to be a king. It wasn't easy for him. He had no opportunities to practise. He had to learn what to do, and win over men who were stubborn in their refusal to accept his kingship. The sheen of confidence he carried is a testament to his resolve, not to his wisdom.'

Now Edmund unwillingly meets my gaze. 'That's not how I remember it.'

'You were a child of four winters. I doubt you remember much as it really was.' My tone is brusque. I must impress this upon Edmund.

He bites his lip, considering my words. 'What is that?' he asks, one hand on the side of his horse, where he prepares the animal for riding, the other pointing towards the book I carry.

At last, I think. 'King Athelstan bequeathed this to you. He accumulated its contents during his life.'

'But what is it?'

'Wisdom from those who lived before him and before you. Insight to teach you how to be a good king.'

Hesitantly, Edmund reaches for the book. I gratefully allow the weight to settle in his hands, not mine. The book is large, at least a foot high, by almost as much wide, and thick with vellum pages. 'You've read it?' he asks, wonder in his voice to think of all that could be encompassed within it.

'I have, yes, and it's worthy of your consideration. It doesn't contain all the answers but it will certainly aid you,' I assure him. 'With careful study of these texts you'll be the man, the king, you're destined to be. Your brother's legacy will live on. He might have been the first king of the English, but you're the second. You must keep England united and her enemies running scared for what they might lose. You fought beside him. You learned politic at his side. He taught you all he could. Don't waste that.'

'Thank you, Mother,' Edmund offers, his tone both quelled and determined, opening the heavy cover to peer at the highly decorated and beautifully inscribed words on the first few pages. From here I can see the neat black writing, the flowing script, the skill of the scribe in copying this material on to folios contained in one huge binding.

'It would have been yours sooner had you attended upon the archbishop.'

'Is this why he wanted to see me?'

'Of course, it was to inform you of more personal concerns that your half-brother left for you in his will.'

But Edmund doesn't hear me. Instead, he settles on a handy stool, absent-mindedly moving aside the brush and hoof pick that wait there for him.

I leave him, my thoughts triumphant and tinged with sadness.

Not only was Athelstan a great king, a vanquisher of the

bloody Norse, but he was also far-sighted enough to plan for the future, even as he lay gasping for his last breaths.

I miss him all over again, feel his loss spring afresh, and allow a tear to trickle down my cheek.

I realise I loved Athelstan, and perhaps not as a stepmother should have done.

18

DECEMBER 939, ST ANDREWS, THE KINGDOM OF THE SCOTS

Constantin, king of the Scots

I grin with delight when I lay eyes on him. Olaf Gothfrithson's my son by marriage, but also a man who sees the future almost as well as I once did. I might not have predicted King Athelstan's death and nor might Olaf, but he's arrived in time to take advantage of the greatest news in nearly fifteen winters.

My keen-eyed son, Ildulb, sighted his fleet off our coast and, without even thinking to ask me, set sail to greet it, despite the tempestuous sea. Once more, Ildulb knows more about current events than I do, but I'm still king. Ildulb can do nothing without my approval, no matter what he might think.

'Jorvik?' I ask Olaf when we're seated before a roaring fire, for it's chilly in my great hall at this time of the year. I'm swathed in fur cloaks and as close to the fire as I can be. My old bones repel heat rather than invite it in.

'Yes. My birthright and easy to take when Athelstan's looking the wrong way.'

I laugh out loud then. Olaf flashes me a look of annoyance. We've not met in person since before the events of the battle of Brunanburh. Perhaps he means to replay all those wrongs. But I hold him off.

'You've not heard the news?' I inquire. His focused eyes glare at me. I note his wind-roughened cheeks and the scars that run over his nose which mark him as a warrior. Perhaps not a very skilled one, if Brunanburh is anything to base that on.

'What news should I have heard?' Olaf glowers with frustration. I didn't believe Ildulb when he informed me of Olaf's ignorance regarding Athelstan's death, but it's evident that he genuinely doesn't know. Olaf had this expedition planned before Athelstan died.

'Athelstan.'

'What of him?' Olaf growls. Perhaps he thinks I'll thwart his plans for Jorvik and towards Athelstan. Already, he eyes Alpin uneasily. He must know that Alpin is a creature of the English king.

Olaf's shrugged off his waterproof sealskin cloak, but I've not yet let him see to his needs and wants. He's redolent of the tang of the sea. He smells of his ancestry. He probably wants to bathe and change his clothes, but I can't let him go yet. I want to tell him the news myself. Behind him, I eye my daughter, Mael Muire, with interest. She was lost to me when she wed Olaf. And then lost again after the failure of the battle. But she still lives, and I know labours to do the right thing for me, and by her husband. Her gaze is fixed on Alpin. Her lips are twisted with distaste. She's not alone in being suspicious of Alpin's presence in my court.

The sea voyage has coloured her cheeks and sharpened her eyes. Finally, she wrests her attention from Alpin and turns to glower at Ildulb: suspecting him, perhaps, of withholding information.

'He's dead,' I say, savouring the two words and letting them fall like pebbles in the stream, curious to see how the ripples will spread. It's the first time I've said the words myself. As each one falls from my mouth into the sudden silence, the reality of what I'm saying sinks in. Athelstan is dead.

King Athelstan of the English is dead.

Olaf's eyes widen.

'Dead? Are you sure?' he questions with disbelief. He won't allow himself to believe it.

'Oh yes, a messenger came with the news. It almost incited my son to war there and then. Ildulb, not Alpin,' I explain, although it's not needed. We all know where my sons' loyalties lie.

Abruptly, Olaf smirks with joy. His task will now be ten times easier. His shoulders relax, all thought of arguing with me about Brunanburh leaving his mind. He reaches for the drinking horn waiting in the hands of one of my servants and swills its entire contents. Then, he demands it's refilled and raises a toast to me. He can barely speak, the grin on his face so wide, the words babbling from him incoherently.

Mael Muire scowls at Ildulb. Ildulb quirks his eyebrows at her. He's a brave man to face her wrath, where she stands, ready to fight, hands on her hips. She'd kill him if there were a blade to hand. Not, I realise, that he's perhaps as brave as Alpin, who sits beside us all as we plot the downfall of a man who must have been like a brother to him.

'You'll join me in retaking Jorvik?' Olaf demands. I want to, but I know I can't. Despite my hopes for meeting the English in battle, I must wait to do so. I've only just begun rebuilding my strength.

'Not me. I'm too bloody old. Look at me.' And Olaf does. He

lingers over my thinning white hair and grey beard, lined face and turned-down mouth, even when I smile.

'I'll allow you that,' he says, without rancour.

'Ildulb will come with you,' I offer, and his grin returns, as does Ildulb's. He'll not be cowed by his sister's fury.

'Good, I'll fill his head with great deeds and glory.'

'You do that, but send him home to me afterwards. I've lost enough children and grandchildren.'

Olaf sobers, but only for the blink of an eye. Neither of us can contain our excitement and anticipation of what the next month or two will bring. What the next year will bring. Athelstan can barely have begun to rot, and already his legacy is in ruins.

'Dead, you say. Of a contagion?'

'I assume so, for he was far younger than I.'

'And his brother is king.'

'Yes, Edmund, you fought him at Brunanburh.'

'Oh, I did, yes, he chased me from the battlefield and to my ship.' Such an admission should cost Olaf, but instead, his eyes brighten with the thirst for vengeance.

'He's young, too young to rule alone, but old enough to, all at the same time. Go, fast and quick, take Jorvik, and hold it,' I caution, but Olaf's staring into the reds and yellows leaping through the fire. I wonder what he sees there. Does he see battle and glory or war and death? I don't know, but he's welcome to both or either.

'Edmund will be a good king,' Alpin counters, his face as flushed as Olaf's and Mael Muire's, for all he's not been on a sea voyage. We all ignore him. We're not interested in his opinion.

I wish Olaf success in his endeavour. It'll be easy to take Jorvik. The people there, more Norse than English and more Northumbrian than English at that, are always keen to assert their independence, to stand aloof from whoever wants to rule them. They'll claim Olaf as their own if he comes at the head of a ship army. But it'll be holding Jorvik that causes the problem. I know that well enough.

Jorvik is easy to win and difficult not to lose. Somehow King Athelstan managed it. Will Olaf have the same powers of persuasion? I don't know, and neither do I much care. The new king of the English will be kept busy; he'll be absorbed by his affairs, and that means I'll be left alone to rule my kingdom and that of the other one, ruled by the son of the feeble Owain of Strathclyde, Dyfnwal.

Whether Olaf lives or dies, I'll get what I want. An English king with no time to interfere in my affairs. And just as importantly, my daughter has been returned to me. I should never have allowed Mael Muire to leave. Not that I think the same about Alpin. I fear for him now. There are too many who hunger for his death. Alpin should have remained in England.

19

EARLY 940, WINCHESTER, THE KINGDOM OF THE ENGLISH

Edmund, king of the English

The hall is a riot of shouting men and fearful-looking women, and over it all I'm supposed to preside with grace and magnanimity. I feel more likely to be the one shouting or crying.

My throat's dry, and my hands shake.

Olaf Gothfrithson of Dublin.

How did he act so quickly? Did he even know or was this attack just happenstance that it occurred so soon after Athelstan's death? I hope it's the latter.

At my side, Athelstan the ealdorman watches on with intelligent eyes. He was tasked with bringing me the news. He'd barely made it to Mercia after the Christ Mass festivities before the news broke. Olaf reclaimed York in a virtually bloodless coup. Even now, he's threatening Lincoln. Olaf means to take back all that he lost when his father was defeated outside York by King Athelstan in 927. He's come to seek revenge for his failure at Brunanburh. And I fear he'll win. England is unprepared for war so soon after Athelstan's death. We believed the victory of Brunanburh would ensure England's survival for at least a generation, not less than three summers. And, it's winter. No one fights during the winter months.

Outside, a harsh storm blasts the royal hall at Winchester, bringing snow which threatens to block all roads, and all my half-brother dreamed of has come undone. I fear for Alpin in the kingdom of the Scots. Does he still live? Athelstan should have sent word to retrieve Alpin from Constantin's court before he died. Now, I worry that Alpin will die at the hands of someone within his birth kingdom.

'Edmund, you must speak. Quell the panic.' Ealdorman Athelstan's voice is insistent. He's correct in his assessment. I know it, but I don't know what words to use, what actions to take. I try and recall the lessons from my brother's book, but I'm sure no one has ever faced such a total reversal so quickly. The letters exchanged between a king and his supporter suggested that my faith would ensure God strengthened me against the pagans, but there's been no time for my faith to be rewarded in such a way.

Bloody Olaf Gothfrithson. The damn Norse take no notice of the weather. They think only of success and triumph.

I stand, filled with resolve, recalling the words my mother spoke to me of the need to ensure Athelstan's legacy survived his death. Instantly, the room turns to silence. My position as king has given me powers I didn't even know I had. My mother watches me intently, willing me on. I take comfort from that. She's not yet steered me wrong. Or, indeed, did Athelstan before his death. Or after it.

'My people,' I begin, pitching my voice so that they must be quiet if they wish to hear my words. 'This news is troubling and unexpected. But we must not panic.' A small bubble of noise greets those words, but others quickly shush the miscreant. 'A choice must be made. Allow this sneaky attack to continue, or face it, suppress it, and drive Olaf Gothfrithson and his Norse allies from our lands once more.'

A stuttering cheer greets my determination. It's unfortunate that Olaf has caught us so unprepared, mourning my brother in the darkest time of the year. But it doesn't mean it'll be easy to hold what he's stolen away.

My other ealdormen and the men of the church left my hall a few weeks ago, alongside Ealdorman Athelstan. They all wished to be within their own homes during the dark time of the year. I felt the same, but I'll have to summon them back to me, no matter the atrocious conditions outside. Their household troops must bolster mine. I have my household warriors, but it'll not be enough to combat the vast horde of men running unchallenged within my lands, to the north and the east. I must hope that only Olaf Gothfrithson is involved. I think of others who might wish to overturn Athelstan's advances. My thoughts turn to the heir of Bamburgh, Ealdwulf, wherever he might be. I hope Ealdorman Guthrum returned to Bamburgh before Olaf's attack, but I've not heard from him. I worry about the people of Bamburgh, and about Guthrum in particular. He's an old man.

I consider Idwal of Gwynedd. He never liked my brother. He'll jump at the chance to enter an alliance against the English.

'Messengers will be sent to recall every ealdorman and every churchman as soon as possible. In the meantime, my cousin, Ealdorman Athelstan, will lead the troops north. His brothers, Æthelwald and Eadric, will support him.'

Ealdorman Athelstan nods at my words. It's clear he expected to be the one to head the advance. I want to be the one to do so but know I daren't even suggest it. My father's vast number of sons has dwindled to just two males, my younger brother and me. Although

I do have some suggestions as to where I might be able to defend my kingdom.

'We'll stop this attack on our people and land. Now, we all have tasks we must be about. Go.'

With my commands given, men and women who moments ago were close to alarm are composed and busy. I must remember this. Men and women need to be occupied to keep their minds from filling with images of mutilation and death when war beckons.

Ealdorman Athelstan stays beside me. We've much to discuss, and in this I'm overly aware that his wife, the Lady of Mercia's daughter, won't be content if her mother's kingdom is overrun. I know she gifted it into my half-brother's safe hands, and took herself to the kingdom of the East Angles, but she'll not wish to see Mercia suffer. She's beloved and has many sons who could rule it one day in her name, as well as a strong husband and his family to support her. For now, Ealdorman Athelstan is loyal to me. I must ensure that continues.

Signalling to my mother, my younger brother, as well as Oda, bishop of Ramsbury, and Wulfheard, the archbishop of Canterbury, the only two holy men who remain in Winchester, I convene a hasty counsel. We'll set events in motion that will protect the kingdom of the English from the onslaught of the Norse.

'How many men?' I demand from Ealdorman Athelstan when we're settled before the hearth, the heat unable to warm me from the chill that's infected my body.

'Too many to count, my lord king,' he offers formally. He always resorts to formality when he can't give the answer that's wanted. 'Too many ships according to reports from York.'

'How many warriors do we have?' I query. I know this answer as well, but I need to hear it once more.

'Upwards of eight hundred. There are over five hundred here, guarding you. The rest are loyal to me or my brothers, but we gave our pledge to you as our king, so they are yours to command.' Æthelwald and Eadric aren't at Winchester. But they'll come. We all know that.

My mother gasps at such a small number of armed warriors. It's insubstantial, but the men are all the best. They've trained for this, and are veterans of the victory at Brunanburh, if not from the fight in Cait where I first became a warrior.

They know how the Norsemen fight. They've faced them before and don't have any fear of them. If I had only fifty of these men to send against Olaf Gothfrithson, it would be better than a thousand green men of the fyrd armed with little more than scythes and farming equipment, with no byrnies to their names.

'Take them. The other ealdormen will arrive soon. I don't believe Olaf and his Norsemen can hope to make it further south in this weather. The roads are blocked. You'll have to fight your way out as you fought your way in.'

Ealdorman Athelstan listens intently to my words. He's a good listener.

'We should consider peace talks,' Bishop Oda announces, my mother opening her mouth to interrupt him, but I stop her with a look. Oda is half-Norse, and a voice of reason. I don't like it, decry the necessity in fact, but I'd be no king if I didn't realise that it might come to that. Archbishop Wulfheard nods at Oda's words. He's clearly in agreement.

'Ensure Archbishop Wulfstan of York is involved. He speaks for the men of York more often than any other.'

Oda inclines his head at my ready acceptance even as my mother harrumphs despondently. If Oda thought I'd argue with him, he's wrong. Planning for every eventuality is necessary. It's not that Oda is a peaceful man, serene in his faith. Far from it. He knows how important it is to fight. But he also understands that my kingship is new and untested.

I'm a new king, a weak king, in a vast land surrounded by enemies everywhere I turn. Many of my people are only newly come to the alliance of the English. Some still think they're Norse or of York, I can't stop that. It's to be expected, but I can guard against it and show myself to be a man of God, peace and honour. If peace must be made, and I hate the thought of it, I'll make peace. Then I can regroup. It'll be a temporary setback, nothing more. It'll have to be, or every one of the kings who swore allegiance to Athelstan at Eamont or Hereford will take similar actions. Idwal of Gwynedd, the new king in Strathclyde, Dyfnwal, Constantin of the Scots, Olaf Gothfrithson. The only assurance I have is that Hywel of the South Welsh will not double-cross me. He assured my messenger Wihtred of his continued support even though he didn't attend my coronation.

My mother watches unhappily. She's been a member of the witan for longer than me. She understands the shifting sands of allegiance and time, the wiles of men and the contrariness of them all. She knows men better than they know themselves.

'This will have been long in the planning,' she finally announces. 'Olaf couldn't have done this in the short amount of time since Athelstan's death. But, it means that Olaf is well prepared with many hundreds if not thousands of Norsemen. He's thought about this long and hard in the last two summers and made his decision on how best to attack at the height of winter and from the north.'

I'm pleased to hear her words echoing my thoughts.

'Everyone, and I mean everyone, will have been caught off guard. The men and women we thought were loyal may have capitulated rather than face their death. It'll have been a matter of expediency, nothing more. Take nothing personally and watch your words with care. There'll be spies and those who'll become spies if they think they might gain anything of value.' She speaks with confidence, her assurance that we will overcome this a comfort. 'There's not even been time for Alpin to send word.' Her thoughts, like mine, have turned to Alpin. He lived in our court for so many years, we've almost forgotten the cause of his arrival here. As with Louis, king of the West Franks, Alpin feels like my brother.

Archbishop Wulfheard of Canterbury observes my mother, weighing her words and mulling them over. He would do well to remember her mind is sharp and finely honed from decades of experience within the witan.

Eadred looks as though he wants to speak but is unsure of himself. I give him an indication that he can offer his opinions. He swallows and stutters a little. He's not used to being brought into my confidence in such a way.

'Brother,' Eadred begins, and receives a sharp glance from our mother for his pains. I shake my head at her. It's right that he should remind everyone of our relationship. Athelstan would have done the same and frequently did. 'I know I may not travel with Ealdorman Athelstan. But, if I can assist in ensuring the loyalty and quick action of our ealdormen, you must speak of it to me. I can travel swiftly through the snow with my horse and a small group of men.' He grins then, all modicum of his fear evaporating now the words are spoken.

I nod solemnly at him and try to decide how best to answer him. I can't belittle his efforts. He's read the situation well, and knows his place as my heir.

'You,' I say, my eyes on my mother as I speak, 'are tasked with ensuring the safety of our mother and the other members of our family, our sisters, cousins and any other I might have missed out. You'll go wherever she goes, as I command. We may have to separate our family to ensure its survival.' Unbidden, my thoughts turn to my half-sisters in East and West Frankia. To King Louis, my childhood friend. But he can't help me. I doubt news of Athelstan's death has even reached him yet. The crossing over the Narrow Sea is a particularly precarious one, and not to be undertaken during the winter months.

Eadred stands proudly at my official tone, a smile on his lips, but something else there as well. This might well be the first time that he's realised what being my heir entails. He must learn to understand men and how our family line can best be served.

I dismiss everyone from our impromptu meeting and watch as my mother gathers her women and sets them to important tasks concerned with warfare and caring for the sick and injured, spindles discarded as they have more pressing tasks than producing woollen threads. Archbishop Wulfheard and Bishop Oda hurry from my hall, causing the door to be flung wide open and a flurry of snow to settle on the wooden floorboards. I shudder in the sudden cold and hope it's not a portent of things to come.

Winter isn't a time to make war.

Bloody Olaf Gothfrithson.

20

JANUARY 940, THE NORTHERN REACHES OF THE KINGDOM OF THE ENGLISH, BETWEEN LINCOLN AND STAMFORD, AND BETWEEN STAMFORD AND NORTHAMPTON

Olaf Gothfrithson, king of the Dublin Norse

Ahead, the sky is clear, but behind, smoke clouds the horizon. These people don't want me as their king. Neither do those unsuspecting people ahead. But they'll soon come under my rulership. There's no one to stop my advance. Already I hold Lincoln with its largely Norse population. In time, I'll take Stamford, Leicester, Nottingham and Derby.

Many are unaware that King Athelstan of the English is dead. My unexpected arrival has shocked them from a quiet winter, waiting for the weather to improve. They were complacent fools in their winter beds, and easy to conquer.

Until I meet some real resistance, I plan on continuing south into the heart of the English kingdom. Any resistance won't come from the new king of the English, Edmund. He's a boy, not a man, no matter the tales of his military prowess. No, it'll be from his people and ealdormen as they raise their household troops.

Edmund won't reach me from his palace in Wessex, where I believe he hides away, not unless he rides out to greet the Norse warriors. I don't believe he'll do so. It'll be for me to decide where I cease the headlong foray into his kingdom. I've been aware of an English force tracking my movements, but they're slow and small in number. I've not countered them. It's better if they witness all of my actions. They can ensure King Edmund knows of my every success.

Jorvik has welcomed me, and the lands of the lords of Bamburgh let me pass. The man who names himself their lord, a lad of few winters, rode to greet me but not from the fortress of Bamburgh itself. Constantin warned me about him. Said he was all talk and no actual warriors or wealth to reward them. I spoke with him, and offered to let him join me, but he was eager to let me pass. I could see that he hoped I'd attack Bamburgh and return it to him. The English ealdorman was apparently missing from Bamburgh, no doubt witnessing Edmund's coronation. If the English king had left any warriors to stave off an attack from the north, they permitted me passage without interference, sheltering on their rocky outcropping, and hiding behind the walls that protect them. The lordling of Bamburgh can fight his own battles. I won't waste my men on what seems to be an attack doomed to fail.

The land south-east of Jorvik, along Ermine Street, was less welcoming. Now, much of it burns in my wake, not easy to accomplish in the winter. I need to ensure that those who live in the south see me coming and know that they can accept me as their king or can suffer the same fate.

I'd prefer a peaceful conquest to enable me to tax the people and live off the land far more easily. If I have to burn more than half of what I see, it'll be a challenging year, and I'll suffer as well, but not as much who those who refuse my leadership.

My warriors hope for blood and violence. I let them have their way some of the time, but their skills are far superior to these men and women who work the land. I need only a score of my men to strike fear into the hearts of those they encounter. Many of them are the descendants of Viking raiders grown soft and used to the good soil and laws that the English kings have given them.

Anlaf Sihtricson rides before me with his group of fifty men. He likes the thrill of being the first to advance. I don't mind if he does. Better to have him at my side than causing problems in Dublin in my absence. Anlaf fights passably and makes my appearance that much more magnificent by comparison. In time, I'll have to honour the pledge given to him before we fought at Brunanburh, but not yet. For now, he knows that if he displeases me, I'm more than willing to gift his possessions to his brother, as happened with Limerick.

While Anlaf wears a cloak of blood and gore, I wear one of shining metal rings, gleaming brightly in the dullest day and a testament to my place as king of Dublin and Jorvik. Soon, I'll be king of much more.

'My lord king.' The cry comes from behind me. I squint into the dying sunlight, wondering who shouts my name and why.

'Yes,' I call, trying to make out the face that rushes towards me and whether the voice is panicked.

'My lord king,' floats on the wind. I recognise my brother, Blakari. I left him behind in Jorvik. Why is he now chasing me along England's snow-shrouded roads? Fear constricts my heart. He better not have bloody lost it when I only just reclaimed it.

'What is it?' I snap.

'It's Archbishop Wulfstan,' he says, when close enough to speak without shouting, his breathing ragged, bringing his horse to a stop beside me, a splash of cold snow flying close to my face so that I batter it aside.

'What of the old fart?' I ask. 'Who rules in your absence?' My words are sharper when I ask after Jorvik. I don't much like Archbishop Wulfstan. He pretends to his Christianity. I don't recognise it from my encounters with the holy men who infect the Irish kingdoms. I've had Archbishop Wulfstan locked up, under guard, until I have more time to decide how to deal with the menace of an English archbishop who looks to the English king in my new kingdom.

'He demands an audience with you. And your son has command of Jorvik, alongside Mael Muire. I thought you'd approve of that.' Blakari quirks an eyebrow from beneath his woollen cap and thick fur cloak. What I can see of his skin is pink from the cold, his beard and moustache layered with icicles, despite the sweat that drips down his nose.

'Why ever would you come running to me with the archbishop's demand?' I question, wondering what's happened to make Blakari hunt me down. I admit, grudgingly, that I approve of him leaving my son in Jorvik. Camman is keen to prove himself as more than just a petulant boy whose father has a new wife while his old one yet lives. Perhaps he and Mael Muire might become allies.

'He promises to get you more land with his words rather than your weapons.' Blakari's tone suggests that the idea perplexes him.

I'm intrigued. The archbishop insinuated none of this when I had him brought before me in Jorvik. Then he was a snivelling turd, thinking only of surviving the threat of my war axe and seax, thinking only of his next meal. He's not just snivelling; he's bloated as well.

'And why would he do that, and how would he do it, more importantly.'

'He says he has the king's ear. He states the English king is a young man, too distressed at his brother's death to beat you in war. He was with the English king at his coronation some months ago.

He promises that with the aid of the archbishop of Canterbury, Wulfheard, he'll extend your borders even further south, and all in the name of his God and peace.'

I absorb the words as I ponder the carnage before me, the smoking ruins, the pale bloodied flesh of those who defied my warriors, the sharp stink of blood and shit redolent in the crisp air. It would be good to take this land without ruining any chance of taxing it. And without destroying the ability of my new people to feed themselves and work to earn more taxes to pay me for protecting them.

'Bring him here. Tell him I want to hear what he has to say,' I eventually announce. It'll take some time to reach me from Jorvik. I can think about this suggestion some more. Even while I allow my warriors to kill as they see fit as we move further south.

Blakari grins more easily, his posture relaxing, as he realises I'm not about to berate him for leaving Jorvik.

'I already have. He insisted that you'd agree to the meeting and in the end, I was prepared to risk your wrath,' he chuckles. I turn then, and realise that Blakari hasn't come alone. Damn him. The archbishop is wrapped in so many layers of fur, I think he'll roll rather than walk when he dismounts.

I knew Archbishop Wulfstan would be trouble. At my side, Ildulb watches me with a strained expression. He doesn't want peace. He wants war. I ignore his angry glower fixed on my brother. Ildulb tells me that Alpin will be dead soon. Alpin can't live while he demands peace with the English and the Scots demand war. I'd pity Alpin if he didn't remind me so much of King Athelstan.

'I'll speak with him later,' I announce, belligerent to be faced with this situation without anything more than grudging assent. 'For now, I've more people to conquer.' If these are the last of the English that I'll get to kill, then I want to enjoy myself.

Turning from Blakari, I follow Anlaf into the smoking ruins of the small settlement. If today is the final time I strike fear into the hearts of the English people, I intend to make the best possible use of it.

* * *

I press on ever southwards, using the roads that run through the kingdom to ease my passage. There are ships as well, streaming down the River Trent, having risked the Humber estuary, cutting a path through the lands of the English. Resistance dwindles. The cold saps the strength of the old and the young, the smell of my bloodied blade driving fear into those who discover they have no stomach for death.

I think myself more civilised than my forebears. I don't burn everything I come across, and neither do I have every man, woman and child who resists me put to death. They'll make sullen subjects, but they'll be productive if their homes and workshops, fields and livestock are left well alone. I crave the coin that their continued existence will bring me.

If I'm lucky, I'll have enough coin to tempt warriors from the ancient homelands of the Norse to assist me in my invasion plans, for this is what I scheme, an invasion of England, and one that will see me as its king. Provided everything goes according to my wishes.

A few years ago, the acquisition of Jorvik would have made me happy. But now that I see how rich and open England is, I yearn to be king over it all. And I'll be a far better man than Edmund. I have experience; I know how to lead men. I even, and as much as I wish I didn't, know how to lose well, how to regroup, how to remotivate men when they're at their lowest.

Not many men have that skill.

I walk through a dead land. Men and women have locked up their homes with the news of my arrival. Some approach and bend the knee, asking for my protection. I give it, but my eyes are turned southwards. I don't plan to stop, not yet. Stamford is mine, just as Lincoln is.

I've spoken to the archbishop of Jorvik, or York as he insists on calling it. He's filled with grovelling respect and assures me that a peace accord between our two nations will ensure I gain much without having to kill. I like the sound of his words, but I trust the blades of my warriors more than I do those words. For now, I'm open to his peace talks, even as I continue my ravages south. At some point, I'm sure, the English must attempt to stop my advances, and if not, then what need do I have for peace?

My outriders return to me, grim-faced. 'The enemy has been sighted to the south-west,' the first to reach me calls, looking red from the passage of his horse through the blisteringly biting wind. The animal steams in the cold air, its legs glistening with melted snow. 'At least five hundred warriors,' the man huffs, an eyebrow arched, as we both listen to the sound of another horse making its way towards us.

'My lord king,' Anlaf Sihtricson shouts, racing in behind my outrider. His expression is murderous at not reaching me first. The landscape here is reasonably flat, the white of the snow merging with the heavy clouds that show more snow will fall during the coming day. If not for the flushed faces of my warriors, there'd be nothing but the weak glow of the sun to break the monotony. 'Northampton's not far from here,' Anlaf announces in a rush. 'It's a walled burh that's held mainly by the Norse. We should go there. They'll let us inside, and we can use it to stand firm against the English force. We already hold Lincoln and Stamford. Northampton will be next.'

A smile touches my lips. The English might be coming, but

there are many loyal to their Norse heritage. Northampton will welcome me with open arms, as so many other places have. I'm sure of that. After all, my trail of destruction and lack of retaliation by the English king reveals who's the better warrior.

'Five hundred?' I demand of Anlaf, checking that he's seen the same as the first outrider. He thinks for a moment, tilting his head from side to side. He could be a handsome man if his face didn't bear the marks of so many skirmishes in the past.

'A large force. Yes, five hundred would be a good approximation. An even match,' he suggests. I consider that. It's taken them weeks, in fact months, to mount any counter-attack, but they have, it seems, taken the time to recruit the number of men they need. I've had to leave men behind in Jorvik, and then in Lincoln, and then on the ships in the River Trent. I started this endeavour with over a thousand and half men. That number has significantly dwindled the further I travel from Jorvik.

'Does the new king lead the force?' I can't deny I'm disappointed not to face Athelstan. It's him who I truly meant to humiliate, but his brother will do, I suppose.

'I didn't get close enough,' Anlaf explains, his expression intense as he continues to glower at the first outrider to speak.

'How long until they find us?'

'A day at the most,' he replies immediately. 'They have many scouts. They know exactly where we are.'

I call the men together, shouting over the noise of horses and the hubbub of excited voices. I meet the gaze of some of my warriors, favouring them with my regard. I see them sit taller in their saddles, the horses beneath them stilling as though aware of my interest as well.

'Northampton,' I call when it's as quiet as it's going to be. 'We go to Northampton and shelter behind their walls until we know more about our enemy.' Cries of acclaim reach my ears. These warriors know to trust me. All we've had so far is success, and they don't believe we can fail. And why would we? Jorvik, Lincoln, Stamford, and all those places in between. They've submitted or been overwhelmed. Northampton will be no different.

I imagine the smell of smoke from the cooking fires in Northampton. Tonight I hope to be warm and well fed inside someone's hall. Archbishop Wulfstan, riding at my side, nods in satisfaction at the news. He's long since stopped complaining about the cold, but only because no one will listen to him. I'll give him leave to try his diplomacy with the men and women of Northampton, but it's a tedious business. He's sent messengers to the archbishop of Canterbury requesting a peace accord. Replies have been slow in coming. Thankfully. War is quicker to accomplish than peace.

I knee my horse to action. He's been stamping his feet in irritation at the persistent snow that mars the land. I too feel the faint tingling of cold feet.

'Northampton it is then,' I decide, and lead the way, following my first rider, trusting him to guide me to the correct place, my eyes watchful.

Quickly, the settlement appears before me. It's not far, the smell of fire and roasting meat directing my gaze.

I don't race towards Northampton as though terrified of the English force, but I do encourage my horse, the thought of holding such a place spurring me on. The wooden ramparts rising from the reasonably flat ground are well maintained. A deep ditch surrounding it is filled with snow. I'm pleased to have found somewhere that offers my men and me somewhere easy to defend from the English forces. Inside Northampton, we'll be safe, and then Archbishop Wulfstan can get on with his slow peace negotiations. When he's done, Edmund will be lucky to rule half the kingdom his brother left to him. Almost all of eastern Mercia is in my hands.

I knew there would be some defence, eventually. King Edmund can hold Wessex. It's filled with Saxons who hate the Norse. I don't wish to be their king. Not until I'm assured of my hold on Jorvik and eastern Mercia.

'We'll ask for admittance,' I inform Anlaf, Ildulb and Archbishop Wulfstan as we come to a stop before the ramparts with a clatter of weapons that clang louder than thunder in the still air. Only then a cry emerges from those behind me, and my gaze rests on Northampton.

A group of warriors emerge through the gateway of the burh, shields overlapping for the foot soldiers, although some are mounted. Behind, the gates hastily close while more men scramble to guard it from the ramparts. I see white faces beneath shining helms, fear and cold combined.

The warriors are armed. I know a moment of doubt as they make it clear they intend to approach me. All the same, I settle in my saddle, and with a flick of my hands, my warriors wait behind me, my brother, Archbishop Wulfstan, Anlaf and Ildulb just to my rear. As my horse moves uneasily beneath me, I force myself to release my grasp on his reins. The damn animal can sense my sudden unease.

'My lord?' the spokesman for the group shouts across the snow-covered landscape as he comes to a stop far enough away that an arrow shot from the ramparts will protect him. His tone is disparaging and heavily laced with his Norse ancestry. I growl low in my throat. Who is this damn fool?

'Brother,' Blakari cautions me beneath his breath, sensing my anger.

'I'm King Olaf Gothfrithson of Dublin and Jorvik,' I retort, chin held arrogantly high.

I sense the change in mood from the men who face me, worried whispers exchanged between them. After all, my reputation does precede me. I relax. In no time, I'm convinced I'll be settled beside a vast hearth fire, my feet warm for the first time since we left Stamford.

The response isn't what I expect.

'What do you want?' the spokesman growls without giving me his name. I should ask him, but I don't much care who he is. Once Northampton's mine, he won't live for much longer. The arrogant sod. He should bow before me, not strut on his horse. For now, I hold my temper in check.

'Use of the burh, my good man. Tell me, was it your mother or father who was Norse? Perhaps we're related,' I ask in a friendly manner. I'm aware that Archbishop Wulfstan nods with approval at my overtures of friendship.

But my words fall like stones from a great height. Blakari coughs, and I turn to glower at him.

'The English are coming,' I explain slowly to the Northampton warrior, although I shouldn't have to justify anything to this damn fool. 'I need to defend myself and my warriors from the feeble English king.'

'Not in my burh, you don't,' the speaker retorts. He glances behind him as though he can see the English force arriving, but instead, he sees the ramparts of Northampton and the great ditch and palisade. Northampton is well-defended, and I recall that some say it was my predecessors who began the fortifications here. If they did, they made a fine job of it.

I can hear the rumble of water close by. Northampton is served by a river. Perhaps I should have sent my ships along it, but I left them not far from Lincoln, safely on the River Trent. Should we ever face the English defence, they're in place to ensure we can retreat safely and to a place of security.

'The English kings leave us alone as long as we pay tax to them. I'm not turning against them,' the man continues. I glance along the line of English foemen as they stand ready to counter my warriors. They showed some initial unease, but now resolve has strengthened them. I consider how quickly my battle-hardened fighters could get to them through the deep snow. Could they kill them all before they got behind the gates? I don't think they could, but I'm tempted to try.

'Don't you know who I am?' I demand, my hand flexing as though I might grip my war axe and seax and end the man's life.

'Oh yes, Olaf Gothfrithson,' he further mocks. 'You're the loser from the mighty battle of Brunanburh. The man who ran home while his men died for him and his wife was left behind, eventually to fall into the hands of a Norseman who took her as often as he liked, before exchanging Limerick for her.' A knowing laugh runs through the mass of men. I feel my rage threatening to spill, not helped by Anlaf's growl of fury at the memory of Haraldr stealing his holding from him. 'I know who you are, Olaf, and I don't bloody care. You can get the hell out of England. I'm not letting you inside Northampton.'

So spoken, he turns his horse. While others protect his back, he continues towards the tightly closed gates, his horse stepping high to plough through the snow. I eye those men, sneering at their cowardly display while the gate opens and they can turn their backs on me as well. Only they keep their shield wall formation. I watch, unsure what they're doing, until I see men scurrying forward and pulling pieces of wood inside the gates as well.

The gates close with a soft sigh. I note the thickness of the wood and the metal reinforcing it, and know I can't beat it. Not even fire will burn through the metal.

Anger rolls in my belly. I've banished the spectre of my failure at Brunanburh. My warriors are fiercely loyal and will do all I demand of them. But this half-English, half-Norse bastard will show me none of the respect I'm owed. If only it were summer, then I'd torch the place and happily listen to the screams of the inhabitants, but it's winter and it takes more than a single flame to get anything to burn. I need old hay – or, better yet, bodies – to start a real fire.

'Your reputation precedes you,' Ildulb mutters darkly, showing no unease at the way his sister's been disparaged. I open my mouth to reply but grimace instead.

How dare the jumped-up little prick speak to me in such a way. I eye Northampton with covetous eyes. I'd like this good burh to call my own, especially as it's so close to London.

'Set camp here,' I shout loudly enough that the men close to me can hear. 'We attack at dawn,' I announce. There's no need to discuss this. I need the burh to frustrate the English force coming to meet me. We'll overpower those inside, just as we did at Lincoln and Stamford.

Ildulb laughs a quiet, menacing sound at my side. 'My lord, one slight, and you plan to attack the place. It's guarded by warriors who fight and speak as you do. If you can't appeal to your common ancestry, then there's no hope for you.'

His words irritate me because I know they're right. We've not yet faced resistance as great as this. I need to counter it or others might start to buck and strain against my lordship. If those in Stamford or Lincoln should hear of this, then I'll be marooned in an enemy land. I sense Archbishop Wulfstan about to speak, but instead, ride closer to the burh, in the tracks of the horses and warriors who escorted the man who taunted me.

Anlaf follows me. I wish he didn't.

'Wouldn't it be better to retreat? There are more defensible locations. We could return to Stamford, or to Lincoln and the ships and counter the English from there.'

'No, it wouldn't be better to bloody retreat. Set the camp and make ready to attack come dawn. Send men to scout the landscape. I want a full report of any possible weaknesses in the construction of the burh.'

Anlaf's expression is pained, but he does as I ask. I hear him shouting for order amongst my warriors. A few complain about forcing a camp when the snow's so deep, but I pretend not to hear. Anlaf's good with the warriors. Not better than me, but good. They'll do as he says. What he lacks is a claim to the number of loyal warriors I have. He has less than a thirtieth of the men who are loyal to me, although, here, outside Northampton, that share has risen significantly. He's travelled with all of his shipmen, unlike me. All the same, should I die here, he'll take the remaining warriors as his own. He's been busy cultivating them by offering rewards and treating them fairly.

I might need to watch him and his ambitions, as well as the English, Ildulb and Archbishop Wulfstan.

Wulfstan promised me peace, but I've not seen much of that yet. War is quicker. With war, I can take Northampton, and it won't matter what the English try to do to counter it, once I have control of the defences.

21

JANUARY 940, OUTSIDE NORTHAMPTON, THE KINGDOM OF THE ENGLISH

Ildulb, prince of the Scots

Olaf's a good companion and a worthy warrior, as I've learned since meeting him in my homeland. I thought him useless and not worthy of my sister as a wife. I believed him inept when we lost at the battle of Brunanburh, but I've since changed my mind. He deserves whatever he gains from marching through these dead winter lands. He's more my brother than Alpin these days. His intentions align with mine, unlike Alpin's.

Yet, I think Olaf's made a huge mistake in pushing so far south from Jorvik and leaving the vast majority of his ship army close to Lincoln. He's exposed to the coming English attack and he certainly shouldn't have taken against this insignificant settlement of Northampton, when the purpose should be to kill Edmund and take all of England.

There have been few warriors to stop Olaf's advance. Until now. He's grown arrogant.

It's bitterly cold, but I don't seem to notice any of it, only my fogging breath reminding me of the chill and snow that lies thickly on the ground. My horse doesn't seem at all concerned by it, but then, he's used to deep snow and driving winds at this time of the year. After all, the land further north of here is a place of extreme weather, pleasant in the summer and frigid in the winter. It makes my people strong.

I've fought in a few skirmishes so far on the way south, along Ermine Street. I've helped people see the advantage of Olaf as their king, but I crave bloody battle. I want to fight the English and see English blood sheeting over the virginal snow. I desire it with a ferocity that surprises me.

However, the coming battle against the people of Northampton isn't what I anticipated. I want the English, not men who live on English land and who yet are also apart from it. Northampton, I know, is a Norse enclave. The nameless man who told Olaf to go home was more than half-Norse, his accent as sharp as the wintry air.

All the same, I obey Olaf's summons to share a meal with him beneath his bleached canvas, bowed under the weight of the constantly falling snow.

'My lord king.' I bow, and he flicks his fingers. I settle on a camp stool, and observe him as he pushes dulled coins in and out of his money pouch. No doubt he has to pay wages, although what the warriors think to spend their hard-earned coins on, I don't know.

Olaf has a few more years on him than I do, but has the bearing of a king. He's easy with himself and confident in his skills, or at least he was until today.

He wears beautiful clothes made of thick wool and a fine coat of mail. His tent's warmed by a brazier, the snow shovelled aside to allow it to rest on the hard-packed ground beneath his feet.

Outside, the rhythmic sound of someone chopping wood can be easily heard.

The food I'm served is warm and plain, seasoned with little more than old garlic and a hint of onion. I almost inhale it in my hunger. I have a massive appetite, almost embarrassingly insatiable in the cold. My fellow warriors tease me about it, and as I eat and eat, I also see the amusement on Olaf's face as his gaze switches to me.

'Your father, how old is he now?' Olaf demands. The wind which has been blowing all day has dwindled away to nothing. Instead, snow silently falls, causing the canvas to sag and strain against the ropes and wooden poles. In the morning the horses will be knee-high in the stuff. If we attack at dawn, as Olaf wishes to do, it'll be a difficult task.

'Almost into his seventieth winter,' I offer, having an inkling of where this conversation is going.

'He's the oldest man I know,' Olaf says wonderingly. I smirk. He's the most elderly man I know as well, and Mael Coluim is most distressed by it, much to my delight.

'And how long has he been the king of your people?'

The answer always amazes people. 'Nearly forty summers.'

'Bloody hell,' Olaf stutters.

'Didn't my sister tell you this?' I ask with surprise. I still recall her furious slap to the face when she heard of King Athelstan's death. I'll carry the scar her weighted ring left on my nose until my death. I don't bloody mind. It was worth it to know something that she didn't.

'Well, yes, but the more people who say it, the more believable it becomes. When someone tells you he's been a king for nearly forty summers, I almost think they must be speaking of one of the fabled old gods, not a man that I know to be mortal and very much alive.'

'Well, he's legendary,' I jest.

Olaf appraises me with a raised eyebrow. 'I should like to be one of those,' he says seriously. I don't want to tell him that it has more to do with luck than skill. My father's long life has been a gift. I can't say he's done anything to earn it, despite his penchant for prayer.

'Is that what you intend to accomplish by taking back Jorvik?'

'No, that's my birthright. I'll become legendary when I kill an English king. No one else can yet claim that, and I want to be the first. My ancestors killed a king of the East Angles, but no one of Norse descent has killed a king of the English.'

I chuckle at the bold statement.

'You don't strive for much, do you?'

'If I don't strive and push and shove my way into England, then no one else will ever do it. I need to do this. This high idea of an "England" that Athelstan brought about and which Edmund is incapable of maintaining goes against everything that's happened before. The Norse, the Viking raiders as they term us, all look towards this island as a place not yet full enough. It has good farmland and good laws and we all want a part of that. If this island becomes English then where will we all go?'

I've not considered this or that Olaf acts for any reason other than his ambitions. To pretend he does this for a higher purpose amuses me. Whatever cloak he covers his aspirations in, I don't much care. As long as he attacks England and rouses Edmund, the murderer of my son, from his royal palace, I'll be pleased.

'What do you desire' Olaf queries, but I'm prevented from answering by the arrival of Anlaf, a grin on his broad face as he removes his gloves and warms himself before the small brazier, stamping his feet to dislodge snow onto the ground.

'Bloody hell, it's bloody freezing out there,' he announces

loudly, not caring that he's interrupted us. 'By tomorrow there'll be snow up to our stones.'

'The snow won't be that deep,' Olaf responds with some annoyance. I wonder how many times they've had this discussion before.

'So you say, but the clouds are full of it tonight and have taken on that strange brightness that means snowfall. You mark my words, we'll not be moving from this campsite tomorrow, and all the men will be bloody moaning, although of course, if we can't move, then the English won't be able to either.'

Olaf's face betrays his annoyance. I watch the two men closely. Olaf's the king, Anlaf his successor, and the son of Olaf's predecessor in holding Jorvik. The relationship is much like mine and Mael Coluim, only masked in some civility for they at least share the same wishes and desires towards England's king.

'Tomorrow we'll attack Northampton, no matter the weather,' Olaf announces defiantly. I think he's a fool for not reconsidering his plans. 'The weather will slow the English and give us more of a chance to get inside.'

'We're not getting into Northampton,' Anlaf counters. 'It's well-guarded, and you've made an enemy without even trying. The men inside are busying themselves for war. They have the advantage of warm beds and well-cooked food in their bellies, and a rampart that we need to crest to get inside. And a bridge, and a river to protect the south of the settlement, if you'd bothered to find out.'

Olaf's face darkens as Anlaf lists the impediments. 'I command here, and we'll attack the northern gate. We'll tear it down, and then we'll murder every last bastard inside.' Olaf's voice rings with conviction.

'We won't make it inside,' Anlaf reaffirms aggressively, as angry as Olaf but keeping a better check on his emotions. 'The English force is coming. We'll be trapped if we stay here, between the hostile force of the men inside Northampton and whichever ealdorman commands the warriors seeking us out from Mercia.'

Olaf stands abruptly, knocking his camp stool to one side. I grab hold of the food on the small table. I'm still hungry. I don't want it to fall to the ground.

'You'll attack as you're told, and you'll lead your men as well as you can. This isn't open for discussion.'

'It's a bloody stupid idea,' Anlaf urges as Olaf moves menacingly towards him.

'Will you fight with me or not?' Olaf growls through gritted teeth, his chest heaving. Anlaf holds up his hands in surrender, although his face is dark with anger.

'Of course, I'll fight with you. But it'll be your defeat. And it won't be the first time that Northampton has stopped a Norse leader from overpowering the English, either.' With that, Anlaf flings open the side of the canvas structure and strides outside, his anger making his steps rigid. A blast of chill air follows his departure. I pull my cloak tighter around me, considering his words. It's hard to decipher much while the landscape is coated in its layer of snow. But he's right. There's a river that protects Northampton to the south and west. There's a small bridge that crests that river, and to this side of the settlement, facing the north, there might well be a gate, but it's a small thing, paltry and only just wide enough for two horses to ride side by side. It's evident that the carts that must visit the place do so from the south, making use of a larger gate and the bridge.

Olaf tries to clear his face and make light of the disagreement, but he's angered by Anlaf's disloyalty.

Silence descends. I don't know what to say. I feel sympathy for him. I know what it's like to have plans ridiculed by another and by the very person you expect to support you the most. It often happens that way with my father.

'I need to sleep,' Olaf finally announces. I incline my head and leave, pleased to be away from the strained atmosphere, even if it means I have to freeze on the way to my tent. I've retained the cooling pottage, so at least I'll eat well.

There's a warm brazier inside, and when I enter, I'm pleased to see my men have seen to my comfort and cleared the snow from the ground so that my bed and brazier sit flat on the ground.

I shiver inside my clothes, and the smell of an unwashed body wafts free. I can't remember the last time I fully undressed. Not since Jorvik, I think. It's too damn cold to remove any layers.

I lie on my camp bed, my thoughts uncertain. I consider what tomorrow will bring.

Olaf better be victorious because, if he isn't, my dream of killing Edmund in vengeance for my son's death will be no closer.

22

EARLY 940, NORTHAMPTON, THE KINGDOM OF THE ENGLISH

Olaf Gothfrithson, king of the Dublin Norse

No sooner has Ildulb left, than Archbishop Wulfstan appears, all smiles and gentle words. I don't want to speak with him, but I try to contain my growing frustration.

I'm speechless that Anlaf would so openly defy me before Ildulb. Ildulb might be my brother by marriage, but I know my every action will be recounted to his father. I don't need Constantin's support, but I want it.

I wish I could kill Anlaf here and now but that would be counterproductive. Anlaf commands the loyalty of a significant portion of my force. I don't want to lose men just because he disagrees with me.

'My lord, Olaf,' Wulfstan simpers. I wish him gone. 'You're set to attack tomorrow?' he continues.

I merely nod. My voice would betray my anger. Why does

everyone suddenly think they command here and that it's acceptable to question my orders?

'What about my attempts at diplomacy?' he presses.

I take a deep breath. 'They can continue. But in the meantime, we need Northampton.'

'Very good, my lord,' he murmurs, and leaves. I consider what that was all about. Why did he seek me out in the darkest of nights and with snow staining his cloak? But I dismiss such concerns from my thoughts. Exhaustion drags me to my bed. I fling as many furs as I can find over my body. My muscles ache with the constant efforts to keep warm. I confess I'm almost at the point where even I think I made a mistake by attacking in the winter. Perhaps I should have stayed close to Lincoln with my ship army after all.

* * *

The new day comes too soon. I'm outside my canvas and ready for battle before everyone else. Small fires splutter in the early morning gloom, doing their best to beat back the still-falling tendrils of snow. I note with some satisfaction that the snowfall the night before has only added a thin layer to that which had already fallen. *Stones deep, indeed*, I think. I only hope Anlaf is wrong about the possibility of success today as well.

Smoke billows above the rampart surrounding Northampton. I've heard tales of this place. I know some of the Viking raiders once made a stand here. What I can't remember is how successful they were, if at all. Anlaf is convinced they failed. I hope he's wrong. I hunger to own the little piece of civilisation amongst so many dormant fields. The men and women of Northampton are good farmers, but there's no need to protect the land when the crop is harvested and safely stored behind those walls for the winter or sheltering deep in the soil, waiting for the better weather.

My men group around cook fires as they wake, stamping life into cold feet and hands. A few cast strained looks my way, but I ignore them. They're my men to command, and I've ordered them to attack Northampton. There's no going back now. Not everywhere was going to be as easy to overwhelm as Lincoln and Stamford.

Quickly, as the daylight builds, driving back the pink-hazed clouds of snow, my men gather in small groups, ready to march across the snow-clad fields. I've spent time deciding how we should begin our assault. A simple and straightforward attack is what I plan. We'll head for the gate that faces us, small as it is. We'll set fire to it, no matter how hard it will be to get the flame to bite, and gain entry that way.

Ildulb and his modest collection of warriors from the kingdom of the Scots await my orders. Anlaf mingles with the men. He's more confident around them than Ildulb, who doubts the Norsemen, but that's because Anlaf's attempting to forge alliances with men who should be loyal to me. Archbishop Wulfstan lingers beneath his canvas. He doesn't fight and no doubt is on his knees praying or pretending to do so. I've not thought to ask if he prays for my success or if he just prays. I'll be victorious, whether he begs his God for it or not.

I signal to begin our advance, men stamping feet and banging weapons on shields, the plumes of hot air before us a reminder of how cold it is.

As one, we prepare to attack. The constant toing and froing through the campsite has melted much of the snow, but further out, closer to Northampton's walls, the snow's much deeper.

At my back, the boys who are too young and men who are too old to join the fighting work their way amongst the horses. The animals have to be kept beneath canvas as well, or they'll grow too cold. If we must make a hasty escape, the horses will be ready and hopefully willing to fight their way through the deep snow. It's cost me enough to keep them fed and to transport the oats and hay that they need to eat each day. I hope their alertness isn't needed, but Anlaf's lack of belief has caused me to doubt my intentions.

Irritably, I push all thoughts of failure away and call the two bowmen I have with me to my side. They know what I want them to do, but it's good to reiterate it. They carry a small brazier filled with flame. They'll use it to set light to the wooden palisade, not necessarily at the gate, but wherever they think they might be able to force a gap or wound men who see me as their enemy. And where they believe the flame has the best opportunity to work its way into the damp wood and earth upon which the rampart stands.

Ildulb and his warriors position themselves in the centre of the shield wall. Anlaf's beside him. The men are mostly silent as they wait for my command to advance. That's a bad sign.

Stepping forward from my place amongst the fifty men at the front of the shield wall, the others behind them in rows, I turn and face them. I must rile them and bring forth the battle rage that'll ensure our victory. The presence of the burh walls and ramparts unsettles them, as do the sullen Englishmen who watch our approach with the arrogance of belief in their success. I don't know where the approaching English force is. They've not been sighted during the night.

Anlaf meets my gaze without flinching, a 'told you so' cant to his neck. Yet, he stands with my warriors. I take that to mean I have his support. He's telling me to ensure those words are good.

'My warriors,' I holler, unsure of what will pour from my mouth. 'Inside these walls are men who share our ancestry, our

Gods, and who speak the names of our heroes. Yet they deny us access and hold loyal to the English king.'

There's a murmur of disquiet from my warriors, some staring at the burh, some looking straight at me with unflinching, hard eyes. They don't care about Gods or ancestry. They care about living through this day.

'We called on them as our allies, and they spurned us without any thought. They may call themselves Norse, but they're English through and through. We'll compel them to capitulate to us. Northampton will be a forward base to continue our attack into the heartland of England, towards London, and Wessex.'

A louder murmur of approval greets my words. Most now watch the burh behind me, lips curling, hands opening and closing on their weapons, resolve settling on their heavy features, despite the cold and the taunting words of those inside which carry far too easily on the brisk, cold air.

'These men are our enemies. We treat them as such even if they wear the trinkets of our Gods and speak our words. They stand in the way of our great Jorvik Empire, belligerent and unyielding. We'll break down their gate and kill the man who leads them. It's he who must die if we're to call Northampton our own. Any man who captures him or kills him will be rewarded,' I bellow as loudly as I can, hoping those inside hear as well as we can perceive them. I know my words aren't the most inspiring, but they're what I have.

Our advance so far south into England has been opportunistic, but I don't plan on giving back anything that I've gained.

'With Northampton in our grasp, we'll hold much of Mercia. London isn't far, and if we take London, we'll hold all of Mercia. With London as our base, it'll only be a matter of time until we strike at Winchester and the boy king who now wears the crown.'

The reminder of our intention has the desired effect. Men's

voices rise and fall, some shouting for blood and others for vengeance. Many of these men, my closest adherents, lost someone to the slaughter field of Brunanburh. I used that to bring them to my side. They hold the English king responsible.

'We attack,' I shout, 'and we triumph.' My confidence, growing with each word I speak, has roused the men from their stupor. Eagerly, I step into the shield wall glancing at my shield brothers to left and right. My bowmen slip through as well. They'll loose their arrows from behind the safety of the shield wall.

I squint to the men we must battle. I note their battle standard, sagging in the chill air, their pinched faces as they watch us approach. If they thought I'd refuse the fight just because it's cold and snowy, they're very wrong.

Immediately, we're moving forward. Not at a jog, which I'd have preferred, but at a steady pace, each man keeping time with those behind and beside him. Over the thick snow, it's an effort to lift a foot, and then force it down while staying upright. Each stride forward is a victory against the elements, as we bang weapons on shields announcing our intentions.

Ahead I see movement on the ramparts. When we're no more than a hundred paces from the gate, my bowmen launch their first two arrows. They fly, blazing through the air, to land with a satisfying thunk on the wooden gate that so resoundingly closed in our faces yesterday. The flames catch but are quenched quickly with a hastily flung handful of wet snow.

Another whoosh of flaming arrows passes overhead. This time one of the arrows connects with something more flammable on the wooden ramparts – the banner, I hope. Immediately, flames spring up high. Then we're too close to be able to see what's happening above our heads. All eyes focus on the ditch before us. We've no choice but to jump into its forbidding depths and fight our way towards the closed gates. The bastards hauled the wooden bridge which made it possible to cross the ditch inside yesterday when they formed a shield wall before the gate. I should, I realise, have appreciated that sooner. I consider why Anlaf didn't tell me. Perhaps his anger was too intense. Maybe he didn't notice.

The trench is deep and wide, maybe two men deep and at least two across. It's filled with deeply packed snow which is far from white and pristine, and who knows what else. No doubt the inhabitants didn't expect a winter attack and have taken fewer precautions than they should, even leaving the wooden bridge out until yesterday.

I call a halt, the noise of men from inside the burh readying themselves for battle impossible to ignore.

I peer down into the ditch once more, thinking quickly about how to counter this impediment. 'It's deep but filled with snow. We can cross it,' I encourage my warriors. I'm dismayed that the bridge is gone, but I'm not a complete fool. I've been expecting something like this. Northampton isn't the only settlement to benefit from a rampart and ditch for protection. From the back of the shield wall, men pass through thick wooden logs. While some chopped wood for fires yesterday, others had another task to accomplish.

One split log is threaded through my hands by the rows of men behind me. I drop my wolf-crested shield to determine how best to position it. It'll be long enough to reach over the ditch, I'm sure, but it'll be impossible to reposition it if I make a mistake now. I won't have the strength to force it upright once it's down. No man would.

Three other split logs snake their way across the snow-filled ditch. I note where the usual wooden bridge must hook on to the far side and angle my log towards it. There's a small dugout. I hope my wood will settle within that gap.

Arrows fly over my head once more. I smell burning wood and hear the sizzle of melting snow.

Only then I hear an unwelcome noise. I rush to raise my shield before me, dropping the log without further thought. Arrows fly over the side of the burh, aimed at my head and those of my warriors. Thankfully, they all miss. We nestle back behind the safety of the shield wall while I curse the mess I've made of setting the log over the ditch. It's down, yes, but whether it does what it needs to do, I'm unsure. It's not hooked where I wanted it to rest.

I rail against the ditch. If only four men can cross at one time, using the split logs, they'll be exposed and likely to lose their life.

There's little option, but still I waver. Should I lead, or send another? The choice is taken from me when first one warrior and then another three step forward, their positions in the shield wall immediately taken by those behind them.

They're weighed down by byrnies and weapons, not to mention the shields they hold above their heads or to the side of their bodies. I watch through the cracks in the shield wall, holding my breath, to see how they manage.

No more arrows fly from the burh rampart. Emboldened by the cries of triumph from the men who've made the crossing, I step out onto the split log, feeling it thrum with my weight. I test it with one foot. It's firm enough.

I want to be the man to hammer through the paltry gateway guarding the burh of Northampton. I hunger to be the one to fling their bridge across the divide and allow my men to dash into the interior without needing to balance on split logs.

I take a calming breath, feeling the wind against my face. I attempt to stay level and guard myself at the same time. The whoosh of an arrow sounds loudly in the air. I hope it's from my archers.

A sudden thought paralyses me. I wobble and gaze upwards. Are they waiting for us to be on their side of the ditch before they unleash a torrent of fire upon us?

Behind, the cries of my warriors intensify. They're starting to enjoy this and see the possibilities of victory whereas before they only saw a vain attempt to gain access to a heavily defended burh.

Even I start to believe in my resolution as their cheers embolden me. Only then one of the enemy warriors is before me. He must have jumped from the ramparts. He's huge, eyes gleaming angrily and maliciously. He wears a beautiful coat of mail, blinding in the glow from the snow and the watery sun. A shining helm covers his face, nose and cheek guards, ensuring I see little but his eyes and twisted lips. He's confident in the abilities of his armour to protect him.

He steps towards the first split log, growling low in his throat, audible despite the encouraging cries of my warriors, to kick it disdainfully aside. It takes surprisingly little effort.

My warrior fights to keep his balance but fails, arms flailing to either side of his body, weighted down by his shield and war axe. Shrieking, he lands at least ten feet below, falling through the soft snow. I hear the whoosh of the air leaving his body even from where I stand and then a sharp crack of bones breaking. His eyes meet mine, but they see nothing. I fight for balance.

My warriors who've already navigated the split logs turn to attack the new menace. The English warrior holds them off without much effort, their blows on his byrnie and shield ineffectual. He kicks the second split log, and the trapped warrior howls with fury as he makes a wild leap hoping to return to the remainder of the shield wall. I watch his arms and legs whirling in the air. Like a man lost overboard, the weight of his equipment tumbles him into the depths of the ditch with another harsh crack.

I stand on the third split log. Hastily, I look behind, considering retreat. Can I make it before the English warrior causes my death as well?

Turning, I launch myself skywards, the wood thrumming

beneath my feet, not daring to look down, only at where I want to go. For a moment, I feel nothing but the weightlessness of flight, and then I land on the stamped-down snow with a clatter of weapons as my warriors create a space for me in the shield wall. I feel the icy hardness of the ground buckle my knees as I land on my arse, the wind knocked from me, while frantic hands reach to enclose me behind the shields.

An arrow slices the air, narrowly missing my hand as it stands upright in the frozen landscape. My battle rage ignites. I will better this lone English warrior.

Standing, pushing my way through the shield wall, I power my way to the side of the ditch, eyeing it with displeasure. Without pause, I lower myself into it, arms entirely outstretched, before dropping down, my knees absorbing the impact, content the snow and whatever else is beneath it will support my weight. With shuffling steps, I creep over it, never lifting my feet clear, keeping them in constant contact with the snow. Dodging the hissing arrows that try to stop me. On the far side, I reach upwards towards the lip of the ditch, my hands fastening on two pieces of overhanging ice. I stretch upwards and grip them, shuddering at the blast of cold that hits my hands, even through my gloves. Hauling myself over the lip of the ditch, to stand on the snow, I face the giant of a man who growls in fury, somehow he's missed my advance.

My men cheer such actions. Some have lowered themselves into the ditch and hasten to support me. I note dispassionately that Anlaf and Ildulb aren't among them. That doesn't surprise me.

My war axe became dislodged from my weapons belt when I fell. I left my shield behind in the shield wall, but I have my sword, and I intend to make use of it.

Smoke billows blackly from inside the burh, making my lungs ache with its acrid stench. I can hear the frantic cries of men and women trying to douse the flames. Fire has been hard to produce of late, that it hungrily devours all it finds inside Northampton is a sign that I'll triumph here, no matter the giant warrior who thinks to defeat us.

The warrior fixes his gaze on me. I beckon him onwards. If I slay this giant before my warriors, they'll see my skills and know they're right to follow me.

My enemy carries a massive war axe. He moves surprisingly quickly for such a huge man and brushes aside my few warriors who think to stop him. They regroup quickly to race for the gateway to drive their war axes and seaxes into its surface to force it open when they realise he means to face me, not them. The ditch was an impediment. The snow's made it less of one, reducing its depths, provided those who cross it do so carefully.

'Olaf, Gothfrith's son,' the man bellows, his harsh Norse accent impossible to ignore. 'You've made a mistake. You'll pay with your life.'

I'd like to say his words don't worry me, but they do. I lick my lips, once more taking in the size of him and his evident skill.

He lumbers towards me, lashing out with his war axe.

'Olaf.' Blakari thrusts a shield towards me from where he's followed me over the ditch. I grasp it quickly, bringing it before my face to absorb the massive impact. It's as though a tree falls on my head. My arm vibrates, and my head along with it. My foeman is as strong as he looks.

The Northampton warrior hits me again before I have time to recover. I hear a sharp crack as the wooden shield fractures.

Angrily, I discard my shield so that it narrowly misses the head of another warrior surging up from the ditch. The monster I face grins with delight and swings his arm backwards, his intentions clear. I dart closer to him and drive my sword in a massive sweep across his body before stepping back again, out of reach of his axe.

I've done no damage. It's hard to dance on the uneven and slick surface, but I manage to stay upright.

His blow misses me, and as he retrieves his arm and weapon, I dash close to him, determined to do more damage. My blade connects more fully this time, slicing his upper arm, although it doesn't draw blood.

Behind the man, I see Anlaf preparing to join the fight. He must have followed me over. That surprises me. I distract my foeman, wondering how Anlaf plans on vanquishing our enemy. He might not have to contend with the war axe, but our foe-man is well armoured and, other than the rear of his legs, I can't see a way to wound him.

Anlaf must think the same. As the warrior steps backwards, and I dance out of the way of the war axe once more, Anlaf ducks low. The man screeches with rage, dropping his weapon's arm to turn, limbs flailing almost comically.

His ire focuses on Anlaf. I look at the shocking red streaks on the man's calves, all the brighter against the backdrop of churned snow, and catch my breath. Bending forward, I land a slashing upward cut with my sword on his leg. Once more the great man bellows with rage. His fist curls, and connects with my face so that I feel the crunch of my nose, and the spurt of hot blood before I can move backwards. Shaking my head, I focus on him, lips curled in pain and fury. Damn the bastard. I want to leap at him, coil my legs around his neck and squeeze the life from him, yanking his warrior's helm from his head and stabbing into his thick skull.

But, abruptly, he forgets both of us, lumbering for the gateway, his gait unsteady because of his wounds. He forces my warriors aside, tumbling three of my men back into the ditch as they cry out angrily, the crack of their bones assuring me they're wounded. With a final glare for me and Anlaf, he flings aside the one man still hammering on the gate, shouting for entry.

The gate opens the tiniest amount to allow him entry, surprising me that such a huge man can slide through such a small gap. None of us is quick enough to join him. It closes with a resounding bang. I gaze around in shock and surprise. The whole thing can't have taken but a moment, yet I feel as though I've lost the battle already.

Anlaf, his shield protecting his head from the projectiles being thrown from the ramparts, anything from a jug filled with piss to a lump of iron, reaches out to grab my arm.

'A good effort, Olaf, but against that man, none of us could ever win. We'd have all been killed trying to beat him if he'd not retreated.' There's nothing but respect in his voice.

I half share his view. I nod as I glare at my warriors on the other side of the ditch. They're still protected by their shields and encourage us to do more. But I don't see what.

The ditch is filled with what feels like frozen rocks, as well as the bodies of my warriors. It depletes a man's strength to wade through it and haul himself out on the other side. The split logs are in disarray. Although I want to order the men to drag them out of the ditch and reposition them, if the giant comes again, we'll only be replaying what's already happened.

Northampton has beaten me with almost no effort. I've only encountered one enemy.

The smell of smoke remains strong, but I can't hear the crackle of roaring flames any more, only the billowing black smoke of a fire being doused with water.

'What do we do?' Anlaf demands, breathing hard, and for the first time on this expedition I'm not sure I have an answer.

'Retreat,' I puff through my cheeks. 'We should retreat towards Lincoln and find another burh, as you suggested. This one doesn't want us.'

'What of the English force?' he queries, reminding me that we wanted to get inside Northampton for a very good reason. They must be nearly here.

'We'll have to outride them.'

Only then do I hear the disturbed cries of my men and finally listen to what they're telling me.

'The English force, my lord. The English.'

Turning to Anlaf, I meet his taunting eyes. Any respect I've won by fighting the giant has been lost already. I signal for a withdrawal and watch as my warriors realise they need to move and fast. We must retreat to our horses before the main body of the English force arrives. I scamper down into the ditch, determined not to look at the bloodied, broken bodies of the men who fell to their deaths, and the others, at least three of them, who took wounds bad enough to kill them and have been kicked aside by those still living.

'Who is it?' I shout to no one in particular as I hasten across the ditch, just remembering to move slowly, but quickly enough, that the hard layer of snow won't disintegrate beneath my feet. When I get to the other side, I grasp hold of the rim of the ditch and pull myself upright, even though there's little strength left in my arms. My lips are clamped tight together, and beneath my feet, the snow finally shifts, threatening to trip me and the others who need to escape.

Ildulb's thick accent answers my question, his hands reaching down to aid me.

'It looks like the sodding king of the English.' Arrows shoot past my ears from inside Northampton. I duck low, even while Ildulb beckons for me to hurry. I grip his hands, and allow him to pull me as my feet scrabble up the side of the ditch.

Damn, this has been a cock-up from beginning to end. I should have listened to Anlaf after all.

Out of breath, my body heavy with fatigue, I lumber from the ditch and meet Ildulb's implacable eyes, fire burning deep in their depths.

'We should stand and fight,' he declares.

'No, we need to withdraw and regroup elsewhere. I can't face the English king now.' I'm cold, bleeding, and my warriors have seen their first defeat of our campaign southwards. They'll be as frozen and miserable as I am. There's nowhere for us to seek sanctuary. I don't know the location well enough to determine on the best defensive or offensive position to adopt.

Anger creases his white cheeks at my explanation, but he saves his words. The men at our encampment ride horses to meet us, too impatient to wait for us to get to them. A sense of urgency fills me. I need to leave this place, and quickly.

The flash of a banner catches my attention, a sparkle of bright summer gold on a winter's day, the slash of red and yellow almost too bright, blinding, and too reminiscent of the blood that streams from my broken nose. Ildulb's right. The king of the English, Edmund, has come to counter my incursion into his kingdom. I can do nothing but run away, my horse steady beneath me.

Damn. I'll not be making this sort of mistake again.

'Where should we go?' I shout to any who'll hear as we race through the white-cloaked landscape. The concern in my voice worries me. I came here to overwhelm Northampton. My complete failure disturbs me. I wanted to reach London, even Winchester, but now I'm rushing north once more, through a wintry landscape. We're not even heading to Stamford, those who lead simply galloping northwards. None would heed my words if I ordered them eastward instead. And I don't want to, the leaden fear in my belly meaning I want the comfort of Lincoln, where my ships wait close by, with Jorvik at my back.

'To the closest burh we find and let's hope they bloody let us in,' Anlaf shouts above the rush of our passage, the fear and frustration easy enough to hear.

I hazard a quick glance behind me. I can't tell if the English king follows our withdrawal. But, as the wooden ramparts of Northampton slowly fade from view, I think how much different today could have been if not for those damn walls and their giant of a warrior. I should have heeded the advice offered to me. I'll be more wary in future, or so I convince myself.

23

JANUARY 940, NEAR TAMWORTH, MERCIA, THE KINGDOM OF THE ENGLISH

Athelstan the ealdorman

I shield my eyes from the low winter sun, hoping to see what I'm being told by outriders concerning Olaf Gothfrithson's current location within Mercia.

Damn the bastard. Couldn't he have let Edmund have a year, maybe even two, before he launched a retaliatory attack? I thought Olaf would never recover from his defeat at Brunanburh. I was wrong.

The English kingdom remains in shock, reeling from the sudden and unexpected death of Athelstan. I little care that Olaf must have planned this expedition without the knowledge of Athelstan's death. Neither can I deny that I'd rather be home in the warmth than watching my breath plume in front of me, hearing my horse's hooves crunch over the crisp, snow-covered ground.

I'm near Tamworth, the ancient stronghold of the Mercian kings and somewhere I spent much of my childhood. Indeed, it's where I met my wife. It's usually peaceful and defensible. I understand why kings such as Penda and Offa chose this location to build their mighty halls.

Olaf's close. His riders have been seen to the north. But where exactly is he?

Has the cheeky cock taken the burh? Has he simply ridden in and sat himself down? Does he even now command Mercian men and women and have them do his bidding? The thought heats my blood, and my anger stirs to something I can barely contain. I want nothing more than to meet the bastard in open conflict and cut him down where he stands.

Columns of smoke dance in the snow-laden clouds overhead. They're the cook fires of the men and women who live on this land.

My eyes narrow once more.

Behind me, my warriors' horses offer reassuring snorts and stamps of impatience. They're just as keen as I am to rid England of Olaf Gothfrithson. Men call to one another, asking the same questions that run through my head. Where's Olaf? Is he within the palace complex? Is he toying with us and hiding in the south? Is he to the north? Have we ridden past him without even noticing?

No, I think he's within the palace. When my wife hears of this, she'll howl with fury. Not that she doesn't know the duplicitous nature of these Viking raiders. She once faced off against one of them. I know she'd do it again if called upon, but this time I can do it on her behalf. I call my brother to me.

'Æthelwald, go with ten of your men. See what you can find out. Only go inside if you're sure to be treated well and you're confident of returning unscathed. If he's in there, no doubt he'll want to make sure we know he is.'

He glares, unhappy to be given a task that might lead to his death, but really, there's little choice. I need to send a man of sufficient rank that if Olaf is within, it'll not offend and cause him to kill the man on sight for demanding entry.

'Shouldn't you go?' he asks churlishly, but I don't respond. He knows the answer.

I watch him ride away over the snow-touched winter fields. I consider what he'll discover. Olaf Gothfrithson won't kill him there and then and neither will he take him hostage if he has control over Tamworth. No, he'll probably feast with my brother and flaunt his accomplishments, happy in the knowledge that King Edmund will hear all about it soon enough.

My anger stirs again. I know that I've sent the right man for the job. Æthelwald will be able to take the mockery better than I would. He'll come out of this alive and then we'll know far more than Olaf might think can be gleaned from a casual approach.

And Olaf will have made an implacable enemy in Æthelwald. He might keep his composure while they converse, but once he's back with me, his rage will fester. Killing Olaf will be the only balm for his soul. And Eadric and I will join him in that.

I stay where I am, on a small rise that overlooks the familiar burh before me. My presence is conspicuous, with the winter-blue sky behind and the white snow beneath me. That's how it should be. I'm not going to hide from Olaf as he seems to do from me. He's killed men and women, children as well. He's burned their holdings and stolen their livelihoods, but these people weren't warriors. Now, he'll have to face the true might of Mercia.

If Olaf has taken the settlement, I want the Mercian people inside Tamworth to see that they've not been abandoned. They know me here. It's not been that many years since I spent much of my time at Tamworth. Most will know my name. They'll certainly know my wife's.

There are few people about on the cold day. Most remain

inside, fighting the dark winter chill, not the enemy that moves amongst them. But someone might see. They might spread the word. So I stay where I am, no matter how cold I become. Behind me, my canvas is being raised. A fire will be set for me, and hopefully some warm food.

The middle of winter, what a bloody time to make war!

A commotion comes from the rear. I turn with some interest, my face frozen in place.

'My lord.' A small voice reaches my ears. I lower my gaze beside my horse's warm body. A young lad stands there, liberally smothered in furs, his face filthy and somehow smudged with mud although I'm sure the ground is entirely frozen, but, as I've discovered, small boys attract mud, no matter what. My warriors jump to surround him. One falls to his knees, his hands outstretched, trying to prevent the lad from coming closer. 'Are you the king?' the boy asks, awe in his young voice. I'm sorry to disappoint him.

'No, I'm Ealdorman Athelstan, but the king sent me here.'

'Ah.' His face clears. He stands more confidently now that he knows he's not facing the king of England. 'Me mam sent me,' he explains. 'She thought you was the king, but you'll do just as well.'

I hold my amusement in place. I'll have to remember to tell Edmund what the lad said. 'And what did she want me to know?' I ask when he seems to have forgotten why he's here.

'Oh, sorry, me lord. Yes, she wanted me to tell you that,' and here his brow furrows and his mouth works as though he's forming the words before speaking them, 'that bloody bastard Olaf Gothfrithson is in the palace.' He mangles the word Gothfrithson, but that doesn't surprise me. It is a mouthful. He breathes deeply then and moves forward to caress the nose of my horse. Luckily, he's a well-tempered beast and doesn't headbutt the precocious boy. I bet his mother has fun with him. His youth reminds me of my own sons – safe, I hope, in Winchester with the rest of the members of the House of Wessex.

'Are you from Tamworth?' I ask, wondering how he's managed to sneak out and we've not noticed.

'No, me lord, well, yes, but I've been hiding out here for the last day or two waiting for someone to come. You got any food?' he queries, his nose working hard as he smells the reasonably appetising aroma of meat cooking back at the camp my warriors are building.

Eadric appraises the lad with an unfathomable expression on his face. As soon as he hears his plaintive demand for food, a wide smile spreads across his face, and he looks at me for permission to take the lad away.

'What's your name?' I ask before he's led away.

'Alfred, me lord,' he replies. I realise that with a name like that, his mother must be a loyal Englishwoman.

'When did bloody Olaf arrive?' I ask, using his words and watching the merriment dance behind his eyes.

'Three days ago, me lord,' he replies promptly, 'and, honestly, I'll tell you more but me stomach is awful empty.'

I wave him away then, a nod of thanks to both Alfred and my brother. Eadric will feed him and extract whatever additional information he carries in his head. Three days, I think, not that long really. Olaf won't be entrenched yet, although he might think he is.

The words of the lad have shot through my small camp. Everyone looks towards Tamworth, malice on their faces. Olaf has chosen to strike at the heartlands of Mercia, and that's made his intentions very clear. Tamworth isn't one of the Five Boroughs, but the Norse have long had a fascination with it. Olaf's no different.

I signal one of my outriders to me with instructions to report to the king, only then I call him back again, for Æthelwald is already returning to me. I can see him and his men riding slowly back across the bleached winter fields.

As soon as he's within sight, I see the black glare on his face and know the news is bad.

'He sits as though he's the bloody king,' he shouts, his angry face belying the horse's gentle canter. He doesn't want to be seen running away from the enemy. 'He sits as though he's the bloody king, pours scorn on King Athelstan and informs me that he plans on being crowned king of England in a matter of weeks. He has Archbishop Wulfstan, and Ildulb of the Scots at his side.'

Æthelwald's rage emanates from him. I feel myself being buffeted by more than the gentle wind that's sprung up. My heart sinks with the knowledge that Olaf doesn't act alone.

'How many men?' I ask, but Æthelwald doesn't know or chooses not to answer, his thoughts elsewhere.

'He has English men and women running around him as though he's the king and they're all smiles for him and his bloody warriors. They glared at my men and me as though we're the damn enemy.'

'Come, you know not everyone can take a sword and strike a man's head from its shoulders.' I try to placate.

'No, but they could look less happy about it all,' he glowers. I wonder who in particular he knows has turned their allegiance to Olaf.

'It's better for everyone if he doesn't kill indiscriminately,' I try to appease, although I'm just as angry as he is.

'I don't give a shit,' he roars. 'Olaf presides in there. He has a huge feast on the go. A scop to regale his men with stories of how crap English warriors are, and he seems about as intent on moving as a slug from a decent green leaf. He barely has anyone standing guard. We just walked right in. He looked surprised as shit when he realised I wasn't a member of his household troops. We should go in there now and take him while he doesn't know his arse from his head.'

I don't want to argue with my brother about the way forward. If I truly believed that Olaf was as unprepared as he seems to think, I'd be in there in a flash. I think my brother might have been taken in by Olaf's use of studied indifference.

Instead of answering, I nod as I listen to everything he has to say.

'How many men do you think he has?' I repeat when I get the chance. He's still ranting and raving about how he just rode up, handed his horses over to some gormless youth and then waltzed into the main building.

'What?' he asks abruptly. It's obvious he's not been listening, so it's just as well that I've not been listening to him either.

'How many men?' I ask once more, patiently.

'Two hundred at the most,' he says without much thought, and my eyes rush to his face.

'Is that all?' I ask, and he nods vigorously.

'Yes, I had my men count, and we all came up with that number or thereabout.'

'Well, it's not very many, is it? Not to make himself king of England.'

Æthelwald stops his complaining for long enough to think that through, his mouth snapping shut on his next complaint. As he does, I see that he's starting to realise that Olaf might have played him for a fool. 'The bastard,' he shouts, 'where the hell are the rest of his men hiding?'

I'm nodding along with him, pleased that he's worked it out so quickly. My brother isn't usually blindsided by what he sees, although he has been on this occasion.

'There's a lad in the camp. His mother sent him to let whoever comes know that Olaf holds Tamworth. I imagine he might know more than that as well, but he was starving, and so Eadric's feeding him up a bit. We should talk to him. In the meantime...' And I signal for my outrider to come to me once more. He's keen to be on his way before the short day ends. I want him to go with more than just the knowledge that Olaf holds Tamworth. 'Did you hear what my brother said?' I ask, and he nods. 'Good, go to the king, tell him everything. And make sure he knows that Olaf is probably hosting an army in its thousands, not just its hundreds.'

He turns to leave, and I call him back one more time.

'Tell the king I'll engage if I get the opportunity to do so, but that if I don't, I'll await his commands.'

It'll be a journey of nearly two days to reach the king where he waits, close to London, and two days to return to me if I'm still outside Tamworth. A lot can happen in four days.

The smoke swirls happily from the thatch on the king's hall in Tamworth. My anger stirs. I might have ordered my brother to calm down, but it won't be as easy for me.

Olaf seems to have treated people kindly within Tamworth, if Æthelwald's impression is the correct one. I want to attack him, send him back to York – or, better yet, Dublin – with his tail between his legs. But for now, he's entrenched. For the first time since Edmund and I discussed it, and since the archbishop and bishop were tasked with the impossible demand, I consider whether it might be better to make peace with Olaf. Give Olaf something, some speck of land, so that he can feel as though he's the victor. Then we can regroup, take back whatever we've given him, and drive him away from England.

Edmund needs time to learn how to rule, and I sure as hell don't believe that Olaf's about to give him that time.

The short winter day turns darker. Rain starts to fall from the overcast sky. It's going to be a grim night under the canvas of my tent, but if it's raining, it means it's not snowing, and that's to be preferred.

I turn away from my vigil over Tamworth, knowing that my warriors will watch it throughout the dark, bleak night. I worry what tomorrow will bring.

24

JANUARY 940, TAMWORTH, THE KINGDOM OF THE ENGLISH

Olaf Gothfrithson, king of the Dublin Norse

The three men I set as watchers over the English force come to me one by one, conveying news of what they've seen and what they think will happen now.

I didn't for a moment believe that whoever led the force would be fooled by the warrior-less state I presented to the man I recognised from Brunanburh. I was correct to think as much. All the same, I enjoyed watching the confused expression on the warrior's face sent to speak with me, as he looked at Ildulb and Archbishop Wulfstan.

I'm unsurprised when one of my watchers assures me that Ealdorman Athelstan is in overall command of the force and that Æthelwald's his brother.

I'm disappointed I didn't make it further south than Northampton. I had dreams of reaching London, and Winchester, but now I hold Tamworth instead after an almost bloodless coup having fled Northampton. The people of Tamworth had no stones for war. They wished to live.

I'm further north than I'd like to be, and yet I know my great-grandfather came this way. Ivarr the Boneless was one of the men who took Repton, not far from here. Anlaf's father wed his Wessex bride here, in Tamworth.

Now I need to decide what to do. Should I be the one to force battle, or now that I'm here, should I encourage Archbishop Wulfstan to carve out the peace treaty he promises with his counterpart in Canterbury? He assures me he can forge peace without blades, and one where I hold what I've taken. I believe some of my men would prefer that. Since the defeat at Northampton, the faith my warriors had in me has faltered. Mercia isn't without its wealth, but it's as hard to pull from the inhabitants as it is water from the frozen ground.

I've seen that the English warriors can predict my intentions. I was found at Northampton, and now Ealdorman Athelstan has discovered me at Tamworth, only a few days after I won the settlement.

I hold Jorvik. I claim much of the land south of Jorvik, including Lincoln. Stamford is lost to me as easily as it was gained, abandoned by the warriors I left there, no doubt, when they heard of my retreat to Tamworth. I'd kill the men who brought me the news, but they did so out of loyalty. I'll have to reward them.

Winter isn't the right time to wage war. Even I know that. Now. Yet it's given me a huge advantage over the English. If I'd attacked in the summer, I'd never have accomplished all that I have. I'd not have reached Stamford, and certainly not Northampton.

Anlaf stamps into the hall, his face pinched and red from the cold, his nose ridiculously bright. He shakes the streaming rain from his great fur cloak and sits before the heat from the great fire at the heart of the hall.

'Bloody hell, it's cold out there,' he shouts, just to be sure I know how inconvenienced he's been by my ploy.

'I'll take you at your word,' I shout back to him, raising my drinking horn to salute him.

He glowers. 'The men are complaining that they've had to stay out all day while you fat lot roasted yourselves and ate and drank what you wanted.' He gestures to my warriors as he speaks. They jeer at him. These are my most loyal warriors from Dublin. Not his, for all he's been my shadow in Dublin since the defeat at Brunanburh. He has yet to win them around with his complaining and moaning, although others have fallen beneath his spell. He's not a man to take anywhere in winter. I wonder if he has the blood of those who once lived in the southern climes. He certainly doesn't act very Norse. Yes, I know it's cold, but really, it's nothing when compared to the frozen northern lands that spit out their men and send them seeking better ground and greater wealth to the temperate south. The land of my ancestors and his.

'Your men can come inside now.' I gesture expansively, but Anlaf remains angry.

'Well, I'm pleased it's bloody convenient for you now,' he hollers. 'If it was all right, couldn't you have ordered our return?'

He has a fair point, but I don't allow it. I won't reveal that I forgot to inform him. That'll just stoke his anger further.

He gestures furiously to a warrior who's followed him inside. The man pauses mid-step, his head swivelling from Anlaf to me, before turning and heading back out into the sleeting rain. I wish it would decide whether to rain or snow. The mush we've been covered in for the last few days makes travel particularly difficult. Clothing gets wet, and the horses hate it when it clings to their coats and takes its own sweet time in melting. It's almost like being rained on twice. I'd welcome the harsh coldness of snow, which surprises me.

'Did it work?' Anlaf demands, stepping closer to me to steal away my drinking horn and slosh its warm contents down his throat.

'Yes, the fool who came couldn't keep the gleam from his eye at the thought of how few men surrounded me. However, I don't think the ruse worked entirely. It's Ealdorman Athelstan out there, so I've been told, and he's more astute than his brother.'

Anlaf nods angrily to hear that. He's been freezing all day. It would appear to have been for nothing.

'Should I recall all the men?' he questions, but I'm shaking my head. I don't want everyone in one place. Not now the enemy knows where we are. When we were racing across the landscape to reach Tamworth, it was acceptable to keep together. But if I'm to hold Tamworth I need to stay here. I don't want all my warriors with me. I need to know that reinforcements can come if required. I can't have everyone together in one place. I must ensure the way to the River Trent is always open to me.

'No, tell them to go to Repton or even to Derby, order the ships to join us there.'

His face flashes angrily once more at the thought of going outside again.

'Not tonight. Ealdorman Athelstan won't act yet. The men can come inside, get warm, sleep and travel to Repton tomorrow.' I try to placate him.

'Am I to stay with you?' he asks with some curiosity. We have an uneasy relationship. Even though we worked together at Northampton, the awkwardness of his fury at my decision to attack hasn't dissipated.

'No, go with the majority of the warriors. Take three hundred of them with you. The others can remain here.'

'How long for?' he complains, and his questions are starting to annoy me.

'Until I send word that I want you elsewhere or the bloody English king drops dead, and I claim his kingdom in his stead.'

My petulance angers him, but he doesn't retaliate, too intent on the warm food brought to him and the seductive heat coming from the fire.

He's an easy man to please.

Sometimes.

I only wish the same could be said for Ildulb and Archbishop Wulfstan. The one demands war, the other peace. But then, neither of them are the king of Dublin and Jorvik. I need to remember that.

25

JANUARY 940, NORTHAMPTON, THE KINGDOM OF THE ENGLISH

Edmund, king of the English

I keep my face bland as I hear the message being relayed to me from Ealdorman Athelstan regarding Olaf Gothfrithson's seizure of Tamworth. I kept Olaf from taking Northampton, and Stamford has been re-secured, but still, he's not run far enough away. I wanted him to leave England once and for all. I held out half a hope that his fearful response to the arrival of the English spoke of his abject terror at finally meeting some opposition. It seems not.

I find myself praying for guidance from my dead brother, Athelstan, more often than I should, opening the book he bequeathed to me every morning, seeking some new piece of advice. It's accompanied me to Northampton. I've never been one to find comfort in words, but I confess, I have done so, my eyes scanning the letters sent between Alcuin, a notable Mercian cleric who lived over a century ago, and the mighty Charlemagne, the man who united Frankia beneath him, even if it didn't last.

Those letters contain knowledge of what it means to be a king, and of how I should rule and protect my people. But there's no advice on how to repel Viking raiders who steal across my kingdom.

My ealdormen, as shocked as I am by the recent events that have befallen my kingdom, were far from Winchester when I ordered them to return to my side. I'm still unsure as to where Ealdorman Guthrum is. The knowledge that the archbishop and Bishop Oda have been tasked with seeing if peace can be agreed with my enemy has created unease amongst them, and only now have they obeyed my summons to attend upon me.

Ealdorman Athelstan stands as my bastion in the Mercian heartlands supported by his brothers, Eadric and Æthelwald. I've taken command of Northampton, keen to use its defences to keep Olaf out. I hunger to attack him, to drive him from England once more. But I'll need the support of all my ealdormen and their warriors to accomplish that. As of yet, and with the terrible weather, that support hasn't been forthcoming, but now that they're here, I can ensure they understand my plans.

I wish I'd been able to chase Olaf further from Northampton when I almost caught him, but I had to listen to the voice of reason that told me to hold Northampton and reclaim Stamford. My role, and that of my brave warriors, was to hound Olaf away. It wasn't my intention that, instead, he should seek shelter in Tamworth. He must know of Tamworth's meaning to my family. He'll have been told that Athelstan grew to manhood there. But, of course, he has Anlaf Sihtricson with him, and Anlaf's father wed my half-sister in Tamworth, on Athelstan's wishes. No doubt it's him who knew his way inside the settlement. Anlaf has given Olaf an advantage.

I hope Olaf knows I was at Northampton. I hope he doesn't think I'm too scared to face him, hiding away in Wessex while my ealdorman counters his attack. I've praised the warriors of

Northampton. I've rewarded the brave man who held against them, and who now lies sweating and feverish, fighting the wound rot that's infected him after the skirmish. I pray he lives.

So what it is I want? Would I be content if Olaf held Lincoln, far to the north? No, but it would mean he was far away from Wessex, and contained to the farthest tip of Mercia. I don't want him to retain Lincoln, but it's also distant from the Wessex heartlands. At least, if I cede it to him via a peace treaty, I'll have the time I need to gather my allies together and win their support.

I take a deep breath and then another. Suddenly, I know what I must do, and although it doesn't please me, it's better than what's happened so far.

I turn to the messenger from Ealdorman Athelstan. 'Tell Ealdorman Athelstan to attack Tamworth. Tell him to encircle it and separate Olaf from the rest of his men, wherever he's hiding them. Inform him that reinforcements are on their way. They'll stand between Olaf and his reserve forces.'

'Yes, my lord king,' he says, head bowed as he recites the words to himself.

'And advise him that once Olaf is as isolated as we can make him, we'll let the archbishops forge their precious peace.'

His eyebrow rises slightly at that, but it's not his place to add any further comments, and he doesn't, instead turning and striding from my presence.

I sit and think about what I've just put into play. Will it work? Will Ealdorman Athelstan be able to separate Olaf from his allies and agree an acceptable settlement with him devised by the archbishops? I don't know, but it's the only option available to me at the moment. Olaf must leave, but if I have to cede a fraction of my kingdom in the process, then I will. For now.

My mother joins me. Her eyes straying to our surroundings. Northampton is no Winchester, but it's comfortable enough, and with her at my side, at least I'm sure of her support. Eadred remains in Winchester, guarding the remainder of my family.

'An excellent decision,' she offers approvingly. She knows how much it costs me to accept we won't be able to overwhelm Olaf. She didn't want a negotiated peace, but even she's come to accept it must be done.

'If I must have peace, I want it accomplished with some aggression.'

She's solemn, nodding in agreement, settling beside me with a swish of thick cloth, her cloak layered with furs against the cold and draughts. 'Olaf Gothfrithson must realise that while he thinks he's made a great victory for himself by attacking the kingdom of the English all he's really done is to ensure our vengeance will be worse. He's taken advantage of us when we're weak. It'll not stand,' she adds confidently.

My mother has a lifetime of experience in contending with the aggressive Norsemen. Some might think she sits comfortably, protected by the might of the king, but if she could, she'd slay them herself. I know that.

'It'll fall to you to counter Olaf Gothfrithson's attacks, and his alliance with Constantin, Anlaf and Ildulb. He might well inspire confidence in those around him who believe his lies, but he's only a man. And you already know that he can be a weak one, as his defeat at Brunanburh revealed. That he ran from England without his warriors and his wife truly shows the sort of man he is.' Her words thrum with conviction. My mother has considered this. Not that I disagree with her assessment of Olaf Gothfrithson.

So resolved, I call those ealdormen to me who've been recalled through the deep winter snows. Ealhhelm, Æthelmund, Wulfstan and, just to add to everyone's confusion, another Athelstan. The name is a popular one amongst those close adherents of my family, even if my brother was half deemed a bastard for much of his life.

These men were my childhood friends, and now we must rule together. Uhtred, Wulfgar and Ælfhere were my brother's ealdormen. Uhtred's a steadying force, a man with more winters to his name than the rest of us and who's used to his place as ealdorman more than I am as a king.

We sit closely together to talk. I watch them keenly. Will these men govern as they should? Will I be able to rely on them in times of crisis? Their seemingly slow response to my summons isn't reassuring, but I don't know how much the weather is to blame, and how much of it might be reluctance.

'Ealdorman Athelstan is near Tamworth. Olaf Gothfrithson has taken command of the burh.'

'And your plans?' Uhtred asks, his voice gravelly and measured. I think he wants nothing more than to join Ealdorman Athelstan outside Tamworth and I don't blame him. I want to be there as well.

'We let the archbishops use their soothing voices to attempt to bring about peace, after we reinforce Athelstan and cut Olaf off from the remainder of his men, and from retreating to his ship army on the River Trent.'

'I'll take my men and reinforce Athelstan and his brothers,' Uhtred announces, leaving no room for debate.

'I'll go as well,' Ealhhelm is quick to offer.

'I need one other,' I say into the sudden silence. The men are considering who'll be the best commander to fight for England. Haunted eyes look one from the other. I want someone to volunteer. I don't want to command these men to their possible deaths.

Ealdorman Wulfgar raises his head and nods to show that he'll be the third to venture to Tamworth. I'm grateful for his agreement.

'I'll also need someone to escort the archbishop to the peace talks. They can no longer be conducted via messenger. Once we have Olaf at a disadvantage, he'll crumble quickly, and want to make peace.'

'I'll escort the archbishop,' Ealdorman Ælfhere offers solemnly.

The talk of defeating Olaf at Tamworth has almost made my ealdormen forget that a peace accord is still the only way we can stop the Norse attack. Reminding them has dampened their enthusiasm. But still.

'Recall, he was overwhelmed at Brunanburh. He fled the slaughter field, leaving his allies dead in his wake. On this occasion, he's caught us out. What we need is to win back Tamworth. If he must hold on to Lincoln for the time being, then that's what must be done. But remember, this isn't it. We'll regroup and attack Olaf. We'll reclaim what he's taken. It's only a measure that must be borne for the immediate future.' I feel the righteousness of my words. I've been scared and humiliated by Olaf Gothfrithson. My kingship has been threatened. England has been endangered. But I finally understand what must be done, and I know we can accomplish it.

I sit a little straighter and feel the same calmness from earlier once more flooding through my body as I say those words. My ealdormen nod in agreement as well. They understand my words. Hands reach for weapons belts, the thought of the future stirring them to battle readiness.

I've chased Olaf Gothfrithson from the slaughter field twice now. I'll do it a third time. Even if that third occasion must come at a later date.

I'm no weak king. I've killed a king. I've killed a king's grandson in the land of the Scots, and I've humiliated Olaf. Twice.

I'll do so again.

26

JANUARY 940, TAMWORTH, THE KINGDOM OF THE ENGLISH

Ildulb, prince of the Scots

I watch the bickering and arguing between Olaf Gothfrithson and Anlaf Sihtricson with amusement. The two men are allies, even if grudging ones. They have to work together, and Olaf has no choice but to belittle everything that Anlaf does.

It almost makes me reconsider my relationship with Mael Coluim, but each time I do, I rethink again. Olaf and Anlaf mutually respect each other and their roles, no matter how much they argue. Olaf is king of Dublin and Jorvik. Once the fighting is over, Anlaf will be his underking in Dublin. Not that it matters. At the moment, Olaf's brother and his son hold Jorvik. Olaf has sent Blakari back towards Jorvik to ensure the path of retreat remains open, should it be needed.

The two men, Olaf and Anlaf, have gained much in a short space of time, and that makes them comfortably uncomfortable with each other.

I can't deny I was worried when the English came upon our force close to Northampton. I was keen to blood my weapon against the impenetrable walls that blocked our way, but seeing the English and their hundreds of warriors chasing us down was a sobering experience, despite my frustration that Olaf didn't stand and fight. But for now, I can enjoy being warm for the first time since I joined Olaf on this expedition south.

I've not sent word to my father about what happened at Northampton. He doesn't need to know all the details of our near capture. When Olaf's secure in his new kingship, and has the agreement of the English king that he can retain what he's conquered, I'll inform my father. Until then he can pray for my safety. He may as well make use of the time he spends on his knees. Still, I might need my father's prayers yet.

My thoughts turn unwillingly to Alpin. His presence in the kingdom of the Scots is unwelcome. His split loyalties are problematic.

'Anlaf annoys you?' I murmur to Olaf, masking my question by leaning forward to help myself to more of the well-cooked meat before us. I can't imagine that Tamworth can afford to feed us so well for long. The poor buggers. Hungry faces watch as we gorge.

Olaf chuckles contemptuously at the question. 'It's the nature of being allies and rivals all at the same time. He annoys me a lot less than Mael Coluim does you.'

I nod in agreement, not prepared to be drawn into an argument where I defend my thoughts regarding Mael Coluim. The hatred between the pair of us is so well known there's no point denying it.

'But you trust him?' I press, curious and wanting to know more about how the Norse work together. The affairs at Brunanburh revealed to me a people who don't wish to ally to achieve a common goal. That doesn't seem to be the case with Olaf and Anlaf. Although, I also know that Anlaf lost Limerick to his brother, when Haraldr Sihtricson used my captured sister to bargain for the settlement.

'I have to trust someone,' Olaf laughs, sloshing mead down his front in the process. 'We Norse. Well, you must know, you've had enough dealings with us. We're loyal to a point and then it's every man for himself.'

'Only the best leaders are the best for so long,' I muse. 'Everyone runs out of treasure and good luck.'

'Is that what you think being a good leader is all about?' Olaf asks, intrigued.

'Why, do you think it means something else?'

'I don't know. I think a healthy dose of fear can go a long way.'

'Fear makes men perform their tasks half-heartedly, just to ensure they don't get punished. Show a man that you care for his well-being, strive to make him rich, and he'll do almost anything for you.'

Olaf laughs once more. 'Is this what your father's been teaching you?'

'No, my father's taught me the importance of luck.'

'How so?'

'He has the good fortune to have lived the lives of three men. Compare him to everyone else we know. Not even Alfred, the so-called 'great', ruled as long as he did. The only man who nearly did is, I think, one of the kings of the Welsh.' It's my turn to slosh mead down my front as I wave my arms about a little too expansively.

'You mean Hywel's grandfather. He only ruled for thirty winters.'

'Only thirty? I think you should reconsider your choice of words. Just think of what can be done with thirty summers to play with when ruling. Most men only live thirty winters – well, if they're Norse and go Viking, they do.'

Olaf considers my words, a glint of amusement in his eye. 'How old are you?'

'Why?'

'Just wondered if you were one of the men who only lives until he's thirty.'

He's goading me. I determine to ignore it. I like Olaf. Now. I find him amenable and appreciate his respectful attitude towards my claim to the kingdom of the Scots. Being the son of a king who's going to give his throne to another claimant makes for uneasy alliance-building. Perhaps the fact he's married to my sister makes him keener to see me as a friend and an ally.

'You think you need treasure to rule?' he continues. He's a Norseman who's spent much of his time Viking. His love of unearned riches is synonymous with his heritage.

'What will you do about the English?' I ask, changing the subject. I don't want to talk about the qualities of successful rulers any more.

'I'll ignore them for now,' he laughs, before sobering. 'I've not fully decided yet. I think there'll be a battle, or I might just retreat to Repton. I already hold so much of the land it seems wrong to throw it away just to hold on to Tamworth. Don't worry though, if I decide upon a confrontation, I'll let you take pride of place. You're a skilled warrior, and your men are loyal to you. It's a good start. Now tell me, what do you intend to do about Mael Coluim and Alpin?' His eyes gleam as he speaks. I know his thoughts must lead him to think that, one day, he could have the kingdom of the Scots, as well as Jorvik and Dublin.

'I'd like to kill them both, but everyone would know I'd done it!'

He roars with laughter at that, his face flushed with heat and drinking. 'I enjoy your honesty,' he says when he's recovered from his outburst. 'I'm sure your father's thought the same throughout his many, many winters and summers about Mael Coluim.'

'Well, if he has, he's kept his opinions to himself,' I mutter, turning away. My good mood has been dampened by the discussion of events at home. And by the reminder of Alpin's presence there. I think I might ask to stay with Olaf in York. Some time away from the constant rumour-mongering at home might do wonders for my opinion of Mael Coluim. But not Alpin. Alpin must be dealt with, and I'm sure my father thinks the same.

27

JANUARY 940, TAMWORTH, THE KINGDOM OF THE ENGLISH

Athelstan the ealdorman

Waiting is the hardest part, it always is, but at last I know what Edmund wants me to do. I'm content with his idea to bring this invasion to an end. His thinking is excellent. I can't deny my shock at knowing it's thanks to him that Olaf isn't encamped inside the burh at Northampton. He was meant to remain inside Wessex.

My men have been busy in the days the messenger was gone, scouting the area and trying to calculate where Olaf had secluded the rest of his warriors. It wasn't all that hard to find them.

Repton, I should have realised. The Viking raiders have always had a strange fascination with the place.

Now I have my household troops arranged and ready to advance on Tamworth while Ealdorman Uhtred and his men have skirted far to the north in order to double back and divide Tamworth from Repton. The distance is perhaps greater than we'd like. There are places where the Norse could slip through our warriors, but I don't believe they will. Their obsession with Repton doesn't extend to the wider landscape. But I know it. How could I not when I spent so much of my youth here?

Ealdormen Ealhhelm and Wulfgar assist me outside Tamworth. Our entire force will attack from the south, over the twin rivers of the Tame and the Anker. Olaf and his warriors will think to escape north, towards Repton, when they realise how outnumbered they are. I wish them luck with that.

I imagine Olaf and his allies laugh with glee inside Tamworth, away from the freezing, driving rain and snow, eating Mercian food and enjoying the stockpile of winter fuel for burning. I could let my anger drive my actions quite easily, but I'm resolved to remain calm, saving my anger for when I need it most. In battle.

As we'll be the aggressors, I've chosen where I wish to fight. I sent a messenger to Olaf telling him of my intent. His response was aggravating. He 'declines' to come and fight for something he already holds.

I want to get this done, get inside Tamworth and feel some warmth seep into my frozen fingers and toes. The men are quiet in their forbearance, but the cold saps our strength. We need to attack.

The youth who met us on the first day outside Tamworth, Alfred, is filled with interesting information. He knows that Olaf sent Anlaf to wait out in the cold when we first appeared and to give the impression that he only had a few warriors with him. He also knows that Olaf and Anlaf treat one another with as little respect as possible. Alfred said that the enemy rode to Tamworth as though lightning struck at their heels. With word from the king, I realise this was because Northampton wouldn't open its gates for them, and neither would anywhere else along Watling Street. They're lucky to have escaped the king and his warriors. It's a pity that Edmund didn't continue the fight.

I'm surprised Alfred knows so much when he escaped so soon after the enemy took Tamworth. I believe, thanks to his insights, that Olaf and Anlaf make poor allies, unable to hide their jealousy from each other even when they're in hostile territory. It's just the sort of rift I'll not hesitate to exploit. Alfred's knowledge that Archbishop Wulfstan is with Olaf unsettles me. Does he support Olaf? Has he turned against the English king? I don't trust Wulfstan, even though he's busy trying to negotiate a peace accord with Archbishop Wulfheard and Bishop Oda.

Now, I toss and turn on my uncomfortable camp bed, aware of every slight move I make as wooden struts creak with the strain. My fur cloak covers me, but still, I can't get warm. The brazier is fuelled for the night, and still I'm cold. Outside, the wind howls fiercely and every so often I hear a dull sound as snow blows against the side of my poor shelter. I hope tomorrow we'll fight and then I can go home.

Æthelwald snores at my side, keeping me awake. I wonder how so much noise can come from one man. He sounds like a herd of horses stampeding over hard summer ground. I'd shake him, but that would mean moving my hand from its warm sanctuary beneath my cloak.

Sleep eludes me. I'd rather have a warm hand and a snoring brother than a cold hand and a quiet one.

My thoughts turn to tomorrow.

Olaf says he won't engage in battle, but I believe that when my shield wall's arranged and ready to attack he'll change his mind. A man such as him will be unable to resist the chance to attack the best warriors within England, and to make good on his defeat at Brunanburh.

If not, we'll be left with no choice but to assault the burh itself. I fear innocent lives will be lost.

Olaf can't stay in Tamworth. It's a shameless ploy on his part, specifically designed to taunt Edmund. Effectively, he's claimed back the principal seat of the ancient kingdom of the Mercians. Essentially, he's pissing in the king's land, and he's bloody enjoying it.

* * *

I wake, head pounding and mouth dry. Æthelwald roughly shakes me. I just manage not to swear at him and tell him to leave me alone. The cheek of the git. He kept me awake with his damn snoring and now complains I'm not battle-ready and prepared to relinquish the warmth of my cloak.

Muttering to himself, Æthelwald exits the canvas, swinging the door wide open and letting in a blast of cold air. I shiver and curse him, Eadric joining me in my complaints as he too rouses to wakefulness.

Stumbling from the bed, I reach for my boots and pull them on. I don't need to get dressed because I've slept in every item of clothing I possess. I only have to remove my cloak and shrug on my byrnie before I'm ready to leave the dubious sanctuary.

Outside, men's voices reverberate in the clear winter air, complaining about the cold. I'd tell them to be quiet, but there's no point. This isn't an expedition of stealth but rather one of brute force. Olaf knows we're here. That he's not yet struck reveals he's playing the waiting game, just as we were. He wants me to take the first steps. He wants me to be the aggressor. He believes that Tamworth will keep him safe. He's wrong, and I'm happy to prove that to him.

I want him gone from Mercia.

Æthelwald shoots back inside the canvas, a scowl on his face.

'Hurry up, you lazy sods,' he complains, reaching for his shield with a gloved hand.

'What's the rush?' I quarrel. Maybe Olaf has chosen to attack after all, and this is Æthelwald's way of informing me. It'd be like him not to tell me outright.

'It's bloody cold, and at least if I'm fighting, I'll warm up a bit,' he counters. My flare of hope dies. This might not be an easy day.

'I'm coming. How are the men?'

'Don't know, everyone's too busy bitching about the foot of snow that's fallen overnight. It's not going to make this pleasant or straightforward,' he offers. I groan. Bad enough when we had slush underfoot yesterday, but with fresh snowfall, it'll make even the smallest movement cumbersome.

I follow Æthelwald into the bright day, shivering, Eadric behind me. The sun's low on the horizon, as it should be at this time of the year. It illuminates an undulating whiteness before me. As far as the eye can see there's nothing but virginal snow. Well, apart from where we're encamped. Muddy footprints mar the surface around the small campfires, and the ground's clear of snow.

The fires hiss and sizzle as clumps of snow are carelessly thrown onto them by the busy footsteps of men going about the business of war. I shiver once more inside my huge cloak and consider if we're doing the right thing. But really, what choice do we have? We can't let Olaf stay here without any resistance. What sort of message would that give him? I imagine he had hopes of riding to bloody Winchester and claiming the kingdom of the English for himself.

We need to make him reassess those plans. Edmund's prevented him from reaching London. I must send him scurrying further north, back to Lincoln and then to Jorvik. I'd like to eject him from there as well, but all in good time.

Tamworth appears to be sleeping. Grey smoke drifts from family homes and the king's hall. A cry from Flodwin, who's been keeping watch all night, and he jogs up the slight hill before us, his face pinched with cold. Only his eyes peer out from beneath helm and above his thick beard and moustache, rimed with ice.

'It looks quiet enough, but they've had a busy night. I heard men talking and horses being led from the stables. They'll make their move soon.'

Flodwin's eyes are gleeful. Far better for us all if our enemy step from their temporary home. Olaf's arrogance will make him sure of triumph, provided he engages with my force.

'Have any of the men come from Repton?' I ask. Ealdorman Uhtred and I decided it would be better to let the reinforcements arrive rather than him standing ready for battle between Repton and Tamworth.

'A few, my lord. No more than two hundred. They were as silent as crows.' Flodwin grins. He was one of King Athelstan's fiercest allies. Now he serves me, alongside Sigelac. King Edmund gave his agreement to the men's requests to transfer their allegiance to me.

That means Olaf has about five hundred men. A good number. He must think that's the strength of my force. Certainly, that's the quantity he's seen living in the encampment for the last week. He doesn't know that I have two other ealdormen in reserve, camping just a swift march away to the west and east.

At least I hope he doesn't know.

'Thank you for your vigilance,' I murmur.

Flodwin stifles a yawn and grins. 'I'd thought to get some rest instead of joining the battle, but I'll stay and fight. These Norse are damn fools, and it'll delight me to kill 'em.'

'You'll be welcome in the shield wall. But if you feel yourself weakening turn aside.'

'My thanks, my lord,' Flodwin gabbles, turning to move away. 'I might have heard digging in the night,' he adds, as an afterthought, 'but I couldn't tell where the noise came from. Would they have been clearing snow?'

'Digging?' I repeat.

Flodwin's lips turn down, and he tilts his head from side to side, and then shrugs his shoulders. 'Or I might have imagined it,' he capitulates, turning aside to prepare for the coming fight.

Æthelwald looks at me with interest. 'What's all that about then?' he queries, but my thoughts tumble. I don't immediately reply. What could our enemy have been doing during the night?

'I don't much like it. Have any of the other night guards reported back?'

'Not yet, no, but I'm sure they won't be long in coming.'

'Go and see if you can find them. I want to know if they heard digging as well.'

Æthelwald stamps off through the snow, his face pensive.

I'm thinking of all the times I lived within Tamworth and trying to determine if I've missed something. Tamworth is an ancient site, but the Heathen Army destroyed much of it in 874. The king's aunt hasn't long rebuilt it, and it's the new settlement that I know. She made its defences formidable.

It'll be almost impossible for my force to attack against the stout wooden palisades and deep ditches that run around the exterior of the site.

Ah, the ditches, I suddenly think. I consider if Olaf had the ditches cleared so that we'd not be able to use the build-up of winter detritus to make the climb easier. Rumour has it that he tried to make use of the filled ditches at Northampton. I wonder if he's trying to prevent us from doing the same.

That sobers my good mood. If he's dug out the ditches, he has no intention of riding forth and fighting us in the open. And I need him to do so if we're to prevail. Abruptly, thoughts of being warm by the evening leave me. This could still be a tedious and long-drawn-out matter.

I glare at the gradually growing billows of smoke coming from the waking burh. I'd have preferred the battle to be underway already. Eadric's silent at my side – no doubt, his thoughts match mine.

Æthelwald returns with news from the nightwatchmen. 'No, the other two men didn't hear anything, not even any horses coming from the north. Can we trust Flodwin?' he asks, and I splutter in amusement. Æthelwald, always quicker to distrust than trust. He'd have made a fine Norse leader.

'It's Flodwin, of course we can,' Eadric confirms.

'Perhaps Olaf was digging out the ditches,' I muse.

Æthelwald's already scowling face settles into a grimace. 'Then he won't be fighting us here,' he complains, indicating where we stand with his gloved fist.

'Perhaps not,' I agree. There's no need to say more.

He harrumphs, thinking of how we can draw Olaf out. I'm doing the same. We need to extract Olaf from his warm hall and force him into the open.

'We could set a fire,' Eadric offers. It might be a good idea, although difficult to accomplish when everything is damp with snow or rain. 'We could set a fire near the animal barn, that would spook all the horses.' Eadric chuckles, considering the panic that would ensue. Horses are bloody valuable, costing more than some men can ever afford throughout their lifetime. Not many ever see more than a hundred silver pennies, let alone have that amount to part with to purchase a good horse. An ox is much cheaper, thirty pence, and more use to men and women who till the land.

It's not a bad idea, but it's too easy a solution. Olaf would never be stupid enough to fall for that. I dismiss it and see what Eadric thinks up next.

His face has cleared, more serious now. His mouth moves although he's not speaking. 'We should send in a small attack force to make a vain effort at getting through the southern gates,' he starts, and I'm looking where he's pointing, trying to see what he does, but I'm too tired to decipher his thoughts immediately. 'While they're all inside the burh, laughing at our incompetent efforts, we send Alfred in. He starts a fire wherever he can. His mother will help him. Perhaps in one of the buildings. In the hall, if possible, but if he can't then it'll need to be in the grain store or something. At the same time, more men travel to the northern gate. Try the same thing there. It'll make Olaf and his warriors panic.'

This is more like it. Make it appear as though the fire is nothing to do with us. That'll upset the superstitious lot inside the protective banks and ditches. They'll see portents in the fires, especially if they blaze despite how damp everything should be.

'We'll need to put on an abysmal show of trying to attack the southern gate, make it seem easy for them to get out here.'

'What about the lad? Will he do it?'

'Oh yes, definitely. He's desperate to be able to say something more heroic than he hid in a ditch for two days until we arrived.'

I take a long moment to ruminate on the idea. It's a good notion. One I've not considered, but then, I always think too literally, always in straight lines. I want to achieve my goal as soon as possible.

'We should do it,' I announce decisively. Eadric looks at me in surprise. He's not expected me to agree to it. Æthelwald's face is drawn into a scowl, but he doesn't object.

'But,' Eadric starts, and I shush him.

'It's bloody freezing, and Olaf's eating the Mercians' harvest. We need to get him out of there, and your idea is a damn sight better than the one I've devised. If we do it your way, we might get our battle without freezing our stones off.'

'As you will, brother,' he says, a little mockingly, but not enough to rile me. He and Æthelwald move amongst the warriors, deciding who'll do what.

The camp becomes even busier as the men chosen for the two attacks make themselves ready. Alfred, bright-eyed and almost jumping with excitement, is brought before me by a grinning Eadric.

Alfred's face is so youthful that for a moment I think we should stop this hazardous attempt, but then I hear a roar of what I think is laughter coming from inside Tamworth. I know we have no choice.

'Are you sure you can get back in without being noticed?' I ask for the third time. He's already assured me twice, but I need to hear it again.

'Yes, me lord, only I know the way. Well, me and my mother. She showed it to me.' I wish I knew more about his mother. Hopefully, when we hold Tamworth once more, I'll meet her.

'And you know what to do when you're inside?'

'Yes, me lord. I'm to set a fire when I hear the fighting. Preferably in the hall or the grain store, but wherever I think would be best.'

'Will you be able to get a brand?' I ask. That's the one part of this plan that could mean its failure before it's begun.

'Of course. I know where they keep all the wood and peat. It won't be a problem. And I can slip into the blacksmith's as well. He'll have a roaring fire on the go. And me mam'll help me if not.'

Confidence oozes from him as he speaks. I let it infect me. This could work.

He slips away then, and in only moments I can't see him even though the landscape is bright with snow. He manages to disappear into the shelter of hedgerows and wickerwork divides that are bowing under the weight of the fresh snowfall.

At my side, Eadric speaks. 'We could use him. You should have him as part of your household.' If he lives through this, I might just do that.

In a far bolder statement, thirty of my men start the laborious task of wading through the snow to reach the closest entranceway into the burh, the one over the bridge spanning the frozen River Tame. The men who'll attack the northern gate have already departed.

We're not sure how long it'll take for them to circle around, especially given the weather, but they have their horses with them. The horses are more sure-footed than men in the treacherous conditions.

The trees are black, the ground white, and the sky a strange combination that heralds the possibility of more snow to come. The men have borrowed cloaks from each other that more closely resemble the landscape they ride through. Gone are the dark browns to be replaced by those lucky enough to have the cloak of a real winter monster, a black and white wolf.

I hold my breath at the thought of their task but quickly have my attention riveted to the scene before me. My warriors near the southern gate, and there are cries of derision coming from inside Tamworth. It sounds like a lot more than five hundred men jeer our efforts, but again, the strange deep winter calm can do that. It amplifies what little noise there is. I imagine a single deer could sound like a herd as it scampers through the snow.

I wonder how many men they think approach them. Do my thirty sound like five hundred?

My warriors bang their shields, probably more to drive warmth into their cold limbs than to scare the enemy. Even from my distance, I can see the fog of their breath and the tracks they've left behind. There's no hiding the marks of their passage.

Æthelwald has his eyes firmly on the southern gate of the burh itself. The sound of the men forming up reaches my ears. The plan is to make a small shield wall, fifteen men long, one with the shield before them and then one above their head, held by the warrior behind. Then they'll rush the gate. We don't believe Olaf will do anything to counter the feeble assault, but then, hopefully, the fire will start. The other force will besiege the northern gate then. There are more men to the north, and word has also been sent to Ealdorman Uhtred to have him ready to reinforce those attacking the northern gate.

Straining my eyes, I see a flicker of flame coming from deep within the burh. Alfred has done what he said. Before there was only smoke, but now I see and imagine hearing the crackle and snap of the flame that's being allowed to work its way up the side of the building it envelops, flames bright in the blinding winter sun.

'Is it the hall?' I query, but Æthelwald shakes his head.

'No, it's the grain store. It's next door to the hall.'

The lad's chosen well. If he lives through this, I'll ensure he's rewarded.

At the southern gate, our warriors make little or no progress. Neither has the gate opened to expel even one of Olaf's Norse warriors from within.

I can't see the north of the burh from here, but I hope the other men have managed to reach it.

A roar of outrage from within the burh signifies the discovery of the fire. It's starting to blaze out of control, and even if it wasn't, the loss of the grain store would hamper the Norse warriors. In my mind's eye, I see the Norsemen surging from the southern gate to stare in stunned surprise at the leaping flames. No doubt they thought it too cold and wet to burn, but the contents of the grain store will always be dry.

Æthelwald grabs my arm. I follow where he's pointing. Another fire has broken out within Tamworth, this one a little further from the hall.

'The stables,' Eadric says with admiration. 'The lad's a thinker.'

Although we're elevated and can see some of what happens inside Tamworth, I decide it's time to move. We need to form our shield wall, ready for when Olaf realises he's under attack from within as well as without.

I've purposefully left the east and the west gates unguarded, but the two other ealdormen are hunkered down, out of sight, ready to engage any who try to escape that way. It's just a matter of waiting for the enemy to scamper from their burning burh.

They don't rush. Even when we hear, on the still air, the cries of the men at the northern gate, the burh stays locked up tight. I begin to worry the ploys we've used won't work. Olaf will never leave Tamworth unless we manage to gain full access and forcibly remove him.

I start to wish I'd told Alfred to sneak out again as soon as he could to show us his secret entranceway. We could have entered by stealth. It would have been more dangerous, but better to attack Olaf where he feels protected, rather than compromise his safety so much that he decides it's better to leave the walls and ditch that protect him.

The day drags, the cold returning to my limbs. The men waiting with me fall sullenly silent from their initial excitement. At the southern gate, the small group of warriors visibly fade in their enthusiasm for the task, worn out by the constant but ineffectual assaults on the southern gate.

Inside the burh, fires rage. As soon as one's quenched, another springs up. I watch with interest as flames work their way around the hall, never quite in it but always just skirting it. Surely, it can't all be the work of one small boy?

I start to consider if Olaf will react at all or if he knows I'm trying to tempt him from his warm lair. He'll stay firm in his disinclination to fight.

And then, finally, my answer comes.

A loud cracking noise reverberates through the air as though a mighty tree crashes to the ground. I watch, surprised, as flames lick the inside of the southern gate. That wasn't part of the plan. Immediately, the right side of the gate flings open. A creature of fire bursts forth from the burh. It's not at all what I'm expecting.

A sharp snap of the wind and the acrid stench of burning hair reaches me, making me retch.

Behind the burning man pour more and more warriors. The thirty men at the gate start to retreat hastily, working their way back while still trying to protect themselves with their shields. The warriors rushing from Tamworth are ready for battle. Was this always Olaf's plan? To keep us waiting until the daylight has nearly drained from the short winter day?

I don't see Olaf amongst the enemy warriors, but as they start to form a battle line, I know my time has finally come. Stamping life into my frozen lower legs, I call the men to attention. Now that Olaf and his men are disgorging from Tamworth, I want to do all I can to prevent him from returning to it. I curse at my short-sightedness for not commanding my men at the gate to slip inside Tamworth and open the northern ones for Ealdorman Uhtred.

The snow sucks at my feet as I shuffle into position, my eyes glued on Olaf's warriors to ensure they mean to meet our attack as we advance from our vantage point and cross the bridge. It's slow going, but finally, we're all where we want to be. I've still not laid eyes on Olaf, but I feel that he's there, hidden under layers of fur and a warrior's helm. I imagine he looks for me in vain, too.

Winter isn't the time to wage war.

Those from the assault on the southern gate join us. Flames continue to lick their way greedily along thatch that sizzles as the snow melts on touch with the hungry blaze. I hope some of Tamworth stands when this is finished! It wasn't my intention to destroy it as thoroughly as the Heathen Army did all those summers ago. I'll have to make reparations.

The steady stream of men coming from the burh trickles to almost nothing. The shrieks of the burning man fade away as his blackened corpse stills in death. Now's the time to attack. I shout for order, and one by one, shields overlap with a crack of wood, weapons of choice to hand.

I can't order the men to run through the deep snow, but I do call for a slow advance. We encounter our enemy with a crash of shield on shield and the harsh breathing of warriors who know this might be their death.

The temperature increases significantly now I have work to do. I'd like nothing more than to shed some of my layers, but it's too late. I'll have to fight as I stand.

Behind our shields, the strain of battle shows on every man's face. Where before I was too cold, sweat beads on my face. The knee-high snow is a problem. We've compelled our enemy outside of Tamworth. Now we need to force them to surrender or retreat.

The comforting weight of the war axe in my hand assures me that, despite my sweat and heave against the enemy, I'm ready for this. I roar with battle rage, swinging my war axe against the shield opposite. I note the emblem on it and smirk to see Olaf's wolf emblazoned there. These are his men from Dublin. I hunger for their deaths. Up and down our shield wall, men follow my actions, a wave crashing onto an exposed shoreline.

The enemy doesn't react, other than to hold firm, which fuels my anger further.

Another crack of my war axe. I can feel the shield I'm facing thrumming with the force of the blow.

Still, there's no response.

Again and again, I try to break through the shield, but it stays firmly in place. Surely, the wood should be brittle in this weather?

What trick is this? Most shields can endure no more than five direct attacks, and yet all these men appear undisturbed by our assault.

Changing tactics, I return my war axe to my weapons belt and reach for my seax. Its edges are narrow and will force me to open the small gaps between the circular shields of our enemy. It's all I can think to do. I've not even seen the face of my foeman yet, and I can feel my strength waxing. Manoeuvring in the snow takes much more effort than fighting on summer-dry grasses.

I lower my shield to sight my target. But my seax meets nothing but fresh air. It's almost as though there's no one on the other side of the shield wall.

A hand on my shoulder and I turn violently to see who disturbs me, fearful the enemy have overwhelmed my warriors. It's Æthelwald, his face darker than midwinter.

'Olaf's gone,' he roars, his voice carrying on the silent air, to be greeted by a loud chuckle from whomever I'm trying to attack.

Angrily, I throw my shield to the floor and yank down the shield obscuring the face of the warrior there. His laughter doesn't falter.

'He sent us out to divert you while he rode away northwards towards more hospitable lands,' the Norse-voiced warrior chortles.

But I'm the one smiling. We'll see how far Olaf manages. He might not have succumbed to my ploy, but he's done better than that. He's fallen into the trap we laid.

I order my men to drop their shield wall and encircle the foemen who've taken part in the ruse allowing Olaf to escape. It's easily done because my warriors from the northern gate have raced through the burh to join the battle, meeting no resistance on the way and dodging the fire as well.

'How did he get out?' I bellow to any who might know the answer, but my words aren't answered.

Content that Olaf's warriors are devoid of their weapons, I have them led back into Tamworth. The ground's slick with water used to douse the fires, and the air's filled with the smell of burning, and not just burning wood.

I see Alfred, a grin touching his cheeks, soot smearing his young face, while a woman stands to the side of him. She's as soot-stained as he is, but looks triumphant. I search her face, but I don't recognise her from my time living in Tamworth. I must find out who she is.

Alfred's smile fades as I walk towards him, but I'm not angry with him. Only with myself.

'Well done, lad,' I say, and his uncertain smile returns. 'Thank you,' I offer the woman. 'Thank you for sending him to tell us of Olaf's advance.' She bobs a curtsey, schooled in the manners of the court. But Alfred speaks before I can say anything else.

'Olaf went that way,' he says, pointing towards the eastern gate. 'He took two hundred and fifty men with him and ordered the others out the southern gate. He plans to regroup at Repton.'

At my side, Æthelwald and Eadric hear everything that Alfred tells me.

'Stay here,' I order them. 'I'm going to search for Olaf.'

I call for my horse and mount up quickly, my rage replaced by a calm knowledge that Olaf can't have made it far. Not in this weather. My household warriors are ready to ride with me. Ealdorman Uhtred will intercept Olaf, and if he doesn't, I'll reach him and end his life. The arrogant Norse bastard.

28

FEBRUARY 940, BETWEEN TAMWORTH AND REPTON, IN THE KINGDOM OF THE ENGLISH

Olaf Gothfrithson, king of the Dublin Norse

Bloody hell, it's cold, I think, allowing my horse to pick its way carefully through the snow-shrouded landscape in the deepening gloom. The joy of knowing that I've just outwitted the English ealdorman almost keeps me warm.

He's got half my most loyal warriors and Tamworth, but he'll not get his glorious battle today, and neither will he keep my warriors. If Archbishop Wulfstan is correct in his assertions that he'll gain more for me with his honeyed words than through fighting, my warriors will be returned to me, and perhaps even Tamworth as well.

I was comfortable in my stolen hall at Tamworth. But it's evident people were working for the English. When the fire spread, it was safer to escape while I could. My men grumbled about the necessity of it, but even they could see the advantages to my plan. Far better to have a lord free to make peace than one captured through cunning.

I hope to make it to Repton tonight and then back into the more firmly held lands along the River Trent and towards Lincoln. Archbishop Wulfstan can expend his time on the peace accord then. Progress has been too slow, but I'll hasten him along now that I've encountered two quick reversals outside Northampton, and at Tamworth.

At my side, Ildulb has lapsed into silence. He's the only one who argued for meeting Ealdorman Athelstan in battle, just as he argued for continuing the fight outside Northampton. His bloodlust is a testament to his deep rage and hatred of the English. I was almost tempted to allow it and send him to fight with those of my men who sacrificed themselves. But if he'd been killed – or worse, taken captive by the English – Constantin wouldn't have been forgiving. Neither would my wife.

'It's better this way,' I call to him through the frozen air, but he's sullen and unresponsive. Sod him, I think. He's not directing this force.

I wonder what he'd have done had the command been his? If he ever stops sulking, I might ask him.

The cries of the aborted battle at Tamworth follow us through the snowy landscape, and it's not long before I wish I'd been less keen to leave Tamworth. It'll be an icy night's ride to Repton.

A shout from in front drags me from my musings. I squint into the dying colours of the day.

What did the warrior roar, voice cracking with worry?

'Warriors, my lord,' I finally decipher in shock. Encircling my group of only two hundred and fifty men, a vast swathe of English warriors menaces us.

'English?' I manage to choke, astounded to realise my plan has been foiled. Ildulb's snarl of anger echoes menacingly.

The enemy warriors are prepared to engage, bedecked in their warriors' garb, and yet they hold only shields in hands, not weapons.

'My lord Olaf,' an English voice shouts, a little thick with the accent of the Northumbrians, but who am I to say anything?

'Yes,' I shout back, trying to find the source of the voice.

'My name's Ealdorman Uhtred, and this is Ealdorman Guthrum, and I believe that you're now our honoured guest.'

Arse. I thought I was winning this game of move and counter-move. Have they had the upper hand all along?

I raise my hands slowly, giving my acceptance to the surrender. My stomach's hollow with failure.

I pushed too far, and now I've been captured, and not even in battle. Worse, along with me, Uhtred also has Ildulb of the Scots, and Archbishop Wulfstan.

Surrounded by four of his warriors, Uhtred rides through the astonished stares of my men until he faces me, his gaze switching from myself to Ildulb, taking in the archbishop at the same time. The fat man looks comical, perched on his horse, swathed in furs to keep himself warm.

'Ah, I see I'm pleased to play host to more than just Olaf Gothfrithson,' he mutters, with a delighted smirk on his lips. 'Follow me, please.' I don't miss that it's not a request we can ignore, not when our hands are bound to our horses, and our horses are bound to one of their warriors. 'We'll ride to Repton, and from there, we'll contact King Edmund of the English and inform him of your detainment.'

Damn. I should have stayed in Lincoln; I shouldn't have gone to Stamford and Northampton. I certainly shouldn't have staked my freedom on this mad dash between Tamworth and Repton, where I hope my ships wait for me on the River Trent.

I open my mouth to speak, to deny those words, to summon my

men to arms. But it's too late. The crash of weapons being flung to the snow-laden ground reverberates in time to my heartbeat. Ealdormen Uhtred and Guthrum have the numbers to overwhelm my loyal warriors, and with my capture, those men won't fight to the death on my behalf. Not when there's no certainty of payment.

I snap my mouth shut, eyeing Ildulb with defiance. I pray he'll keep silent.

I can already hear Archbishop Wulfstan and his protestations of peaceful intentions. I hope his words win over the glint of iron and sharp blades.

29

FEBRUARY 940, NEAR REPTON, THE KINGDOM OF THE ENGLISH

Edmund, king of the English

Snowfall has delayed my journey to the peace conference. My men and I are cold and miserable. The chill makes each shiver painful.

The two archbishops have been hard at work, forging peace that'll be acceptable to both me and Olaf Gothfrithson, even though Olaf's my captive. I don't envy the men their task, but the fact that Olaf's my prisoner eases my fears a little. I'm more than pleased that Ealdormen Uhtred, Guthrum and Athelstan were able to contain Olaf. At least he's now nearly out of Mercia. Olaf's successes have been many and varied but not decisive, other than in Jorvik and Lincoln. I curse the loss of those settlements.

All the same, I can't erase the thought that, even though Olaf's my captive, he's going to demand more. The spectre of the ancient Watling Street border my grandfather once agreed upon with Halfdan looms large, and not just because Ealdorman Athelstan has warned me that Olaf is arguing his right to much English land. But it won't be the Watling Street border this time. Olaf's reversal at Stamford, and his failure at Northampton and Tamworth, mean that while Lincoln might be lost to England, the Five Boroughs are not to become Norse once more. Perhaps the border will be that of the River Trent, as it forges a path through the northern Mercian landscape. I can afford the loss of Lincoln. For now.

I've been cautioned by my mother and advised by Ealdormen Athelstan, Guthrum and Uhtred to be more conciliatory than I want to be. Olaf has his men left behind in Jorvik and Lincoln ready to attack what remains of Mercia, although his ships were prevented from coming further south by Ealdorman Guthrum and his warriors. His brother, Blakari, and son, Camman, command Jorvik. His other brother, Gothfrith, holds Dublin. No doubt they have many loyal warriors there. And Anlaf's brother, Haraldr, possesses Limerick. It might take time for the Irish Norse to mount an attack to reinforce their brothers, but it will come, eventually.

This isn't how I imagined I'd be making my official survey of the kingdom of the English.

I'm not the victor, which upsets me. These people are used to seeing King Athelstan triumph over the Norse. I can't lay claim to that. Not yet. My kingship has begun in a blaze of failure. With the help of the terrible wintry weather, the Norse have run roughshod through my kingdom, leaving a trail of death and destruction, fear and anger. While Olaf is now my prisoner, that doesn't yet place me in a position of great power. If he should escape before a peace can be agreed, Olaf will come back. If I refuse to yield, he'll return with the forces of Jorvik, Dublin and Limerick. This then, my mother assures me, is a balancing act in which I must prove proficient.

Finally, Tamworth comes into sight as we make our way along Watling Street before branching out to follow one of the lesser roads to Repton. I eye Tamworth from afar. It's not as destroyed by fire as Ealdorman Athelstan fears. That pleases me.

I rein in my horse as Repton draws near and take a long moment to compose myself. I need to be kingly when I greet Olaf. I can imagine his smug expression, even though he's my captive. The last time we met, at Brunanburh, he was running away in defeat, desperate to reach his ships and escape my wrath. How have three winters brought about such a giant reversal in our fortunes? How has he made it as far as Northampton and now holds Lincoln?

I wish my half-brother were here. King Athelstan would have oozed composure, no matter the enemy he faced.

Instead, it's Ealdorman Athelstan and his brothers who greet me when I'm in sight of Repton, alongside Ealdorman Uhtred, and the welcome sight of Ealdorman Guthrum, who ultimately captured Olaf, Ildulb of the Scots and the archbishop of York. The church of St Wystan's rears up from the ground, the surge of the River Trent escaping the confines of its icy surface to thunder through the landscape. Ealdorman Athelstan's breath puffs before his face. He's covered almost from head to toe in thick furs, as are his brothers, and Ealdormen Uhtred and Guthrum. I don't blame them. Only my eyes peek out from the layers that cover me.

'My lord king,' he offers formally. I roll my eyes at him, and he immediately reverts to his usual self. 'It's good to see you, Edmund.'

'How's Olaf?' I inquire. His face blackens.

'He's an arrogant bastard. You're going to have to watch everything you say to him. He has a way of twisting a man's words so that they seem to mean something other than what you intended.'

I store that piece of advice away. 'He's been a pleasant prisoner?' I ask more for something else to say than because I want to know.

'No, he's done nothing but bitch and moan, and his men are the same. They're hardly being kept in any discomfort, but they're unhappy all the same. Being inside Repton as prisoners upsets them all when it's so easy to see the defences their forebears once erected to claim the settlement as their own.'

'It's a reminder of what can happen, and very quickly,' I murmur, thinking how closely these thoughts resemble mine in regard to the success of the battle of Brunanburh.

'I suppose so, and for future reference, we need to remember how much the Norse and the Irish hate this place.'

'And what of the archbishops?'

'Wulfheard is his usual talkative self. Wulfstan. Well, I'll let you decide. He's a slippery eel, and I don't know that I like him. I thought he was English, but he doesn't seem to have our interests at the forefront of the negotiations. And perhaps not Olaf's either. He's adamant that his position at Olaf Gothfrithson's side was only so he could help secure peace. He prayed there would be no more war.' Ealdorman Athelstan's words thrum with fury.

Ealdorman Uhtred looks no happier as he speaks. 'We've agreed on peace in all but the finest details. The River Trent will be the border above Repton. Remember it's not forever,' he offers hastily. His eyes bore into mine, as momentary panic grips me. My breath comes too fast through my dry mouth at hearing my fears spoken aloud.

'We'll get it back,' Ealdorman Athelstan wants to assure, but his words fade away, and I can barely hear him, or see the nodding and determined expressions on the faces of Ealdorman Uhtred, Eadric, Guthrum and Æthelwald. 'We'll get it back,' Ealdorman Athelstan repeats more loudly and with more confidence this time, as though he's convincing me. I grab hold of that thought. Slowly, I feel my calmness return. Ealdorman Athelstan is right. I only hope that everyone else realises the same. This is a temporary setback and one that we'll start working to reverse before the ink is even dry on the vellum it'll be scrawled on.

'Lead on,' I manage to command. With a look of sincere sympathy, Ealdorman Athelstan escorts my men and me into Repton. It's an ancient place, the old church in magnificent condition, its curved stone roof a wonder to behold, and yet there are scorch marks on it, and the heavy wooden door is scoured with what seem to be axe marks. There was a battle here, perhaps more than one. The Norse lost Repton. I know that.

And then before me, emerging blinking into the bright light of the snow-shrouded day, I see the arrogant smirk of a man I'd hoped to kill three summers ago. Olaf Gothfrithson.

He doesn't wear chains, but ten of Ealdorman Uhtred's best warriors encircle him, iron glittering from their weapons belts, their byrnies bright and shimmering. Their eyes watch his every move. I almost pity him such intense scrutiny, even as I seek out the familiar face of Ildulb of the Scots.

I slide from my horse and hand the reins to Ealdorman Athelstan. He passes them on to Æthelwald, and then joins me before Olaf. I hesitate for barely a moment.

'My lord Olaf, I'd like to say it's a pleasure to meet you. Sadly, I find you too deep within my lands for it to be anything but unpleasant.'

His eyes lighten at my tone. I might hate him right now, but it doesn't mean all my kingly graces need to be forgotten as he inclines his head towards me, and I reciprocate.

'My lord Edmund,' he rejoins, 'I return the greeting and only wish I wasn't currently detained at your convenience. Or my allies, Anlaf and Ildulb.' I risk a glance towards Ildulb. He glowers, licking his lips, his hand returning time and time again to an empty weapons belt. Anlaf, I realise, is shockingly similar in appearance to Olaf. They're cousins, not brothers, and yet. Well, perhaps their mothers were closely related as well as their fathers. Anlaf thought he was safe at Repton, but Ealdormen Uhtred and Guthrum captured him as surely as they did Olaf, Ildulb and Archbishop Wulfstan.

There's a bustle of activity behind Olaf. Before we can speak more, the archbishops join the grouping. Wulfstan's a short man, a little too rotund around the waist, whereas Wulfheard's rigid, tall and thin, almost as though he'll break with a huge gust of wind. Bishop Oda is also in attendance.

They wear serious expressions. This peace accord is to no one's liking.

The hall's filled with men and women, whose conversations all lapse as I enter. I stand taller, endeavouring to appear as though I'm the conquering king and not come to beg for my kingdom.

A series of benches are arranged around the large fire at the heart of the hall, and it's towards them that Olaf walks with confidence. I stop and look around. I don't want to be seen as his meek follower. I beckon for Ealdormen Uhtred and Guthrum to join me while I take the time to see how Olaf reacts to being kept waiting.

Ildulb and Anlaf escort Olaf. Seeing them together makes me realise my position is stronger than it might appear. Olaf is my prisoner. If I wanted to, I could slit his throat and he'd be dead. It would be that simple. There's nothing his warriors could do other than kill me in retaliation. I don't believe my loyal Englishmen would allow that. But I came here with a promise of peace not war, a peace that's been determined by the two holiest men upon our island.

Satisfied that Olaf's aware this will be done in my time, not his, I walk and sit before the fire, beckoning for the archbishops to join us.

Wulfstan of York does so quickly, almost waddling along in his haste.

'My lords,' he begins in his grating voice. I wish Wulfheard of Canterbury had spoken first. It's him I trust, not Wulfstan. 'I welcome you to Repton and hope that we can make a lasting and binding peace here, ratified in the magnificent church next door.'

I nod to show I hope the same, even though I don't. Into my hand has been slipped a warm beaker containing wine. I don't drink it, but I welcome the heat that makes my fingers tingle.

I'll make this peace only because Olaf and his allies were captured while retreating, and because they still hold Lincoln. I'd rather Olaf had been killed in battle, but that didn't happen.

'I agree,' Olaf smirks triumphantly. 'I wish to be gone from this place. My warriors are outraged that I'm being held against my will. My brother, my son and my father by marriage will march to recover me if I'm not allowed my freedom.'

I don't rise to the bait, although I see Ealdorman Athelstan curb his temper. If Olaf's warriors were so furious, perhaps they shouldn't have succumbed to the English force so quickly.

'If you raid another man's land then I'm afraid you take the attendant risks,' Archbishop Wulfstan counters, not fearing to upset Olaf. His tone speaks of familiarity. That confirms my suspicions. Wulfstan is too closely allied with Olaf, for all he seems to chastise him. We need to be wary of him.

'If you'll ride directly into my armed force with too few men, I'm unsure what you expect to happen,' I interject. I want the sly grin to be wiped from Olaf's face. It's my desire to make him worry that events may not play out as he'd hoped they would.

His eyes flicker to my face. I hope he sees nothing there but contempt. I've banished my worry.

It's Archbishop Wulfheard's turn to speak to soften the edges of our anger. I listen with half an ear as he attempts to appease, but I find my glance turning to Ildulb time and time again. I killed his son in battle. It was a fair fight, but still, I know that he doesn't see it as such. He hungers for my blood, and my position as king doesn't daunt him. If looks could kill, I'd be dead, and my young brother king in my place. But I'm also perplexed, for Ildulb looks so similar to his brother Alpin. And Alpin was almost my friend, not my enemy. He carried no grudge towards me for killing his nephew in battle.

I want to ensure Alpin is well in the kingdom of the Scots, but fear it will merely create problems for him. I hold my tongue.

'My lord king,' Archbishop Wulfheard addresses me.

I look to him in puzzlement.

'My lord king, Edmund,' he reiterates, 'I was discussing the damage that's been done to the people of Mercia and how Lord Olaf will need to make reparation.'

I nod in agreement, but Olaf must be expecting the discussion.

'Lord Edmund needs to understand that he should have protected his people better if he didn't want me to attack them,' Olaf retorts almost before Wulfheard has finished speaking. Olaf tries to wound me with his slights, but I brush them aside.

'My lord Olaf needs to appreciate that, as the king of the English, I can't allow men to attack my people, kill, maim and destroy the winter stores without compensation.'

Olaf laughs then. 'Is that all this is about? Money?' He leers at me. He's an unpleasant man when cornered. I'm also surprised. The Norse have only ever assaulted my kingdom for money or treasure.

'Why are you attacking us?' I ask. He settles back on his bench, his right leg crossing his left and his hands cupping his right knee.

'I'm here to claim back Jorvik.'

I understand that, but it doesn't explain his presence in Repton. 'If my geography doesn't fail me,' I begin, 'York, or Jorvik as you term it, is far to the north of here.'

His smug smile drops. Has the man not realised he can't argue for Jorvik when he sits in Mercia?

'I found the people pleased to call me their king, and so I pressed on.'

I laugh, a low noise that builds slowly. His argument is weak, and he knows it. This might be easier than I thought it was going to be after all.

'I understand that the *people*, as you term them, tried to stop your attack and that you've left a trail of burning homes and dead animals as you've rampaged through my lands.' I stress 'my lands'. It's important for Olaf to understand I'm not relinquishing my claim to anything despite the talk of the River Trent as a boundary between his people and mine.

Olaf looks shocked. He's been expecting some gentle-worded soul who's going to beg for his land back. He forgets that I'm as much a warrior as he is. I might look young, but I know the power of my position.

'You'll need to pay the wergild for every person you've killed,' I state.

He sucks in a startled breath. I worry that he's killed hundreds and hundreds of people and that Ealdorman Athelstan hasn't told me of all his atrocities.

'And you'll need to leave here and never return.' His shoulders relax at that. After all, the money doesn't concern him. He'll be rich, holding the wealth of York. But his freedom does worry him.

'You'll cede Jorvik to me,' he states boldly. 'My men hold it, and as the archbishop will tell you, the people are pleased to call me their king. They enjoy being part of my kingdom of Dublin and Jorvik. The trading opportunities are immense.'

Now I feel uncomfortable. I knew I'd have to do this. In fact, this should be the easy part of the negotiations, but I'm not happy to be talking about giving away parts of my kingdom that have only recently been reclaimed by my half-brother.

'York will be yours, provided you govern the people well. Any disquiet from them and I'll march to the gates of York and overwhelm your warriors, taking it back into the domain of the English kingdom.'

I'm not bluffing, but my words fall flat. I'm embarrassed that my great statement of intent sounds so weak.

Olaf watches to see if I have anything further to add. I don't. He's been ceded a huge swathe of land, but there's nothing I can do to take it back. Not right now. Ealdorman Athelstan's words resound in my head: 'we'll get it back.' The knowledge holds my back straight under the scrutiny of my enemies, Olaf, Anlaf and Ildulb, and it seems Archbishop Wulfstan of York as well.

'And Lincoln?' Olaf persists. It takes all my effort to maintain my posture. I don't want to give away Lincoln but, once more, Olaf grips it firmly. I have no choice but to relinquish it to him.

Luckily, Archbishop Wulfheard interjects, his smooth voice saving me from trying to answer when speech seems to be beyond me.

'The border will be the River Trent. That will give you command over Lincoln, and the River Trent as far as Repton, but not including it, and no further south.'

'I agree but on the stipulation that it lasts only as long as Olaf holds the kingship. Upon his death, Lincoln will revert to the English. It'll be a land transaction, nothing more. You may keep your possessions for the duration of your life, as is the custom of the English.'

Anlaf glowers at my words. Olaf smirks at his success. He apparently thinks he's immortal. A man should be more aware of his mortality when he makes a treaty. Look at King Athelstan and Eamont.

'The bishopric of Lincoln will remain neutral,' Archbishop Wulfstan murmurs, but I doubt that, especially if events here are anything by which to judge.

'Agreed,' I announce quickly. I don't want to discuss this further.

'As do I,' Olaf confirms after a momentary waiver.

I feel soiled by the brief discussion. I hunger for the summer months, when the men of the fyrd will be at my back, as well as the household troops of my ealdormen and king's thegns. Then, we'll be able to counter anything that Olaf Gothfrithson and his allies throws our way.

Conversation mills around us from those witnessing these discussions, for what needed doing is done. The lands of the English are being carved up. I only need to add my mark to the prepared vellum that sets out the terms of the treaty, and then I can leave this place. The terms aren't as onerous as those agreed by my grandfather with Guthrum when so much of what is now England was lost to the Norse.

I can recite those boundary clauses easily. They've long been scored into my memory, a promise that the same would never happen again. 'First concerning our boundaries; up the Thames, and then up the Lea, and along the Lea to its source, then in a straight line to Bedford, then up the Ouse to Watling Street.' That treaty saved my grandfather's life, but ever since then, the English have been fighting those stipulations, desperate to overturn them. Until now, there had been great success, but there will be a border along the River Trent, as far as Repton, for the foreseeable future.

But I linger a moment longer. Wouldn't it be easier if the English were friends with Olaf? Wouldn't it be better for the people now under his rule? Perhaps, I think, I could suggest a marriage with one of my unwed half-sisters to Anlaf? After all, that's how Athelstan managed to take York in the first place.

In other circumstances, Olaf might be a good ally. But not now. Not when he's proved himself so intent on violence within England. And if we're friends, it'll be that much harder to face him in battle where I hope to either cut his head from his shoulders or watch his backside running for his ships once more as at Brunanburh.

No, Olaf and I can't become family.

We can't even be friends.

We're mortal enemies. And there's only one way to resolve that.

30

FEBRUARY 940, THE BORDERLAND BETWEEN LINCOLN AND ENGLAND AGREED AT TAMWORTH

Athelstan the ealdorman

King Edmund managed well when he signed the accord with Olaf Gothfrithson. He was magnanimous although his hasty departure showed just how much the peace troubled him.

In his place, he left Ealdormen Uhtred, Guthrum and me to see to the final details and ensure that Olaf was deposited back to the land relinquished to him, along with his warriors. We've stood guard and watched him ride away at the start of a crisp, wintry day.

I thought Olaf might linger, toy with the men, perhaps even slink back across the newly agreed border to try our resolve, but he didn't. With a cheeky grin and a wave of his untied hands, he turned his heel and left with no further thought, his warriors calling cheerily to one another as they were reunited.

With Olaf gone, hurrying northwards along the River Trent, Uhtred, Guthrum and I watch the landscape before us. The snow has yet to clear. The winter's proving to be harsh and long, the blackened skeletons of trees a testament that the warmer weather, and the promise of summer, are far away.

'We need a more secure border,' Uhtred announces into the companionable silence between us. Horses neigh and nicker, but other than that, all is peaceful. It's as though we can breathe for the first time since Olaf's incursions into England were first reported. 'The River Trent is too convenient because it's a designated marker, but the Norse have their ships, and so a river is no impediment to them, especially one that runs so far through Mercia. While the Viking raider Guthrum might have recognised the border he agreed with King Alfred in his day, I doubt Olaf will respect the intent behind this accord. No hostages have been exchanged. Olaf hasn't even been forced to accept baptism with Edmund as his godfather. It was a treaty of equals.' Ealdorman Uhtred's voice is matter-of-fact as he recounts his worries.

This has always been Mercia's problem. To the west, Offa built his dyke, stretching between the Welsh kingdoms and Mercia. To the south west, Wansdyke performed a similar task between Mercia and Wessex, with the River Thames providing the rest of the border further south east. But there's little to separate Mercia from the ancient kingdoms of the East Anglians, while the Northumbrian kingdom, divided now between Norse-held Jorvik and English-held Bamburgh, is demarcated by the vast River Humber, which the River Trent meets. The two, combined, and if overrun by our enemy, could easily deprive England of its northern extent. The building of the burhs within Mercia did slowly push the Norse back to the extremities, banishing them first to York, and then back to Dublin. But it's not proven to be a final resolution. At the moment, it seems far from that.

A slow smile works its way across my face. Uhtred raises a quizzical eyebrow.

'Burhs,' I murmur, wondering why I've not thought of this

before. Indeed, why King Athelstan didn't consider them for he was a clever man. 'We need to refortify the old ones and build new ones, pushing ever further north until we meet the River Humber. That way we'll have a defensible border that doesn't rely on rivers.'

Uhtred and Guthrum consider my idea for a long moment, gazing off into the distance. Eventually, Uhtred grunts in approval. 'We just need to convince the king,' he warns, with an arched eyebrow on his weathered face. That might not be easy, hangs unsaid in the air. Then, because we're all happy that Olaf, Anlaf, Ildulb and the archbishop of York have buggered off home to Jorvik, Uhtred kicks his horse and begins the long journey south to join the king at Winchester, Ealdorman Guthrum accompanying him.

I'm to stay behind to repair Tamworth and guard against any further opportunistic attacks. But already, I'm thinking ahead. For now, Olaf won't return. None of his men wish to continue their fight during the winter weather. But come the summer or next winter, when the cold of the recent invasion has faded from their memories, it'll be different.

The fortified burh system, I realise, that's what we need, further north, just as my wife's mother, Æthelflæd, had built throughout Mercia, at Stafford, Tamworth, Derby and elsewhere. With that in place, as with in the past, we can ensure the Norse never again set foot in England. Or the Welsh. Or the Scots. Or any of the Dublin Norse either.

And, with the burh system, as at the height of the Viking raider attacks, we'll protect the people of Mercia, and build a solid boundary that the Norse won't be able to break through. We'll take back what's been stolen. And this time, with the burhs, we'll hold them for all time.

31

EARLY 940, THE KINGDOM OF GWYNEDD

Idwal, king of Gwynedd

I smirk as I hear the latest news of King Edmund's defeat brought to me by my brother. I nod along as Cadfan speaks.

'Peace, with Olaf Gothfrithson. Agreed by the archbishops.' My brother smiles, his eyebrows dancing above his bright eyes.

'Edmund's a pathetic image of his brother,' I murmur, a frisson of excitement running through my body. 'We can rebel now, and refuse to do all that was demanded of us. Edmund can't impose his wishes over us. He can't even compel Olaf to hand back Lincoln and Jorvik.'

'What do you plan?' my brother queries.

'Immediately, we cease our payments to the English king. That way we can ensure our warriors are better provisioned. I'll also seek an alliance with Olaf Gothfrithson.'

'What do you have that he wants?' my brother questions with a downturned curl of his lips. I don't appreciate the disdain.

'He wishes to crush King Edmund. This is only the start of it. With our support, Olaf will be able to take more than just Jorvik and Lincoln.'

Again, my brother nods, finding the idea appealing. Only then he spoils my good humour. 'And Hywel?'

'Hywel has stolen his last kingship from my fellow warriors. He's moved as close to Gwynedd as he's going to get in this lifetime. I'll reinforce the other kingships, send them aid if need be. Tewdwr ap Griffi ab Elise might have allowed Brycheiniog to fall into the hands of Hywel, but I'll ensure Gwent and Glywysing remain free of his interference.'

'Morgan and Gwriad will agree to your assistance, will they?'

I glower at my brother. Of all the people here, I expect him to be the one to support me most fully. I don't like his questions. Or the fact that they're quite so pertinent. 'Yes, they'll agree to it,' I offer patiently. I won't show any doubt.

'They won't think you're about to do the same to them as Hywel plans to do?'

'No, because that's not my intention.' And here I feel the smirk once more on my lips. 'I mean to help Olaf Gothfrithson overpower Edmund. I've no interest in my fellow Welsh kings' possessions. I'm not as ambitious as Hywel in that regard.'

Once more, my brother nods, but he's still not quite as enamoured of my suggestions as I might hope.

With a huff of annoyance, I speak the words I know I'm going to regret. 'What would you do differently, brother?'

He licks his fat lips in anticipation and leans towards me to whisper. 'Olaf and his brother, Gothfrith, they should send an attacking force from Dublin to harass Hywel's coastline. That'll keep him on his toes.'

Grudgingly I admit that my brother might have something there. 'And you'll be my mediator?'

'Of course, brother, it would be my pleasure.' His grin is impossible to contain.

'It could be dangerous,' I suggest, but he merely shrugs his shoulders.

'Everything is dangerous, and anyway, these men, they want the same thing that you and I desire. The end of the English king's dominion.'

'Very well,' I agree. 'Should it be to Dublin or Jorvik?'

'Dublin,' Cadfan offers into the silence that falls between us. 'Easy to avoid Edmund and his ealdormen that way.' What he leaves unsaid is that Gothfrith, Olaf's brother, is likely to agree to the offensive without waiting for his brother's agreement. Rumour has it that Gothfrith holds power in Dublin, with the support of Olaf's first wife. That'll be interesting should Olaf ever be forced to return to Dublin. It might be very interesting. But, for now, it means my brother is correct. Gothfrith Gothfrithson is the one to approach, and then, when that alliance is forged, it'll be as though we're Olaf's allies anyway. He'll welcome my support, and I'll be just as eager to provide it.

32

SUMMER 941, NORTH OF THE KINGDOM OF JORVIK

Olaf Gothfrithson, king of the Dublin Norse and Jorvik

I bring my horse to a stop and take the time to admire the view before me. I enjoyed my journey to the south when I claimed Lincoln last winter, but I've been forced to turn my attention north to quench the battle thirst of my warriors and myself. Edmund of the English guards his borders with an enthusiasm that dampens my ardour for conflict. He has many more warriors than I thought he did. Where they've come from, I'm unsure. I hear rumours that his involvement in the affairs of East and West Frankia is at an end, that he and his cousin in Flanders are enemies, not allies. Something to do with a woman. I don't know. I don't care. The information that reaches me is muddied and confused. But, perhaps then, some of his warriors have returned from whatever they were doing to support King Louis, the fourth of his name. Wherever they've come from, it's impossible to raid south as I'd like to do. The warriors on the border are fierce. Edmund's positioned ships close to Repton along the River Trent. I can't even break through that way.

I've considered more friendly overtures towards him to enable me to exploit our peace accord. Perhaps I could wed Anlaf to one of Edmund's half-sisters? Perhaps even my oldest son? He's old enough to need a wife. Reports persist of Edmund's intention to claim back Lincoln. Every time I get close to calling for Archbishop Wulfstan to send a messenger on my behalf, I reconsider. I see now that's how these things are done between brother kings. Edmund and I should send messengers between one another when we have such ideas. I know that's how Hywel keeps abreast of affairs in England. Not, I realise, that Edmund would name me as his equal.

Not even the support of Idwal of Gwynedd can tempt me to incite war on my southern borders. And Idwal is very keen for me to overrun Edmund, as his overtures of friendship to Gothfrith in Dublin have shown. And that's why I've had to force Gothfrith to my side. He can't make alliances as though he rules Dublin. He must remember who's the king, and who the king's brother.

And to attack Edmund, I need more than Idwal of Gwynedd, and Constantin of the Scots, or rather, Constantin's son. I require warriors from Ireland as well as the Norse homelands. Idwal and Constantin, despite their fierce denials, are still too much under the sway of the English. Even with Edmund's losses, they simper and bow to his messengers, and send their tithes, or as little as they can get away with, all in the hope that Edmund will stay his hand and not retaliate. I know Idwal planned to cease all reparations, but he's not as determined in his resolve as those words imply. He's weak.

It's not as easy as it sounds, either, raiding in the north. Constantin of the Scots is vigilant on his borders. He doesn't expect me to attack his lands when we're united through my marriage with his daughter. And he extends that to the kingdom of Strathclyde as well, which he governs through the use of one of Owain's sons, Dyfnwal. The people of Bamburgh are jealous of my every movement, although maybe my attack on the monastery of Lindisfarne didn't help me. Bloody fools. Perhaps if they guarded it better, my men and I wouldn't have been tempted to assault it and steal away their treasure and cattle last summer. Not even the outraged complaints of the son of the dead lord of Bamburgh made me regret that decision. He's a weak thing, Ealdwulf. And Edmund has yet to repopulate Bamburgh with enough warriors for them to counter my attack. I know that Ealdorman Guthrum once held the north for the English king, but no longer. Since our unfortunate meeting at Repton, he's died, and as of yet, Edmund has sent no one to replace him. He shows himself as timid in that regard.

No, the land between Jorvik and the kingdom of the Scots is wild and unclaimed by the English. But, in Ealdorman Guthrum's place, there are many who think it should be theirs. I include myself in that, as does Ealdwulf, who'd like to name himself 'of Bamburgh,' but can't.

At the moment I hold Jorvik and Lincoln with the aid of my brothers and son. Gothfrith has relinquished Dublin to Anlaf Sihtricson, and both have been advised alliances can't be reached without my accord. They'll not use my name and reputation to act independently. After all, that was our agreement before the battle of Brunanburh. Sadly, Gothfrith brought my first wife with him from Dublin. I wasn't pleased to see her. And neither was Mael Muire. She's visiting her father, or so she told me. I didn't have the heart to argue with her. She grows round with my child. Should the boy live, I'll be more interested in her.

And while she's escaped my first wife and Jorvik, I've been

forced to do the same. It's not just to keep my warriors happy. It's also because I can't abide the snappiness of my first wife, or the relationship she's formed with my brother. Now, I ride through these nearly empty lands where every day sees so many different weather conditions I can go from wearing my cloak to riding tunic-less, and then be drenched by rain, between one meal and the next.

It might be raining first thing, full summer sun by the time I reach my destination and then windy by nightfall. Hills can be masked by cloud in the morning, and enticing with their bright sunshine by the afternoon. It's a hard place but at least not as bitter as the far northern lands of my ancestors. Or so I tell myself. It took nearly half a year for the cold to leave my bones after my expedition into England.

I've ridden far to the north, almost to the borders with the kingdom of Strathclyde. It doesn't hurt to bait Ildulb and my father by marriage a little. But now I'm returning to Jorvik. I plan to banish my brother and my first wife, or rather, to reward them for their loyalty with some possessions far from Jorvik, but not in Dublin. I need to keep them close, but not too close.

The horses are heavy with stolen goods; precious metal, jewels and whatever else of value we could take from the people we raided. I imagine they hoped Archbishop Wulfstan would protect them as he holds the land. When Wulfstan finds out, he'll be furious, but what can he do to me, a warrior with a bloodied blade? He's proven himself fickle in the war between Jorvik and the English. I don't trust him as far as I can throw him, which isn't far. I imagine he'd squeal if I went close to him, just like the pig he resembles.

Behind us a small herd of cattle complain as they follow on, being shepherded along the path by my warriors. My men are attentive and relaxed. I enjoy the moment. I've killed many since my raids into England but not as many as I'd have liked. I've ruled the combined kingdom of Dublin and Jorvik successfully, but I still hope for more. I'm a young man, and I want to gain an epithet for my name similar to Alfred's or, perhaps, my great-grandfather, Ivarr the Boneless. What a fabulous name for the scops to conjure with?

The outraged cry of one of my men has me reaching for my shield and war axe. I didn't expect to be set upon here, but I can see mounted men racing towards us across the vast expanse of moorland that we traverse. Perhaps, I realise, these cattle did belong to someone who could do something about it.

'Bollocks,' I exclaim. Quickly, I slide from my horse and urge my warriors to do the same. Our enemies have come to claim back what we took, and they have us surrounded. We can't escape to the north, or the south. We'll have to fight them. I'm not about to barter with them. They should have protected their cattle better in the first place.

An opportunity to fight to the death will wake me from my growing lethargy knowing that the coming winter will see me trapped inside Jorvik's walls, perhaps with my brother and my first wife. And Archbishop Wulfstan. But not my second wife, or the babe she carries in her belly.

'Shields,' I urge my warriors. Not that I need to tell them. We all have more than enough experience. These loyal men, who followed me from Dublin to Jorvik, won't fear a few angry farmers.

The cattle we protect low and bellow at being forced to stop, whereas before we've been urging them ever onwards. The horses wait patiently, their reins tied close to their saddles so they can decide whether to run or not. I hope they don't. I don't want to ride a cow back to Jorvik. My brothers would enjoy seeing me cast so low. My first wife would taunt me. I'm not going to allow that.

The men who race towards us are well armoured, their iron

shimmering beneath the streaks of sunshine that currently light the sky, although dark clouds promise more rain will fall soon. Hastily, I reconsider. These aren't some wild men from the northern lands. They might even be from Bamburgh. Are they the English king's warriors from Bamburgh? Has he finally sent a replacement for Ealdorman Guthrum? I don't recognise them. Instinctively, I tighten the hold on my shield. They outnumber me. I don't like the uneven odds although I thrill at the possibility of another great victory against whoever thinks to hobble me. If these are the English king's men, thinking to overwhelm me here, I'll take great delight in sending their decapitated corpses to Edmund.

Cries of derision from my warriors to those men who are even now forming up to attack us float in the air. The foemen wear good clothes and have well-made shields and weapons. They must be from Bamburgh. There's nowhere else close by they could have come from. Without pausing for thought, I call the advance. No matter the identity of the enemy, we'll triumph.

Our two forces crash together like summer thunder echoing through the high hills.

I hold my war axe but swiftly change it for my seax as I press my shoulder into my shield. My enemy's surprisingly strong.

'Hold firm,' I bellow, wishing my feet didn't scrabble for purchase on the summer-dry grasses beneath them. 'Hold firm,' I call again when it appears to have no effect. No matter how hard I call for greater efforts, I know a moment of worry. It quickly solidifies when a young voice shouts in terror from where the horses and cattle are being watched. I can hear the cries of more and more of my enemy. Their shield wall thrums.

Unless I triumph quickly, I fear we'll have to make a hasty retreat. I don't want to die today. Not to keep some stinking cattle safe. It hardly speaks of a mighty warrior vanquishing his foes. I won't make it to Valhalla if I die for a cow.

The press against my shield is unbearable. At my side, my favoured warriors grimace with the effort to keep upright and in position. Slowly, shuffling footstep by shuffling footstep, I know we're losing ground, not helped by the men, and I include myself in that, who slip on the yellowing dry grasses.

'Attack,' I roar. Those behind remove the shields covering our heads and we lash out with seaxes and war axes, trying to pull down the shields that protect our enemy. But the men we face aren't at all concerned by our change of tactics. They hold firm. I don't even draw blood. I think of my bowmen, but they're in Jorvik, and they'd be no help here, anyway. 'Hold firm,' I bellow once more. The shield above my head is back in place. Breath burns in my throat and between my dry lips.

I feel a blade sneaking its way between the shield that protects me. I swing my seax at it, but it keeps coming, its point sharp and snaking closer and closer to my eye.

I grunt and grit my teeth, forcing my shoulder as hard as I can against the shield in the hope that it might lift it higher and trap the blade.

But the blade's advance doesn't stop.

I shout to the man who guards my back, Asl, but he doesn't hear me above the thunder of battle.

Left with no choice, I step back, disturbing the men to either side of me, but at least I'm out of the reach of that damn blade.

Asl realises what's happening. 'To me.' He hollers for others to come to my defence, but three of the enemy race forward, into the gaping hole left by me abandoning the shield wall. Their faces are filled with murderous intent.

Asl steps before me, in the absence of any other, but the first enemy doesn't even break step. He raises his war axe and hammers it down on Asl's helm. I watch as my warrior stumbles and falls to his knees.

Our foeman ignores him, stepping around him and aiming for me again. Asl isn't worthy of his attention. The men Asl summoned before his death attempt to batter their way to me, only more of the enemy have dropped the pretence of the shield wall. They mingle with my warriors, weapons drawn, all eyes on me.

'To me,' I bellow, but my warriors don't sense the danger.

I'm going to have to defeat the enemy warriors myself and show the fools how it's done. If I can. I take a calming breath and glance once more at the view I'd been enjoying only moments ago. If it's the last thing I see, I want to savour it. Although I'm sure I can better them. I'm Olaf Gothfrithson, great-grandson of Ivarr the Boneless. I won't meet my death here.

I heft my shield and seax so that I'm protected. A bellow of fury leaves my mouth as I dance into their attack. I surprise the first warrior with my keenness to engage. I land three quick blows on his shield. But it doesn't disintegrate at my attack. It does slow the warrior down for a fraction of a moment. I use it to watch one of the others rush behind me.

Spit flees from the first warrior's open mouth. I slam my elbow into his teeth when he steps closer to me, his seax to hand. His teeth fracture, and he rears back in shock, his weapon arm dropping with the movement, mouth filled with blood.

I turn then and face the bastard at my back. He swings his axe from side to side. I wonder how quickly he can make a tree trunk into logs for the fire. I imagine he's probably the quickest in his settlement at the task with the size of his arms. He leers at me.

'Who are you?' I shout, but he doesn't answer. Instead, he hastens towards me with his war axe above his head. I sidestep the movement, causing him to overbalance when he strikes at me. I lash out with my foot to kick him out of the way. He stumbles and falls, but I don't have the time to finish him off because the third warrior is before me.

He grunts on realising the other two men have accomplished little. My confidence returns. They thought it would take three of them to kill me, but I'm winning. I am, after all, worthy of my ancestor.

Not that I have time to enjoy it. My enemy attacks me with his sword, the blade already shimmering with the vivid red of blood. It's a massive thing, far longer than usual. Its reach means I can't get close enough to attack without the risk of being injured.

The man's stately in his movements. It's obvious he means to kill me. I just wish I knew who he was, but the enemy are strangely quiet in their attack. None shouts one to another. Is it Constantin of the Scots? Has he finally tired of me? Is it Edmund of the English sending mercenaries to cut me down when I'm far from Jorvik? Is it Anlaf Sihtricson, my cousin, unhappy with being given Dublin to rule when he really wants Jorvik? Is it any other that I've wronged in my life? Perhaps these are Danish men, come to avenge the loss of their prince, Ivarr, at Brunanburh?

I scamper aside from his reach, but my focus is so intently on the third man I don't even realise one of the other warriors has regained his feet. The first indication is the burn of metal that scours my back.

I gasp in pain and shock, the warrior facing me, grinning with delight.

'I know who you are,' he shouts, the accent impossible to determine over the roar of his rage. 'My lord, Olaf. You killed my family, and now I take your life in payment.'

The man behind me yanks on his sword. It grates over my bones as I scream in agony. I'd rather have faced my death in any way other than this. To die with a blow to the back isn't the warrior's way.

Blood pours down my back, drenching my trews, as I stumble to my knees, clasping my blade tightly.

'I killed a hundred men's families,' I roar, for his words mean nothing to me. I don't recognise him. I don't see anything about him that lets me know who has killed me. He wears no symbol on his clothing or shield. I don't remember killing this man's family.

He grins. Another blow strikes me. My head's forced towards the left, where I see my warriors have all succumbed to their wounds. I'm the last one left alive, and that won't be for much longer. I feel the blade through my skin, inside my body, sawing through my organs. I'm the king of the Norse. I can't die here, in such ignominy, but that's what's going to happen. My arrogance has killed me. It almost killed me at Brunanburh, but at least such a death would have found my name written into the English king's scop song. But this death? This death will not even be written about. None will find my bones.

I think of my wife, Constantin's daughter, and of the child she carries in her belly. It's taken a great deal of ploughing to get it there, mostly enjoyable, but now I'll never know if the boy lives, or if she survives the birth. My sons won't rule Dublin and Jorvik after me. Anlaf Sihtricson will claim Dublin in my stead, and Jorvik. Will he allow one of my brothers to be his underking? Will he kill my son, a much easier way to remove rival claimants? Will he triumph against King Edmund of the English where I've failed?

As pain surges through my body, I tighten my grip on my seax, even as my shield falls lifelessly to the ground.

I think of all I've achieved and all I hoped to accomplish.

I once cursed my father for his failings. Tears sting my eyes as I realise I'm no better.

I've failed Camman.

I've failed my unborn son.

I've failed my living brothers.

I hope Anlaf Sihtricson enjoys being king of the Norse, because I know one thing: King Edmund will hurry to retract the terms of the peace accord. For as long as I lived. It's not been long, not at all.

33

SUMMER 941, ST ANDREWS, THE KINGDOM OF THE SCOTS

Constantin, king of the Scots

I sit within the vast hall at St Andrews, for once pleased to be away from the silence of my church. My son by marriage, Olaf, sits proudly in Jorvik and his ransacking of the English king's lands has left Edmund of the English as a defenceless lamb with no one to turn to for aid.

I thought Edmund might demand a new alliance with me but he didn't. It's not that I mean Edmund ill will or even want his land, not any more. Far from it. I simply don't want his gaze turning towards the land of the Scots ever again. He's had his fill of the blood of my warriors and my family. He killed my grandson. And Cellach died at Brunanburh.

Around me, the men and women of my court feast, laughing and talking. I'm almost tempted to join in and call one of the women to my side, but I don't. Such wants and needs are no longer mine.

I sit back in my chair and simply enjoy the moment. I'm an old, old man but tonight the young people infect my nagging bones and drive the aches and pains from my head. Well, either they do, or the vast quantity of mead I've consumed is responsible. I don't much mind which.

A rare smile covers my hoary, bearded face and I wish I were fifty winters younger and able to mount anything I wanted to, beast or woman, without thinking of my knees, my back or my bladder.

It's not a pleasant thing to grow old and live so long. Perhaps it would have been better to have died at Brunanburh. But then I'd not have lived to see Olaf Gothfrithson achieve so much.

My daughter keeps me company tonight, her belly rounded and full, a gentle smile on her face as she absent-mindedly runs her hand over her prominent bump. The babe will be along shortly, and I'll be a grandfather once more. This child will have a claim to rule Jorvik and Dublin, which amuses me. No doubt, its father thinks it'll allow it to claim the kingdom of the Scots as well, but that'll never happen. I know my daughter escaped Jorvik because of discord with Anlaf's first wife. I wish I'd realised the woman still lived before I agreed to the union between the two of them, but still, at least she's here, with me, and this child will be born a Scot.

I'll have the child baptised in my church and named appropriately before it even meets its father. Olaf might not approve, but Wulfstan, his archbishop of York, will, and that will make the child a suitable heir for Jorvik when the time's right. I hope Olaf reigns as long as I do and that he bedevils Edmund of the English for many long summers and winters to come.

Alpin also accompanies me. His presence unwelcome and welcome, all at the same time. I consider if we'll ever reconcile. Perhaps I should just be pleased he's not demanded a return to

England, and that his support of Edmund has grown so quiet he never voices it any more.

The night's long and joyful, the fire at the centre of the room spitting out wave after wave of superheated air, enough even for my old bones to feel too warm. Then, just as I'm nodding in my chair, I'm an old man and allowed to sleep in my hall, a blast of chill air touches the room, guttering the fire and sending it spinning wildly out of control.

Not that the cool air isn't welcome for it is, serving to calm tempers and passions in equal measure.

I don't recognise the man who steps into the room, even though he wears only light summer clothing and a cloak. My eyes are weak. I only see well at night when candles are lit or when I venture outside. My eyes have been overstrained, just like the monks I see peering intently at their scripts as they copy them on to fresh vellums.

At my side, my daughter gives a gasp of fright. My drink-sodden eyes turn to meet her wild-looking ones. Her hand remains on her belly as she half stands. I'm almost calling for the woman who'll escort her through her birth when I realise her gaze is fixed on the man entering the hall, not on her well-being at all.

My good mood evaporates, and instantly I'm alert.

What's the bloody idiot done now?

'My lord king, my lady, my lord,' the man says, dropping to his knee before me.

It's my daughter who finds her voice first and who knows the warrior's name. 'What is it, Eric?' she asks, fear lacing those few words.

'My lord,' Eric says, looking at me with some desperation, and I appreciate he brings the worst possible news.

'My dear,' I say, turning towards my daughter, understanding in my voice, but she already knows and is finding her seat, gesturing

Eric to continue, while she tries to stay upright, to hear the worst that she could.

'My lord king, my lady, my lord, I carry grave news of the murder of Olaf Gothfrithson, king of Dublin, Jorvik and Lincoln, while out raiding. His body was recovered, and it was,' and here he swallows thickly, 'clear that he was very definitely murdered.'

My daughter pants in shock and dismay, a cry of grief as she covers her face with her hand, the other hand firmly clamped to the small life she carries inside her. The heir to her now-dead husband. It's taken them too long to conceive this small life, and now, the father will never know it. It's a pity.

'Who bloody murdered him?' I demand, but Eric shakes his head, his hands to either side of his body as he shrugs his shoulders.

'We don't know, my lord. His body was found in the far northern land of Northumbria.'

Now's not the time to be debating something as trivial as this and I grit my teeth in annoyance that Olaf was so obviously raiding on my borders. The damn cock.

'But who do you suspect?' I persist. I doubt he lacks suspicions.

'The people of Bamburgh, perhaps, although it's not certain, with the aid of the English king, or perhaps Ealdwulf, the last lord of Bamburgh's son,' he offers without hesitation. I thought Ealdwulf a worthless fool when his father died. I didn't support him, and I regretted that. He made a fool of himself at Brunanburh.

'Why?' I ask, but once more Eric shrugs his shoulders.

My daughter glowers at me.

'My apologies, my dear,' I belatedly say. 'My sorrow on your loss. He was an excellent king and a good husband.' I hope my alignment of priorities doesn't antagonise her too much. She is, after all, very pregnant, and I've already been the victim of one of her evil tempers this day. Carrying a child isn't becoming on her.

She nods without speaking. Her expression softens at my description of her husband. Ildulb has belatedly realised that all is not well. He stumbles to the table I sit before.

'Father?' he demands.

'Eric brings grave news of Olaf Gothfrithson's death,' I announce without preamble. My daughter sobs once before containing her emotions. It wasn't a marriage of love but one of convenience, but she must have learned to care for him. I'm pleased that the union didn't make her unhappy, even after the failure at Brunanburh, and her captivity. She still won't speak about that. She won't let me seek vengeance against Haraldr Sihtricson either.

Ildulb's mouth moves without speaking. Abruptly, he chuckles. I stare at him in shock, his sister glaring at him. 'The bloody idiot,' he says, tears pouring from his eyes as he laughs.

I fear some strange affliction has taken my son because it's clear he's grieving even while he laughs.

'My apologies,' he gulps, holding his mouth together so that his hysterical laughter can't escape. 'Sorry, sister, I just, I can't believe the damn bloody idiot is dead.'

He slumps to his knees before me, his body wracked with sobs. I pity him. Ildulb thought he'd found a man who shared his viewpoints and desire for action against the English. He's suddenly been robbed of one of the few men who treated him as more than the son of a king who would have no power once I'm dead.

If I could, I'd reach out and touch my hand to his head, but it's my daughter who needs me now.

'Edmund will show his stones now,' Alpin offers, a rare smile on his face, undoing all the good will he's cultivated since Edmund's defeat. I wince to hear his delight. And it's too much for my daughter. I motion for her women to come forward and escort her away from the feast and into the privacy of her rooms.

She's as white as snow at Alpin's words. She screams with rage and reaches for his eating knife, stabbing him before I can even shout a warning. 'You bastard,' she shrieks. 'You bastard,' she repeats. Alpin falls to the floor, the blood pooling so quickly around him that I know his sister has killed him. His face is contorted in pain, and I hear his soft words of prayers, even as I sit, immobile. Stunned.

My eyes sweep to my daughter's face. She's panting, blood shimmering on the knife she still holds. I imagine that by the morning, my grandchild will have made its way into the world, kicking and screaming and demanding justice for its father. But her brother will be dead. I can hardly comprehend what's just happened.

Eric watches with miserable eyes and a look of fear on his face as Mael Muire is bundled away by her women, and some of my hastily summoned guards. Ildulb watches his brother dispassionately as he stills in death.

I take a deep breath, offer a soft prayer for my dead son. And then another one. I've struggled to come to terms with the murder of my grandson in Cait and the loss of Cellach on the battlefield of Brunanburh. How am I to reconcile with what's just happened here? I knew Alpin's return would cause problems. I knew the death of Athelstan and the defeat of Edmund made his existence precarious. But his own damn sister? I never imagined such as this. But I am the king here. While servants rush to our aid, water to mop the blood away, a splatter of it resting on my cheek, almost a tear, I allow my eyes to rest on Alpin. His face is slack now. His pain and sorrow for Athelstan's death is gone.

As much as this troubles me, perhaps it was always the only solution for poor Alpin. Damn Athelstan. And damn Edmund. It would have been better had Alpin died in England at their hands.

'My thanks for bringing us this sad news,' I offer through tight lips. I want to weep. I want to pray. I want this to never have happened.

Eric nods solemnly, trying not to watch as Alpin's lifeless form is carried away while silence fills my hall. The joy of the evening is gone.

'You'll be rewarded with a fine horse and coins.' I promise, even though the evidence shows the exact opposite, and my voice sounds strangled. 'Is Anlaf Sihtricson now king?' I seek normality from the chaos of moments ago.

Eric nods as I hand him my own drinking horn and gesture for him to drink deeply. It might be the end of summer, but it's turning cool in the evenings; a sign that winter will be coming soon.

'Yes, my lord king,' Eric replies, eyes tracking the progress of Alpin's body.

'And do you serve him?' I ask, wondering why the task has fallen to him, and determined to be distracted from all that's happened here. I wipe the blood from my cheek, watching it on my old-lined hands. My son is dead. I can't truly comprehend it.

'I will now, my lord king, but before I was Olaf Gothfrithson's man.'

'When did he die?' I ask, suddenly remembering that I don't know. All questions of how Olaf died have been driven from my mind.

'I didn't want to disturb your daughter,' Eric explains, 'but it was some time ago. The body was in a very bad way, or rather what little of it remained. It had been savaged by the wild beasts of Northumbria.'

I stare sharply at him then, recalled to the problems of Olaf's death. 'You've not seen his full body?'

'No, my lord, but believe me, enough blood has drenched the ground to make his death an absolute. He was cut from behind, that much can be seen from what little survived.'

I swallow around my bitter thoughts. Olaf is dead. And so is my son. The hope that England will falter has been taken from me, just as my son has been. I curl my fists in anger.

The first time my hall has rung with the cheer of a feast since the failure of Brunanburh, and this is what happens. Tomorrow I'll be back on my knees, praying for the dead members of my family, and Alpin must now be included in that number. I might remain there forever.

I hear the scream of a woman over the silence of the hall.

Ah, as I thought. News of two deaths and then a birth all in one night. And all, somehow, the fault of the English king.

PART III

PROTECTOR OF WARRIORS

'Here King Olaf [of Jorvik] passed away'

— ANGLO-SAXON CHRONICLE, E TEXT

34

SUMMER 942, THE KINGDOM OF JORVIK

Anlaf Sihtricson, king of Jorvik

Archbishop Wulfstan's shown into my presence, wringing his hands with worry. I suppress my exasperation at seeing him in such a state. He's a good man. I think. But he's not my sort of man. He irritates me with his constant sighing and general exhortations to his bloody God. I wonder what he's come to object about now.

'My lord king,' he simpers. He doesn't bow before me because, so I've been informed by my men when I complained to them, he sees himself as my equal before God and need not show me any greater respect than that which he conveys with his voice and mannerisms.

'Archbishop Wulfstan. You're well?' I intone loudly, hoping to wake the man who sleeps slumped over the table at my side. My predecessor's brother and my under-king is a man who likes his women and his mead. Blakari Gothfrithson stirs, and his head snaps back on his neck as he gazes around, instantly alert and on edge. His eyes narrow as he looks between Archbishop Wulfstan and me. Recognition washes over his face. He doesn't like Wulfstan and hides it poorly.

'As can be expected, my lord king,' Wulfstan continues, his tone honeyed although I know his ways. This could mean anything.

'What ails you then?' I demand, my tone abrupt. His games of knowledge can be tedious, serving only to remind me that he has more spies than I do, a fact of which he's inordinately proud.

'It's the English king,' he says with anticipation. I glare at him without comprehension. I think he hopes I'll already know what he's come to discuss. But I don't. What has the young fool done now? Offered me the whole of Mercia to go with Lincoln? On reflection, I'd like that. More land to call my own. I grin at the image that forms in my mind and then straighten my face.

Archbishop Wulfstan glances around then, looking to see who watches us. With his simple robes and their elaborate decoration dragging over the clean wooden floor, he comes to stand in front of me to whisper his words.

The top of his head is shaved, as it should be. He brings with him the smell of inferior fabrics and rich foods. The combination sets my teeth on edge. He might well be wealthier than me, but he masks it and always appears humble and penitent. My wariness of his great God and the demands he places on his followers grows every time I consider this inconsistency.

'The English king is rumoured to be in Tamworth, amassing his warriors. I believe they mean to take back Lincoln.'

My good humour evaporates in a moment. I jump at Blakari's harsh *ca-caw* of laughter ripping from his mouth. He thinks even less of Edmund than he does of Archbishop Wulfstan.

'He can try all he wants, but he's no King Athelstan. He'll not have my possessions back.'

Archbishop Wulfstan flashes intelligent eyes to Blakari's glazed ones. Wulfstan's disgust is evident to see. He doesn't like a man who gives in too quickly to his wants and needs, and Blakari is notorious for his desire for instant gratification. The irony is never lost on me.

'I hear that there are over two thousand men and they mean to reinforce the old burhs running through the borderlands, the ones King Edward made use of in his day. I understand Ealdorman Athelstan is behind the suggestion.'

Now I'm more alert. Those burhs or forts, or whatever men and women term them, I've been warned about them before but paid little attention to their existence. Some of them are barely more than a few struts of rotting wood in a muddy pile. But they're all in strategically good locations, even I admit that. And they're not far from Jorvik. If King Edmund is doing as Wulfstan implies, I'll need to raise my warriors and make my way south to counter the threat. And quickly.

'How long ago?' I demand, not caring that my words are harsh and without preamble. Wulfstan flinches at my less-than-kingly tone. We've had this argument before, all couched in 'my lord's and 'your grace's and now isn't the time to revisit it.

'The messenger arrived this morning, bringing news of no more than four days' age.'

Why he couldn't have just said four days ago, I'll never know. I have an inkling that the Latin words he reads and mumbles within his great church make it impossible for him to speak the plain truth if the possibility of twelve words for two exists.

'Just the one messenger?' I quiz further. I know that Wulfstan has many followers. I appreciate that he thinks himself a friend of the English king as well as of me. He's often told me that we're all God's children and, therefore, all subject to his kindly ministrations. That he's conniving seems to pass him by entirely, playing one king off against another.

'No, my lord king. Three, all one after another, and then a fourth, from the English king himself, asking me to arrange a peace treaty with you so that blood won't be shed. He wishes to be reunited with his lost lands and orphaned children.' Wulfstan speaks as though his words are unimportant, the calmness of his tone belying the threat behind them. I wonder if he's working for the English king already.

Damn the bloody man. And then I glare at Blakari. He avoids my eye. He's only just returned from assessing the southern borderlands. Why didn't he see anything or speak of this new incursion? If Edmund has an army of that size, it must have been visible when he left to return to me. Instead, Blakari returned with news that Idwal of Gwynedd sought an alliance to overwhelm the English king. I've been considering it, but no more. After all, why would I want to risk all I hold when I already possess it? But if King Edmund means for there to be war, perhaps Idwal will prove to be a worthy ally. Certainly, it would be wise to entice him to the border with the English kingdom. Better, should he lose his life in any fighting than me.

Blakari and I are uneasy allies, but I don't blame myself for that. It was his arse of a brother who got himself murdered on a raid into the far northern lands last year. It's not my fault that, as is the way of our people, it's the son of the previous king who inherits, not the brother of the current one. He'd like my place as king of Jorvik, but he'd fritter it away. He has no skills for diplomacy, only for whoring and drinking. I'm only grateful that the other brother, Gothfrith, has taken himself back to Dublin. He was a real trouble-maker. It doesn't help that Blakari and Gothfrith suspect my involvement in their brother's death. Equally, I suspect theirs. No one has claimed responsibility, which only allows the rumours to whirl.

'And you've come here now to do what?'

Wulfstan's eyes are intent as they switch between Blakari and me. He knows what uneasy allies we are.

'To do as King Edmund asked and to offer you my counsel, if you so desire it.'

I still haven't asked him to sit or offered him refreshments. I know I'm remiss in that. As much as I don't wish to discuss this with Wulfstan when he has so many more facts than I do, I call for food and drink and gesture for him to take a seat beside me at my table.

A faint smirk covers his old face at my capitulation. I doubt he'll still be smiling when our discussion is done.

'You have the messenger with you, or was it written down?'

'The messengers are with me, and the king wrote to ask me to intercede on his behalf.' Wulfstan's taking his time settling on the bench beside me, making the old timbers creak and groan under his weight. His words are distracted as his head swings from side to side, ensuring he's decently covered on the hard bench and that his robes don't show any of his wobbling flesh.

Food and wine appear before him. He reaches for a tasty piece of baked fish, his fat little fingers hovering over which morsel to choose. Now, it's my turn to look away from him.

'You have the English king's letter with you?' I've allowed a few moments to pass so that I don't have to watch him stuffing food into his rotund little face.

Wulfstan gestures to someone to come closer. One of his attendant monks steps from the shadows, in his hand a rolled script held firmly. He takes his time unrolling the parchment, which creaks and threatens to snap, before clearing his throat. All the time my fingers are itching to be busy, perhaps around the man's neck, but I hold them tightly within my other hand.

Wulfstan's a man who understands the importance of anticipation. He knows how much I detest it and that just gives him perverse pleasure to extend the moment even longer.

'Archbishop Wulfstan,' the young monk finally coughs out, his mouth working hard to form the words. I've not seen this monk before, not that it's always easy to tell the men apart in their similar clothes, but I have the feeling that Wulfstan has brought the newest member of his scriptorium to practise his skills. No doubt it'll take a long time to hear the entire message.

At my side Blakari shifts on the bench, reaching around me for some of the fresh wine that's been brought for the archbishop. He swallows loudly and repeatedly before the monk continues.

'King Edmund of the English greets the Archbishop Wulfstan with friendship and requests his assistance in interceding with Anlaf, king of York, regarding the lands between Lincoln and the English kingdom.'

I hide my annoyance at the flamboyant words. It wouldn't do to be angry before I've even heard what Edmund intends. I also note that he says 'king of York', not pretender to the throne or anything so incendiary. Perhaps he's learning diplomacy at last. Although, he does say York and not Jorvik. The English are so arrogant.

'The lands were ceded by a treaty organised by Archbishop Wulfstan and Archbishop Wulfheard, with the previous king, Olaf Gothfrithson, latterly of Dublin and York. Following his death, the treaty is no longer valid.'

Blakari barks in outrage at my side. I feel my temper begin to fray. But I gesture for the man to continue his stumbling way through the letter.

'As such, I request a meeting at a location convenient to both parties and under the auspices of the archbishops of York and

Canterbury, to reconsider the treaty. We hope that Anlaf Sihtricson will agree to our sincere request, as he is like a brother to us, and that you will convey our sincerity in the matter. In the name of Almighty God, King Edmund, adorned and elevated with no small dignity, lord and protector of the English people, the Britons, the pagans and the Christians.'

The monk stops speaking then, and I glance at Archbishop Wulfstan in surprise.

'Is that it?'

'Yes,' he speaks around the food still crammed into his mouth. You'd think he'd not eaten for forty days, as he often discourses on at length. I imagine he ate just before he left his hall and is now just filling in any tiny gaps that might still exist. The man should have a barrel for a stomach.

'There's no mention of war.'

'No, not in his letter to me, but the messengers have seen the English men, and they're amassing in high numbers, the fyrd and the king's warriors and those of his ealdormen.'

'So he asks you to arrange a peace conference while at the same time showing his forces?'

'Yes, he does. A good tactic and one that I think he might have learnt from you and Olaf Gothfrithson.'

I ignore that little jibe. My people prefer war to talk, as do I. Better to act and rue the consequences later if you're still alive!

'We should ready the men,' Blakari announces at my side. I agree with him. I don't want to talk about the land Edmund claims. I want to reinforce the right to the settlements that Olaf has already staked as belonging to Jorvik.

'Yes, we should. Go and spread the word. We'll ride out the day after tomorrow.'

Blakari, his aching head gone in a moment, stands abruptly and slips from the hall. He's a man of action when he wants to be. I ignore his teetering steps. He'll sober up and lead the men, or he won't, and then he'll fall from his horse and die, and I'll be without his nagging presence. I can't see how I can lose here. I still suspect him. Did he know of the English king's designs on the old forts? Is he playing games with me? I'll be more wary of him from now on.

'And you, Archbishop Wulfstan. Send word that it's acceptable for us to meet at Lincoln in a month's time.'

Wulfstan nods to show he understands his command and gives nothing away about how he feels at my response. He thrusts his hand out to grab the last piece of baked bread and pops it into his mouth before standing and bowing his head, just the smallest fraction, in deference.

'I'll do as you say immediately. I'll be accompanying you.'

Of course he will. The snake in the long grass is always vigilant and ready to exploit any little weakness he finds. I must remember to have one of my trusted men watch his every move. It's better to be pre-warned when Archbishop Wulfstan gets an idea into his head.

He leaves me, and I watch him with angry eyes.

Peace. There's never enough of it to enjoy my hold on Jorvik. But this is my birthright, and I'll defend it against any who thinks they have a greater claim.

The English won Jorvik because of my father's untimely death. I have no intention of allowing them to take it back, and they can't have Lincoln either.

35

942, TAMWORTH, THE KINGDOM OF THE ENGLISH

Edmund, king of the English

Messengers rush to and fro as I sit within the rebuilt hall at Tamworth, its rafters stained black with smoke. They were one of the only parts of the original burh that remained after the attack by the Heathen Army all those years ago and have been hoisted back into position, a testament to the might of the Mercians, and now the English.

The bloody Norse, with their eyes on jewels and silver or lands that belong to another. The story always stays the same, and yet I remain surprised by it. Just as I continue to be astounded by the speed of the reversal of my half-brother's victory at Brunanburh. I thought it would last forever and there have been many times that I've blamed myself, sunk low on my failures, and questioned whether I'm the man to be the king of the English. But I know better now.

The Norse are bloodthirsty, lethal warriors, happy to take advantage of any small display of weakness.

Show frailty, and they'll piss all over you and steal your fur cloak at the same time, and your silver jewellery, your shield, sword, and, if they can, your horse and your hound.

I don't hate them all, but right now, my anger serves me better than my understanding of them.

I'm the king of the English, and I intend to remain the king of the English and demand back my poor brethren who've been forced to live under a Norse yoke for these last two summers.

Damn the archbishops with their honeyed words and exhortations to God that made me accept a peace accord. I've not enjoyed pretending to tolerate a peaceful resolution to this matter of the broken accord either. But my new archbishop, Oda, was determined on it. He's been a man of war in the past, fighting at Brunanburh. But in this he thinks peace is the answer. As such, a message has been sent to Archbishop Wulfstan, with the suggestion of meeting peacefully. I hope Anlaf Sihtricson refuses. Then we can have war, no matter Archbishop Oda's reservations. I'm busy preparing for it.

And damn bloody Olaf Gothfrithson. His death has merely seen him replaced by another, who sits at York as the king of the Norse. These Norse warriors are interchangeable. They all have the same ambitions.

Such anger will ensure I regain what was taken from me. I'll recover my half-brother's legacy, and this time I'll hold it against the ravages of any other who tries their luck against me.

Ealdorman Athelstan and the other ealdormen are my constant companions. The English witan has effectively moved north to stand as a bastion against the depredations of this new menace from York and Dublin for the summer months. Anlaf Sihtricson is the son of my half-sister's husband, Sihtric. I didn't know him. I was too young when they wed, but I've heard her speak of him and to all intents and purposes he was a bastard and his son is the same.

One skirmish too many amongst the northerners and Olaf's life was snuffed out. He's gone for good now. That should please me, but of course, there's always another to step into a dead Norse king's boots.

'My lord King Edmund,' Ealdorman Athelstan murmurs at my side.

I meet his gaze. I've been avoiding his eyes for much of the morning because I don't want to hear what he has to say. I hunger for triumph against Anlaf and the Norse. I've called my warriors together, my ealdormen and their household warriors, even the fyrd of Mercia is preparing for war.

'King Edmund, what do you think? Should we reinforce the burhs, and build a new one in the gap between Kexburh and Conisburh? Then we'd have a strong point to muster or retreat to, or, if God smiles on our enterprise, from which to push forward into the kingdom of York.'

His idea is good. To repair and make habitable the burhs and forts along the old border of the Five Boroughs and the lands of the Norse kings of York. He's been speaking of it since the settlement agreed at Repton with Olaf Gothfrithson. But I'm impatient. Understanding flashes across Ealdorman Athelstan's face. He knows me too well. He appreciates that I want to push on into the kingdom of York, and take back Lincoln, the thought of delaying while building work takes place frustrates me. But Ealdorman Athelstan realises that to hold what we gain during our endeavours northwards, we need forts along the border. They'll help the local population if Anlaf retaliates. Yet the peace accord said the agreement would only last as long as Olaf lived, and he's dead. I should just retake what was lost without the need to refurbish the broken-down burhs.

'Yes, yes. Give my assent for the work to be done, but have it done quickly.' I eventually capitulate. I dream of the future where Olaf Gothfrithson's depravations within England are long forgotten about. But there's a difference between dreaming and guaranteeing it. I must ensure the task, once completed, will never need to be done again.

Ealdorman Athelstan flashes a brief smile at my words. 'The men and women say that the work can be done in a matter of weeks. In most places, some remnants of a previous burh can be reinforced and new structures attached. Only in one location must the new burh be constructed from beginning to end and even then, there are available vantage points to build upon. The work will be completed quickly, and then York will be returned to us. And if not York just yet, then certainly Lincoln.'

Ealdorman Athelstan dashes from my side almost before he's finished speaking. I watch him with amusement. He's had his own messengers on hand for the last two days, ready to flee to those holding firm at the sites that have been identified. They're as impatient as he is to be busy with their work. In fact, I imagine most of them have already begun work without my express orders. Ealdorman Athelstan will have given them assurances that my agreement would be forthcoming for the building work at Kexburh, Conisburh and Mexburh. Ealdorman Athelstan knows me too well.

Ealdorman Æthelwald stands with me, a faint smirk on his face. Æthelwald now governs the lands of the people of Kent on my behalf. Eadric is ealdorman of the southern Mercian lands. We were once warriors together, fighting side by side at Cait and Brunanburh, but now we're all burdened with more responsibilities. I consider how much different it would have been had King Athelstan lived for longer.

'My lord king,' Ealdorman Ealhhelm calls, striding into the hall with purposefulness about him. He's been tasked with finding out all he can about Anlaf's movements from York.

'Ealhhelm, you have news?' I'm instantly curious. I want to know that Anlaf fears me. After all, we're almost relatives; his father married to my sister. It's a fine way he's thought to repay our familial links.

'Yes, my lord king, I do. He's mustering to move south. His men are amassing.'

'Good,' I say to the assembled room. My warriors are keen and ready to fight. The defeats of two winters ago have left a wound on all of us. 'Anlaf comes to meet us with his warriors. We'll have our people and our land back.'

There's a rousing cheer from those assembled, busy at their work and yet with an ear to their king, and I feel a swirl of confidence. I welcome the coming clash as much as they do. I admit, it helps to know that while we fight Anlaf, Ealdorman Athelstan's burhs will rise like bastions over the landscape of northern England. With them, we'll drive Anlaf further and further north, and then, without the aid of King Constantin of the Scots, who's not kin to Anlaf, he'll have no choice but to leave Britain's shores for Dublin.

The prospect of success emboldens me.

I will prevail.

36

942, ST ANDREWS, THE KINGDOM OF THE SCOTS

Constantin, king of the Scots

I seek the solace of my church, only to find my prayers interrupted by men in byrnies, carrying blades at their waists. I hold my frustration in check. It never pays to snap when they determine to prevent my prayers.

Ildulb steps forward. Of late he's become the spokesman for this small group of men who cling ever tighter to my kingship. How little they know! I don't want the kingship most of the time. But I'll not yet hand it over to my successor, no matter how much Mael Coluim desires it. I might not crave it, but he's not to have it while I still breathe. Instead, I'm burdened with this group of men who stick to my fragile rule as though it'll last another century or more.

'There's news, my lord king,' Ildulb says formally. He knows how little I like to be disturbed from my communications with my Lord God. I'm aware of how my resort to prayer annoys him. He thinks I should spend my time governing my realm, not seeing to my soul for when I'm no longer here. I'm wary of his formal approach.

'What is it?' I ask with some asperity. It'll be about one of two things, either Anlaf Sihtricson in York and Dublin, or Mael Coluim, my successor. I don't much wish to hear about either of them.

'It's Edmund of the English. He's marched north against Anlaf Sihtricson.'

Ah, I was half wrong. The news is only partially concerning Anlaf and more about Edmund.

'And where does he march to?'

'The disputed border with Anlaf, the one agreed only two years ago with Olaf, which gave him the command of Lincoln and Jorvik.'

Ah, Olaf Gothfrithson. My son by marriage and the man who led me to such a monumental defeat at Brunanburh. Even now, a year or more after his death, I feel belligerent towards him. Did I love him? Admire him? Or was I just a bloody fool who allowed myself to be led around by the noose and, in doing so, destroyed my peace of mind? My daughter still grieves for him, while his small son thrives. But other than that, I'm perturbed by the memory of him and my alliance with the Norse. I don't like to recall the night I heard of his death. Even now, I pray for Alpin. My daughter has no remorse for murdering him. I'm still far from reconciled to it, and so I mourn him, as I should, allowing myself to forget the means of his death.

'It's no concern of ours then? It's about the English lands. It'll have no impact upon us here.'

Ildulb bows respectfully at my words as though he expected them. 'With respect, my lord king. With Idwal of Gwynedd also in rebellion, I think we should lend our support to this endeavour.

Finish the English king. He's involved himself in our affairs one too many times.'

Ildulb hides his rage towards the English behind a mask of civility that I expect my loyal adherents to wear.

'Mael Coluim's encouraging men to go,' Ildulb finishes defiantly. I think him irresponsible for allowing his aggravation to temper his words. No one needs to hear again how he feels about Mael Coluim.

'Then they don't go in my name, only in his. They don't act for our kingdom and our people, only for themselves. Or Mael Coluim, if you wish to be pedantic.'

A huff of annoyance comes from Ildulb. I raise a cautioning eyebrow. This isn't good statecraft.

This might be my church, peopled by my monks and priests, but there are always men who'll run to Mael Coluim with tales of anything that might concern him. They earn his high regard, and sometimes because I can, I feed a little sliver of misinformation just to check who's no longer loyal to me.

It's interesting. It changes monthly. Mael Coluim doesn't always inspire the loyalty that he should.

'If you wish to go, then go. But you'll go as a solitary military leader, and negotiate with Anlaf Sihtricson for your share of the spoils.'

Ildulb wasn't expecting my response. It's clear he's very tempted by the idea.

When he went south with Olaf two years ago, he took my warriors with him and my blessing. This time will be different. Olaf accomplished much for himself, but little for Ildulb and my kingdom.

Ildulb looks behind him, hoping to catch the eye of the other men who've come to demand my involvement in the affairs between Jorvik and the English.

He nods as though it's the first time he's considered the possibility of making a personal journey south. I don't think it is.

Ildulb has few weaknesses, and few blind spots, but Edmund is, and always will be, one of them. At least his rage has grown old and cold, not hot and fiery. He wants his revenge, but it isn't his only concern these days.

'My thanks, my lord king.' He bows, eyes flashing in the light from the candles arrayed around the church. 'I'll think about it and inform you of my decision.'

I nod in acceptance and return to my prayers, listening to his departing footsteps.

He'll go, I know he will. He doesn't know he will yet, but he will. The possibility of killing Edmund, fantasy though it might be, looms too much in his thoughts. He was denied the opportunity two winters ago. I imagine he will be once more, but maybe it'll be good to have eyes on what happens between Anlaf and Edmund. Perhaps, if I'm lucky, they'll kill one another, and I'll rule all of their kingdoms as well as that of the Scots. I don't deny the thought is an enticing one. And it would certainly aggravate Mael Coluim if, instead of being the king of the Scots, I'm the king of the Scots, Jorvik and the English. Then he'll have to stop voicing his complaints, which he thinks I don't hear, of how I'm to blame for the failure at Brunanburh.

37

942, THE NORTHERN KINGDOM OF THE ENGLISH

Athelstan the ealdorman

The plans for the refortification of the burhs along the border with Anlaf's kingdom have been long in the planning. Edmund's pitied the people living under the rule of Anlaf and, having seen Anlaf's idea of government first-hand, I'm inclined to agree with Edmund.

Olaf Gothfrithson's death the year before, the news delayed to the English witan by the onset of one of the harshest winters I recall, has made the matter urgent. Now's the time to move against Anlaf Sihtricson. Now's the time to have the disrespectful peace accord redrawn. The settlement agreed at Repton wasn't Edmund's finest moment, even if it was necessary.

Edmund's reputation grows daily. He's a father, husband and son all would be proud to call their king and their friend. He might have been forced to fall back on the use of words in 940 as offered by Archbishops Wulfheard and Wulfstan, but now he's ready to employ sword, shield and seax. He's ready to lead his men and make up for his lack of two winters before. Now that he's a father, he must fight for the future of his son as well as to reclaim his half-brother's lost legacy.

I know how much that failure galled him. He hadn't just failed himself, but the people who looked to him and pledged him their allegiance. Edmund knows that Olaf and Anlaf aren't the harshest of rulers, but they are 'other'. The men and women of York counted themselves as English. Athelstan had ruled them for over ten summers before Olaf Gothfrithson landed with his ship army and laid waste the area with the support of Anlaf and Ildulb.

The people of Lincoln might share ancestry with Olaf and Anlaf, but they were content with their English king. They've sent messengers to him throughout Olaf and Anlaf's tenure, keeping him informed of any changes made by the two men and crowing with delight when Olaf Gothfrithson met his death in the wilds of the north. Even now, the truth of Olaf's death in unknown. I consider if it will ever be discovered.

And I? Well, I'm the ealdorman of East Anglia. Our border abuts the land held by the Norse, and my people want to be reunified with their kin and no longer forced to pay taxes to York in order to continue their trade. The temporary border is just that, temporary, provided we bring it down now. The border, making use of the River Trent, isn't an impenetrable stone wall for us to breach. It's not the ancient wall that runs from one side of the land to the other, above York but below Bamburgh. There's to be no permanent remembrance of this temporary hold. Provided Edmund now destroys Anlaf Sihtricson.

As King Athelstan had to overwhelm his half-brother, Edwin, all those years ago, Edmund now needs to do the same to a man who could have called him his nephew by marriage but chose not to do so.

There's no reason why Edmund won't succeed. He has his plan, and he'll abide by it, no matter how Anlaf tries to force him from it. There'll be a battle, perhaps more than one, and people will die, but in the end, Anlaf will be left with nothing. At the very worst, he'll be pushed back to his stronghold in York, and I almost think him welcome to it.

I smirk at the thought. I'm a man of God, most assuredly, but my enemies must be eradicated for England to become whole again. I accept that. Perhaps too willingly, but that's no problem for my conscience.

The Mercians will garrison the forts. They fight for what they've lost, and are anxious to do so.

I ride quickly through the slumbering countryside. People have drawn back from the River Trent boundary that separates the English from those ruled by Anlaf. They know there's little point in planting these disputed lands, not until they're safely back in Edmund's hand. It's too likely that the Norse will make a dash across the river and take their wealth.

Hedgerows lie, not in ruins, it's not been long enough for the work of hundreds of years to fall into tatters, but they're in need of maintenance. The wicker fences require rethreading; the wooded areas need some care before mature trees overpower the smaller saplings.

These lands are sleeping, waiting for me to reclaim them for my king.

The birds make merry in the full hedgerows with their gluttonous harvest of berries and fruits. It's early in the season, but the neglect means that they carry a far heavier load than normal. If nothing else, when this battle is won, there'll be fat pheasants, blackbirds and crows to help themselves to the farmer's resown crops.

My musings amuse me. Here I am riding to war, and all I can think of is the wildlife and the farmers. But then, that's whom I protect. The fragile land that feeds us all has failed in the past. Terrible droughts and famines have stolen the lives of the weakest. Bad enough to die in battle, ten times worse to die of an aching emptiness in the stomach with nothing to sate it.

I might have men who carry out my instructions on my behalf, but I tend the land as well. I must still feed my family, learn when to till and when to leave fallow. I must pray to my God for a good harvest, for summer storms and winter rains to keep the soil well drained and filled with goodness to allow the plants to grow. I have to recognise which sheep will give good lambs and which cows can be milked. I must understand when to have the correct charms spoken over my fields and animals.

Admittedly, I'm also required to comprehend which weapon will kill my opponent in battle, how to swing my axe, sword and shield, and how to repair them should they be damaged in the thick of a fight.

I'm a man with as many roles in life as my king. He's obligated to govern his people, watch the borders, and ensure fair trade, good justice, and that the word of God is spread. But at the same time, it's necessary for him to hold firm against any coming strife and any shortfall in the harvest. He's obliged to have the wherewithal to raise funds to outfit his warriors, and he must gain their respect, for who will fight for a man they don't revere?

The king and his ealdormen are required to be builders, warriors, fathers, husbands and sons. We must be farmers. It's our requisite to be fair, righteous, able to enforce our laws, and have the strength to carry out the punishment. We're compelled to do all this and yet rule with equanimity. It's imperative we inspire men to die on our behalf, to listen when we speak and to want the same things that we do.

In short, we must do everything and nothing. We're no more important than the man who simply farms and plays his part in the fyrd, the wife who minds her house, creates thread from sheep wool, stitches clothes, grinds grains for flour and raises her children, the monk who prays for everyone's soul, the children learning to swing their swords.

At my side, Æthelwald is conscious of my deep thoughts. It's obvious from his silence that he allows me to think. I imagine he believes I'm devising strategies and that I need to concentrate. I little believe he realises where my musings actually lie.

Æthelwald is a warrior of renown and close to the king. But his views on England and her future are simpler than mine. I almost envy him. I wish I wasn't cursed with the ability to see so many different points of view, to understand each and everyone's motivation even when it goes against everything I want to accomplish. I'm afflicted with magnanimity, and with my genuine belief in the sanctity of all life.

'Will you kill him?' Æthelwald finally breaks the silence. I grimace at the blunt question. I think he wants to kill Anlaf himself.

'If the opportunity presents itself.'

'It bloody better,' Æthelwald growls with annoyance. The thought of doing all this, moving all these men and it all being for nothing, is something he can't truly comprehend. He still scratches his head with wonder and tries to work out how so much of England was lost so quickly when Olaf Gothfrithson invaded.

'What of you?' I query.

Æthelwald grins, pondering his perceived involvement in the coming altercation. 'I'd prefer Blakari myself, but any piece of Viking scum will do for me.'

I shake my head at his battle joy. I've no problem with fighting, killing, decapitating my foe, but I don't dream of it. Not like they do.

'Ah, brother. You need to think less and do more,' Æthelwald comments with a hint of anger, because we've had this argument before. I don't rise to the intended slight. We all think we're the better men. Only time will prove one of us correct in our interpretation of how men should live. I follow our father's approach to life; my brother follows our grandfather's. Both men could hold their own at the king's witan and on the battlefield. I'm proud to be their descendant.

'And you need to think more and do less,' I reply promptly, no rancour in my voice, just a statement of fact.

Æthelwald raises his eyebrows at me and urges his horse to ride a little faster so that he's not beside me.

His very action is an indication that he might agree with me, but there's no way he'll put a voice to that. I grin as I watch his broad back sway before me.

We're brothers, and we act as one. In all things, even if in private, we sometimes disagree.

Still, I hope to kill Anlaf. That'll annoy my brothers, and I believe it's about time I took the life of one of England's enemies.

38

SUMMER 942, THE ENGLISH / WELSH BORDER

Hywel, king of the South Welsh

I've not seen Edmund since shortly after his accession. Times have been testing and too busy, but we're to meet today at the borderlands as prearranged by Wihtred. We've relied on Wihtred for the last two summers. He's kept us reliably informed of what the other does and when they do it. And if he's added their own insights as well, then that's benefited both of us.

The death of Olaf Gothfrithson last summer has shifted everything once more. The players of our game have changed and my cousin, Idwal of Gwynedd, hopes to gain.

I sigh deeply as I look out over the fertile farmland before me. The English lands are welcome and enticing. Yet, I turn with more joy to the wooded hills and barren slopes of my homelands, dotted with the backs of white livestock, as though they're clouds. I love the majesty of our hills and the mystery of our valleys. Edmund can keep England. I want the lands of the Welsh. All of them.

I've brought my war band with me, more than three hundred men, with my sons each leading their contingent, but I don't think I'll be using them.

My cousin, Idwal of Gwynedd, has marched east to join Anlaf Sihtricson, Olaf's successor. These Norse and their similar-sounding names. It's enough to make a man forget who they are. My sons and I have journeyed here to close the gap through which Idwal might retreat, if he lives after he's beaten, and to offer my support to Edmund in person.

Edmund's faced many perils. King Edward would be proud of him, not that such information will please him. I imagine he has no recollection of his long-dead father.

King Athelstan would admire Edmund as well. He might even apologise for his untimely death that allowed an already riled Olaf Gothfrithson to sneak in the back door of York to retake Lincoln, and the English kingdom to the east of the River Trent. King Athelstan thought to win with peace, and was forced to turn to war. Edmund had war thrust upon him and was forced to accept a peace accord to prevent more of England disappearing beneath the rising swell of the Norse.

But now, with time as his ally, Edmund has a vast army arrayed along the boundary dividing the Norse-held lands from the English-held ones. That he has a force of thousands to enforce his claim ensures Anlaf Sihtricson will know Edmund isn't to be dismissed as irrelevant.

When we meet today, I'll assure Edmund of my support against Anlaf Sihtricson. I'll also make it clear that I have no love for my cousin, Idwal. I have my eye on Idwal's kingdom. I hope to hold it by the end of the year.

Owain, my oldest son, sidles his horse next to mine. He reminds me of a much younger me; only he's more respectful than I ever was and far less powerful. At his age, I had lands to rule and govern in my name. He doesn't. Not yet, but he would be capable if the need arose. If I died abruptly, here and now, he'd rule in my place, and many might not even realise they had a new king, not unless they met him in person. Then they'd know, for my son lacks my grey hair and lined face.

'Idwal has been sighted far to the north. He's crossing the border close to Chester.'

I consider that piece of information. Would I have done the same in Idwal's place? Chester is the most northerly point that he could have chosen. Does he intend to hasten to York and meet Anlaf, or is he, and here I wonder whether I've underestimated him, planning on meeting with the new king of Strathclyde, Dyfnwal? Has he, against expectations, found himself a new ally to assist him in joining with Anlaf to counter the threat of the English?

I doubt it because Idwal doesn't like to rely on others. He's a man who governs alone and through fear instead of tact. He's done things I'd never have considered. He takes responsibility for his deeds, not because he should, but because he thinks he's a great king. He wants no one else to steal his acclaim. He's known as Idwal the Bold which unfortunately doesn't refer to his lack of hair but rather his decisive actions and daring manoeuvres.

I find him a bore in my old age, but, well, the scops of his court will find some way to praise him. Being bold might be a virtue, although I think it might just be another word for impulsive and a lucky bastard.

My cousin's a fool, but I'll deal with his land when it becomes mine and then the Welsh, as the English call us derisively as though we're foreigners in our lands, will be united under my rule. Perhaps then, when my borders are secured, I can turn my gaze towards the kingdom of the English. Maybe. Not that I think I'd like to rule that vast land. Or perhaps I would.

A commotion in front of me, and the shape of King Edmund of the English and his troops start to form in the churned dust of the road. He's not late; I was merely a little earlier than I intended to be.

As his horse nears mine, I observe him with interest. How have the years being king changed him?

Immediately I see it, and I'm impressed. Edmund's adopted the noble bearing of his half-brother, and he carries it well. There's still some room for improvement, but I imagine that his victories in the coming month will give him the total assurance King Athelstan possessed. Whatever happens behind his eyes, and if he's like King Athelstan in that regard there will be much, he hides it well. He has deep blue eyes, long ragged blonde hair. I narrow my gaze and see him with a crown there. I find it's an image I'm comfortable envisaging.

He breaks into a grin on seeing me, his face instantly transformed to the young prince I used to know.

'Well met, my lord Hywel,' he shouts, sliding from his horse as I do the same. We should meet as equals on the grassy rise.

'And you, my lord Edmund. Well met.' We clasp arms. I feel his strength and his vigour. He's much younger than I am. Indeed, he's younger than my sons. 'To business,' I announce when we've embraced and commented on how well we both look. I know he lies about my vigour, but I allow it, as old men will do when greeted by such youth. We're handed elaborate drinking horns, and we offer each a toast in the centre of our swirling mass of warriors who raise their voices in acclaim at seeing us so united and friendly with one another. 'Idwal moves to the north. He intends to cross at Chester.'

'I've sent Ealdorman Athelstan north. He's desperate to prove the prowess of the new burhs and forts that guard against the Norse in the northern lands. He'll allow Idwal to travel to York and meet with Anlaf Sihtricson, as we suspect his intentions are. Or, if Idwal means to force a fight, Athelstan and his brothers will be on hand to quell his attempts.'

I remember Ealdorman Athelstan. He fought at Brunanburh. I think Edmund has made a good decision, but I don't tell him that. He's not my son to be complimented when he delegates efficiently. No, as the king of the English he instinctively needs to know that his decisions are just and correct.

'Is it your plan to follow on behind?' Edmund questions.

Edmund and I have discussed this via Wihtred, but it's good to speak in person.

'Yes. It'll either be to block his return or to take control of his kingdom. I don't expect him to live through any battle against the English. He's not a warrior, although he thinks himself one.'

'So you say, and I wish you well in your ambitions on his kingdom. You'll govern and rule it far better than he ever did.' Edmund's words are calm and reasoned and laced with iron. He and I share similar visions for our people. 'Just as you do in Brycheiniog.'

I don't miss the caution in Edmund's words. He must know I mean to build a kingdom of the Welsh. After all, that's why I must take the kingdom of Gwynedd as well.

'So you've heard nothing of King Constantin's intentions?' I redirect the conversation.

'No. Rumour is that Constantin does nothing but wear his old knees down to the bone praying for his sons and grandson.' He winces as he speak. The death of Alpin at the hands of his family has become well-known. I consider if Edmund mourns him or feels responsible for it.

Edmund glances towards the lands of the Scots as if it were possible to see Constantin praying from here.

'I hear similar tales. What of his heir?' I question.

'Mael Coluim is desperate to be king in his stead. I don't know if he can even think of anything else. And all the time Ildulb grows his own collection of followers. Whenever Constantin dies, Ildulb will be ready to move against Mael. Perhaps Constantin sees his long life as a curse. He's outlived almost everyone. My father, my brother, your father, Olaf Gothfrithson, his uncle and his father, and of course, Owain of Strathclyde. I wonder if he has any allies left at all.'

Now that Edmund has named the dead so eloquently I take a moment to think of them all. Constantin is older than us all, and yet I'm not that far behind, not any more. I'm probably nearly as old as he was at Eamont when I thought him almost in his grave. It's strange how my perspective on age has changed as I've aged. Edmund is little more than a child. Constantin's old and past his prime. Hopefully, I'm still a virile man. But we didn't come here to talk of Constantin.

'And where will you be?' I ask Edmund pointedly. This we've not discussed for fear that Wihtred might be intercepted.

'I'll be waiting close to Lincoln, not that far from the line of forts, in all honesty. I'll send a messenger and let you know if anything changes.'

'I hear so much about Lincoln.'

'Yes.' Edmund's voice has turned to stone. 'It's filled with the descendants of men and women who decimated Northumbria and Mercia before settling the land. My aunt, Lady Æthelflæd, won Lincoln, and the other four of the five boroughs, back for Mercia, King Athelstan claimed them for England, and then Olaf Gothfrithson stole Lincoln. And now, Lincoln seeks to return to the kingship of the English, as discussed at the peace accord in Repton.'

'So you intend to bring this about peacefully?'

'I do, but only after we've defeated Anlaf. We must have a

battle, and I must win it. Then I might make peace, or I might not. I might hound Anlaf's arse all the way to York and besiege him inside it.'

I laugh at the confidence in his voice. Edmund quirks an eyebrow my way. My sons look at me in shock. I don't think they expected this to be a jovial meeting.

'I wish you luck with it. Personally, I prefer to benefit with a little bit of stealth, but sometimes a point must be made. I think now is one of those times.'

Edmund's tense posture relaxes at that. I hadn't meant to offend, but I forget he's still largely untried in the art of directing battle. He has his dreams of what will happen when he meets Anlaf, and he also has to face the reality that he's not done it yet.

Anlaf. I know more about him than I know him. He's a warrior by trade, more so than his predecessor. I consider if Edmund appreciates that he'll be a harder man to beat. I think he does. I think that concerns him.

Anlaf snapped at Olaf Gothfrithson's heels, and now I hear his underking is keen to govern in his name as well. Anlaf needs to keep Blakari Gothfrithson close enough that he never has the opportunity to plot his downfall. As I understand it, there's little hope of it ever happening. Blakari drinks and talks in his sleep. He couldn't keep a secret even if his life depended on it.

No, Anlaf is quite secure in Jorvik, and Edmund must know that.

'I take it I can't tempt you to join an alliance with me?' Edmund asks into the companionable silence. His words offer no censure. He's aware I won't ally with him, not yet and not openly, but I am a friend of England, I've made that clear. I think he just says the words so that we both know they've been spoken.

'My lord Edmund, I do what I can from here. My sea borders are vast in comparison to my people and resources. I'm obliged to remain removed from the coming hostilities for fear that Dublin will dispatch her warriors to join with Anlaf. After all, he's king there as well. He is the king of the Norse.'

Edmund quirks a smile at my candid answer. There's no point lapsing into politic. My reasoning is sound and accurate. My sea border with the men of Dublin is far harder to guard than Edmund's land border, albeit an ocean divides us.

'I understand. Your failure to support England's enemy speaks volumes for your allegiance. I thank you once more. Now, we must be away, towards Lincoln. When we next speak, and may it be in less time than five years' time, I hope to be, once more, king of all the English.'

'And I hope to be the king of the British, or the Welsh as you would have us known.'

We both weigh up one another's ambitious words, but there's nothing there that the other didn't already know. That I speak my aspirations openly doesn't offend Edmund.

We part as friends with shouted words of encouragement from our warriors. We would be a deadly force if we fought together, but once Anlaf is gone, and York is again in Edmund's hands, there'll be no one to fight but Constantin of the Scots. And really, he can keep his land. It's as hard and rocky as mine, his land borders are vast, and his coastlines even longer. It's a sign of its perceived barrenness that the Norse haven't simply overrun its rivers and mountains. I hear them say it's too like the homes they've fled.

No, I only want my cousin's lands. Nothing more. For now.

39

SUMMER 942, NEAR CHESTER, THE KINGDOM OF THE ENGLISH

Idwal, king of Gwynedd

'My lord king.' An outrider rushes towards me. I turn my eyes to take in his appearance. If he rides easily on his horse, it'll be good news.

His eyes glow with excitement, and I take it to mean he's found our enemy.

'They've been sighted, my lord king, but far away from here. Nearly three days journey to where they've made their camp to wait for us or for Anlaf Sihtricson. I'm not sure.'

The news is good and bad in equal measure.

'Do they face towards us, or away from us?'

'I couldn't tell, my lord king. I saw their camp and smelt their fire but went no closer. Dafydd stayed behind to gain further information. I came back to inform you of our discovery.'

Those were my orders, but I'm frustrated to only receive half the knowledge I need. Based on this I don't know if the English expect an attack from me or if they're only waiting for Anlaf Sihtricson.

'You've done well. Did you see any other men?'

'Just a few stray outriders, scouting the area as I was.'

'But you led none back this way?' I ask sharply.

'No, my lord king. I laid low in a ditch for some of the day and waited for them to pass me. The horse was tethered amongst a herd of farm animals so it wouldn't give me away.'

I admire the man's initiative. He's done well to cover his tracks.

'Where exactly are they?'

'I don't know the names of the villages well, my lord king, but I think near to the southernmost tip of the lands the Norse claim, but not quite in the kingdom of Jorvik. Tanshelf?' He makes it sound too much like a question.

I know his words sound vague, but my people are not overly familiar with the English lands. What I do know is that this location is on the regular route to reach Anlaf's holdings from his stronghold at Dublin. It's clever positioning by the English.

'Did you see the king in person?'

'No, I didn't, but as I say, Dafydd may well do so when he returns.'

I signal that he can leave, and I ponder what his words mean.

I wanted to take Edmund unawares, but it's difficult to do when he's already preparing for battle against Anlaf, not against me.

Anlaf's predecessor, Olaf, took Edmund spectacularly by surprise when he reclaimed Jorvik and Lincoln. I'd have preferred to emulate him. Now I worry that the English will be too well prepared, whether Edmund looks northwards or westwards towards my warriors.

I consider the problem.

My intention is to join Anlaf Sihtricson and his summer campaign against the English. I want to attack King Edmund, and visit my revenge on the heir as I never could on King Athelstan for the embarrassment of those peace terms agreed at Hereford and reinforced after Brunanburh. But should I take the risk and attack alone? Should I wait for Anlaf Sihtricson or reveal my military prowess by triumphing alone?

I want victory. If I defeat the English, and Anlaf comes against them as well, we can hold the area that runs from my kingdom to Jorvik. We'd have more control than anyone in recent memory. It would place me on an equal footing with Anlaf and even my cousin, Hywel, to the south of my kingdom. It would make Hywel reconsider his stance towards me.

Hywel thinks I'm a weaker king than him, but I know I'm stronger. I've not relied on the passive acceptance of another to forward my plans of a united land of the Welsh. I've not relied on deaths and happenstance to take another man's lands.

That's the heart of the problem. Hywel seems unstoppable. If I misstep here, and my death comes, will my lands remain in the hands of my sons or will Hywel claim them as well?

I glance towards where I know Hywel's kingdom lies, almost as if I can see him on the horizon. He hovers there, a constant reminder of what he's taken to date. First the kingdom of Dyfed, and then slowly but surely, one death at a time, he's extended his borders so that they meet with my mine. The two kingdoms of Dyfed and Deheubarth are now one great realm, and he's not finished yet. Hywel was once known as the king of the South Welsh, but now they say he's the king of the Welsh.

If he could he'd have England and her possessions as well. Perhaps that'll be his next move. Maybe he pretends friendship with Edmund and yet covets his kingdom. Hywel's travelled on the continent; he's visited the Pope. He knows what's possible and he's met great men and wants to be one himself.

What to do? What to do?

There was never really a choice. Not when I've urged my warriors to war, and called on the words of the scops to unite my Welsh warriors with those of Anlaf's Norse.

I call my brother to me and tell him of my plans.

'We move towards the waiting English force. We'll follow the road to Jorvik.' He nods. He encouraged me to ally with Gothfrith Gothfrithson, and now he urges the same alliance with Anlaf Sihtricson. But, if we can overpower the English, then that will be all the better.

I've long been subject to the English king's whims. Before Brunanburh, I distanced myself from the English, but then, when Athelstan's victory was so decisive, I was once more forced to bend the knee. Now I plan on reclaiming my independence. Gwynedd will cast off the yoke of the young English king, and then I can contend with bloody Hywel as well.

40

SUMMER 942, DERBY, THE KINGDOM OF THE ENGLISH

Edmund, king of the English

My meeting with Hywel went well, as I expected it to, and in my absence from the rest of my ealdormen and warriors, little has happened. But I know battle is coming. I can feel it. Somewhere, and some-when soon, Anlaf or Idwal or both of them if I'm lucky will force the issue and attack me.

My outriders have found Idwal. He travels alone with only his men. He's not allied himself with Anlaf or Dyfnwal of Strathclyde as far as can be seen. He comes alone, and he's riding straight to where Ealdorman Athelstan waits for him at Mexburh, one of the new forts to hold our boundary against Anlaf during the upcoming engagements.

Mexburh is a small place, close to the River Don, but eminently defensible. It's a long way from Idwal's homeland and will allow Hywel to cut off any retreat he tries. Whether Idwal dies at Athelstan's hands, or at Hywel's, I don't much care. His death is all that's needed. I simply hope that he doesn't plan on joining with Anlaf first.

Once Hywel's king of all the Welsh, I'll once more have the submission of the Welsh, as my brother did while he lived. Idwal's treachery doesn't surprise me. He was reluctant to make peace with Athelstan in 927, and he tried to disrupt the settlement when Athelstan arranged to meet the kings of the Welsh at Hereford. Idwal's always been a problem.

He's loved within his own lands. Idwal's people are content with his rule despite his greed and jealously towards those who have more than him. But I don't trust him.

'My lord king.' A voice recalls me to where I am, as opposed to where I've been.

'Yes, Eadric,' I reply, watching him as he walks inside my tent. He's dressed as though the battle will come at any moment, and sweat beads his forehead. He looks uncomfortable in the midday heat of the early summer. Not that we're complaining. Better to be too hot than too cold.

'We've received a response from Archbishop Wulfstan of York.'

I look up in surprise. It's been near enough two weeks since I sent to Archbishop Wulfstan. I'd expected an immediate reply. I've taken it as sign that Anlaf Sihtricson was simply set on war to hold on to the lands lost to Olaf at Tamworth, after all, I received intelligence that Anlaf was gathering his forces. With Olaf's death, Lincoln should once more be mine. I'm prepared to fight for it. In fact, I want to fight for it. I'd almost forgotten about the mooted peace conference at a mutually agreeable location to resolve the issue.

Eadric's holding a carefully folded and sealed document in his hand. My household priest steps forward to take it from him. I can read, but I have my scribe to deal with the tedious details of running the witan and the country while I'm away from my main scriptorium. My mother sends missives at least once a day if not twice or even three times. She isn't ruling alone in my stead, but with my brother at her side, although she seems to think it's all her.

'Who brought it?' I ask with interest. Where's my messenger, Sigeric? He's one of the most trusted men in my household. He knows secrets few others do.

'The messenger's seeing to his horse. He'll be along as soon as he can. He has a verbal message as well,' Eadric assures me, and I relax. I'd be unhappy if I lost Sigeric. I like and respect him, and more, I trust him.

I'd hoped for a spoken response, and so I turn expectantly to my scribe, determined to wait for Sigeric to arrive. My priest's brow is furrowed as he mouths the words to himself. 'Apologies, my lord king,' he says when he realises I'm waiting for him. 'My lord Edmund, king of the English, Archbishop Wulfstan sends greetings and prayers for your safe keeping.'

I hope Wulfstan hasn't filled his letter with words of courtesy, stolen from some letter written decades ago, and which he reuses to make him sound even more holy. I know it's the way of bishops, popes and archbishops to do just that.

'Anlaf, King of Jorvik and Dublin, has listened carefully to your request but has, with deep reservations, refused it.'

My priest's eyes open in shock at the words, but Eadric and I grin at each other. We didn't want a peace talk. We desire war. We thought we were going to get one.

'Is that it?' I ask, but the priest shakes his head as he reads the words before speaking them out loud.

'I will continue to speak with King Anlaf on your behalf. And then the letter ends with exhortations to God on your behalf.'

'Thank you,' I say, gesturing to be handed the letter. I wish to see the words myself.

My priest strides the few steps to me and offers it. 'It's not as you hoped?' he inquires, and I wonder how he can know me so poorly after all this time.

'No, it's as I expected. Anlaf might think he has nothing to lose if he doesn't act, but we can simply overrun the land as Olaf did, only this time, we'll have the forts to reinforce us, and we'll not lose them again.'

My priest is a man of peace and God. I hide my amusement at his consternation. He sees the world only regarding the words of the scriptures, and they're not always a realistic portrayal of facts. Even as devout as I am, I know that what happens between men and their enemies rarely runs as the scriptures would have it.

'We'll make ready to advance northwards. Make our claim to Lincoln before Anlaf realises what's happening.' The priest looks at me with dismay although he doesn't speak again. Then Sigeric arrives.

He enters the tent without any preamble. He's travel weary, but his eyes are bright and alert behind his deep blond beard and moustache, a hint of amusement playing there. He's the son of a Norse woman and an English man and has always found humour in most situations. He's invaluable for he knows how the Norse think and also how I do, an Englishman, and what's more, he knows how Norse women think too. The women can be more contrary than the men and far more determined.

'My lord king,' he offers, bowing low and helping himself to my mead before drinking thirstily. 'Archbishop Wulfstan treated as earnestly as he could on your behalf, but Anlaf wasn't interested, not at all. He's called his warriors together and is trying to raise his allies, who may include Idwal of Gwynedd. He'll be moving south already. I don't know what Blakari Gothfrithson said to him, but it seems he was unaware of our advances. Perhaps he hopes Anlaf will die and then he'll be king in his place. These Norse are as loyal as a flea in a pack of hunting hounds.'

'Is that what Archbishop Wulfstan wanted me to know?' I query, smirking at his description.

'Yes, and also that he'd side with you as soon as you've made your presence felt in the north. He thinks you might encounter resistance in York, but the rest of the land should capitulate soon enough. He says Blakari isn't to be feared. He lives only to drink.'

That intrigues me. 'There's unrest even in the heartland of York, and Wulfstan knows about it?'

'Archbishop Wulfstan knows everything, my lord king, as you should be aware. He probably has a spy within this tent even now.'

His words fall like stones into a suddenly chilly silence, and even though I don't mean to, my eyes settle on the priest, and he glares back at me. He's been with me since I became king, I do trust him implicitly. I raise my hand as an apology, and he nods to accept it, but Sigeric still glowers at him. He sees conspiracy everywhere, but that's his role in life, I can't blame him for that.

'Let's hope not quite within this tent,' I say, trying to deflate the tense atmosphere. 'Did he say anything else?' I ask. I can't imagine that the archbishop left it at that.

'He did, yes. He has details of Anlaf's intentions, and he also says that Constantin knows what's happening.'

'You trust Wulfstan?'

Sigeric grins at that.

'Not all the time, no. And certainly not where Anlaf's concerned. He and Wulfstan pretend to hate each other, but I'm not always convinced. Wulfstan almost thinks himself the king in York. I don't believe he welcomes Anlaf there, but neither does he want you or Blakari.'

As I say, Sigeric is a man who speaks his mind and says things others would hesitate to. Not that he's telling me anything I don't already know. Archbishop Wulfstan holds great power within England, or Norseland, or whatever it should be termed while Anlaf's king there. Olaf's capture of York means that Archbishop Wulfstan stands aside from England while also a part of her religious organisation. I'm not surprised that he plays both sides to his best advantage.

'Are you to return to him?' I ask. Sigeric sometimes makes plans with Wulfstan without my consent. And not only Wulfstan. He has contacts throughout the territories I lost two years before.

'Not unless I must.' His voice is carefully neutral. He knows I'll command him no matter his desires.

'For now, I think you should stay with me, or move around on the other side of the border, as inconspicuously as you can. Remain in touch with me in case I need you.'

Sigeric grins at that, relief washing over his face. 'My thanks, my lord king.' He stands abruptly. 'You know I don't like battle.'

'I do, and you have my permission to stay away.'

He nods and leaves without so much as a backwards glance.

Eadric opens his mouth to speak and then shuts it again. He stayed quiet while Sigeric and I spoke. 'You trust him?' he finally forces past his set jaw, mirroring my words to Sigeric about Archbishop Wulfstan.

I consider his words. Do I trust Sigeric? 'I do. He's been faithful throughout the last two summers and before then too, although I didn't know what he did.'

'He's comfortable with kings and archbishops?' he asks, and I see where this might be going.

'Sigeric can use words better than you can a sword. Don't let him worry you. He says what needs to be said to those who need to hear it, and the rest of the time, he's simply a good listener.'

Eadric looks unconvinced, but I wave his concerns aside. I know Sigeric, and that's all that matters.

'And now to greater matters, Eadric. Athelstan is meeting with Idwal at Mexburh, or thereabouts, and we need to decide on a position for ourselves. Where shall we set our sights to engage Anlaf?'

This question has been plaguing me for some time. By rights, I feel that it should be at Tamworth, the place where Anlaf's father once allied with King Athelstan, but I don't want him so deep within my kingdom. Olaf's invasion took him to Tamworth. I don't want to endure that again. If Anlaf comes to Tamworth, he'll have gone past Mexburh, and there's always the possibility that Idwal will not die but retreat. I don't want him to have the chance to reinforce Anlaf.

'I thought we were moving northwards, towards Lincoln,' Eadric says at my side, as I peer over the neck of my priest at the map he's scratching on to a piece of parchment. It shows where the forts are on the current border with the kingdom of Jorvik. He's placed Ermine Street, Watling Street, Ryknield Street and the Rivers Trent, Don and the Idle on it, and I could curse him for that, but I need to understand the lay of the land.

A map is an invaluable tool.

'We are, but I want to direct him to one place where we can be ready and waiting for him. I want my outriders to tempt him to follow them and bring him to his destruction at a position of my choosing, not his. This will be our triumph and we will decide everything about it.'

Eadric peers over the map as well. A faint smile on his lips. 'I know, my lord king.' He points to one particular spot, and I smile as well. Eadric has an eye for terrain, and he knows a good position to hold. Anlaf certainly won't be expecting it.

41

SUMMER 942, MEXBURH, THE NORTHERN KINGDOM OF THE ENGLISH

Athelstan the ealdorman

Mexburh is to the left of the River Trent, but above Lincoln, which is a good two days' ride to the east, involving crossing the River Don and the River Trent. I'm very firmly in English territory, and now the defensive location is about to be tested, but not by Anlaf Sihtricson, who rules Jorvik. The death of Olaf Gothfrithson last summer has once more changed the political realities. While Olaf thought he was the victor, taking Lincoln and Jorvik from Edmund in the early days of his rule, the peace accord has provided Edmund and the English with exactly what we needed. The time to regroup and build.

No, it's Idwal of Gwynedd who thinks to make a name for himself. I have no reservations that his actions have been encouraged by Anlaf Sihtricson. My eyes narrow as I watch Idwal's advance. No doubt, he thought to travel towards York, to join with

Anlaf, but has veered aside from the York Road upon hearing of my presence.

Mexburh is now a fort, its wooden ramparts rearing up from the deep ditch that surrounds it. It's defensible, and a means of protecting the people who live close by, should Anlaf Sihtricson think to try the same tricks as Olaf Gothfrithson. And it's not alone. A collection of burhs, or forts, stretch their way between the River Trent, across Ryknield Street, and towards the River Ouse. News of Idwal's arrival has already been sent to me. While the forts at Kexburh and Worsburh haven't engaged in battle with the Welsh king, purposefully forcing him to travel further away from the might of Jorvik, we've been preparing for his arrival.

A Welsh warrior rides towards me. He's small and wiry, sitting atop a massive horse that dwarves him. I smile a little at the image and then settle my face to one of mild interest. I'm surrounded by five of my most skilled warriors. But I've ridden outside the fort to meet the messenger. I don't want him to see all that Mexburh offers the English as a means of attack and defence.

'My lord?' the man calls as soon as he's close enough to do so. His Welsh accent is impossible to ignore. He comes alone, and looks warily between me and my warriors.

'Athelstan,' I reply, and hold in place my smirk of amusement when the man does a double take. He hadn't been expecting that, for he knows King Athelstan is long dead.

He flounders for words while trying to make sense of my name and his expectations. He glances over his shoulder to where his king waits for him to return, wondering if this has all been a terrible error. For just a moment, he doubts himself and all he's been told.

'Ealdorman Athelstan,' I correct myself.

His expression instantly clears and his mouth only just stops from forming into a large 'O' shape.

'And who are you?' I press.

'Caddac, my lord. I'm a messenger for King Idwal.'

'And what would your message be?' I ask, amused by the man. He's not the best messenger. Perhaps he's not used to such a position.

'He wishes to engage you in battle, claim back his independence from King Edmund.'

'Is that all?' I ask, wondering if I can goad him.

A light wind springs up, ruffling the growing crop in the field we stand beside, and I look outwards to where I know Idwal must be setting up either a camp or a battle line.

'Well, he'd rather face the king,' Caddac admits with a shrug of his shoulders. 'But I've heard of you. You're the king's cousin by marriage. It'll be as good to kill you first and then move on to the king.'

The man's cockiness doesn't amuse me. I consider what tricks he thinks to play and where Idwal must be hiding his other men. There's no chance that he'd have come with only a hundred or so warriors to face the English king, or to join with Anlaf Sihtricson. Perhaps he hopes to imitate Olaf Gothfrithson at Tamworth two winters ago. We all know how that ended.

'With only a hundred men?' I ask, but Caddac doesn't respond vocally, although his eyes fill with suppressed amusement. It's all the confirmation I need that Idwal has warriors elsewhere than at his side. He intends to trick me.

'With only a hundred men,' he confirms. He glances at the sun, squinting to see where it lies in the sky. 'We'll attack at dawn. I look forward to it,' he announces before turning and riding away.

I watch him go without any misgivings. It might be the strangest attempt at diplomacy that I've ever been a party to, but really, I think Idwal was just trying to determine if I was Edmund or not.

Now he knows I'm not the king he'll think me just a prelude to the main battle. I intend to finish it for Edmund. There's no need for him to face Idwal in battle. Idwal has been a pestilent boil ever since Edmund became king. He pays only what he thinks to get away with of the tithes agreed at Hereford, but if he thought his alliance-building with Gothfrith Gothfrithson and Anlaf Sihtricson had gone unnoticed, he's mistaken.

I return to my men.

'We need outriders throughout the night, and men to watch our enemy. We'll fight in the morning.' No one argues. We've been waiting for just such an opportunity.

Only my brother Æthelwald shows some interest in exactly how we'll fight our enemy. 'Will we make our shield wall inside the fort or outside?'

It would be good to take advantage of the defences of the fort, but I also want to kill Idwal once and for all. I know there is another, more loyal to Edmund, who'll gladly govern Gwynedd. Hywel hungers for Idwal's death. I must be more aggressive in my approach to Idwal and his force of warrior men if that's to happen.

'Outside, and then, if the worst should befall us, we can retreat inside, but I'm not convinced the defences will be tested against him. His messenger wasn't conciliatory. He simply wanted to know if I was the king or not.'

'Idwal's always been a fool. He thinks to be a mighty king allying with the Norse, but he's forgotten about his overlord and other enemies closer to home.'

'He'll be dead tomorrow so it little matters,' I counter. Æthelwald grunts in agreement before turning away to see to his battle preparations.

I scowl from the rampart looking towards where I can see Idwal and his men in the growing gloom. I wonder what he plans.

I'll find out soon enough.

42

942, MEXBURH, THE NORTHERN KINGDOM OF THE ENGLISH

Idwal, king of Gwynedd

Caddac languidly guides his horse back towards me, and I groan at his delaying tactics. I just want to know if the man I see is the king or not? His slow pace makes me think it's not and that he's delaying giving me the news, but until he returns I just don't know.

I hope I've not come this far to meet some subordinate. I want to kill Edmund of the English and have this done once and for all. I'll prove my worth to Anlaf Sihtricson, king of Jorvik, and be rewarded in being treated as an equal. I know Hywel plots my demise with his overlord, Edmund, and plans to take my kingdom upon my death. Hywel's plans are too presumptuous. I intend to kill Edmund first and then bloody Hywel.

Cousin or not, Hywel can't take my kingdom. He already rules an empire to rival that of our grandfather. I always assumed he respected me more than any of the other petty kings he's ridden roughshod over. Apparently, I'm wrong. I'll make Hywel pay for his ambitions. When Edmund's dead, Anlaf will support my desire to conquer all the Welsh kingdoms. I'll see how Hywel enjoys such a reversal.

'My lord king,' Caddac's finally within shouting distance, 'it's not King Edmund but Athelstan.'

Something flashes in Caddac's eyes at the use of the word, and I startle too. I'd not expected to hear that name today, no matter how common it is amongst the English.

'Ealdorman Athelstan,' he corrects eventually, coming into talking distance, not shouting. I narrow my eyes at his little trick.

'Is the king coming?' I demand.

'I don't bloody know,' is his abrupt response, sliding from his large horse to land before me, handing the reins to one of the young boys who travels with my force. 'I told him we'd kill him and then move on to Edmund.'

His flat eyes crease at that. I chuckle at his tone. He can be a surly bastard, all wiry, hard muscles; sometimes he makes me wonder why I have him in my entourage. Only then he'll surprise me, in a good way, and I remember all over again.

'He thinks you only have a hundred men.'

'Good, long may he believe that, at least until he's bleeding to death with his entrails hanging from his belly. Does he suspect?'

'Not at all. I think he's a cocky bugger, keen to kill you.'

'At least we share that in common. I want to kill him as much as he wants to kill me. Well, I do now I know he's here and not Edmund.'

'Did you find a suitable position for us to attack from?'

'I did, but I believe he'll abandon the protection of the fort and meet you in front of it, so he can retreat if need be.'

I turn to glance at the intended battlefield. I can't decide if it'll be to Athelstan's advantage to stand outside the new fort or within it. Certainly, it'll make it easier for my men to attack if the English aren't inside. We've ridden past a number of such burhs to reach Mexburh, having left the York Road. They made no effort to stop us. I think they lack the number of warriors required to adequately defend such a place. The English king has thought to build his forts as a means of expressing his power, but he lacks warriors. And what use is a fort without warriors to defend it? Perhaps, when this battle is won, we'll overwhelm all of the forts. They'll be mine, and Anlaf Sihtricson can pay me handsomely to have them handed on to him.

'They don't suspect my other warriors are here?'

'Not as far as I can tell. We need to watch them, see if anyone sneaks out to check the numbers you command.'

I nod consideringly. 'How many men would you say he has?'

He looks at me with disbelief. 'My lord king, I barely made it much further than we are here. I couldn't tell you how many men, women, children or goats they have. Hopefully, not enough.'

I glower at his annoyance. I know I ask too much of him. I'd prefer more information, but I'm not going to get it.

I wish it were Edmund within the fort, not Athelstan. It's Edmund I hunger to kill. It's the English king who's thought to humiliate me by standing as my overlord. I won't countenance it for a day longer. I want this done. Then I can go home and kill bloody Hywel myself.

'My apologies,' I say to Caddac. 'Tomorrow will be soon enough to know everything.'

'It's going to have to be,' he responds disagreeably, and wanders off without so much a bow.

I stand and watch the fort for signs of life for some time, but there's nothing. Like the other forts I've passed, this one seems surprisingly little populated. I might just have the measure of this Athelstan. I'll find out tomorrow.

* * *

The morning is warm and damp all at the same time. I shiver with anticipation of the battle to come. Strangely, I've slept soundly and deeply, having to be woken by an annoyed Caddac who demands to know if I intend to fight today or if I'm too much of a weakling.

I ignore his disgruntled tone and notice the deep grey under his eyes. I've had the benefit of sleep that's been deprived him.

It's still gloomy when I set about readying myself for the coming day. My men's voices drift through the air, muted but busy. When the sun peaks over the horizon, I intend to be in position and ready to meet the ealdorman and his small force of warriors. And then I remember.

'Caddac, did anyone leave the fort during the night?'

He looks at me with his sleep-deprived red eyes and shakes his head. 'I'm no witch or mage to see in the dark. But no, I didn't see any brands or hear any noise.'

'My thanks for your commitment to duty,' I offer, but he's not to be soothed with ingratiating words today. His aggression pours from his tight body. I wonder if he'll even be able to raise his sword and shield with the tension that holds him rigid.

Before I slept last night, I sent word to Cadfan who leads my other warriors that the original plan still held. I'm hoping he's ready to support me when I need him most.

I'm handed a piece of bread and some cheese that I eat hungrily. Battle always makes my belly hollow. I know I need to eat and drink beforehand, but this morning I'm impatient and eat only enough to take the edge from my hunger. I'll feast later when Athelstan's dead or nearly so, and I hold Mexburh.

By the growing light, my men and I, over a hundred in total, make our way to my predetermined battle line. The horses have been tethered away from the bloodshed, and those who don't fight but who travel with my warriors are gathering together our possessions. I don't like to countenance that we'll be defeated here, but clearly, they're thinking ahead.

I watch as they load the horses with what meagre supplies we brought with us along the York Road. I shrug away my moment of fear. If we lose, they'll probably still live, and if I win, well, the camp will be ready to move into the fort.

When the sunlight finally breaks its way over the horizon, I experience a jolt of shock. Athelstan's men must move more quietly than mine for they've formed up in front of their fort, all tranquil and battle-ready. Not even their weapons have given away any telltale clangs and bangs. Perhaps they've covered them in sheep's wool to mute any noise they might make.

Either that or my harsh breathing has masked the sound.

They stand beneath a banner of the Wessex wyvern, the yellow of the beast evidently dyed repeatedly to make the thread so bright. Against the red background, it seems to breathe fire.

It makes my banner appear pathetic in contrast, it's colours old and sun-bleached. Perhaps they don't even realise the creature is also a dragon, depicted in black against a white background. But I banish the thought. I will triumph here.

Caddac looks at the men and then back at me with a slight gleam in his eyes. I question if he knew what was happening and simply didn't tell me. As much as he wants to win this battle, he'd still be happy to show such spite.

The two lines of warriors eye one another with interest, calculating the size of my force and theirs. My men are all warriors; they'll not baulk at what's to come, although I sense unease rippling through the line of warriors. We've not fought a decent enemy for many years. We didn't join the fight at Brunanburh. My alliance with Gothfrith Gothfrithson has kept the Norse from Gwynedd's shoreline, and the English rule over my kingdom peacefully. We've not drawn blood in anger for many, many summers.

My brother would have some comment to make to calm the men, to stiffen their resolve, but Cadfan leads the other half of my force. I should have asked him for his advice before we split it.

I've been king for twenty-six winters. My warriors all know and respect me. They want me to be their king. My sons are too young, and untried. They're at home in Gwynedd. I spare a thought for them, hoping they're not bickering and making trouble in my absence.

My long tenure doesn't mean I'm the most verbose of men.

Ah, sod it, I think, the men know why we're here. They'll fight no matter what I say.

Caddac leans toward me.

'That's Ealdorman Athelstan with the coned helm.' I glance where his eyes point and see a man with a gleaming helm, finely embellished with an intricate design but strong for all that. My eyes narrow. I want to face him, kill him, beat him, but he's not directly in front of me. When we clash in the next few moments, another will likely have the honour of first blooding him.

I can't move either. He'll have marked me as the king, for I too wear a beautiful coat of mail and have a helm polished with sand. It would make my intentions far too visible if I faced off against him.

'I see he's outside his fort,' I conversationally offer Caddac.

He barks his harsh laugh. 'He has somewhere to retreat to now. That's good. It means he's not confident.'

I appreciate his reasoning, and suddenly words are flooding from me as I bellow at my men. 'For too much time the English king has tried to lay claim to us, for too long he's made us subordinate to him. Today we fight for our freedom, as the scop told us, we will subdue the interlopers, drive them into exile, bring an end to the dominion, and make them food for the wild beasts. There will be no return for the tribes of the Saxons.'

A roar of approval greets my words. I smirk as I ensure my helm is tight on my head.

My warriors.

Fiercely independent and always happy to be reminded so.

Swords and axes hit shields with the thunder of a herd on the move. We're moving forward towards the enemy.

Today the English will die and then tomorrow perhaps Edmund will. Either way, Hywel isn't to have my kingdom. And I will benefit from my Norse alliance.

43

SUMMER 942, MEXBURH, THE NORTHERN KINGDOM OF THE ENGLISH

Athelstan the ealdorman

The Welsh face us, and I think they're surprised by our readiness. I cautioned the men to silence but felt with each muffled whisper and bang of a weapon on the summer ground that there was no way our presence would have been kept a secret. I was wrong.

Suddenly, I realise it's unlikely they even know I sent outriders last night to scout the land using the south facing gateway. In which case, they won't know we're aware of their other force.

Our victory grows more assured.

I've met Idwal before, but I doubt he'll remember. After all, I was just one amongst many at Athelstan's witan. I'm glad I know him by sight. I want to do my king the honour of killing this man for his false promises.

The people of Gwynedd are always happy to shout about their heritage, freedom and independence. I expected nothing else from Idwal. After all these years, his treachery, double-dealing and indifference, he deserves to know that the English kings aren't fools. I'm looking forward to this battle.

I've positioned my men outside the fort. My intention is to prove that while the fort is needed to maintain order on this borderland, to stand a guard against any incursions from York while it remains outside our sphere of influence, it's not required to overwhelm our enemy. Battles should be fought in the open.

A cry from the line of well-provisioned men before me and they're rushing towards us. My men, quiet for so long while we assembled, are now roaring their battle rage. I let them. Men should hear their voices before battle. It might be the last time.

I spoke words of reassurance to them last night. I urged them to take victory for their king, and not one of them trembled at the thought that today might be their last.

'Advance,' I bellow, Æthelwald echoing the cry from his position in the shield wall.

Advancing, my shield overlaps with those to either side of me, Ælfsige and Ælfric. In only a few steps, I encounter an enemy shield. No arrows have been shot overhead from the enemy, not yet. Neither have my handful of bowmen loosed their arrows. Spears have fallen on the ground behind us, a waste of a resource when they don't find a target.

My men, those less proficient in warfare, too old to be of great use, or too young to yet stand in battle, collect the spears and hand them to the fighting warriors. It's the ultimate betrayal when an enemy dies at the hands of their weapon. Young Alfred from Tamworth is amongst their number. I've begun the task of training him to be one of England's finest warriors. He has the quick wit needed to be a battle commander one day.

Spears snake their way under or even over the tightly held shield wall. The hustle and bustle of the men, the heave of their effort in keeping the shield wall tight and together, can be heard in the cries of elevated voices.

It's the intention to push Idwal and his men back before fully engaging with blades. I want them to lose ground without our weapons being used. The ringing of an axe on my shield has me biting my lip in concentration. The attack's fiercer than I thought it would be. The rage of the Gwynedd warriors heats the space between us. I redouble my efforts. I can't buckle under the onslaught.

With the shield quivering in my hand, my seax ready in the other, I use my shoulder to force my shield into the enemy line. 'Attack, you damn fools,' I roar at my allies. Again, Æthelwald mirrors the cry. I feel the shield wall stagger a step forward. A smirk crosses my face. These are the right words to use to force my warriors to even greater efforts.

We surge forward again, three steps this time. Up and down the shield wall of a hundred men, cries can be heard from the enemy trapped by the onslaught. The rear shield carriers use their weapon of choice to dispatch the victims with sickening thuds when they appear at our feet, cries of dismay on their faces at having fallen beneath the force of our offensive.

My shoulder strains, as we take another step and, with my seax, I reach for a leg, cutting at the exposed calf of my foeman.

A screech of outrage, and suddenly I have half a man beneath me and my fellow warrior, Ælfsige, uses his sword to slice open the man's exposed belly. A scream of terror crashes into my ears, but it's too late. The man's dead, and my feet are covered in his slippery blood.

The body's pulled behind me. The advance continues.

It's almost too noisy to hear anything above the furious shouts of men and cries of pain. Eventually, another handful of steps forward, and it's Æthelwald who shouts for us to drop shields and attack. My shield falls to the left. With my seax I'm ready to dispatch whoever stands before me.

Fear-crazed blue eyes meet mine. I step towards the man, his shield loosely held in hand, shocked by our sudden movements, his axe hanging in the other.

Belatedly, my opponent raises his shield, but it's too late. I slice my seax across his weapon arm. His blue eyes blaze with pain as his forearm opens up and blood pools onto his hand. His weapon slips with the oily liquid. That's all I need. Even closer now, I raise my elbow and slice across his neck.

He gurgles for air, but it's a quick death.

As his lifeblood flows onto the hard ground, his knees buckle. He kneels before me, as though in prayer. I kick him backwards, out of the way.

I wipe my blade on the back of my trews and turn to the next warrior. It takes a moment to recognise him behind his helm, but then I do. Idwal, the king of Gwynedd, and for too long a problem for Athelstan and Edmund.

His eyes flash with delight, even though I'm sure his men are losing ground. I echo his joy. I want to kill him as much as he thirsts to end my life.

Idwal smirks with pleasure as the noise of the battle fray doubles, but I know what it is. I don't let his reinforcements disturb me. His brother and warriors can do all they want to try and sway the battle. In a moment it'll all be irrelevant because Idwal will be dead.

Only he doesn't seem to realise that.

Idwal rushes me, his coloured shield before him, sword in hand. It gleams with blood as the burgeoning daylight flashes on it. For a moment I'm distracted by the knowledge that he's killed one of my men.

Idwal takes advantage of my momentary diversion. Before I

know it, his sword is on my shield, words pouring from his mouth that I don't hear because everything has gone silent around me. I'm suddenly deaf.

Angrily, I shake my head, only to hear a buzz, as though a hive of bees is near, and as his sword strikes my shield once more, his eyes delighted by my lack of defence, I raise my shield and return the blow.

His eyes flash dangerously with the realisation this won't be as easy as he thinks. But, confidently, he evades me and replaces his sword with a vicious-looking axe, the edges hooked and sure to inflict damage if it gets anywhere near my skin.

I think his weapon is a poor choice. I prefer my seax.

Raising my right arm, I aim not for his shield but his axe. I'd rather knock it out of his hand now before he gets any ideas.

Intent on his actions, he pays me little heed, aligning himself to swing his axe at my exposed side. Holding firm to my seax, I circle it so that it meets the axe with a jarring thud along my arm. His axe is caught, my seax wedged between the teeth and handle. If I angle it just right, I'll trap his hand and slice a few fingers off. But that's not my design here. A fingerless Idwal is still an alive Idwal. I want him dead.

Abandoning my seax so that Idwal has to spend time freeing it from his axe, I reach for another seax, sharper, lighter, easier to manoeuvre, on my weapons belt. We're standing close together. I can stab it into his arm or chest or slice open his neck as he tries to free his axe.

He senses my movement. His body judders as though he wants to evade my reach but his feet are entangled, one behind the other. He wobbles precariously, his neck coming forwards and meeting my blade, with almost no effort on my part.

All colour drains from his face as he sees death on that sharp edge. I could step away. I could let him fall to the floor and then stab him, but in that instant, I decide the easier way is the right one.

His body weight will force him onto my seax. He'll cut his neck. I stand firm, waiting to feel the heat of his blood sheeting my arm.

Only it doesn't come.

Belatedly, I realise he's regained his balance and managed to turn away from the shimmering blade. My seax hits his back, doing no damage against the byrnie he wears.

Cursing, I examine his position anew. Idwal spins to greet me. His axe, now free from my other seax, slices quickly through the air between us. I step back. The weapon makes an audible sound as it passes me.

Damn the man. He must have been praying as he fell. Surely, only the intervention of the Almighty Lord could have saved his life.

I flick my shield before me once more, holding it firmly as he assesses me in the same way that I do him.

Now isn't the time for tricks and feints. I just need to use my skill to kill him.

The sound of the battle slowly filters back into my consciousness. Shouting men and crashing swords, but more as well. Those who came to reinforce Idwal have moved to join the primary battle. Now, more of my men pour forth from the fort where they've been watching and waiting.

The fight's evenly balanced. But Idwal doesn't realise, the smirk returned to his lips. He's only heard his reinforcements. He doesn't know that I also held many in reserve. His face is streaked with a stray slither of blood that covers his chin. Is it the blood of the English, or his own? I growl low in my throat at the thought, and then remember myself. I step back twice, calm my breathing, allowing my composure to return. Rage won't win this battle.

Idwal menaces towards me thinking I'm retreating, but I'm not.

He's misread the situation. With a glance to either side to check no one will get in the way, I pool my weight onto the balls of my feet and balance a moment, readying myself.

My muscles bunch. Then I move, lightning fast. Twisting to rush around Idwal, my blade bites into his neck, before he can turn and meet my unorthodox attack.

Blood covers my hand. I drive my seax deeper and deeper, Idwal's choked cry dying on his lips.

Behind me, I hear Æthelwald's voice raised in triumph. He must have been watching me closely. As Idwal's body slides from my blade, crumbling to the floor, a cheer works its way amongst my warriors. They fight with renewed passion as Idwal's warriors try to decipher the words that rush like fire from man to man telling of their king's death.

Idwal's dead.

Idwal is dead.

I breathe harshly, watching the light of life drain from Idwal's slack face, the surprise clearing as he settles in death. But I've only a moment to myself before another takes his place.

I don't know this man. His look of horror directed at Idwal's lifeless body tells me this is his brother seeking revenge.

He's out of breath and panting as he circles at a wary distance. He's rushed to get to me, perhaps hoping to save Idwal, and now takes time to consider his next move. His eyes are shadowed and hooded as he glances towards Idwal's dead body.

Sword in one hand and shield in the other, he faces me. Leather gloves protect his hands and a padded byrnie his body.

I step over Idwal, ensuring I purposefully crush the still face into the blood-drenched ground, a resounding crack assuring me that Idwal's skull has caved in under my weight.

A howl of rage erupts from the new warrior. He moves towards me, his shield before him but his weapon only half raised. I wonder what he'll do when we clash.

He surprises me by ramming his elbow towards my face. I only stoop at the last moment. I'd thought he was going to attack me with his blade, not his body.

I sidestep his movement and use the time to lift my seax into an offensive position. My arm quivers with the exertion, but I ignore it. I've won half of this battle. Now, I'll win the rest.

His sword narrowly slices the air behind my back. I'm relieved I wear such a well-made byrnie.

I turn quickly, seax carving through the air. My speed surprises him. He's not ready. I slash my blade over the top of his, causing them both to vibrate. While he fights to free his sword, I thrust my shield into him, forcing him to take not one but two steps backwards.

Our weapons part. As I reassert my grip on the hilt, I see the perfect chance. I drop my seax and reach for Idwal's discarded axe, wrestling it from his death grip.

My enemy's chin is low. I lash out with the axe. It hits just below it. I yank it upwards with as much force as I can. He grunts in agony as blood spurts from the wound, the crack of fractured bone loud. I cover my face but still his blood lands on my lips before my mouth's shut. I spit the hot liquid away, only narrowly avoiding his flailing sword as he tries to kill me – even as he stands dying.

'Bugger off,' I howl into his still-staring eyes. I knock him to the floor with my shield. He's dead. That's all that matters.

Once more Æthelwald's voice echoes over the battlefield. It takes me a moment to understand what he's saying. It better not be retreat, not when I've killed Idwal and his brother.

A hand on my back and I spin, axe raised menacingly. I drop it just as quickly, a look of shock on Æthelwald's face.

'Apologies.' I stagger.

'I was the bloody fool who startled you.' Æthelwald says just as quickly. 'Didn't you hear? They're retreating.'

I look before me for the first time since encountering Idwal and his brother, noting the sun's fully risen. The field's a bloody mess of broken bodies. A few straggling men rush away northwards, desperate to keep their lives. I note the messenger, almost decapitated, not far from where Idwal lies dead. Good, he was an arrogant fool and deserved to die beside his king.

My men don't chase them, but they watch wearily, panting and recovering from the fight. There are too few survivors. We need some to run to Anlaf Sihtricson and tell of our success.

'Have we lost many?' I demand.

'No, not as many as the enemy,' Æthelwald confirms. I nod as I wipe sweat from my eyes and remove my helm when that doesn't work. I can't get my hand through the nose guard and eyepieces.

'Idwal?' Æthelwald queries, kicking the body before him.

'No, another, Idwal lies there.' I point and Æthelwald turns with interest to stare at the body.

'Are we sending him back to his family?'

'No, we'll bury him here, with his men.'

'Good, I don't much fancy making sure he's all in one piece again.'

Æthelwald's eyes glints with amusement as he speaks, taking the sting from the reminder of my handiwork. I don't like to kill, but I will when I must protect England and the English from the enemy.

44

942, ST ANDREWS, THE KINGDOM OF THE SCOTS

Constantin, king of the Scots

Mael Coluim strides into my presence, and I hold my grimace in place. I imagine his angry stance, his hand hovering near the seax at his belt, has something to do with Ildulb. He's made no effort to hide his intentions, and I almost wish I'd told him to do so. It would save this interview now.

'Mael Coluim,' I begin, deciding it's better to get on with whatever he's come to say to me.

'My lord king,' he replies, inclining his head to me in a perfunctory way. He doesn't mean any respect, in fact, he means exactly the opposite. 'Are the rumours correct?' he demands aggressively, and for the tiniest fraction of a moment, I'm tempted to deny it or play dumb, pretend I don't know what he discusses. But I decide against it. I want him gone from my church quickly.

'Yes, Ildulb has gone to assist Anlaf Sihtricson against Edmund of the English.'

His blazing eyes shine a little brighter. I think he's doing well to keep his anger in check. 'Officially?'

I consider how to answer that. Again, I'd like to string Mael Coluim along. In the past, I would have done so. 'No, personal vengeance,' I murmur, walking towards the front of the church to run my old, grizzled hand over the magnificent book on display. I hardly recognise the hand as mine. It shivers and shakes. I don't know the last time it didn't tremble.

The decoration on the manuscript is stunning, the gold lettering flashing in the candlelight. I feel honoured to be able to handle it as I do. Mael Coluim's steps follow me. I can almost feel his heated breath on my neck.

'We should have sent an official delegation,' he barks, and my temper flares. I know full well that if I'd sent an official delegation, he'd have berated me for that too. He's a master at making every action I take appear wrong. And anyway, Ildulb informed me that Mael Coluim intended to travel south. I'm surprised he's here, arguing with me. My son has more stones than him.

'We should do what's being done, nothing more. Anlaf needs to prove himself before we ally with him. Ildulb will bring back valuable information about how Anlaf copes with the attack.'

Mael Coluim cracks a laugh. 'He's a Norse king, he'll beat Edmund, or he'll die in the fighting. There are few enough options open to him.'

'He might well reach an accord with him, another Eamont.'

'Eamont was nothing. Even Brunanburh was bloody nothing.'

I hold my temper in check at what Brunanburh cost me personally. Mael Coluim throws it in my face as often as he can because he knows how much it upsets and disturbs me. It's a low blow.

'It was a temporary stay, nothing more. King Athelstan is dead. Olaf Gothfrithson is dead.' He leaves unsaid the next section he wishes he could say, *Constantin is dead*, but I hear it anyway. Mael Coluim needs to learn to mask his thoughts better.

'Another Eamont then perhaps,' I say with a wry smirk. It was Eamont that led to Brunanburh. That comparison might make Mael Coluim smile.

'And all those other treaties that went before,' he says sourly. He knows his history of the lands of the Saxons almost as well as our own. He knows who's allied with whom and who's double-crossed whom. I know as well because I've lived through it all, but he prides himself on having learned it all as though it's a lesson to recite by rote. He doesn't truly feel what those treaties cost me. 'Anlaf is no Olaf, but he just might hold his lands and kill the English king. We should have an official delegation there to gain an overview of what happens.'

I'm almost tempted to allow Mael Coluim to have his way and let him go south as well, perhaps even with the official sanction that he's so desperate for. Ildulb won't like it, but Ildulb has to learn to cooperate with Mael Coluim, and it will ensure Ildulb knows I'm aware that he wasn't entirely honest with me about his endeavours.

I pause for a beat; maybe it's five. My mind's working frantically to seek out all the nuances of what I could set in play now. Should I send him? Should I allow him to go and do what he so desperately wants to do?

'And you want to be the official delegation?' I query, just to hear him say it. It's interesting to see the fleeting need that flashes across his face. He wants to go.

'Yes, I do,' he states blandly, as though we discuss the weather or what we might hunt today.

My eyes narrow as they flash away from him. What harm could come from allowing this? Ildulb will be angry, but that's hardly a concern for the governance of my land.

'Go then, with my royal sanction. Seek out Ildulb and inform him that you come with my agreement. Make a treaty with Anlaf if you think it would be advantageous but offer nothing of importance, no more than five hundred men, no money, and certainly no wife.'

Mael Coluim can't hide the glint from his eyes or the quirk of his smile. He thinks he's finally being allowed to do what he wants to do. Even though Ildulb has already ridden off, I know that he'll intervene if it's necessary. Perhaps, and here I'm hoping, it'll be Mael Coluim that loses his life in the coming battle. I should have allowed him to fight at Brunanburh. I rue that mistake every time I see him.

'My lord king,' he says, his bow far deeper this time as he tries to rush from my presence.

'Mael Coluim,' I call as his back faces me. He turns to me reluctantly. 'Remember you labour for your people and our land, not for yourself.'

His eyes flash angrily, but I don't regret my words. He needs to be reminded of who he is. He thought to triumph over me, but he hasn't. Not yet. Only my death will allow that to happen.

45

SUMMER 942, NEAR LINCOLN, THE KINGDOM OF THE ENGLISH

Edmund, king of the English

News of Ealdorman Athelstan's victory and the death of Idwal of Gwynedd runs through the encampment. Men rejoice or are pensive. I know how they feel. This victory is momentous and significant, and yet it means that we must now be as successful against Anlaf Sihtricson.

Athelstan's brother, Eadric, rushes to and fro from my presence whenever some new piece of news reaches him, or he thinks of something else that I should know or that needs to be asked. His questions make me consider our plans. Do they need to be changed in light of what's happened?

It was Æthelwald who was tasked with news of the victory. He's ridden non-stop from Mexburh, swimming across the River Trent with his horse to reach my side, rather than riding to a crossing. As the colour drained from the summer sky, he arrived, face flushed, his victory flung about him like the most expensive cloak a man could ever wear, his eyes bright for all he shook with exhaustion.

Before he even spoke, I knew he brought monumental news. He travelled with his warriors, depriving Ealdorman Athelstan of half his force; a sure sign that victory had already been achieved. I consider when Athelstan will return to me. For now, I want him where he is, mindful of any retaliatory raids from the defeated men of Gwynedd, those few who yet live. Or perhaps from Anlaf Sihtricson, who might be riled to battle because of the death of his ally. The king of Gwynedd might be dead, and his brother too, but he'll have had his firm adherents. Not every warrior from Gwynedd perished near Mexburh. I hope King Hywel will be well placed to prevent any warriors riding from Gwynedd to reach York and Anlaf.

'My lord king?' A voice at the doorway and I turn, distracted, to see the face of my priest. 'A rider, my lord king,' he explains in his monotonous tone, 'from the north.'

Ah, another rider. I wonder what news this one brings.

The man who enters my tent is Sigeric. I give him a quizzical look. I thought he'd distanced himself from the coming conflict.

He smiles ruefully and shrugs his shoulders. 'Sometimes my sense leaves me, and I meddle where I shouldn't.'

I smirk at his tone. I understand his sentiments.

'Anyway, my lord king, I had a feeling that everything wasn't going quite as to plan as we thought.'

'And what have you discovered?' I ask, intrigued, sitting forward on my camp stool, my elbows on my knees and my head on my hands. I wonder what he might have devised from watching the actions of Anlaf that my other spies have missed.

'Anlaf's split his forces, sent Blakari away to find Idwal. Archbishop Wulfstan travels to Lincoln alone.'

This I didn't know. Well, I knew about Archbishop Wulfstan

heading for Lincoln, after all, that's where we're supposed to be meeting. And I knew that despite Anlaf's refusal to attend, he'd send someone in his place. I didn't know about Blakari. A sudden foreboding fills me with dread. If Blakari finds his way to Mexburh, Ealdorman Athelstan will need to make extended use of his newly rebuilt fort. He's so proud that he didn't need to use it when he fought Idwal but Blakari is another matter entirely. His reputation as a womaniser and a warrior is almost equal in measure.

'When did this happen?' I ask, trying to calculate if there's time enough for Æthelwald to return to Mexburh with his warriors.

'Just yesterday. They were near to Gainsborough when Anlaf made his move.'

'And how do you know this?' I ask. I don't think he lies, not at all, but I'm curious as to how he came by his information. He's always very slow at revealing his informants. He's a man you want on your side. He'd make an uncomfortable enemy.

This time, however, he only laughs. 'I staked him out and watched. I saw Blakari and his men go one way, and Archbishop Wulfstan and his warriors resume their journey along Ermine Street. Anlaf stayed at the site of their original camp, but I'm sure he has something planned. There's no other reason why he'd split his force in such a way. He wants Blakari and Archbishop Wulfstan out of his way so that he can act without their knowledge.'

That worries me. 'And you didn't stay and watch what he did next?'

'I already know what he's going to do.'

'What does he plan to do, and how can you be so sure?' I'm frustrated that he might have come to me with half a story, but I should have known better.

He smiles at that. 'Anlaf Sihtricson is a Norse king, they all think the same.'

'And how's that and why don't I know?' I wish he'd just tell me, but he often makes me decipher the meaning of his words myself.

He ponders that for a moment and then shrugs. 'You do know; you just don't realise it.'

'So tell me what he's going to do.'

'Do you want me to tell you or are you going to take a moment and work it out?'

I know that many men would be outraged at his tone, but I'm grateful he speaks to me as he does. He keeps me grounded, and I do as he suggests. I take a moment and think about Anlaf, and Olaf and all the other Norse warriors I've heard of, the stories from my youth, of great men and heroes who fought against them all and tried to keep Wessex out of their greedy hands. What is it that they all do? What is it that makes them so predictable to my messenger friend?

And then I realise and I smirk at him. His face mirrors mine.

The Norse all share one thing in common, one thing that makes them great if it works, and dead if it doesn't.

'He'll fake his intentions, pretend to go to Lincoln, and instead head for the Mercian heartland, perhaps using the River Trent.' I've had ships on the Trent since my defeat. We made use of them to cross the river closer to Nottingham. But there aren't many of them, not any more. No more than five. If Anlaf uses his ships, it'll be too easy for him to overwhelm my small force. I curse my arrogance in depleting the force so greatly.

'Where he'll hope to meet a combined force of Blakari and Idwal.'

'Only Idwal's dead, and Blakari will encounter Ealdorman Athelstan, not Idwal.'

'Exactly,' he adds with a deepening grin.

'We should send word to Ealdorman Athelstan, have him move from Mexburh.'

'I already have.'

I grin once more. I admire his confidence. 'So we should move, return to Tamworth, and expect to meet battle there.'

'I'd think so, my lord king.' He offers a bow, as though he remembers that I'm his king and that he might have been a little remiss before when he spoke to me. I shake my head at him to make him understand I'm not offended and that I appreciate his bluntness. 'The Norse have a strange fascination with Tamworth and Repton, they always have.'

I'm nodding with conviction as he continues to speak. The past is a strange place; I don't often consider it, knowing that it's populated with mere men who've become legends throughout the lands. My grandfather, his enemy Guthrum, my father, my brother, they all live in the past, with violent men, pagans and Christians alike. But it does teach me something important. I understand Sigeric's confidence now.

'My lord king,' he says, bringing me back from my musings. 'We need to play him at his own game. We must give the illusion that you're continuing to Lincoln as well. He'll have scouts watching what you do. Everything needs to be done with stealth if you wish to confuse him completely.'

Sigeric has done well to remind me of this. I was a hair's breadth from calling Æthelwald to me and having him race back to Ealdorman Athelstan with news of where he needs to position himself now. Instead, I'll need to be less conspicuous. I'll have to cover my movements as well, perhaps send someone else in my place to Lincoln, with Archbishop Oda.

I lapse into silence. Sigeric stands quietly while I think. I gesture once more that he can sit or leave, drink or eat. As he helps himself, my priest stumbles into the tent and glances between the pair of us. Without a word he turns and leaves and returns with Eadric, Æthelwald, and Archbishop Oda.

I smirk at them all as they file in with interest, noting Sigeric and somehow realising that something monumental is about to be decided.

Hastily, I have Sigeric recount what he's seen, and then I tell them what we're thinking. Æthelwald's the first to speak, his words slow and pensive.

'I don't like it,' he grumbles, but Eadric shushes him quickly with an apologetic glance my way.

'It'll be perfect,' he offers instead, meeting Æthelwald's furious glare with his one of resolution. 'You must see it, brother,' he says, as though they're arguing over slices of meat and not the place of battle. 'He's trying to trick us, and thanks to Sigeric, we'll have the upper hand.'

Æthelwald pauses his angry retort as he considers the words. I leave him to his thoughts. He'll come around, eventually. It might not be tonight. He stifles a yawn as I try not to watch him. He'd be mortified if he knew I'd seen his exhaustion.

Archbishop Oda is a battle-hardened man, but his face shows unease. 'I'm to be the bait?' he asks, trying to process all he's been told.

'Not the bait, no, the diversion.'

'That sounds a little better,' Oda capitulates. My priest's watching him as though he can't believe his agreement was so quickly given. I think he too easily forgets that when warriors come rushing through our lands, it's the religious men who suffer first, along with the women and children.

'I'll go to Athelstan,' Eadric announces. 'Æthelwald needs to rest and recuperate.'

'I'll go to Lincoln,' Archbishop Oda announces just as decisively.

'And I'll stay here and pretend to be you, my lord king,' Æthelwald says with a renewal of interest.

'But how will we move all the men?'

'At night,' Æthelwald speaks with confidence now, 'that's what we did at Mexburh. Idwal was completely taken by surprise.'

'Anyway,' Sigeric says, 'Anlaf won't have spies deep inside your lands. He'll only be able to find out information from his scouts. Take the men south a little, as though you're retreating, and then bring them through the heart of Mercia. Anlaf will have no idea that you've deciphered his intent. He'll believe you're weak because he'll see what he wants to see.'

'What of our original plan?' Eadric queries.

'I think we keep with it. Use it as a reserve in case Anlaf somehow escapes from Tamworth or comes right through our line of defence.'

My leading ealdormen and the archbishop nod in agreement.

I meet their eyes.

There's much at play here. We must ensure that England triumphs over the Norse as it has over the men of Gwynedd.

46

942, MEXBURH, THE NORTHERN KINGDOM OF THE ENGLISH

Athelstan the ealdorman

The joy of my victory is slow to dissipate, guiding my actions through the next day as we dig a mass grave in which to toss the bodies of our enemies. Even Idwal and his brother are given no special treatment. I'd wish to be buried with my men if they died in battle for me. I hope he thought the same. It might appear callous, but the priests are in attendance, saying the prayers as they should. We try our best to reassemble those missing parts of their pale bodies before consigning them beneath the churned earth.

It's a gruesome task, this reminder of what it means to battle and kill men. The only consolation is that they wished the same on us. They wanted to be the ones doing this, and the realisation that I'm alive and not dead is a heady tonic. The comprehension that they wanted me dead hardens my heart against the young and old faces alike, the grizzled warriors and those almost too immature to grow facial hair.

It's still a grisly task though, and one I take part in alongside my men. Only a bad commander would expect his men to carry out such a difficult endeavour without helping as well.

I don't know how many men survived from Idwal's force, and so I did make one small concession, and sent a messenger to King Hywel. It should be he who takes the news to Idwal's court. It ought to be he who knows first so that he can take advantage of the power vacuum that's been created. That's the harsh reality of this skirmish. Less than five hundred men fought here, but a whole kingdom will now be in disarray.

I don't want that to happen to my England.

My brother's gone to Edmund with the news of our victory, but more than anything, I want a message from Edmund, and not one of congratulations either. I want to know where Anlaf is. I need to know if he's heading for Lincoln or if he too might try and attack Mexburh, or one of the other newly fortified burhs.

I know Edmund wishes to vanquish his defeat of three winters ago. But the rotting flesh turns my stomach and the gaping grey wounds of death, infested now with maggots and buzzing with flies, are too potent a reminder that it could have been me, or even Edmund, being buried today.

Death's a terrible business, especially when it's on such a large scale.

I hurry through the task. As I look at the fort I've had built and repaired at Mexburh, I take the time to feel some pride in what I've accomplished here.

It might have resulted in mangled bodies and severed heads, but they were the enemy, they were here to kill my king and my men. They wished to kill me.

I'm pleased now that I coerced the king into building the forts and reinforcing those that were old and decaying. I'm glad Ealdorman Uhtred put the idea into my head. England is surrounded by enemies, but here, on the borderlands between her and the lands of the Norse kings, I want to know that she can defend herself and keep herself whole against any would-be Norse kings.

'My lord?' A voice sounds at my shoulder and I turn to meet the questioning eyes of Ælfsige with whom I'm hauling a body to the grave. Somehow my thoughts have stilled my feet. I stand in the middle of the battle site, hands firmly around the ankles of a dead man with staring eyes and a grey, protruding tongue.

'My apologies, come, let's get him buried.'

Ælfsige grunts in agreement, and we struggle our way to the side of the grave. It's near full enough now, and only a few bodies remain at the farthest reaches of the slaughter field. Soon we'll close it and move on.

I shake my thoughts from my head. I need to know what's happening with the king, where Anlaf is, and what I should be doing next. It'll take time for news of this victory to reach the king. Until then, we'll remain vigilant.

47

942, NEAR REPTON, THE KINGDOM OF THE ENGLISH

Anlaf Sihtricson, king of Jorvik

Repton holds a special place in my heart, as it does many Norse. This place was where we almost took the island of Britain from the Saxons, from the English as they call themselves now. This was where the ancient kingdom of Mercia became our territory, no matter how briefly. It's here that my ancestors shattered Mercia in two, making half of the lands Norse and half Saxon.

I'd hold it under my power if I could and so would everyone I command. The men grumble and mutter as they eye it with the same acquisitive gleam that I do. I've been held in captivity here, by King Edmund, when Olaf was king. I'll banish that spectre by reclaiming it for myself. I might even rule from here. Jorvik is safe in the care of my son, Rognavaldr. It would be delightful to rule my Norse kingdom knowing the English are so very, very close.

I'm disappointed in Idwal. His death shows he wasn't the ally he promised to be. The bloody fool. He should have joined with my force first, and not thought to take the English on alone. I know what his intentions were. He meant to make himself my equal. It didn't go well for him.

It's a blow to my plans but one I'll manoeuvre my way round, now that I've managed to dispatch Blakari and Archbishop Wulfstan on their own endeavours.

And anyway, it seems that my erstwhile ally is soon to be replaced. Initially, I feared terrible news from Jorvik when riders were reported gaining on us from the north. I even feared that the English had discovered my plan. But no, those rushing towards me are from the kingdom of the Scots. Not just Constantin's son but also his heir-to-be: the delightful combination of Mael Coluim and Ildulb. I imagine Constantin's enjoying the peace that will soon be deprived to me when the quarrelsome pair arrives. But I'm pleased all the same. They might carry the official sanction of the king of the Scots. Constantin has been wary of any alliance with me since the death of Olaf Gothfrithson. That wariness has come to an end.

'My lord king.' A voice at my side distracts me from my musings.

'Yes, what is it?' I ask with annoyance. I wish to be left alone.

'Another messenger. This time from Archbishop Wulfstan.' The old windbag has been sending messengers by the half-day, as though he's desperate to prove his allegiance to me by forwarding every tedious bit of intelligence my way.

I don't much care what Edmund's doing as long as he's heading towards Lincoln, leaving Mercia open to me. Repton is inside the English side of the precious border agreed with Olaf. I'll show Edmund that trying to steal Lincoln from me, regardless of any peace accord, will merely result in the loss of more for him.

I certainly don't need to know his every step. I consider if Edmund knows he has a spy within his midst reporting directly to Wulfstan. I also wonder whether he's playing me at my own game.

All men double-cross and think only of themselves. It's learning to read the truth from the half-truth that helps.

'What does he want now?'

'He wouldn't tell me, my lord king.'

It must be something secretive if the messenger won't speak of it to any but me.

'I'll see him. Bring him to me now.'

In only a few heartbeats the messenger is stood before me, appraising me in a way I'm not used to. He's not one of Wulfstan's monks. In fact, he looks as friendly as I'm feeling.

'My lord Anlaf,' he says, barely bowing at me and raising my ire. Does he think he's equal to me? Even Archbishop Wulfstan makes more effort than that.

I hold my temper in check, wondering what he has to say.

'Archbishop Wulfstan sends his good wishes and hopes to find you before you meet the English in battle.'

'Is that all he sends?' I ask, wishing the man would get to the point.

'No, my lord, not at all. We've been watching the English king, Edmund, and we have some unsettling news.'

'I know of the battle with King Idwal already,' I drone, annoyed to be receiving the news twice. 'I know of his death at Mexburh.'

'It's not about Idwal,' he interjects, 'rather about Edmund himself.'

'What of him?'

'He's not going to Lincoln.'

'Where's he going then?' I query. How dare the English king attempt trickery? He demanded a meeting, and I named the location as Lincoln, why is he now reneging on that?

'We don't know. He's disappeared south, using Ermine Street, and we've lost sight of him.'

This I find interesting and perplexing. The English king has been robust in his battle preparations. Why would they flounder now?

'Quick, tell me everything.' I want to know exactly what Wulfstan understands.

'Someone is going to Lincoln,' the messenger qualifies, 'and with all the pomp and ceremony as though he were the king, but he's not.'

My brow furrows at the news. What's Edmund planning? Surely, he knows of Idwal's death.

'Wulfstan thinks he might be meeting with Hywel of the South Welsh, that they mean to conquer Gwynedd between them, and then, when Gwynedd's quelled, resume their attack towards Jorvik.'

My thoughts freeze for a moment as I contemplate what sort of damage could be done to me if the men from the farthest reaches of the English lands, and the lands of the Welsh, all descended on my kingdom at Jorvik. They could annihilate us all, stop us from retreating.

I feel a cold sweat sheet my forehead.

How dare he? How dare this English king put all my dreams and hopes into such stark contrasts?

'Did Archbishop Wulfstan say anything else?' I ask eagerly, but the man shakes his head.

'No, my lord. As soon as he knew of this, he sent me to you.'

'So this news is more than a few days old?'

'Yes, my lord king, I'd say it was at least five days old by now.'

I'm thinking hard, looking at Repton with greedy eyes. The recounting of the massive force that came here is a favourite amongst the scops who grace my court with their stories and poems. How they sing of what happened at Repton over fifty summers ago when my ancestors took it as their own after their great raid through the lands of the ancient kingdoms of East

Anglia, Mercia, Wessex and Northumbria, the days when the Norse almost claimed every Saxon kingdom. Ah, I wish I'd been born then. I crave warriors like those heroes to assist me now.

I wish the English kings were as gullible as the men who'd once ruled Mercia and East Anglia. My task here would be far easier then.

I wish I knew what to do now.

Should I continue to Repton, the place I'd hoped to make my stand against Edmund, or should I chase him across the rest of England until I find him?

I need more information, but one thing's for sure, I can't focus on claiming Repton, not if my kingdom of Jorvik's threatened. With a last longing look at the small church and its ancillary buildings in the near distance, I know I need to leave. Just as I did when Olaf and Edmund made their treaty. The only problem now is whether I should retreat northwards to the disputed borderlands where I know Ealdorman Athelstan of the English is hovering inside his fort at Mexburh or go to Lincoln, and attend the peace accord with whomever pretends to be King Edmund, as though that were my intention all along.

My thoughts whirl with indecision, I turn my horse about and remove the tantalising glimpse of Repton from my vision.

I need to rethink everything I'd hoped to accomplish.

Damn the bloody English king.

Damn Idwal of Gwynedd. His death has just become more than inconvenient.

48

942, ST ANDREWS, THE KINGDOM OF THE SCOTS

Constantin, king of the Scots

My daughter watches her young son toddle across the floor with acquisitive eyes. The birth was hard on her, coming as it did at the same time that she learned of the father's death. I've tried to treat kindly with her, but her mood swings and imperious demands are draining on us all.

My servants and warriors avoid her when they can. She has only one servant who'll tolerate her, and I pay her handsomely to do so. The servant's a good woman, and she assures me that one day my daughter will smile and enjoy life again. She informs me that my daughter's anger one moment and sobs the next can be the normal result of becoming a mother. She doesn't make mention of what happened to Alpin. It remains unsaid.

I'm grateful the mother of my children wasn't so inclined. I'm devastated that grief haunts my daughter even now, over a year after Olaf's death. I could weep for her sorrow. I already weep for her actions towards Alpin.

Olaf wasn't even my son, and yet I mourn him, just as I do Alpin and Cellach, as though he was of my flesh and blood. It's not just to make my daughter happy for a brief moment when she realises that someone else misses him as much as she does.

The little boy reminds me of Olaf. His looks, his mannerisms and his deep blue eyes. He also has his tenacity. He makes me chuckle when he refuses to give up on his quest for whatever item he's decided he must have, no matter how lethal it might be.

Ildulb has been gone for much of the summer, and I worry about him as only an old man can. I wake in the night and think of little nuances he might not have considered. What will he do if Edmund captures him? What will he do if he has to kill Anlaf to stay alive? What will he do about Mael Coluim?

I can only hope he knows his mind well enough to make the right decision. I don't mind whether Anlaf lives or dies. But, it would be far better if he lived and continued to act as a buffer between Edmund and me. When King Athelstan held York, I was always worried he'd turn his attention to the land of the Scots. In the end, I was proved right. I much prefer knowing that Edmund's far from York.

The traders who come this way have brought stories of Edmund's military plans for reconquering Lincoln. It's clear he isn't about to accept the peace he forged with Olaf three winters ago. No, it's obvious to me that Edmund intends to be as land-hungry as his brother.

I sigh deeply.

I'm far too old for matters of state and politics.

I watch the little laddie before me. Another Olaf who'll one day demand vengeance for his father's death. Will there ever be peace on our island?

49

SUMMER 942, THE NORTHERN KINGDOM OF THE ENGLISH

Athelstan the ealdorman

We've caught Anlaf in an unenviable position. It's clear to me he was trying to flee from his decision to take Repton. But we've found him, and now my men ready themselves for another fight. King Edmund hurries to reinforce our small force, no more than a hundred and fifty men and the handful of warriors that Eadric brought with him.

What we can do is stop Anlaf from slinking his way northwards to York to hide behind the walls of the settlement. A small skirmish will make our intentions clear. He must agree to the peace being discussed at Lincoln, or we'll kill him. As with Olaf Gothfrithson and his attempts to reach Repton from Tamworth, it'll be easy enough to capture Anlaf. I'd prefer to kill him, I confess, but if we do that, another Norse bastard will simply try and force their way into York to replace him.

When my outriders told me that Anlaf had been sighted, I

turned with a grin of delight to Eadric. He's not yet had the opportunity to blood his weapons. I know he wants to. Given half a chance, I think he'd take his men and conquer any he could, anywhere other than in England.

I wish I knew where Blakari Gothfrithson was but I have men searching for him. He'll appear soon. He'll be able to sniff out this little clash.

My men are armoured and ready for the coming fight. I've decided that a lightning-fast assault is the best way forward. Anlaf and his men are hidden from our sight by a helpful hill. When we race around it, as soon as I give the command, he'll not have the opportunity to arm himself and make a decent defensive line.

It's midday. I won't wait any longer. Beneath me, my horse is restive, as though smelling the tang of blood already. With a determined glare at my men, I kick my horse to a fast canter, my shield steady in one hand, the reins in the other.

I imagine Anlaf's fear as my warriors and I appear. I leap from my horse and rush towards the enemy, my warriors and brother at my side. Within only a few horse lengths of Anlaf's camp, my men and I form a shield wall that bars their way.

I focus on the confused expressions of foemen who don't know what to do. I want them to form a shield wall to attack mine, but no one's giving the orders. Where's Anlaf?

The mass of swirling, confused bodies slowly parts. Anlaf has been playing at subterfuge. While his camp followers gave the impression of disorder, a fully prepared and well-provisioned shield wall has formed among them. Now it rushes forward through the gap. I grin with battle lust. Anlaf expects to fight here. He hopes to win. I'm going to prove him very wrong.

Eadric hollers further along the shield wall, his voice loud, clear and sharp as he informs Anlaf's men of what he thinks of them. I grin despite myself. Where did my brother devise such wonderful phrases?

'Engage,' I bellow when he's finally finished. As one, my men and I advance at a gentle run, our shields locked in place, our movements so coordinated that I imagine we could be one body, not a hundred and fifty.

We lock shields with the enemy quickly. These men are far better than Idwal's, their power far greater than I encountered at Mexburh. But I'm so confident in my abilities after killing Idwal that I don't worry about it. I don't have a fort at my back to retreat to, but I won't need one. The king's coming, with his fyrd and Ealdorman Uhtred along with my other brother, Æthelwald and his men. It's essential to hold off the enemy until there are more of us.

We don't even need to use our weapons if our shields suffice.

The last messenger I received from the king was yesterday. He was close. With the remainder of his ride yesterday and what he'll have done this morning, I expect his arrival at any moment, as do my men.

We heave with effort all the same. There would be a perverse pleasure in capturing Anlaf and delivering him to the king. The men on the other side of us apply as much pressure as we do and then a cry ripples up and down their battle line, and one by one, the shields are dropped, and the men attack us with their weapons.

I think Anlaf remembers events from the winter of two years ago. He doesn't want to be captured.

I howl with the full joy of battle, all efforts at maintaining the enemy in their current position gone. I want to kill them just as much as they want to see my death.

My sword's in my hand, but I quickly exchange it for the axe I took from Idwal of Gwynedd, and take a mighty sweep at the man before me. He raises his shield quickly, but not before I've managed to dent the edge of it. The shield rim buckles under my onslaught, but my foeman doesn't notice, driving at me with his sword. It's a vicious-looking blade, flashing in the sunlight. The edges have been honed to as cruel a sharpness as the main point of the blade. This warrior likes to use all of his sword.

I avoid his blade, and land another axe blow to the already weak shield. This time my punches impact another part of the shield, half of it impaled on my axe. The warrior laughs derisively as he discards the weapon. I have no choice but to do the same, slamming my shield into the warrior's face while I fumble for another blade.

My shield collides with his nose guard. I grit my teeth against the uncomfortable tingle that rushes towards my shoulder, but my sword's in my hand now. I step back, and he does the same before two-handedly driving his sword against my shield. I block the blow and lash out wildly with my weapon. I don't expect to meet flesh, but I do. I lower my shield and look in shock.

Opposite me and with a grin on his face stands Edmund, battle-ready and with a bloody sword in his hand. The warrior before me stands for a moment, looking down at the tip of the blade that's pierced his chest. Then he stumbles to his knees and tumbles face first onto the hard ground, but I'm not looking at him but at the mass of men who block any retreat for Anlaf's army.

The only way they could go now is forward, through me and my mere hundred and fifty men.

Edmund grins at my confusion and steps forward to embrace me, uncaring of the men who still fight around us. It won't be much longer before they realise that's all the fighting they're going to get today.

'My Lord Athelstan,' he shouts, thumping me on the back in his exuberance.

'My lord king,' I answer, but then we're both laughing, tears of relief streaming from our eyes. So few deaths and yet Edmund will have back Lincoln and, if he wasn't such a man of honour, the lands of Jorvik as well. But in victory I know he'll not be underhand. No, once Anlaf has signed his name and agreed that Lincoln no longer falls under his jurisdiction, he'll be allowed home.

If the people of York will have him.

50

SUMMER 942, BETWEEN REPTON AND MEXBURH, THE KINGDOM OF THE ENGLISH

Ildulb, prince of the Scots

My frustration must be showing in my every word and action. I've been here before, and I don't want to have a repeat of past events.

I sure as hell don't want to become a prisoner of the English king.

I understood when Anlaf chose to retreat rather than face a combined force of all the English at Repton but his failure to adequately scout the area towards Jorvik has led to this shocking defeat only half a day's ride from there. He'd have done better to stay at Repton.

This clash of blades is no battle, and no one will remember it or write about it. No, the only battle now will be between the two premier religious men of England in Lincoln as they hammer out a peace treaty that can only be advantageous to one man.

Once more, the king of Jorvik isn't going to live up to my expectations and deliver what I'd hoped he would. The English king,

Edmund, the murderer of my son, will continue to live his life and I'll be left with my rage and my grief.

I wonder when Mael Coluim will realise that everything from here will be no more than a flurry of words before returning home.

I've made my excuses, and now my men gather around me.

I don't want to make an enemy out of Anlaf but neither can I remain his ally. Not now. If Mael Coluim wants to, then he can deal with the consequences.

My loyal followers are as furious as I am. As we flee Anlaf's coming failure, I fear I'll never have the opportunity to kill Edmund.

This was my chance and I've accomplished nothing. I've not even had to clean my sword or wipe the blood from my face. I've done nothing but eat and drink and bemoan Edmund and his brother Athelstan. I could have done that if I'd stayed at home.

On the way north I plan on calling at Bamburgh. I've not yet heard all the details about how Olaf Gothfrithson died, and I have a good idea that the people of Bamburgh may know a lot more about it. My father hasn't asked me to make the detour, but it's something I feel I should do. If Bamburgh was implicated in the death of my sister's husband, I should know about it, and let her know it was a conspiracy and not a freak accident.

It's a grim task, but it may bring me more peace than my useless trip to Jorvik and then to the borderland with England.

I must advise my father that the illusion of England is more lasting than we'd thought. He might wish to change his tack when dealing with King Edmund and his overtures of friendship.

But I won't. Ever.

51

942, NEAR LINCOLN

Edmund, king of the English

After all the bluffs and counter-bluffs, it's come down to this. Within Lincoln, the two archbishops sit and feast and talk about peace, whereas out here, on the flat land that surrounds Lincoln, two armies face each other, the one hobbled.

It's the height of summer. The men of the fyrds are keen to return to harvest their crops. I'll let them go in a handful of days, but first, I want everyone battle-ready and standing to attention.

Now that I've rewritten the history of the beginning of my reign, I want to ensure it stands. For decades or even centuries this time, not a few small years.

A commotion and Archbishop Wulfstan hastens towards me, his face red although he rides a horse and doesn't labour up the hill himself.

'My lord king,' he intones, bowing his head and calling for my attention.

I'm almost tempted to have him dismount and bow low as he really should, but watching the man's excruciating movements is too much for me to bear when my mood is already so unsettled.

'Archbishop Wulfstan?' I ask, intending it to be more a question than an acknowledgement of him. He tests my patience. Is he a man of God or a man of politics? Sometimes I wonder.

He gives me a funny smile, as though conceding that I understand his motivations, but continues without commenting further. 'Anlaf Sihtricson, king of Jorvik, is defeated. He knows it and wishes to extend the hand of friendship to you.'

'My thanks, Archbishop Wulfstan, but I know he's defeated. I was there when we bettered him in battle.'

'Of course, my lord king, I apologise. I have more words than just those.'

I gesture for him to carry on talking, hoping he'll get to the point sooner rather than later.

'He wishes to make a treaty with you. One where the border between your two kingdoms is demarcated, preventing the need for future bloodshed and loss of life.' I ignore the irony that I agreed a border three winters ago and have since overrun it and that I first suggested this peace accord.

'And where would he want this border to be?' I ask. I know full well where I expect it to be.

'Where your new forts already sit.'

So Anlaf means to accord me land by a treaty that I've just won with force. I don't miss that this is similar to the peace I forced upon Olaf Gothfrithson.

Archbishop Wulfstan watches me with his too-curious eyes. My stomach clenches at the sight of him. He's no Archbishop Oda of Canterbury. I don't like him and his strange ways.

'I'll agree to a treaty, but the boundary must be at the River Humber. North will be under Jorvik's domain. Beneath it, mine.'

Wulfstan sucks in a breath as he absorbs my words. He opens his mouth and then closes it again. I enjoy seeing him so discomforted. 'My lord king,' he finally manages.

'That's my final word on it. And he'll be baptised and become my godson.' I should have insisted on these provisions with Olaf Gothfrithson. The position of godfather is almost akin to making us family, only without losing one of my half-sisters to the bastard.

Defeated, Archbishop Wulfstan ambles away on his horse. I watch him go, trying not to smile at his slumped shoulders. Whatever the damn fool promised Anlaf, he's not able to provide it. I imagine that will make for an interesting discussion between them.

52

942, LINCOLN, THE KINGDOM OF THE ENGLISH

Anlaf Sihtricson, king of Jorvik

The hall I'm summoned to is sumptuous. I was always proud of it in the past, but I've yielded it to the English king, and I doubt I'll ever sit within it again.

Lincoln might not have been mine to keep on the death of my predecessor, Olaf, but that doesn't mean I didn't want it. Pity that Olaf caused such a commotion with his invasion three winters ago. He made the English king reassess everything about his relationship with the parts of England that had only recently come under his control.

Now Edmund holds them, as though with iron, a series of forts and burhs stretching across the landscape.

Archbishop Wulfstan's effusive in his welcome and manages not to comment on the fact that all my plans have come to nothing. Olaf wasn't always fond of the fat little man, and neither am I, and yet he's a friendly face in a mass of sullen English faces.

Somehow that makes me grateful to him for his continued support.

Blakari's more petulant than the English, and even Mael Coluim has deserted me and retreated to the land of the Scots, following on when Ildulb left before meeting the English king in battle. The Scots, it seems, are far from being my allies.

If only bloody Idwal of Gwynedd hadn't been killed before my attack had actually begun. I might have stood a chance then, but not now.

At least Edmund's not made it as far as Jorvik. It's a small consolation but one I take anyway. Olaf secured Jorvik against the English, and now all I need to do is rule it. Wulfstan will keep the men and women of his church happy, and the added trade from the connections with Dublin serves to make the agreement a good financial one. There's no reason for anyone in the town of Jorvik to want the English king back. No matter that the coinage is still mostly that of the English kings. I'll have to see to that when I return north. It would be better if my face were on the coinage, not Edmund's.

The English king has played an excellent game in subterfuge. He agreed to meet at Lincoln. Then he seemed to be retreating, only for him to appear, almost out of the blue at Repton, with another force coming from the north under the leadership of Ealdorman Athelstan, the man who killed Idwal of Gwynedd. Hemmed in from all sides, my warriors succumbed to the greater numbers the English had. None of us wished to die that day, not when Archbishop Wulfstan had promised peace.

I'm not as foolhardy as Olaf Gothfrithson. I have no option left but to submit to Edmund's wishes. This way I'll remain king of Jorvik, and I might even be able to force a friendship with Edmund, one of mutual support, perhaps against the fickle Scots. I'd like to repay Constantin for his lukewarm assistance.

I'm never happier than when I hold my shield and weapon, but right now, I'll be glad to return to Jorvik where I can decide on my next course of action.

I'm thinking of going to Dublin, visiting my other domain once more. I can leave Blakari and my son in Jorvik to deal with the unease and expense that warring with England has incurred. I'll think about it and decide when the weather starts to change for the coming winter. It'll be easier for me if I don't see the pitying expressions on the faces of the inhabitants of Jorvik.

Archbishop Wulfstan greets me deferentially and leans towards me.

'It won't be a pleasant settlement, but I take it you'll be happy with retaining Jorvik?'

I wonder how long he and Oda have been debating the finer details of the treaty, but for now, I nod in acceptance. 'I understand, Archbishop Wulfstan. Do the best you can. My hoped-for ally is dead, and King Hywel will be taking Idwal's kingdom even as we speak. I'll be happy with Jorvik.'

He nods emphatically; I think he's pleased by my ready acceptance of his words. The negotiations are complicated. I've nothing to barter with other than myself. I'm not strong. I'm weak and Wulfstan tries to do what he can for me.

I'll sign my name to almost anything. I just want to go home, lick my wounds and decide what the future holds for me.

My father would have done the same.

I'll call on our family connections when Edmund appears. It's always good to remind someone that my father, Sihtric, bedded his sister, Edith. Hopefully, it'll make the terms less humiliating.

Wulfstan leans over to me again.

'Edmund demands that you become his godson, and have yourself baptised before you leave.'

I glower at Wulfstan in disbelief. All this and all Edmund

wants is for me to accept the word of God from one of his priests. It's almost laughable.

Wulfstan watches my face intently. 'The relationship will be a problematic one,' he advises. I tilt my head to one side trying to determine how that can be. 'As your godfather, he'll expect you to turn to him for advice.'

'And not attack him?' I ask, finally working out just what Wulfstan's trying to tell me.

'Exactly, my lord king,' he confirms, turning away, his attention caught by one of his priests who mills around the hall, carrying pieces of vellum or scratching away at them. No doubt a beautiful embellishment will front the document when it's ready.

I think about what Wulfstan said. I feel more hopeful than I have since my men and I were trapped in a pincer movement.

Edmund might well have his land back, as far as his new line of forts, but he's still treating with me, still trying to show that we're almost equals. I think he's recognised that if we're to rule the lands separately, we might have to work together on occasion.

I smirk a little. Wulfstan pivots back and watches me with understanding on his face. He's already had the same thoughts that I have.

I wonder if Edmund has another sister I could take to wife? Then we'd be brothers once more.

I might suggest it. If one of his sisters was good enough for my father, then I'm sure one would be suitable for me as well.

53

942, THE WELSH BORDER WITH ENGLAND

Hywel, king of the South Welsh

The messenger from Ealdorman Athelstan is too late to be the first to tell me of Idwal's demise, but I appreciate the sentiment all the same. Athelstan didn't need to inform me. It wasn't part of the agreement I reached with King Edmund.

I'm pleased I stationed my warriors on the border between Mercia and Gwynedd. It's allowed me to intercept the men who survived the engagement as they try and sneak home. For the most part, I detain them, not in unpleasant conditions, but so that they'll not rush to the court of Idwal and inform those of the calamity that's befallen their king.

I must get there first and be the man to tell them that their king is dead. Then I can inform them that I now rule in Idwal's place because we were cousins and this land was our grandfather's. And Idwal's children are too young to rule at this turbulent time.

I know many won't like my encroachment, but it's better to

reunite all of the Welsh, just as Athelstan sought to unite the ancient Saxon kingdoms into his vision of an 'England'. United, the Welsh will stand firm against the Norse, and the men of England should Edmund succeed in recovering all of his lost territories and look elsewhere.

Idwal's sons might be a problem, but soon they'll realise they can't rule without my help. I prefer my takeovers to be peaceful, but I have two hundred warriors with me, probably the number that Idwal lost in battle. I have the greater force to impose my will over the people and the court. Idwal won't have left his court unprotected, but it'll be the old and the young who strut around as though they're warriors when they're not.

I look out at the border with the English, once more noticing the great rift that dissects the land, the work of an ancient Mercian king who saw the Welsh as a race with whom to demarcate a firm and fixed boundary. It's a pity it's not always worked. Maybe this time it will.

The English king and I are almost friends and could make natural allies. The work I need to do in Gwynedd to establish myself will be far easier if I know the border's quiet.

Once more I ask the messenger to repeat what happened at Mexburh. I relish the details. It sounds as though my cousin was as bold as normal, attacking without thinking, and assuming he'd win by employing a little bit of subterfuge.

If I'd been in Idwal's place, I'd have sneaked north and found a way to meet Anlaf Sihtricson before encountering the English. With a combined force of men, it would have been far easier to overpower the enemy. They might then have retreated inside their fort and stayed until reinforcements arrived, but it would have given the aggressors time to undermine the fort.

Buildings are all well and good, but they make it impossible to see everything the enemy's doing, and there's always a weakness, whether it's a well or a small escape route that one of the children inside the fort might have constructed.

Buildings and forts can always fall. Eventually.

Perhaps Idwal did the best he could.

No, I disagree with myself; Idwal did what he always does. He acted with thoughts of glory and an easy win. He ought to have learnt by now that the English always have tricks to play.

Idwal should have taken the time to learn from the English as opposed to detesting everything they stood for.

I wonder how Anlaf fares.

Not that I care. Anlaf isn't interested in Gwynedd. The Norse don't much like the kingdoms of the Welsh. They've made some attempts to conquer us, but the land is too harsh for the warriors, a fact I find amusing as I know from speaking to the Norwegians and the Danes that their ancestral homes are even more forbidding. They have huge mountains that surround deep, chill rivers. In some places, the snow never melts, and the farmland is poor.

My land's more forgiving than that.

And now I have the lush, flat lands of Gwynedd to call mine as well.

I nudge my horse to attention and set out to claim the next piece of my birthright. Gwynedd will soon be mine.

54

942, LINCOLN, THE KINGDOM OF THE ENGLISH

Edmund, king of the English

In the far distance, I see what I assume are Anlaf and his most loyal men. They're clustered together, protecting each other and especially their king, as though there will be a fight and not a meeting of men agreeing on the return of Lincoln to English hands peacefully.

I thirst for his blood, my battle lust thoroughly roused, and yet I know that I'll not have the overreaching victory that I want. Not now.

I've reclaimed Lincoln. Ealdorman Athelstan defeated Idwal at Mexburh, and I've defeated Anlaf close to Repton, and taken him as a prisoner, although he was released into the care of Archbishop Wulfstan quickly enough. Suddenly, the desire of the witan to reinforce or build the forts anew along the northern border makes good sense. My men can stand as guards, ensure Anlaf's trapped in York and I can build on my gains.

York might not be mine today, but I know it's coming. Day by day, step by step, I'll take back what my brother won, and Olaf Gothfrithson stole back when I was deep in grief and too young to realise what was happening.

The thought's a comforting one. I know it will see me through the coming days. Where others see two great victories, I only see the disappointment that I didn't gain all I wanted.

As a king, I must speak words of congratulations to my men, thank them for their great sacrifices, mourn those who've died, and yet… and yet I'm disillusioned.

Where did we go wrong? What did I do wrong?

King Athelstan would have removed Anlaf Sihtricson from the face of the earth. He'd have used his men to drive Anlaf to the coast, to have him drown in the rushing tide before he could make it to the protection of his ships.

Then I take a deep breath and reassess what I've done, and what my men have accomplished.

It can't be denied that my brother, Athelstan, took advantage of his good fortune, that deaths fell to his advantage, that Olaf Gothfrithson and Constantin of the Scots didn't command such accomplished warriors. Athelstan was my brother, a great king, a religious man of conviction. I was in awe of his prowess, and his constant success, but it fell to him as though he had the right to it, almost with no effort on his part, despite my mother's words to the contrary on that long ago day which filled me with conviction to make more of my unwanted kingship. Athelstan was a man who had the luck of God on his side. The Norse would say he had the luck of their Gods on his side. I don't much care which God it was, all I know is that he had it and I don't.

Every victory is harder fought, every slight from my brother kings throughout the island of Britain is ten times greater than anything they did to Athelstan. Athelstan ruled over a Golden Age when men wanted peace, and I know I'll spend much of my life trying to regain what he had and what Olaf Gothfrithson took from me.

I suppose I should be grateful that I have the opportunity to make my name as my brother, father and grandfather did, but really, I want to claim more, not reclaim something that was stolen from me.

Better to have stayed the same than to lose and recover it.

Anlaf might well still be alive today, but there's no reason he should still be a week from now, a month from now, or even this time next year.

I'm a young man. I've got years left to rule.

I'll get back the kingdom of York.

And then.

Well, then I'll decide where to turn my eye next.

I'll have my victory as great as Brunanburh, and I'll hold it firm this time. I'll vanquish my brother's losses.

One day.

HISTORICAL NOTE

In keeping with my use of the scop song to incite the great battle of Brunanburh, I have then 'allowed' the same scop to compose the 'Battle of Brunanburh', which survives as a poem in the *Anglo-Saxon Chronicle*, an almost singular occurrence in a prose piece of writing.

The *Anglo-Saxon Chronicle* is an infuriatingly complex source to understand, as I've mentioned before. But this poem is deemed to be near contemporary to the period it was written about, at some point between 946 and 955, so within seven to sixteen years of the battle taking place. There's some argument as to whether the poem was written for the *Anglo-Saxon Chronicle* or whether it was included having been written for a different purpose – and here is where I've employed it. We don't know who ordered the construction of the poem. It's my assertion that it might have been King Athelstan, but this can't be proved. The actual identity of the scribes who penned the *Anglo-Saxon Chronicle* are unknown – while it's possible to trace their handwriting, the individuals themselves are strangely absent, despite how much we are in their debt in trying to understand the period.

After the entry for 937 and the 'Battle of Brunanburh' poem, there's nothing further in the Anglo-Saxon Chronicle until the death of Athelstan on 27 October 939. What happened in the immediate aftermath of the victory is unknown – although we do know about events in East and West Frankia. Unfortunately, there's also a gap in the charter evidence, which can be used to reveal the Welsh kings witnessing Athelstan's charters until 935, but then there's no account of this happening again until c.946. This is perhaps due to a lack of surviving charters, or it may reflect the political reality of the time. Athelstan's successes may have caused unease. Edmund was unable to reverse the losses for some time.

In 939 we're told that Edmund succeeded his brother. There's again no other entry until we are given another poem, 'The Capture of the Five Boroughs' in the A text of the *ASC* under 942, although the D text adds under 941 that, 'Here the Northumbrians belied their pledges, and chose Olaf from Ireland as their king.' (This Olaf is Anlaf in my story, I've changed Olaf Sihtricson to the Old Norse version of the name, Anlaf. To modern readers it appears an entirely different name, although it wasn't at the time.)

The Capture of the Five Boroughs poem reads as follows:

'Here King Edmund, lord of the English
Guardian of his kinsmen, beloved instigator of deeds,
Conquered Mercia, bounded by The Dore,
Whitwell Gap and Humber River,
Broad ocean-stream, five boroughs,
Leicester and Lincoln,
And Nottingham, likewise Stamford also
And Derby. Earlier the Danes were
Under Northmen, subjected by force
In heathens' captive fetters,

For a long time until they were ransomed again,
To the honour of Edward's son,
Protector of warriors, King Edmund.'

I have not allowed Olaf to take all of the Five Boroughs with his attack. I considered the idea of the Watling Street boundary agreed in the Alfred/Guthrum treaty, but decided it was too massive a reverse for Edmund, and for Olaf to gain. The Alfred/Guthrum treaty saw almost the whole of the east of what we know of as England fall into the hands of Guthrum, and created the Danelaw – an area where Danish law co-existed with English law for many years, even when 'England' was 'England'. The law codes of later time periods show this divide in how the law applied differently to those deemed as Danish or English. I've allowed Olaf only Lincoln and Jorvik.

William of Malmesbury (a later Anglo-Norman source) informs that Idwal of Gwynedd and his brother died in Wales. William isn't always the most reliable of sources so I've ignored him and moved them to Mexburh. William was born c.1095, not far from Malmesbury, Wiltshire. He was of mixed Norman and English parentage. He entered the monastery at Malmesbury and stayed there all his life. Both *Gesta Regum Anglorum* (The Deeds of the Kings of England) and *Gesta Pontificum Anglorum* (The Deeds of the Bishops of England) were completed by 1125.

Killing Idwal at Mexburh fits more with the idea that Idwal and Anlaf were working together against Edmund which, in place, fits more with the idea that Britain was home to a set of warring kings who were all trying to outdo each other but who were happy to ally with each other if they thought it might suit them. Michael Wood has written about the 'forts' across the northern parts of England. His article, 'Brunanburh Revisited', can be found on jstor.org. It's quite old now, but the map provided was invaluable, even if there is now general agreement – for most, but not Michael Wood – that Brunanburh occurred close to the Wirral and not in the north-east.

The details of the Alfred/Guthrum treaty have been taken from *English Historical Documents: Volume 1* edited by Dorothy Whitelock. I have the first edition. It seems there's also a second edition which is somewhat different in its contents.

The idea that King Athelstan may have had a book of 'kingly advice' which was gifted to Edmund is not my assertion but rather inspired by the belief of Professor Joanna Story of the University of Leicester that such an item existed. I've twisted this to fit my narrative and provide Edmund with some much-needed reassurance from his brother beyond the grave. The letters of Alcuin are a fascinating source, surviving from the later eighth century, when he had a friendship with Charlemagne and seems to have spent much of his time writing to all and sundry, and he didn't mince his words. He was quite happy to give a firm telling-off to those he deemed were failing in their religious duties. He wrote to the queen of King Offa, as a way of gaining the ear of that great Mercian king.

Athelstan's will does not survive, although it's possible to trace many of the books he 'owned' as they have inscriptions in them showing which people and establishments he gifted them to.

I have slightly mangled a few names, such as Conisbrough, to make it clear that they are burhs, just as Brunanburh was.

Quotations from the Anglo-Saxon Chronicles are from M Swanton's fabulous, The Anglo-Saxon Chronicles, my constant companion to Saxon England. Those of the Annals of Ulster and the History of the Kings of Alba are from Alex Woolf's 'From Pictland to Alba.' While I'm much less well-versed in the Irish and Scottish annals, as this is a story of Ireland, Scotland, Wales and

England, it feels only right to include them. Equally, it has never been my intention to portray any of these men as weaker or more evil than their fellow kings. I simply wished to tell a 'rounded' story of events in the British Isles at this time. However, I hope we all have our favourites.

ACKNOWLEDGEMENTS

As ever, thanks to my editor, Caroline, for pushing me to get this story right. It's not always easy to get the historical 'facts' to fit a satisfying narrative, especially during these uneasy times at the beginning of Edmund's reign. I confess, it's not always been very enjoyable.

To the whole team at Boldwood Books. Wow. Thank you for all your endeavours.

A special thank you to Ross, my copy-editor, for catching all those pesky mistakes and made-up words I'm so fond of using. I assure you, I will never change. And to Jack for his final read-through. Thank you.

To my other half, EP, thank you for putting up with all the huffing and sighing this book created. To my fellow 'support' authors, Kelly Evans, Elizabeth R Andersen, Eilis Quinn, J C Duncan, Donovan Cook and Peter Gibbons, for freely sharing tales of angst, woe and triumph.

To my readers, thank you for joining this journey into the complicated period of the middle tenth century. I have had occasion to regret my decision to attempt something so complex, but it does give me a real rush to know you appreciate it, and more importantly, enjoy it.

And a side note for King Athelstan on the 1100th anniversary of him becoming king of Mercia, and then Wessex, and then 'of the English'. I have no idea what sort of man he was, but he deserves to be remembered for his accomplishments. History can be a real bitch.

ABOUT THE AUTHOR

MJ Porter is the author of many historical novels set predominantly in Seventh to Eleventh-Century England, and in Viking Age Denmark. Raised in the shadow of a building that was believed to house the bones of long-dead Kings of Mercia, meant that the author's writing destiny was set.

Sign up to MJ Porter's mailing list here for news, competitions and updates on future books.

Visit MJ's website: www.mjporterauthor.com

Follow MJ on social media:

x.com/coloursofunison

instagram.com/m_j_porter

bookbub.com/authors/mj-porter

ALSO BY MJ PORTER

The Brunanburh Series

King of Kings

Kings of War

Clash of Kings

The Eagle of Mercia Series

Son of Mercia

Wolf of Mercia

Protector of Mercia

Warrior of Mercia

Eagle of Mercia

Boldwood

Find out more at www.boldwoodbooks.com

Follow us

@BoldwoodBooks

@TheBoldBookClub

Sign up to our weekly deals newsletter

www.ingramcontent.com/pod-product-compliance
Ingram Content Group UK Ltd.
Pitfield, Milton Keynes, MK11 3LW, UK
UKHW012250290726
14090UKWH00016B/566

9 781837 511990